A Winter Hope

Sheila Newberry was born in Suffolk and spent a lot of time there both before and during the war. She wrote her first 'book' before she was ten – all sixty pages of it – in purple ink. Her family has certainly been her inspiration and she has been published for most of her adult life. She spent forty years living in Kent on a smallholding with her husband John, and has nine children, twenty-two grandchildren and seven great-grandchildren. Sheila retired back to Suffolk where she still lives today.

Sheila NEWBERRY

A Winter Hope

ZAFFRE

First published in 2000 as *The Family at Number Five* by
Judy Piatkus (Publishers) Ltd.

This edition published by
ZAFFRE
80–81 Wimpole St, London W1G 9RE

A CIP catalogue record for this book is
available from the British Library.

ISBN: 978-1-78576-189-8

Also available as an ebook

1 3 5 7 9 10 8 6 4 2

Typeset by IDSUK (Data Connection) Ltd
Printed and bound in Great Britain by Clays Ltd, Elcograf S.p.A.

Zaffre is an imprint of Bonnier Books UK
www.bonnierbooks.co.uk

For Gladys Pattemore,
a staunch friend and
inspiration to her fellow writers

PART ONE

1932–39

CHAPTER ONE

THE ROW OF RED BRICK Victorian villas with sash windows and formidable chimney stacks seemed to stare aloofly at the cheerful terrace of pebble-dashed new houses opposite. The occupants of the older properties had lost their status, such as it was, when developers demolished the crumbling mansion house and began building on the site of the old orchards. This was in the few optimistic years after the war, before the General Strike. All that remained of what had been almost the last vestige of the pastoral past was a lone apple or pear tree in each small, square back garden. This was not due to sentiment on the builders' part: more a sop to halt indignant protests from the villa residents.

When the Hope family moved in to Number Five Kitchener Avenue, they discovered that the old tree was blighted and the fruit scabby and sour. Rather like the expression on the face, which appeared between twitching curtains upstairs at Lahana House over the road.

Fred Hope opened the front gate, set in the middle of a neat privet hedge, with an exaggerated flourish. He winked at Miriam, his young wife, heavily pregnant with their first child, leaning, pale and perspiring against the closed door.

'O be joyful!' he encouraged cheerfully. 'Here we are – in our new home, and in time for Christmas, just as we'd hoped. Just five minutes from the station and all downhill from the Jubilee clock in the High Street. But, we're on the up, Mirry, never mind the mortgage, eh?'

'Fred dear, it's £750. It's 1932 now – it'll take twenty-five years to pay that off . . .' She thought that the proximity to the station and shops was all that had concerned Fred. What had clinched it for her, only she couldn't tell him so, of course, was The Palace, with that sure promise of dark, hazy magic within. Mirry was a devotee of the Pictures. When they were in the poky London flat, she had visited the cinema most afternoons, brushing her hair with eau de cologne afterwards to disguise the tell-tale lingering smell of smoke. Not that a cigarette had ever passed Mirry's lips. However, going to the Pictures would soon be a rare treat, for didn't babies take over your lives?

They were among the fortunate few. They had married during the Depression, which, of course, was not over yet. Fred was a civil servant, with a secure future. This move showed his confidence in that.

Barbara, Mirry's fourteen-year-old sister was to live with them. Mum was moving in with her sister and brother-in-law. It made good sense, to share living expenses, now they were retired.

Bar already had a job lined up, at the new Woolworths in the High Street. She had gazed openly at the curtain twitcher, as they waited there for the estate agent to arrive with the key and the pantechnicon with their modest worldly goods. 'Not as grand as they'd like us to think they are, I reckon – what's that board say, behind that straggly hedge?' she wondered.

'Don't stare, Bar,' Mirry reproved her, but knowing that Bar would, anyway. She hoped it wouldn't prove too much of a responsibility taking her on. It had been Fred's idea, of course – she couldn't help being jealous of his fondness for her pretty young sister – fancy him thinking Bar would be a help in the house after the baby arrived . . . she was already showing signs of becoming far too fond of going out and having fun. It wasn't fair: Bar had naturally wavy dark hair in a thick bob, green-flecked eyes and deep dimples in her unblemished cheeks. Mirry, at twenty-two, still sighed over the odd spot. She determinedly twisted pipe cleaners in her fine mousy locks each night but, at the first suspicion of rain, the curls unwound and hung limply. If only she could pluck up the courage to have a permanent wave; but she worried about being literally plugged into the electricity supply. There was a hairdressing salon next door to The Palace – you could hardly miss the pungent smell of ammonia mingling with scented setting lotion. Mirry hated having to wear glasses, but they were essential. No one notices I've got nice eyes, too, she said to herself. Fred's so handsome, whatever did he see in *me*?

Bar concluded, having had a good squint at the inscription on the board, for she wouldn't admit that her eyesight was not exactly perfect either: 'Ooh, it's a dancing academy; ballroom, ballet and tap . . . Beatrice Boam, Proprietor. That couldn't have been B.B. at the window though, unless she forgot her wig. It might be a bit livelier round here than I thought –' Bar had been reluctant to leave the lights of London.

'Here's our chap, and the key,' Fred interrupted, as a motorcycle spluttered to a stop by the kerb. 'Let's hope the water and gas are on. Good thinking, Mirry, to bring the kettle with us . . .'

'I wrote to remind them,' she said. She saw herself as the practical partner, well, except for daydreaming in the Pictures.

'Can't lift you over the threshold, Mirry,' he whispered, with a grin, 'but it's home sweet home for us at last.' He squeezed her hand instead.

'Homes Fit For Heroes', the faded, peeling billboard at the beginning of the estate still proclaimed. There *were* heroes, Mirry thought, not far from here: ex-servicemen begging in the streets. Legless men wheeled in home-made carts to their pitches; some selling matches, some just holding out greasy-rimmed caps to invite pennies; men staring sightlessly, turning the handles of ancient, wheezy barrel organs. Cards dangled from strings round their neck: 'Army Veteran', 'No Hope!', 'Homeless', 'Out of Work', 'Large Family', 'Help!'

Sudden tears spilled from her eyes as she waited for the kettle to boil. She took her glasses off and wiped her eyes on her pinafore. She had remembered to bring that, unlike Bar, who blithely ignored the maxim that good clothes must be taken care of. Fred's arms went round her from behind, his hands gently caressed the taut swelling of her front. She felt embarrassed, supposing someone came in the kitchen and saw them? The baby kicked in protest. She sighed. It must be a boy, she thought, and wearing football boots.

'Pity you couldn't fit a chair in your bag, Mirry – but at least you thought of the cups . . .' he joked anxiously. 'You all right, dear?'

'Just happy Fred, to be here at last,' she assured him. 'Where's Bar?'

'Looking out for the removal men, she says, but chatting to the agent,' he told her, ruefully.

The shrill whistle of the kettle, the steam dislodging the cap on the spout, made them both jump.

'Not much room for a scalded cat in here,' Fred rinsed out the jug in lieu of a teapot. Mirry produced tea leaves in a screw of paper, likewise sugar and a bent teaspoon, worn at one side where it had been held over the gas flame, to caramelise sugar to brown gravy. She carried on with all

Mum's little economies. Like Fred's mother, her mum had been widowed in the war.

'It's a kitchen*ette*, Fred,' she touched the shiny taps over the deep sink with pride. 'Hot and cold, we won't know ourselves . . .'

'Only hot, when the fire's going,' Fred pointed out. 'We should save up for a gas heater over the sink – the bathroom geyser will cost a fair bit to heat, I daresay, we'd best just use that for baths, once a week. You can rinse the little 'un in the sink for a year or two, can't you?'

She nodded. 'I do like the green and cream paint, in here, don't you? You'll need to fix me up an airer as soon as you can . . . Call that girl in for her tea, do, Fred.'

Mirry sat outside in an easy chair, under the apple tree. She shivered a bit, because it was early September, after all, and the afternoons soon drew in. Fred had promised to light the fire when the men departed. 'You stay out of the way, Mirry, there's a good girl, you mustn't overdo it – I'll slip 'em a bit extra to help put the beds up, and Bar can sort out the linen. She's popped round the local shops for a few things – I feel like a good fry up, don't you?'

The very thought made Mirry feel queasy. 'Only if *you* do the cooking, Fred . . .'

''Course I will. You know me – a lump of lard, thick rashers, nice fat sausages – there, doesn't that sound just the ticket?' He brushed a leaf from her hair and kissed the top of her head. 'Have a little snooze, I should . . .'

The fire stubbornly resisted all efforts to set it alight, and the fall of soot meant that the departing family had not kept their promise to sweep the chimney, but the gas stove was obliging.

Much to her surprise, Mirry *was* hungry, and Fred really was a dab hand with the frying pan. He'd learned to cook as a lad, when his mother was at work.

They sat at the table in the recess of the bay window. Mirry didn't protest at the lack of a cloth, because Bar had put out cork mats. She didn't even ask her sister if she had washed the crockery when she removed it from the straw packing in the boxes.

It was a pity Bar had to mention that the butcher had the tips of two fingers missing. 'Mangled 'em in the mincer,' he said, when he saw me looking.'

'Not today I hope, when he was making the sausage meat?' Fred joked.

It was a good-sized room, just right for every day. Fred had fixed the mirror over the mantelpiece, but Mirry longed to see her ornaments all in place. The big armchair by the fire was reserved for Fred, when he listened to his wireless: there were two smaller easy chairs for Mirry and Bar. They would have to buy a shade for the light. Woolworths was the place for a bargain. The linoleum struck cold to her feet. But their budget wouldn't run to carpets yet awhile.

The three-piece suite, Mirry's pride and joy, was in the front room, together with the piano, inherited from her grandfather, who had paid for her to have music lessons as a child. This room would be strictly reserved for Sundays, or entertaining.

They had saved hard and bought good-quality modern furniture from Arding and Hobbs at Clapham. Mirry often felt guilty that they had so much, when so many were on the dole. But what could she do about that?

Their mahogany bed had an unyielding base. Mirry missed the comfort of the feather mattress she had shared with her sister before her marriage. Fred said they weren't hygienic. He was very fastidious.

Mirry hadn't yet read her *Daily Mirror*. She was tired, but past sleep it seemed. Fred snored beside her, satisfied that the day had gone so well. She heard Bar turn over in bed in the room next door. Oh dear, the walls must be thin . . . She sat up cautiously. She must visit the bathroom shortly, what a relief it would be when the baby no longer sat on her bladder. At least there was no need for a chamber pot here, under the bed. She fumbled for her glasses on the bedside table, switched on her lamp. Five minutes reading – with Fred oblivious she could turn to the cartoon strips before the news.

Some time during the night, Fred awoke. He unhooked her tortoiseshell glasses, removed them gently, turned off the light. He eased her down in the bed and cuddled her lovingly and carefully. He felt so proud. He was twenty-six-years old, he was a householder, and he was almost a father. He could provide for his family. *His* generation was ready to change the world . . .

CHAPTER TWO

FRED BROUGHT BAR A CUP of tea first thing. 'Well, I'm off, to join The Band of Hope – cheer-ho! You'll look in on Mirry before you go, won't you?' He blew her a kiss at the door, winked. 'Enjoy your day at Maison Woolies!'

Bar grinned, sipping her tea. She appreciated her brother-in law's sense of humour. She suspected that her sister some-times did not. She could picture the small army of men in carefully brushed dark suits, bowler hats, polished shoes, chins jutting above their sternly starched detachable col-lars, which were changed daily, marching steadily uphill to the Jubilee clock, wheeling right to the station to catch the London train. They emerged from the new houses and strode shoulder to shoulder, as some of them must have done during the war, each with a rolled newspaper under his arm. They greeted each other by surname, passing a comment or two about the weather.

Mirry was exercising her expectant mother's privilege of a lie-in. Since the move Fred insisted she must only rise early on Mondays, when he lit the copper first thing, then there was a busy time ahead with the washboard and rubbing with hard green soap. Today was Thursday.

''Bye Mirry – don't do too much!' Bar peeked round the bedroom door. 'It won't be *today*, will it?'

'I hope not, nearly two weeks to go, the nurse reckons.'

'You look as if you'll burst long before that.' Bar said candidly. 'Call in to the shop today, if you get time, we've got some lovely new china in . . .' Of course, Mirry had all the time in the world, being home all day, Bar thought, but without resentment.

She was always in a rush, eschewing breakfast, but gulping a glass of milk, before she dashed out of the front door. Today, she just avoided colliding with the Galloping Major, out for his early morning constitutional with his dog. Why he had to cross the road and walk on *their* side, was a mystery to Bar. She wasn't aware of just how attractive she looked; more grown up than her tender years.

The soubriquet was, naturally, another of Fred's. The Galloping Major was part of Mirry's repertoire at the piano during their Sunday evening singsongs.

'Hey, hey, clear the way, here comes the galloping major . . .' she hummed audaciously under her breath.

Apart from raising his hat, revealing the shiny, scarred bald head which had intrigued her when she caught sight of him the day they moved in, Major Boam didn't waste time, but indeed galloped off on long legs, pursuing his bull terrier, trailing his leash. The major was forced to relinquish his grip on this, when he made his gentlemanly gesture, for it was obvious he only had the use of his left hand. Bar had already deduced that his right hand, clad in a sinister tight-fitting black glove, was artificial, for it hung, motionless from his sleeve at his side. As usual, the major wore his military greatcoat over jodhpurs and high, laced boots. He was making for the Grove, the local park. 'Bridger – stop!' the major called in vain. Still, there was no traffic to worry about, Bar thought, as there was in the High Street. The milkman with his horse and cart had been along at dawn, likewise the newspaper boy on his bike.

Bar was dying to meet the major's daughter, to ask about ballroom dancing lessons. Mirry had actually spoken to her in passing, yesterday, at the shops.

'What did she look like, Mirry – like the major?' Bar had asked eagerly.

'She has plenty of hair, if that's what you mean, Bar. A pretty coppery colour – not cut, but in a bun. She seemed quite friendly.'

'How old is she?'

'No idea, Bar – well older than me . . .'

Musing about the major and Miss Boam – she'd beaten Fred to it this time – *La Bohème*, as she called her to herself – Bar arrived at Woolworths, at the heart of the bustling High Street.

She donned her smart overall, combed her hair, and then joined her fellow assistants in all the tasks that must be performed before the doors were opened to the public. She was happy to be behind the crockery counter. Everything 3d. and 6d. A jolly, curved teapot for the larger amount and its lid for the former. She thought Mr Woolworth was very clever to juggle the prices like that. Nearly every home she could think of had a Woolworth teaset with square plates patterned with poppies more orange than red. It was a best-selling line. Bar was glad she had insisted on leaving school as soon as she could, though Fred had said, seriously for once, she'd regret it, because she'd got brains. Mirry had sulked after that, because no one had said that to her: *she'd* left at fourteen, she said sharply, because mum needed her money coming in, each week, to help feed and clothe annoying little sisters . . . Anyway, Bar was enjoying her new life as a working girl.

She was not too grown-up, however, not to glance longingly at the sweet counter when hunger pangs struck her at around ten o'clock. Miss Phillips, her senior, who appeared prim and unbending but was really very kind, slipped her a humbug and hissed: 'Don't crunch, don't let the manager see – just suck slowly, Barbara.'

About this time Mirry heaved herself out of bed reluctantly, and looked at her pasty face in the dressing-table mirror. Her arms ached from stretching up to unwind each pipe cleaner curl. Her hair badly needed a wash. Maybe she'd ask Bar to help her with this, tonight. She felt a little sick. She had surreptitiously let the fried egg, which Fred had solicitously presented, slip down the lavatory pan and had flushed it away. It took two yanks of the chain to do so. Oh why did Fred insist she must eat for two?

It was an effort to dress herself. She struggled with her maternity corset – bent awkwardly to fasten the suspenders. She felt a sudden rush of fierce loathing for the navy dress with its coy tucks and elastic inserts; she'd been wearing the beastly thing for months now. It was in dire need of dry cleaning, past sponging. Never again, Mirry thought as she eased her feet into low shoes. Ouch! Her ankles were really swollen this morning. Then she gulped, clapped her hand to her mouth. Would she make it to the bathroom?

As she heaved her heart up, she experienced the first niggling pain and knew her time had come . . .

It shouldn't be like this, she told herself, dismayed. Mum had offered to come next week to hold the fort: she'd promised to stay on while Mirry was confined to bed, with the nurse still calling in daily for two weeks. The things she needed for the birth were still waiting to be unpacked but were thankfully all to hand, in the big case Fred had pushed out of sight under their bed. Mirry had intended to fix the curtains on the old cradle this weekend, but that, and the pram, were still in Aunt Alice's spare room. Uncle Stan was bringing them over in his motorcycle sidecar tomorrow evening. Fred had wanted to pack the baby things in the van with furniture: she had dissuaded him. 'I'm not having them all scratched and dusty, Fred. I'm surprised at you suggesting it – you and your hygiene!'

Now, she tried to take a few deep breaths, to calm herself, to work out what to do first. The pains were insistent now, much too close. Mum had told her just a little of what would happen, the nurse not much more. In fact, Mirry had met the midwife only once, two days after their arrival, when she and Fred went to book her for the birth. No sense in wasting money in visiting the doctor, they agreed, apart from the early confirmation of her pregnancy, when he informed her that she was a strong, healthy girl, despite her slight figure; that her heart was normal and she need only return if there were any problems. The nurse agreed. First babies weren't usually in a hurry, she smiled. Mrs Hope should get plenty of warning.

When the next contraction faded, she didn't wait to put on her coat or hat, but made for the front door. She gritted her teeth and managed to get through the gate before the next pain caught her.

She clung to the gatepost – there was no way she could force herself to walk down the road, round the corner and then several hundred yards more to the midwife's house. She was unaware that she was screaming as her legs buckled under her and she collapsed in a heap on the pavement.

Then strong arms lifted her, almost carried her back to the front door. She had left it open.

'I was just crossing over to see you, I thought it was about time I introduced myself properly – I am Anna Boam from Lahana House . . . In here?' the husky voice asked.

Mirry could only nod as her saviour turned the knob on the front-room door and led her towards her precious threepiece suite. But she was past caring. Her shoes were eased off, her legs swung up on the sofa.

There was a knock on the door. Miss Boam motioned her to stay where she was, and went to answer it.

Mirry heard a man's voice: 'Saw you from the window – anything wrong?'

'Our new neighbour is in labour, will you go *post haste* for the nurse, Father?'

The Galloping Major, Mirry thought, bemused.

'What can I do to help, my dear?' Miss Boam bent over her, stroking her forehead with a cool hand.

'Could – could you fetch a towel from the kitchen and – lay it under me . . . just . . . in case . . . and, then . . . hold my hand, *tight*, please, till the nurse gets here . . .'

CHAPTER THREE

FRED QUICKENED HIS STEP when he saw the light in the
front bedroom window. Surely it couldn't be the baby?
He had followed his mum's advice obediently, keeping
a torch handy in case things started in the middle of the
night. They usually did, she added wryly. He had really
wanted to be there for Mirry when she went into labour.
Even though the nurse had said firmly she didn't hold
with fathers being present during the actual delivery.
He'd be much more useful stoking the fire and making tea. Thirsty work, bringing babies into the world.
Men were the weaker vessels, she had laughed, she really
couldn't be doing with stepping over a new father passed
out on the floor.

As he fumbled anxiously for his key, Bar opened the
door. 'Fred!' she cried. 'You've missed all the excitement!
The baby's come – this morning, would you believe it – and
Miss Boam, from Lahana, is here, she's been with Mirry all
day, and the nurse is waiting to see you – and Mirry said

not to tell you what the baby is, 'cause she wants to tell you herself.'

Fred's coat landed on the floor at her feet. He took a deep breath and leapt up the stairs, two at a time.

Miss Boam met him on the narrow landing. They came face to face, unavoidably close. 'Oh, good, Mr Hope, you're home at last – please excuse me, but I must get back to see to my father's supper now . . .'

The electric light gilded her smooth auburn hair. He was tall, but she was almost of a height. What a good-looking woman she was, what a graceful figure, he thought. She exuded a strong sultry perfume.

'Thank you, I understand you have been most kind,' he said formally. Fancy noticing another woman at this time, he chided himself. It was a weakness which he knew Mirry suspected and resented. She always needed his assurances of undying love. 'Cheer-ho,' he added.

She smiled. 'I'm sure we'll meet again very soon,' she said softly.

He guessed that she was well aware of the disturbing effect she had had on him. He stepped aside, allowing her to pass. 'Cheer-ho,' he said again.

'Isn't she beautiful, Fred?' Mirry whispered, revealing the tiny baby at her breast. Quite unconcerned she was, for once, that he should see that part of her unclothed. Fred fondly accepted that she was prudish. Without her glasses, with her hair bunched, she looked scarcely older than Bar. Fred caught his breath with love for her.

'Knows just what to do, she's a hungry little soul,' the nurse was just as proud. 'I'll leave you three together for five minutes, eh? Mrs Hope behaved like a real trouper, Mr Hope. We only just managed to get her upstairs in time . . . Just a small tear, not enough to warrant stitching, but the doctor will call tomorrow to make sure. I'll see you downstairs. I believe your sister has made the tea . . .' she closed the door behind her.

'Are you pleased, Fred, it's a little girl?'

'You *know* I am.'

'Miss Boam sent a telegram off to Mum – got to the post office just before it closed. Bar's going to make the baby a bed in the linen basket, for now.'

Fred leaned and kissed her, then the baby's pulsing head, warm and still damp, like ruffled down. He cleared his throat. He felt distinctly odd, just as if he might burst into tears. And cheated, of sharing in the most important moment of their lives.

'Gladys?' he queried. He'd get his late mum's name in first. He wasn't so keen on Elsie, fond as he was of Mirry's mother.

'Oh, Fred dear, d'you mind? I suddenly thought of Gloria, and Anna for her second name, that's after Miss

Boam to say thank you for all her help. I *know* we thought she was Beatrice, but that was her mother, apparently . . .' Mirry's voice faded. She couldn't go into explanations now, she really just wanted to go to sleep. She wasn't going to tell Fred, either, that she was disappointed, oh, just a bit, at missing Gloria Swanson swanning at The Palace that afternoon.

'Band of Hope and Glory!' Fred exclaimed. 'Glory and the Band of Hope. I like it, Mirry – Gloria – Glory Hope!'

Bar felt a bit ruffled, too, on Saturday evening. She'd worked hard all day and arrived home to no waftings of supper. She found Mum upstairs cooing over the baby, and Fred lounging beside Mirry on top of the bedclothes, wriggling his socked feet and displaying his big toe through new holes. He needn't think *she* was going to offer to darn them. That was a dutiful wife – or mother's – task. Fred was lucky, she thought, he only had to work Saturday mornings. This was her busiest day in the shop. Wednesday afternoons off were no real compensation. There was nothing much on in the way of dances, midweek: she liked something more active than the Pictures.

However, she dutifully admired little Glory. Really, any-one would imagine the baby had grown in just two days. How could the others say she was beautiful? She looked all red and her eyes were screwed up. Bar wasn't too sure she was happy about being under Mum's thumb again for a bit, either. Mirry kept unbuttoning her nightie and nursing the baby every time she opened her mouth to wail, and Fred didn't take his eyes off her for one second. They didn't seem to care that this made Bar feel all hot under the collar.

Mum – they were alike in looks, so Bar could guess exactly how she'd look when she was nudging fifty, only not so plump, her daughter hoped – had the same thick, springy hair. Only Mum had been dyeing hers black for years now. I suppose I'll be grey before my time, too, Bar sighed to herself. And I haven't *lived* yet. You wait, I'll show 'em ... I want much more than being a 'little wife and mother', as Mirry's magazines coyly put it.

The reproachful sigh caught Mum's attention at last. She reached for her handbag, which went everywhere with her, even under the pillow at night. 'Bar, ducky, you must be starving.'

'I am,' Bar said, with feeling. 'I'm still growing, you know.'

'Here, run along to the fish shop and get us all some rock eel and chips, will you? Get 'em salted and shake on plenty of vinegar – and get a pickled egg or two if there's enough change – then we can eat straight from the paper – no washing up ...'

'I'd rather have cod,' Bar said. She sighed heavily once more, all too aware of her throbbing feet. She'd only just walked home from the High Street and now Mum expected her to trudge there and back again. Still, this was a supper she always enjoyed, so . . .

A quick visit to the bathroom saw her nearly falling over a full bucket of soaking nappies. She wrinkled her nose in disgust. 'The only soaking I intend to do, is my poor old feet – then I'm off dancing,' she said aloud.

* * *

The lights were blazing from the upstairs dance studio at Lahana. Bar could hear the music as she crossed the road. Tonight, it was slow and seductive, cheek-to-cheek stuff, she thought with an anticipatory little shiver of excitement. 'Always get a good number on a Saturday evening,' Miss Boam had told her, the day the baby arrived. 'Why not come over this Saturday? You'll be sure of a partner, even if it's another lady – it was so different before the war, when Mother started the classes . . .'

'I can dance, well, just a bit,' Bar said. 'I'm really keen to improve.'

Her knock on the door went unanswered. The music was too loud. She was rather late, of course, due to the fish and chips. Seven o'clock, Miss Boam had said, and it was nearer seven-thirty. She peered through the coloured glass fanlight in the door, down the hall. There was a line of light showing under the door at the end. Bar crunched round on the gravel path to the side entrance. She could see through the uncurtained window into the huge kitchen. A figure was slumped in a chair by the old-fashioned range: a dog sprawled across his feet. The Galloping Major ... She felt like a Peeping Tom. Then, her eyes widened. On the table, next to a half-cut loaf on a crumby board, and a wedge of cheese, was – The Hand. Still covered in the black glove ... It was poised as if ready to seize the almost empty bottle behind it. She shivered.

Bar felt a gentle tap on her shoulder, a shush! not to scream. 'I thought I heard someone knocking – so I came to see. Father's dropped off, it seems – best thing, when we're all dancing, eh? Come back to the front door, and I'll show you the way.'

She followed Miss Boam obediently. The hall was brightly lit now, and she hoped that she didn't betray her surprise when she saw what the dancing teacher was wearing. An expensive frock, obviously: oyster-coloured satin, with floating gauze panels suspended from the waist, sparkling with diamanté. Not new, even unfashion-able, with little catches in the material, even a gaping split at the side seam. A rope of pearls dangled almost to Miss Boam's knees, as milky as the expanse of bosom revealed by the daringly scooped bodice. There were thin gold ban-gles on her bare upper arms, but she wore elbow-length net gloves. Her hair was piled high, and, Bar saw – she'd painted her face.

'Hang your coat here in the hall, Barbara – oh, don't you look pretty tonight! Did your mother make your blouse? Up the stairs – you're just in time to learn the tango.'

Fred was waiting up for her. For once he looked a trifle reproving. 'Your cocoa's gone cold,' he said briefly. 'We thought you'd be in by ten – Mum was weary, she went to bed.' He looked at the clock. She was nearly forty minutes late. Miss Boam had insisted on making up for the time Bar had missed, after all the others had gone. Why should she tell him that?

'Sunday, tomorrow, Fred,' Bar said dreamily. 'We can all lie in, can't we?' She gave him a quick peck on the cheek, as she always did, to avoid a kiss on the lips. There were limits. ''Night!'

He smiled back, wryly. 'Well, *you* can – there's a new baby in the house – remember?'

He poured the cocoa down the sink, rinsed the brown fluid away, then washed the cup and placed it face down to drain. He hoped that Mirry's reservations were not about to come true. It was a responsibility, a girl of Bar's age, and they had another priority now, of course, their own baby daughter, Glory.

The scent Bar had been wearing lingered in the hall. On an impulse, he picked up the chiffon scarf she had worn

26

over her hair and smelled it. It was the perfume he had noticed when he had encountered Miss Boam outside his bedroom door . . .

Bar, he thought, was already a very attractive young lady. She was bound to turn many heads shortly. That sophisticated scent made him think that perhaps the process was already beginning.

CHAPTER FOUR

IT WAS MIRRY'S FIRST OUTING with the baby on her own. She still felt a bit wobbly on her legs. Ten days was an awfully long time to be in bed, she thought.

'Get to know the neighbours, I should,' Fred had suggested when she told him of her plans for the day.

'Oh, I know Miss Boam, don't I?'

'You haven't much in common with her,' he said briefly.

'*Fred*! She couldn't have been kinder, the day Glory arrived and she came to see me twice, and brought me those lovely black grapes, and Mum said how nice she was and, she's teaching Bar to dance, isn't she, for a special rate, Bar being in her first job?'

'I'm not sure if it's such a good thing, Bar going over there twice a week. Your Miss Boam is much more worldly than our young Bar, Mirry. She's growing up fast enough as it is.'

'There's no harm in it.' Mirry was upset, for it was unlike Fred to be pompous. 'At least we know where she is, don't we? I'd rather she was there, than out with some young tearaway on the back of a motorbike . . .'

Anyway, to mollify Fred, Mirry decided to call at next-door-but-one and make herself known. The young woman who lived there had a toddler and a baby a few months old. They had said 'hello' when they were shopping, before Glory was born, but had not been introduced.

'Oh, come in do. Fancy a cup of tea? I'm Laura Sims, and this is Donald, he's nearly two, and this is Junie, see, in her pram in the hall, for her morning nap. I brought it in from the porch, the sun having deserted us. Don't leave your little one outside – what's her name? I know you're Mrs Hope, but I don't know your first name.'

'This is Gloria – we call her Glory,' Mirry said proudly, lifting her beshawled infant from her cosy nest in the pram and feeling pleased that she had dressed her in the pink pram suit Mum had knitted, with the fluffy angora bonnet. 'I'm Miriam,' she added, 'and they shorten my name too: do call me Mirry.'

'Our husbands catch the same train to London each morning, I believe,' her new friend remarked. She was a tall, willowy girl, wearing smart, high-waisted tailored slacks in dark blue linen with a matching jacket piped with white on the reverse. She had cropped fair hair and round, slightly prominent blue eyes which were repeated, in both the solemn, thumb-sucking Donald, and when Junie awoke, Mirry saw, in her daughter, too.

Laura held Glory while Mirry slipped off her coat, but kept on her neat cloche hat. She couldn't help noticing the gleaming Black Cat cigarette machine by the hallstand. She felt rather shocked, but concealed it she hoped, at such flamboyance. Laura, fortunately, interpreted her look as interested surprise.

'Jim tells me he can keep track of his tobacco consumption with this, but I'm not so sure. It's always empty for several days before the man calls to refill it. More likely, I tell him, that he got talked into it, by a clever salesman, eh?'

They sat in a dining room furnished in very much the same fashion as the Hopes'. They ate shop buns from Woolworth plates, for Laura said frankly she was not much of a cook, and drank their tea from matching cups.

'How long have you lived here, Laura?' Mirry asked.

'Most of my life. I was born in one of the villas. Mum and Dad were against the new houses being built at first, but in actual fact, they bought one before we did. Mum admits they are so much easier to run. Of course, I worked away from home for a few years.'

'In service?' Mirry ventured. That was usually the only reason for leaving home before you got married.

'Good gracious, no! My parents sent me to a secretarial college. Maybe they thought no one would marry me,' she joked. 'I enjoyed being an independent girl. My last job was as secretary to a film company – that was in Surrey.' She sounded wistful now. 'I've got this impossible dream, Mirry, of returning there one day . . . I met all the stars and I had secret hopes that my boss would look at me and say:

"There's just the part for you, Laura, in our next picture!"
But he never did, of course, though he did say I was the
best secretary he'd ever had – then I met Jim, and that was
that. I really had no intention of getting married – I was
almost thirty – but here I am, three years later, mum to
two, back in the very same place I thought I'd escaped for
ever . . . More tea, Mirry?'

'Please.' *Escaped*? Mirry thought, puzzled. We believed
we'd escaped from London to a better place, here in the
suburbs, when we moved into Number Five.

Later, as she laid Glory back in her pram, Mirry asked
diffidently: 'Would you like to pop round to my house,
Laura, one afternoon? I could ask Miss Boam if she'd like
to join us.' Fred would be pleased, she knew, that she had
made the effort to meet Laura. He couldn't say they had
nothing in common. Laura's husband worked in a City
bank; like Fred he was a white collar worker.

Laura opened the gate for her, shooed Donald back into
the garden. She didn't look at Mirry as she replied: 'It'd be
nicer if it was just us; yes, I'd love to come. Mind, Don's
just at the age when he touches everything, and if your
husband is as houseproud as mine . . .'

'Don't you like Miss Boam? She was so kind to me when
Glory decided to come in such a rush . . .'

As if recognising her name, the baby gave a wail.

'Uh-oh – feeding time. You'd better hurry home, I'll see
you soon,' Laura said.

Bar had eaten her dinner with undignified haste and departed for her dancing lesson. Mirry's own meal was interrupted yet again by her baby's demands.

'I'll lay her down, you eat up, dear,' Fred said, wiping Glory's milky chin with a muslin piece. 'You look really tired,' he added, concerned. 'Bar might have waited to do the washing up.'

'Oh, Fred, she works hard, you know, she deserves to do something more exciting than swishing her hands in greasy water.'

'So do you. I tell you what, you go to the Pictures on Saturday afternoon, I'll enjoy looking after the nipper.'

She scooped her peas onto her fork. Sometimes she forgot she was a woman now, and anyway, Mum wasn't there to admonish her. 'What if Glory wakes up and needs feeding?'

He grinned. 'I'll sing to her. Didn't I charm you when I was in *The Gondoliers*, when we both joined the Operatic Society, and you got roped in to play the piano? If that doesn't work, I'll try pushing her round the block in her pram – and if that fails, I'll dip that dummy your mum insisted on buying, in the honey pot . . .'

I was the envy of all the girls, she remembered, Fred being so tall and good-looking – he still is – with that curly hair and his silky moustache. 'I do love you, Fred,' she said suddenly. It was good to be on their own this evening. She would tell him about Laura, who she was sure would become a real friend even if she was older and more educated than she was, although Mirry had diligently studied book-keeping at evening classes to better herself. However, Laura was definitely younger than Miss Boam, and, of course, she and Laura had the children in common.

It was warm, almost steamy in the studio. There was no visible heating that Bar could see. She didn't realise that the atmosphere was generated by perspiring bodies, by excitement. There were wooden chairs all round the perimeter of the dance floor, freshly french-chalked to enable the dancers to glide. The heavy, dusty plum-red plush curtains were not closed, perhaps because they were faded in stripes from the sun, she thought.

She had changed into her dancing slippers in the Ladies' Powder Room. There was indeed bright pink powder provided, to cover any hectic flush, in a cut glass bowl, with a rather grubby swansdown puff. Coats and hats were left downstairs, but there was a swinging mirror in a gilded frame and more bowls containing hairpins and hair-combings. Bar did not fancy these, or the brush and comb. Cold water trickled from the hot tap, and the soap provided in the stained hand basin was a mere sliver. These things persuaded her not to venture into the water closet. Anyway, there was no need, she only lived over the road. Miss Boam obviously had no help in this big house.

Bar had realised, on her first visit, that she was the youngest pupil. Miss Boam tended to call out, if she was demonstrating new steps with her regular partner: 'Bar dear, would you mind winding up the gramophone?' Bar always rushed to oblige. The gramophone was encased in mahogany, with a great fluted horn. There were the latest records, so different from Fred's collection, for he preferred light opera, and Mirry's piano pieces were rather old-fashioned. There was a piano here, in a corner, but obviously no pianist.

There were sixteen pupils this evening, she counted; there had been half that number at the last session. Bar didn't expect to get a partner. Miss Boam sometimes guided her round the floor, but women outnumbered men as usual. She wore a new dress tonight, which she had concealed under her coat when she left home. One of the girls at work had asked if she would like to buy it: 'I thought I'd get slim enough to wear it, but Mum makes too many steak and kidney puds and I'm too weak to resist 'em, so . . .' she said ruefully. The dress had cost ten shillings, was a bargain at seven-and-six, but even that was beyond Bar's means. 'Shilling a week, would that help?' her colleague suggested. 'Take it home and try it on. Let me know tomorrow.' So here she was, in purple rayon, with bare arms like Miss Boam, and fantail pleats to the skirt so that it swirled deliciously round her knees when she twirled.

The tango! Miss Boam moved away from her partner after they had displayed the moves. Someone dimmed the lights. Miss Boam's partner unexpectedly bowed politely to Bar. 'May I have this dance?' he asked formally.

He was supple, skilful, but he held her much too close. One hand seemed to burn her back, the other clasped her own damp hand and jerked her arm into the required position. Bar felt his breath fanning her throat as he bent her backwards: she smelled his cloying brilliantine, and averted her gaze from his smiling, red lips, which were accentuated by the thin black pencil line of his moustache. 'Da-da-da-da, de-da-de-da-da,' he murmured encouragingly to the beat. She was a natural dancer: with an expert partner to guide her they moved in unison. She was completely oblivious to the fact that the other couples had gradually moved aside, and that they were left to dance the final sequence on their own. Flustered, Bar mumbled, 'Thank you,' and made for her seat, as she heard the spontaneous applause.

He didn't ask her to dance again, but gallantly presented himself to the other ladies in turn. Bar was relieved, because although she had discovered that she really could dance, with the right partner, there was something about Miss Boam's friend that made her feel nervous. He was plainly several years younger than the dancing teacher, but he was an older man, to Bar, and all of a sudden, she felt like the fourteen-year-old she was.

She was in the hall, putting on her coat, the last to leave, because the other coats had been piled on top, when she heard Miss Boam and her friend on the half-landing above. She heard Miss Boam give a gurgling little laugh. 'Too young and innocent for you Chas, I can see I'll have to keep an eye on you. Are you sure you can't stay tonight? *I* need you, you know that . . . I've got plans for that girl, anyway.'

''Night!' Bar called out, praying that they wouldn't realise she'd overheard. She opened the heavy door, rushed back home over the road. She'd tell the girl at work, sorry, the frock didn't fit, anyway her sister said the style was too old for her. A shilling a week was too much to pay for growing up before you were ready.

CHAPTER FIVE

MIRRY TROD SLOWLY UP the wide steps to the glass doors of The Palace, savouring the prospect of a thrilling afternoon.

She shook the drops from her umbrella on the top step, and closed it. The rain had been relentless, but her hair had been protected by her headscarf. She wore a blue rubber mackintosh, tightly belted to show off her newly restored waistline, and black galoshes over her best court shoes.

She joined the small queue in the foyer, moving slowing towards the ticket office. There was no hurry. The main feature didn't start until two. There were framed photographs on the walls, of past and present stars of the film world. Nearly all from America, but some were British born, of course. She liked those with intriguing accents, like Greta Garbo and Fredric March. Did his wife call him Fred, too? Her ticket was punched – pushed through the slot under the grille by a limp white hand with blood-red nails. 'Next ...' said the refined voice of the blonde behind the glass. She looked uncannily like Jean Harlow, one of her favourite film stars, Mirry thought.

Now, she pushed open the swing doors, the curtain parted and she stepped uncertainly into the sudden darkness. A girl with a torch shone a powerful beam as she led the way, allowing the light to sweep across the rows in search of an empty seat. Startled faces turned towards them, looking cross at being disturbed, eyes blinking. 'Here, do, dear? Room for one in the middle – would you mind letting the young lady past, please?' Fred had insisted she buy a ninepenny ticket, because the cheaper front rows meant a crick in the neck, being so near to the screen. They were also in close proximity to the Ladies and Gents, with their overriding smell of strong disinfectant. The swinging of those particular doors was distracting to the avid screengazer, as children went in and out endlessly.

The seats, the tip-up sort, were quite comfortable, but Mirry always obeyed Mum's strictures not to rest her head on the back of the seat. The Palace looked nice and clean, but she wasn't going to chance an itchy head.

There was another beam of light from above, focused on the screen. At the back of the cinema, aloft in the projection room, the reels rolled smoothly, but the projectionist had to remain alert to possible breaks in the film. He had to keep calm and ignore the stamping feet, the whistles, the angry calls when the whirring ceased abruptly and the screen flickered spasmodically.

Mirry missed the piano accompaniment: the stirring music was no longer necessary now there was sound with the pictures. However, all the newer cinemas, and this was one, had electric organs, and that was a real treat to look forward to, in the intervals. The huge cinemas in London had great organs which rose up into view, with the organist already seated at the instrument. The Palace had a modest version below the screen – those in the front seats had to put their fingers in their ears.

She settled down with her bag of nuts and raisins, a favourite cinema snack. There was a smell of wet mackintoshes, of noisily crunched peardrops, of peeled oranges. She was thankful there were no large hats obscuring her view ahead, then she suddenly spotted a bald head, dented on the crown rather like a celluloid ping-pong ball, gleaming in the projected rays, two rows in front of her. The Galloping Major? Surely not . . . She was glad, anyway, that she was sitting behind, so that if it was him, he wouldn't be aware that she was at the Pictures too.

The big picture was a tear-jerker. Mirry was not the only one sniffing and wiping her glasses. Then came the advertisements, the lights went up, the organist flexed his fingers, and the seats tipped up and down as folk hurried to buy ice-creams and chocolate bars from the girls with their trays in the aisles. Mirry reluctantly decided against leaving her seat for this purpose, as she didn't want to meet her neighbour. She was sure now that it was him, because he had turned and she had seen his profile.

The second film was full of gangsters and wisecracking girls with rigidly waved hair and smart dresses, even when they were supposed to be living in what the Americans styled as doss houses, with the dregs of society. Mirry had actually begun to yawn during this picture, for the plot was predictable, when there was a sudden commotion in front. A woman screamed, the usherette came running from the back, and necks craned as attention was switched from the screen to real-life drama. There were angry voices, then the manager appeared. The film wound on, and the lights remained dimmed. Someone was being manhandled along the aisle, protesting vehemently, and as he passed, Mirry was shocked to see it was the Galloping Major. Following was a sobbing woman, being comforted by the usherette.

'Horrible it was! A heavy, black – thing! On my knee! I want me money back . . .'

'Heard it all before,' the woman next to Mirry volunteered, crumpling her chocolate wrapper. 'Says he don't realise he's doing it, 'cause it's an artificial hand, like . . . Poor old sod! Mind, he always gets away with it.'

Mirry came out into the cold night air. Thank goodness it had stopped raining, she thought. It was past five, the street lights were glowing, but the shops were not yet closed. She'd go along to Woolworths and buy some sweets, she decided, to take the sour taste out of her mouth. Maybe she'd hang on for Bar, it was almost time for her to finish work, then they could walk home together. She suddenly felt guilty. Glory would be hungry, poor little soul, and Fred would probably have had quite enough of trying to cope with her on his own. She'd leave it a while before she went to The Palace again, she decided. And there was no point in upsetting Fred, or Bar, with the sordid details. After all, she tried to convince herself, that poor woman hadn't been touched by flesh and blood . . .

'I must think of my future,' Bar said grandly, when Mirry asked her why she had stopped going to her dancing lessons. 'Miss Phillips reckons I ought to go to evening classes, there's that business college along the London Road, a couple of nights a week. I can't afford to do both things. I could walk it, I'd be on the way, if I went straight after work. Her nephew started there in September, he's a junior reporter on *The Norwood News*, but I'm sure I could soon catch up. Miss Phillips suggested I do shorthand and typing: I should have stayed on at school another year as you and Mum begged me to. Didn't see the point then, *now* I do.'

Mirry felt that familiar irritation: it seemed that Bar always disregarded *her* advice. 'Dark evenings now . . .' she pointed out. Fred would have to turn out again to meet her off the tram on her return, she thought, with a little exasperated sigh.

It was Wednesday afternoon, and Mirry was making lemon curd while Bar held the baby, who was grizzly, at her request. She liked to make the curd for immediate use. Fred had hinted that he fancied one of her lemon tarts for pudding tonight. It was a lengthy process, you couldn't hurry it, but the results were so delicious, even if the curd was not brightly coloured like the shop pots.

Bar sat down on the kitchen chair and watched. Mirry was a good cook, but a slave to the kitchen. You wouldn't catch *her* making her own preserves when – if – she married, for now she'd decided on a career, she'd need to be singleminded.

Into a jam jar, already set in a pan of gently bubbling water on the gas ring, Mirry spooned butter and granulated sugar. When the butter melted and mingled with the sugar, she grated the rinds of two lemons into the mixture and squeezed in the juice. Finally, she stirred in two beaten eggs. She turned the heat low. 'You must cook it slowly until it thickens . . .'

'Smells wonderful,' Bar murmured. 'Unlike your daughter,' she added with a grin. Glory was red in the face.

'Oh dear, not again! She seems to have the collywobbles, must be something I've eaten, I suppose.' Mirry sighed. 'Shall I make the pastry before, or after I change her?'

'Well, she's gone to sleep at last, so I should knock up the pastry quick while you can.'

Mirry washed her hands again, mindful of Fred's strictures on cleanliness in the kitchen. She shook flour onto the well-wiped top that fitted over the copper. 'What really made you change your mind Bar, about the dancing, I mean, you seemed so keen. Nothing happened to, well, upset you, did it?' She couldn't help recalling the episode in the Pictures. As she so often reminded Fred, Bar was their responsibility now.

Bar immediately looked wary. Mum questioning you was one thing, your big sister didn't have the same right. She said finally, fiddling with the bow at the neck of Glory's matinée jacket: 'As I said, I want to get some qualifications. I don't want to be a shop assistant for ever, even though I enjoy it now.'

'I'll talk to Laura Sims,' Mirry decided. 'She had a very exciting job before she got married, in a film studio, just fancy that.' Bar hadn't answered her question about the dancing, but she told herself that Bar was her usual cheerful self. Better not to pry. After all, she had a secret or two to keep to herself, too.

*   *   *

'I didn't call before, because I know how busy you must be, with Glory,' Miss Boam said. 'I just wondered if Bar has changed her mind – such a pity if she has, for she has a natural talent – about the dancing lessons? She's missed two, now.'

'She's been very busy at work,' Mirry floundered, 'and the subject of evening classes came up – she might have to concentrate on those, for a while . . . I'll remind her she should tell you, one way or the other.'

Miss Boam produced a present for the baby from her bag. A fine silver chain bracelet, which she asked if she might fasten on her wrist.

'Of course,' Mirry said, a little flustered, aware that she hadn't dusted the room for at least three days. Maybe she should have ushered Miss Boam into the sitting room: then she remembered the last time they had been in that room together, when Miss Boam was so kind, holding her hand like that. 'Thank you,' she said now, meaning it: 'The bracelet is lovely.'

'No weight, on that delicate little wrist.' Miss Boam straightened up from the pram, which Mirry parked between the easy chairs when she was busy in the living room. 'She's such a pretty baby, Mirry – you don't mind if I call you that? And of course, you know I am Anna . . . She looks just like you.'

'Oh, I'm not pretty,' Mirry insisted. Well, only Fred thinks so, she thought: if only she'd taken after Mum, like Bar, instead of her paternal grandmother . . .

'Of course you are! Mind, you deserve a new wardrobe of clothes after your Trojan effort. I'd be glad to advise.'

Mirry wished she wasn't wearing her pinafore, and that she'd curled her hair last night, but she'd been too weary to make the effort. Besides, they were on a tight budget, now they had a mortgage and train fares for Fred to find. New clothes were out of the question, apart from those she could sew for herself.

Anna immediately interpreted her expression. 'Of course, how tactless of me, babies are a big expense,' she sighed regretfully. 'Something I have no experience of, alas. Could I alter that maternity dress for you? I noticed what good quality material it was when, forgive me, I helped you to disrobe . . . It could be quite transformed with a touch or two of white piqué – what d'you think? I enjoy altering clothes.'

'It needs cleaning,' Mirry faltered. She had intended to put the hated dress away for 'next time'.

'Oh, don't waste money at the cleaners. I have my own economy – I steam all my clothes. Mother taught me that – all those lovely stage clothes, ballgowns . . . Let me steam your dress – do fetch it now.'

Reluctantly, Mirry went to do her bidding. She knew she would always be aware of the original purpose of that dress, however much it was 'transformed'.

On her return, she caught Miss Boam bending low over the pram. She straightened quickly. 'I imagine you will be having her christened soon?' she asked wistfully.

'I only just stopped myself from inviting her to be a godmother, Fred,' Mirry told him, when they were in bed, that night. 'What with the bracelet and us naming the baby after her – it was obvious what she was hinting at. I felt really mean, after all she did that day.'

'*La Bohème*, eh? Well, I'm glad you *didn't* ask her.' Fred finally bestowed the nickname which Bar had guessed he would. 'I imagine,' he added drily, 'that was also the reason for offering to renovate your dress.'

CHAPTER SIX

'ONLY TEN MINUTES' WALK, BARBARA,' Miss Phillips told her, walking briskly along the pavement. Her shoes squeaked, Bar couldn't help noticing, which Fred always said meant they weren't paid for, although that naturally couldn't be true in this case. In the evening damp, Miss Phillips's smart fox fur gave off a whiff or two of something rather unpleasant, not that Bar could place it.

It was Monday evening, not a busy day at the store, and the time had dragged a bit. Bar was glad to be going out this evening: she wouldn't miss the endless nappies steaming on the clothes horse obscuring sight of the fire. Every day was wash day now, she thought. She was curious about Miss Phillips's abode, for she'd been cordially invited for 'a bite of supper, before Clive escorts you to the evening classes', though she couldn't help a little frisson of regret at not going dancing instead. Had she been rather hasty in this respect? Miss Boam had slid a little perfumed note through the letter box: Miss you, Bar, come and see me soon! Anna Boam.

All the houses along the London Road were old. Substantial, but down-at-heel. Here and there, were shabby old shops, already boarded for the night, or maybe, for good. People hurried home, heads down because of the drizzle, swung open creaking gates, inserted cumbersome keys in stiff locks.

The trams rattled past noisily in the middle of the road. When they reached the far end of London Road, the passengers would alight; the driver would leap out, change the connection on the overhead wire, while the conductor tipped all the wooden seats to face the other way. When the driver again had his hand on the lever, at the opposite end, a new crowd would step up into the tram for the clanking return journey. Boneshakers, trams.

'Here we are,' Miss Phillips said. 'Like you, Barbara, I live with my sister; she's long been an invalid, I'm afraid. We have a good neighbour who looks in on her while I'm at work and rustles up our supper. That's a great help.'

Bar followed her down the steps to the basement flat. 'We used to have the whole house. I worked in Bournes then, in London, as assistant buyer. But when my brother-in-law died some years ago . . .' Miss Phillips opened the door. 'Mind Clive's bicycle, he tends to leave it in inconvenient places.' She sounded more fond than cross. 'Hang your coat here, Barbara – a narrow passage, I know, but we have to make use of every inch of space.'

A door opened and Clive, a long, thin boy with a shock of dark hair, cheerfully invited Bar to enter a low-ceilinged room with dingy wallpaper and brown paintwork, and a newly-lit fire spitting in the grate.

There was a sudden explosion of harsh coughing from a room situated off a short flight of stairs above the hall. Miss Phillips paused. She did not follow Bar into the living room. 'Excuse me, please, Barbara – my sister is letting me know that she is aware of our arrival. I must pop up and see what she wants. She *might* like to say hello to you after supper. It all depends . . .'

'I'll look after Barbara, Auntie Iris,' Clive offered. Bar looked at him openly, as he had regarded her. His shirt was not long enough in the sleeves, his bony wrists protruded, he wore a badly knitted Fair Isle pullover and baggy trousers which obviously needed both belt and braces to hold them up on his skinny torso. His angular face was like his aunt's. Amused at her scrutiny, he raised his eyebrows. He had hazel eyes with surprisingly long eyelashes for a boy, she thought.

'Bar, everyone calls me Bar,' she ventured, feeling shy, unusual for her.

'Except Auntie Iris, of course,' he put in, grinning, and he pulled out a chair at the table with a gallant gesture and she warmed to him because he had good manners, like Fred. 'Shepherd's pie,' he added in a conspiratorial whisper: 'Don't expect too much. Dear old Edie next door can mince up yesterday's mutton, but that's about all. It must have been a grey, ancient shepherd. I'll dish up, Auntie won't be long. Mum's rather fractious, that's understandable because she's in a lot of pain. And she knows it's my night out tonight.'

Bar, glancing at the slices of dry bread already on the side plates, felt sorry for him. If learning shorthand and typing was Clive's idea of a night out, well . . . She had a sudden bright idea. 'Do you dance, Clive? I've been taking lessons. I – I could do with a partner of my own age . . .'

He looked at her keenly. 'Been going to that dancing academy near you?' he asked. 'I *might* be interested, if I can get away. The editor says I could do with some social graces, having to cover the local hops from time to time. I might even graduate to the town hall dinner dances next year. I'm a bit older than you, though – sixteen,' he said with pride. 'I've been working for the paper since July, when I left the grammar school. I'd have had no chance of the job if I hadn't got matric. Education's so important, particularly for you girls now things are at last becoming more equal – you're doing the right thing, Bar, joining night school.'

'Oh,' she exclaimed. She couldn't think of anything else to say. But she knew she liked him, and his opinions. He was a good sort, clever and ambitious, like Fred.

* * *

'How about an early night?' Fred asked casually. Cold meat and bubble-and-squeak, plenty of homemade chutney, the usual Monday night dinner. Hardly exciting. But at least they had the house to themselves. Miss Phillips's nephew was walking Bar home after night school. She had her own key. They could leave her a sandwich and a glass of milk in the kitchen.

'Fred! It's not eight o'clock yet,' Mirry exclaimed, going pink.

'Not expecting any callers are we?' he joked, but Mirry could see that look in his eye.

She folded up the ironing board, unplugged the iron from the light socket, replaced the bulb, then switched the light on again. She was weary, but it wasn't fair to Fred, she thought, always making that excuse. Glory was nine weeks old now. Nurse had said tactfully, when she called in the other day, that it was all right, resuming normal married life. It was just that, well, she found the whole thing rather undignified, and . . .

'Don't worry,' Fred's arms slid round her waist, tightened, as she fiddled with the pile of linen. 'Glory is enough family for us, right now . . . You've got your hands full, little Mirry, I'm well aware of that.'

She turned then and hugged him back. 'Thank you, Fred,' she said gratefully. He did understand one of the reasons for her reluctance, she thought, and maybe she'd overcome her other inhibitions in time. 'Yes, it'll do us both good – an early night . . .'

From the outside, the college looked grim, very institutional. Inside there were large, lofty rooms, with long rows of desks and tables marked with ink and scratches. Diligent seekers after further education filed eagerly, willingly, into class. The courses were subsidised; in some cases, discreetly offered free. Bar filled in the entry forms, paid the modest fee, advanced to her by Fred, and was welcomed by a kindly teacher into the shorthand class. She slid into the seat beside Clive, who gave her an encouraging wink.

To her surprise, the hour passed quickly. She received help whenever she raised her hand. Clive was transcribing an article into shorthand outlines, with much chewing on the end of his pencil. Bar continued practising the strokes, while the rest of the class took simple dictation at a steady speed. There was homework to be done: but the instructress told her she should soon catch up with the rest of the class.

Clive accompanied her to the typing room. 'The machines come out of the ark, Bar, but the keyboard's the same. You won't have any problems learning to type. *I* had to learn how to untype,' he told her ruefully, 'I'd been stabbing the keys with one finger, but here you learn to touch type. You can get up to great speeds, they say – court reporters take down verbatim.'

For Bar this evening, there was certainly no speed, just uncertain searching for the keys under the cover placed over her hands. At the end of the lesson she really felt she preferred the shorthand.

Clive pushed his bike alongside her and they chatted as he walked her home. They stopped with one accord at the fish and chip shop. 'I'll treat you,' Bar offered grandly, guessing he would not refuse, being a believer in equality between the sexes, 'as I saved the tram fare, and Miss Phillips gave me supper.'

They dipped into their newspaper cones of red-hot, fatty, delicious chips and munched the rest of the way downhill from the Jubilee clock.

'See you on Thursday, then,' Clive said, swinging on to his saddle, outside her gate. He paused for a moment, feet straddling the pavement. 'That's the dancing place, isn't it – all lit up over there? I don't suppose Mum'd mind if I went on a Friday night: Saturdays are out because I often have to cover events for the paper then. Would that suit you, too? I can't afford more than once a week.'

'That's about all I can scrape up now, with the evening classes – Friday would be a good night, as it's payday. Thanks ever so much for seeing me home. See you Thursday,' she repeated. She waited at the gate to wave him on his way.

The light was on in the hall. All was quiet. She went into the kitchen. She couldn't manage the ham sandwich after the chips, but it was kind of them to think she might be hungry. She wrapped it carefully in greaseproof paper and put it in the larder cupboard. It would do for lunch tomorrow. She downed the milk. Poor old Mirry and Fred, she thought, it must be a blight on their love life having her always around. Though she suspected that Mirry would be embarrassed if she suspected that Bar felt sympathetic on that score. Well, they'd soon have Friday nights to themselves, too.

Glory gave her first hungry cry of the evening. Mirry disengaged herself from Fred's warm clasp, bent to give him a fleeting kiss. Not that he was aware of it. He was already asleep.

'Up you come, lovey,' she whispered, lifting Glory and getting carefully back into bed.

'I'm in, 'night,' Bar's voice from outside the firmly closed door.

"Night Bar,' she returned dismissively, 'tell me all about it tomorrow, eh?'

CHAPTER SEVEN

MIRRY SCRAPED THE SOLE OF HER shoe vigorously on the patch of grass bordering their hedge. 'Oh no!' she exclaimed wrathfully. Major Boam had allowed Bridger to do his 'business' as Fred termed it, right outside their gate. She'd say something, she thought irately, next time it happened – the problem was, the major really was always at a gallop. She repeated the cleansing process with the pram wheels, just in case. Then she set off to call for Laura, for they were going to the Grove.

It was early afternoon, the end of November; they went out directly after lunch these days in case the fog came down. It would be Christmas soon and a familiar nip was in the air. The Hopes had settled in well to their new home. She turned her mock fur collar up and adjusted the cover on the pram. No sitting by the pond today, feeding the ducks, while Donald launched his little sail boat, no music from the bandstand, no inclination to ignore the warnings and to step over the little railings on to the grass – just a brisk walk round the park and then head for home.

'They say it's lucky,' Laura said, as they pushed their heavy prams side by side.

'How can treading in anything so foul be lucky?' Mirry asked.

'They're a strange family,' Laura pulled Donald's hat over his ears: the little boy sat on the step of the pram, drumming his heels impatiently whenever they slowed up. 'He was badly injured in the war, of course, that's when his hand got blown off by a shell, they say.'

'Nothing wrong with his legs.' Mirry was still indignant.

'No, but a problem with his head – haven't you seen that awful dent in his skull, when he raises his hat? He spent a long time in hospital after the war, a special hospital – she brought him home just before Madame Beatrice went.'

'Died, you mean?'

'No, she disappeared. There was a lot of talk about it at the time – I wasn't at home then, but my mum and dad heard all the rumours, of course. Went off with her daughter's fiancé . . .'

'Oh!'

'You'd have mistaken them for sisters, Mirry. My parents used to hint darkly at what they thought really went on at the dancing school. I certainly wasn't allowed to go there for ballet lessons as a child, despite all my wheedling. Beatrice was not at home much before the war – she toured quite a bit as a professional dancer. Anna was a lonely child, I guess, with her father away too. Then her mother came home and started the academy, and taught her daughter to dance and, in her teens, she began to help with the classes. Mum said they were very busy during the war, with the major safely out of the war at the Front.' She looked meaningfully at Mirry.

'Miss Boam's had rather a rotten life, it seems.'

'Maybe, but she's her mother's daughter and she rules the major with a rod of iron.'

'How d'you know?'

'Eyes and ears,' Laura laughed. She lifted Donald down and set him on the path. 'There, get rid of a bit of energy, my lad! I'm not usually one to repeat gossip, you know – but perhaps you ought to be aware, well, that you should be on your guard a bit with Miss Anna Boam – your sister, too. I keep forgetting that Donald's all eyes and ears too, Mirry, until he repeats everything to Jim when his daddy comes home at night.'

The little boy jumped in a pile of leaves. 'Rod 'n iron!' he shouted gleefully.

'Bar, how nice to see you again!' Miss Boam beamed, opening the door to Bar and Clive on Friday evening. 'And you've brought a friend with you to boost the male contingent.'

'This is Clive Joy. I work with his aunt,' Bar told her. She hoped that Clive would not be too bowled over by Miss Boam's powerful perfume, the same one which she had squirted Bar playfully with the first time she attended a class, telling her that a touch of scent gave you confidence. She also hoped that he would not notice Miss Boam's magnificent bosom.

Miss Boam caught her wide-eyed look at this. 'One of my mother's stage dresses, it seems such a pity not to air them. Of course, some of them are quite fragile, but then I don't risk them disintegrating at the cleaners. I steam them, you see.'

'I know,' Bar hung up her coat. The steaming had indeed taken out any marks on her sister's altered dress, but they had agreed that it couldn't possibly make clothes smell fresh. Bar felt dowdy beside Miss Boam. She was wearing her pink jumper with the short, puffed sleeves, fitted to the waist. Mum had sewn silver bugle beads on the smocked yoke, and she had thought it went nicely with her grey, pleated skirt, until . . .

'You look very smart tonight,' Clive whispered unexpectedly in her ear, cheekily flicking her hair to one side so she could hear.

She felt that her cheeks must match her jumper at this compliment. As Clive was dressed exactly as he was the last time they met, she could hardly say the same in return.

'Leather-soled shoes, I hope, Clive?' Miss Boam asked. 'The floor, you know . . .'

'Yes,' Clive said, unabashed, as they went upstairs. 'I did wipe them well on the mat.'

The slow foxtrot was the main dance tonight. After the demonstration, Miss Boam invited Clive to partner her.

'I do like to take the new men through the steps. Chas, will you dance with Bar?'

'My pleasure,' Miss Boam's regular partner said smoothly. As previously, he held Bar too closely and guided her backwards, thigh to thigh. This was in the rules of dancing, so she could hardly complain. 'You were born to dance, young Barbara . . .' he murmured.

Over his shoulder she could glimpse poor Clive stumbling valiantly, being jerked round the corners by Miss Boam. He looked unhappy: she wondered if he would want a repeat performance.

They danced the Last Waltz together. Bar whispered, 'One, two, three, one, two, three . . .' trying to inspire confidence. Clive held her almost at arms' length, watching his feet. The big light was switched off, only the side lights glimmered. Other novices, who had fallen over their own feet during the past hour, relaxed at last, and shuffled round and round. Miss Boam gave a final turn to the handle of the gramophone, while chatting to Chas in the corner.

Quite unexpectedly, the door burst open and the room was immediately flooded with light. The dancers slewed to a standstill, turned their heads, blinking and looking foolish. In the doorway, the major loomed, swaying. 'Dancin' in the *dark*, eh?' he shouted thickly. He had removed his boots and stood in his stockinged feet. And Bar guessed that the gloved hand had been left by the bread board in the kitchen.

Miss Boam's voice was loud and clear. 'Thank you all for coming. Please see yourselves out. Father, you are not dressed to be in company. Kindly go downstairs and wait for me. I will not be long . . .'

Someone squeezed Bar's arm. Startled, she turned to see Chas smiling at her. 'We really must try the tango again soon. Goodnight, Barbara – goodnight – I can't recall your name?'

Clive spoke for them both. 'Goodnight.' Then he slipped his arm firmly round Bar's waist and led her away.

'I don't suppose you'll want to come dancing again, after that,' Bar sighed.

'Of course I will. Someone's got to keep an eye on you with lechers like that about . . . Anyway, you're going to be a really good dancer, even I can tell that – and you can help me to be the same, though I guess you'll have your work cut out, Bar.'

*　*　*

Iris Phillips helped her sister off the commode and back on to the bed. It had been the usual dreary evening, listening to Maisie's complaining, the repeated: 'Shouldn't Clive be back by now, Iris? You allow that boy too much leeway.'

'You're only young once, Maisie,' she said once again. 'Clive deserves a break, it's no fun for him being at home with us.'

'That girl . . .'

'She's from a most respectable family. Doing well at work. She won't lead Clive astray.'

'I hope not. It wouldn't be the first time, would it?'

Iris suppressed a sigh. 'No, as you say, it wouldn't be the first time, Maisie.' How long did one have to go on paying for a single mistake, she wondered.

Fred opened the door: 'You're early – care to come in for a cup of cocoa, Clive? Mirry's just put the baby down, and we wouldn't say no to a bit of lively company.'

Bar still seemed to feel the reassuring warmth of Clive's hand around her waist. He'd steered her away from that smarmy Chas – *he* really gave her the shivers. She wondered what was going on in the kitchen at Lahana. There had been a nasty twist to Miss Boam's mouth when she reprimanded her father. It made her think. Mirry had passed on Laura's warning about Miss Boam.

'Yes, come in, Clive,' she said. She wanted Mirry and Fred to approve of him. Particularly Fred, because she supposed he was a sort-of father figure to her, as her own father had been killed near the end of the war, before she was born.

CHAPTER EIGHT

MIRRY DETERMINED THAT BAR SHOULD not be the only one seeking self-improvement. She joined the local lending library and brought home a basketful of books for herself and Fred each week.

Mirry was able to leave Glory sleeping in the pram in the entrance. Even in the children's section there were notices requesting 'Quiet Please'. There was a reverent hush, just like being in church.

Fred liked a bit of light reading, like Westerns, especially those written by a genuine frontiersman like Zane Grey. Mirry selected these swiftly first, without glancing at the contents, for she patronised the shelves near the outer door in order to keep an eye on the baby. Her choice naturally fell on authors from M–Z. While she missed A.J. Cronin, Conan Doyle, L.P. Hartley and D.H. Lawrence (whom Laura had recommended as a shocking read), she took out Somerset Maugham, Frank Swinnerton, Hugh Walpole and Dornford Yates.

There was also the travelling library. A small van drew up outside the house once a week, and a portly man would stagger up the path carrying a brown cardboard case. He opened this with a flourish, then spread the contents in piles of two or three up the stairs. It would not be proper, Mirry thought, to invite him into the dining room to display his books on the table. It never occurred to her that it might seem a little improper for him to ascend her stairs. He then waited patiently in the hall, asking permission to smoke his pipe, while Mirry worked her way up, sitting on each stair, dipping in and out of the pages, spoilt for choice. She limited herself to three love stories for sixpence. These books were easy to read and were exchanged midweek with Laura. Pearl S. Buck, with her stories set in China, was a joint favourite. Concubines and mandarins, exotic settings, mystery and mastery ... The combination was irresistible. Mirry read when she nursed the baby. 'You'll flatten her head!' Fred grinned, catching her at it one day with the open book almost obscuring Glory. When he opened the front door on cardboard-case day, he sniffed and said: 'Old pipe-smoke, I presume?'

Another sixpence would actually buy a paperbacked novel. It was sometimes a toss-up between one of these, or a visit to the Pictures, but Fred often treated Mirry to the latter. Once a month they went together, of an evening, while Bar looked after the baby. Mirry always felt a trifle apprehensive, wondering if she would see that shining bald head, but she never did.

* * *

Before the Hopes knew it, it was Christmas Eve. It had snowed heavily overnight, but Fred, like the neighbours, cleared the front path and pavement outside. Being a civil servant, he had a week off at Christmas. In the front garden he'd put a small Christmas tree in a tub and fixed lights to the branches, to welcome visitors and passers-by. He'd promised to do the Christmas cooking, so Mirry could relax.

Bar had to work on Christmas Eve in Woolworths, but she didn't mind, because there would be bargains on the rapidly emptying shelves, and she'd been saving up. Mirry lent her galoshes to put over her shoes, and made her wrap up warmly. When she left Number Five, Bar smiled as she heard excited voices. Laura was out in the garden with little Donald, making a snowman. 'Got any carrots?' Laura called. 'For a nose!'

'Mirry will find you one!' Bar called back.

Woolworths was a sight to see, and a joy to explore. Miss Phillips greeted Bar with a hug and whispered: 'I put a few things aside for you, and a poke of humbugs. They'll warm you up inside!'

There were crackers in a slightly dented box, shining coloured glass baubles for the Christmas tree and a fairy doll; another box of Christmas lights and tinsel, which had got in 'a bit of a tangle, so no charge,' Miss Phillips said. Bar bought her Christmas presents, all half-price . . . She chose a plush teddy bear with a squeak hidden in its tummy and a floppy ear, but Bar was sure Glory would love this cuddly little teddy. She hesitated at the tin toys but thought: she's not big enough for those yet . . . Bar chose jigsaws for her grandmother, Aunt Alice and Uncle Stan who'd join them on Christmas Day; a game of *Shove Ha'penny* for Fred, which all could enjoy; also playing cards, and for Mirry, her favourite *Swap Cards*, featuring film stars, including Gloria Swanson . . .

Miss Phillips said diffidently, 'I expect you'd like to give Clive a present, and he can't resist chocolate, so . . .' She produced a box of Cadbury's Milk Tray and added, 'He'll pop round later with something for you, and this is from me . . .'

Bar thought: Warm, fur-lined gloves, just what I need! 'Thank you.' She said shyly.

She moved on to the crockery section and bought a little cream jug for Miss Phillips. 'This is for you! You are so kind and helpful. Happy Christmas!'

Miss Phillips had a tear in her eye, but she said briskly, 'Thank you, dear. . . . We must get behind the counter now as we are about to get a crowd coming in, despite the snow!'

On Sunday, Christmas morning, naturally the baby had the most presents, though Bar had the pleasure of unwrapping them along with her own, which included a red rubber hot-water bottle from Mirry and Fred.

Fred insisted: 'You are not to do a thing, Mirry, Bar will help me, and our visitors should arrive shortly. The turkey went in the oven at midnight,' he cleared his throat, 'after Father Christmas filled the stockings! These cards are from your new friends, Bar, I expect!' He tapped the top card: 'From La Boheme I presume, by the scent – did you send one from us, Bar?'

'I poked it through the letter box on my way home from work,' Bar admitted. She'd seen Clive approaching, and when they wished each other Happy Christmas, she'd grinned as he handed her a box of Milk Tray. 'Snap!' she said, and he admitted, 'I had one of my chocs earlier!'

When it was time for for Christmas Dinner, all enjoyed the feast. Fred and Bar had worked hard preparing vegetables and timing the Christmas Pudding. Mum added mince pies and sausage rolls she'd baked.

Fred provided half a dozen bottles of R White's lemonade, respecting Mirry's wishes for no alcohol. 'This'll make us belch,' he said, earning a disapproving look from Mirry.

After pulling the crackers, they donned paper hats and read mottos. Then, they gathered in the front room round the fire, which Fred had lit first thing, and Mirry settled on the settee, to feed the baby, with her feet up on the velvet covered pouffe, her gift from Fred, alongside Mum and Aunt Alice. They admired the decorations and another Christmas tree, sparkling with baubles, tinsel and colourful lights, (though the fairy looked a bit tipsy!), thanks to Bar. Fred, Uncle Stan and Bar tackled the washing up in the kitchenette, then Fred brought in the wireless. This year they heard the first ever Royal Speech, written by Rudyard Kipling, by King George V from Sandringham.

Bar broke the silence to say, 'How about a game of Shove Ha'penny?' She provided the coin and now her purse was empty . . .

*   *   *

Clive questioned Bar continually. 'Why?' 'What d'you think, Bar?' He tried to interest her in politics worldwide. To Bar, Adolf Hitler was a silly little man on the newsreels at the Pictures, mesmerising the masses with his harsh voice and that mad gleam in his eyes. He strutted about stiffly in the goosestep, waving his arms and affecting that arrogant salute. He was certainly stirring things up in Germany: Clive enlightened her, at length. Sometimes she wished he wasn't quite so earnest, but he threw himself heart and soul into everything he did. She might have given up the evening classes long ago if he hadn't made her stick to her studies.

She was fifteen in the May of 1933, the year Hitler was appointed Chancellor of Germany by Hindenburg. There was the burning of the Reichstag in February and the terrible persecution of the Jews in Germany began. It was shocking, frightening of course, but it was all so far away, Bar thought.

It was also the year she became a keen cyclist and joined a local club with Clive. They went out for a spin to the countryside where Suburbia had not yet advanced, most Sundays. The dancing classes were not held from May to September, so she welcomed a new interest.

She bought her bicycle with the five shillings Mum gave her for her birthday. It was a sturdy Rudge model, with drop handlebars, a shrill bell and a handy saddlebag for the necessary puncture kit, spanner, oil rag, bottle of water and pack of sandwiches. Clive was the proud owner of a custom-made bike from Balham, fitted to his specifications. He needed something speedy, showy but reliable as a roving reporter, he said.

One Sunday morning, Bar donned her new drill shorts, a cool blouse, short socks and plimsolls. She tied her hair back and rubbed Pond's cold cream well into her face, arms and legs. Windburn was a problem, and she wasn't used to so much fresh air. She rolled her mac into a sausage and fastened it to the carrier. It was lovely weather, but better safe than sorry.

Mirry made tomato and cheese sandwiches and a thermos of milky, sugared tea. She split a bun and buttered it, then added a small bar of chocolate peppermint cream to the lunch pack.

'Thanks Mirry! Don't worry about supper, we intend to stop off somewhere for a cream tea – or we might have something on toast, like Welsh rarebit. What are you doing today?'

'We're going with Laura and Jim and their two to find out about the new municipal tennis courts in the park. Fred says we all need to take more exercise. We might even take a picnic tea ourselves . . . listen to the band, if the children allow us to. Take care, Bar, there might be a lot of traffic on the roads . . .'

Bar ruffled Glory's soft fair curls. She could pull herself up now, rocking on her feet, looking most determined. Fred reckoned she'd be walking well before she was a year old.

Glory chewed on her bone-shaped rusk, hanging from a ribbon round her neck. She had four teeth already, and more were obviously on the way.

''Bye all of you, I'm off then,' Bar told them.

She wheeled her bike outside the gate. She glanced round: she hoped she wasn't being watched, as mounting was still a bit hit and miss, without the faithful Clive to hold it steady, she thought ruefully. But she could pedal with the best of 'em, even if she hoped her legs wouldn't become too sinewy. Clive had not only taught her to ride, he'd shown her how to mend a slow puncture or what to do when the chain came off. Women wanted equality, eh? All right, then they must wield a spanner too.

Some of those who lived nearby had already departed for early church; many were still lying in; others were eating a gargantuan breakfast. Bar was meeting the other members of The Venturas Cycle Club at the Jubilee clock at eight.

Something prompted her to look up. Framed in the window upstairs at Lahana was the major. He held the curtains in a bunch in his sound hand. He looked more comical than shocking, in his cream wool combinations, which covered every portion of his anatomy. Bar just couldn't resist it: she gave a cheery wave, before she put her head down and cycled off up the road. 'I'm happy when I'm biking,' she sang loudly, and didn't care who heard. Just a small liberty with the words of the song, for she would be doing some hiking today, too, she thought.

'What d'you keep giggling about?' Clive asked curiously as they cycled two abreast. Mirry needn't have worried, there wasn't a soul, or vehicle about, just a long line of bikes.

She told him.

'If that's all he revealed, poor old devil, I should forget it. Not quite right in the head, as we know . . . It's a long ride, Bar, I hope you won't be saddle-sore at the end of the day.'

'Well, I never sit at work, so as long as I can stand on my feet tomorrow . . .'

'I like your shorts,' he approved. He didn't add that he also admired her shapely long legs.

'And I like yours! I began to wonder if your legs were too spindly to show off, as you always keep them covered,' she retorted at his cheek.

'It wasn't warm enough to bare all, till now,' he grinned.

From Godstone to Hanging Wood they wheeled their bikes in single file along a neglected part of the Pilgrim's Way. There was much crunching of juicy apples and dodging of the deftly thrown cores. Wild flowers were abundant in the wood. They ate their lunch on a grassy bank by a great beech tree, leaning against the vast trunk. Some of their fellow cyclists went ostensibly to pick sheaves of bluebells with drooping heads and blanched stalks to take home to their mothers. Other couples, hand in hand, looking sheepish, disappeared into a denser piece of woodland. Their bicycles were abandoned, propped against nearby trees.

Bar and Clive were left by themselves. The long grass was busy with insects. It was very peaceful. Feeling drowsy, Bar allowed her head to incline towards Clive's shoulder. He still wore that baggy pullover. He must be sweating, but probably his aunt had insisted. She smiled at the thought.

'Your hair's coming loose,' he said lightly. He pulled the ribbon off, untied the bow and smoothed it into a coil round a finger. He glanced down at her smooth, pale legs, the now grass-stained plimsolls, then averted his gaze quickly. He'd never kissed a girl; it wasn't that he was shy, but there had been no opportunity to do so. He seized it now.

His lips were warm on hers, the pressure uncertain. She opened her eyes after a brief moment, colour flooding her face. She sat up instantly, pushed him away. He fell over in mocking surrender, hands raised.

'Don't be so soppy, Clive,' she said flippantly, but her sparkling eyes told a different story.

'Just wanted to see if you were really asleep . . .' he said.

This marked a subtle change in their relationship. Bar acknowledged that to herself, as she turned over gingerly in bed that night, and lay on her stomach. She felt as if her bottom was black and blue. Did she really mind? She wasn't sure. All she knew was that her easy camaraderie with Clive was very important to her.

Mirry had dusted her down. 'You're all crumpled – grubby. You look as if you've been . . .'

'Rolling in the grass,' Fred supplied lightly.

Bar didn't resent the worried look they exchanged. After all, she thought, she knew she'd done nothing to be ashamed of.

CHAPTER NINE

FRED HAD RISEN A COUPLE of grades in his department. It was a slow process, but eventually he knew it would be rewarding. In 1936, he could afford to buy his first motor car. It had taken nearly three years to save £100 for the not quite new Morris Eight saloon. Fred extolled the virtues of the four-cylinder side-valve engine and its hydraulic brakes to anyone who would listen. Mirry and Glory were much more interested in being transported to pastures new – Epsom and Goodwood would do nicely for a start, Mirry told her husband. Laura's Jim, who had bought his Ford some months earlier and now considered himself an expert, was only too pleased to offer advice on maintenance. Clive also wasted time, in Bar's opinion, discussing engines with the two men and revving up his own new motorcycle outside the house, while she sat on the pillion and waited for him to roar off.

Bar was going up in the world, too. Her diligent studying had certainly paid off. She had enjoyed her three years behind the counter but now she was a junior typist working in London. She caught the bus which stopped at the end of their road and was delivered almost to the door of the publishing company she worked for. She certainly wasn't sedentary in her new job because, as the humblest employee, apart from Terry the office boy in the post room, she dashed out on deliveries, deputised on the telephone switchboard and in reception and made the cups of coffee and tea for her superiors. Apart from fearing that her shorthand would become rusty, she tackled it all with great enthusiasm.

Glory, coming up to four years old, was a lively child, with round green eyes like her mother and aunt. 'Just like Shirley Temple!' an acquaintance exclaimed one day, to Mirry's joy, admiring the cap of strawberry blonde curls which Mirry encouraged secretly with a sticky lotion called Curly Top. ('Just comb through and your child will have the most amazing curls . . .') 'Glory won't need to use rags or pipe-cleaners at night,' Mirry said with satisfaction to Laura, having graduated to grim steel rat-traps, as Fred ruefully called them after coming into contact with them.

All cinemagoers seemed to adore little Shirley Temple in her miniscule dresses. Mirry cut out her pictures from the movie magazines and made her own versions of the clothes for Glory. She became expert with her whirring sewing machine. They were simple styles, comfortable to wear. These children's clothes bore no resemblance to the stuffy garments worn by Mirry in her youth, or even Bar, not so many years ago.

Women's fashion had undergone yet another revolution, too. Hair was longer, softer in style but still curled, with a feathery fringe. Skirts were more graceful, longer; waists were back in place, emphasised by wide belts. Hats were small, saucy, veiled; shoes were strappy with heels. The boyishness of the late twenties had given way to the feminine look. Fred, for one, thoroughly approved. Mirry was more curvy since she had the baby. She might be wistful about the rounding of her figure and the need for a proper brassière; he certainly was not.

It had been a year of change, beginning with the death of King George V in January. The first intimations of his illness had come just three days before. Just after midnight, silent and sombre crowds waited for the official notice to be posted outside the Palace. The exodus was equally quiet, a drifting away into the darkness. At home, Fred, Mirry and Bar listened, stunned, to Sir John Reith on the wireless. 'He whom we loved as King has passed from our midst.' The king's last broadcast to his people had been from Sandringham at Christmas.

But 'Long Live the King!' was soon proclaimed in London. Fred joined the throng listening to the heralds at St James's Palace.

The king's subjects wore crêpe armbands or a sewn-on black patch. It all seemed unreal, bewildering to them, for just last year there had been the celebrations for the Silver Jubilee.

When the Spanish Civil War began in July there were already strong rumours that the new King Edward might abdicate for love of an American divorcee . . .

At the beginning of November, on a Saturday, Mirry followed what was now a pleasant routine. She and Glory caught the London bus to meet up with Fred after his morning in the office. This was the only time he used the car to go to work. On fresh autumn days they visited Green Park before making their way to Whitehall. Bar usually went straight to visit Mum after her morning's stint, so Mirry did not have to worry about lunch.

Mirry was elegant in her smart tweed costume. Glory wore a black-and-white checked coat with velvet collar and buttons like shiny liquorice cuttings, and a matching tammy, because a bonnet would have flattened her curls. While it was now the weather for liberty bodices and woolly stockings, Glory had not yet had to wear the cumbersome leggings which completed her new outfit.

Fred opened the doors of the little car with a flourish. 'In you go, girls!' He produced a bag of rather squashed jelly babies from his pocket and presented them to Glory, sitting on Mirry's lap in the front, so she could see out of the window.

Mirry bit back a mild protest. She supposed jelly was better than chocolate, but Fred never realised that children always wiped their sticky fingers on their best clothes.

Back through Brixton toward Streatham they bowled, mindful of the trams, and pedestrians who suddenly took it into their heads to dash across the busy road. They stopped at Sainsbury's to buy familiar treats for tea, like chocolate wafer bars sandwiched with red jam, and a cherry cake. While they were about it, Mirry took the chance to buy some of their special butter, shaped with wooden pats on the marble counter. Fred lifted Glory up to watch. Their local shop sold butter cheaper, but Fred rudely compared it to axle grease.

They had just passed the common, when the fog descended very suddenly. One minute it was dull, but with visibility, the next they were caught up in a swirling, evil yellow mass which obscured everything.

They slowed to a snail's pace. They could hear scurrying feet, loud coughing, panicky voices. The beam from the headlights was not powerful enough. The whine of the approaching tram made them start. Fred reached over and deposited Glory on the back seat.

'Open your door, Mirry,' Fred remarked in a matter-of-fact way, determined not to alarm them: 'I shall need your help . . . Stretch your leg out, feel for the pavement with your foot, then "walk it". I'll drive as slowly as I can, steering by the kerb: you must warn me if you feel the car veering out. Grip the glove compartment tightly. We'll allow the tram to draw ahead and follow it as closely as we can but we must steer clear of the tram lines . . .'

'I . . .' Mirry felt her throat constrict painfully as the smell of the fog permeated the inside of the car. *I can't Fred*, she wanted to scream, *I can't.*

'Daddy,' Glory wailed plaintively, 'I can't see.'

'Be a good girl, don't worry, just eat your sweeties and keep quiet,' Fred told his daughter calmly.

If only she hadn't put on her smart shoes, Mirry agonised, as her heel scraped the pavement, inch by inch. She felt as if she was propelling the car along by herself. She was terrified of being sucked out, of rolling under the traffic trailing them, in turn.

It must have been at least an hour before they arrived at the Jubilee clock. Here the street lights flickered feebly in the gloom and here the tram continued on its journey along the London Road. They stopped beside the clock.

Fred switched off the engine, turned to Mirry. 'You've been a real brick – are you all right?'

Her leg felt numb. She could only nod.

Glory awoke from an uneasy snooze. 'Mummy, I want you,' she cried this time.

'Now what do we do? Abandon ship and walk home?' Mirry asked.

'I'm not sure we should leave the car here,' Fred worried.

'See us across the road Fred,' she said impulsively, 'we'll go and get Jim, he'll have gone straight home before the fog came down – he's got a storm lantern.'

She hoped that Fred didn't see that she was limping badly, as she and Glory walked cautiously away from him. She hardened her heart to the plea: 'Carry me, Mummy! I don't like this fog. I can't see, Mummy.'

She cannoned into someone as she thankfully turned the corner into Kitchener Avenue. She gave an involuntary shriek, echoed by Glory, clinging to her coat.

'Whoa! Steady!' It was the Galloping Major. Something hairy, breathing heavily, brushed against her ankles. Of course, the dog . . . Old and arthritic now, Bridger no longer ran off when he felt his leash slacken. A hand groped for and touched her face, then slipped from her shoulder to her arm. 'Mrs Hope?' he questioned. The whiff of spirits almost knocked her back.

However, Mirry was past caring whether she had seized the Major's real hand or not. She was about to ask for help, when she heard the unmistakable sound of a car coming cautiously round the corner. Two cars! Fred had an escort, a police car, and a kindly policeman walked ahead of both cars, with a powerful searchlight. She couldn't help suddenly crying with relief.

'Come on Bridger, we aren't needed after all. Good after-noon, Mrs Hope,' the major said quickly. Then he crossed the road and continued on his walk.

Only the major, Mirry thought, would dream of taking a constitutional in the fog. Or had he been hoping for an encounter of a different sort? She couldn't help remembering the episode in the cinema when they first moved here. That really made her come over all goosepimply . . .

There was quite a big headline in The Norwood News:

WOMAN ASSAULTED IN FOG IN PARK

Miss Enid Smith, taking her usual short-cut home from serving lunches in the Dog and Fox public house, was found in a distressed state by her brother, who had come to escort her, but been delayed by the density of the fog.

Miss Smith told PC Sandman that she had rested momentarily on a bench to get her breath back, and her bearings. She did not realise she was not alone on the seat. Her clothing was disarranged, but she used her handbag to good effect and made her escape. She could not describe her assailant, but there was a dog barking in the vicinity.

A search of the park revealed nothing. It was deserted on such a bad day. Women walking on their own must take care, the police warn.

* * *

Two women fetched scissors and neatly cut the column from the newspaper before relegating it to the pile for lighting their fires. Both folded the cutting and put it away in a drawer, wondering . . .

I don't know that he went on to the park that afternoon, Mirry thought. If it was the major, well, he just seems to like to touch. Miss Enid Smith has a broad smile on her face in the newspaper photograph, she doesn't look much like a woman who's had a nasty shock. But, if I told Fred, would he say I must report my suspicions? The major might be pilloried for something he didn't do, because of me. Better to forget all about it, she decided.

In his room, the major stood as usual at the window, and watched the comings and goings of the two young women in the house opposite, while his daughter also kept her suspicions to herself.

CHAPTER TEN

GLORY HATED THE NIGHTLY RITUAL of being plucked from her warm bed and being sat on the cold-rimmed chamber pot. This was more an outrage than a comfort like closing your eyes to the soft voice of your mother, or the deeper tones of your father reciting familiar bedtime stories, even the ones where something frightening occurred, like the black panther pouncing on the zebra, because then she cried quickly, 'Turn over the page' and she knew there would be a happy ending . . .

Tonight was different. She was lifted in her mother's arms, clung to her determinedly as usual in an effort to avoid the putting down, but instead, she was carried into her parents' bedroom at the front of the house, where she blinked as she discerned her father and Bar at the window. The room was in shadows, the bedside lamps not switched on, and the dressing table had been shifted to one side.

Her father took her from her mother, held her so that her face was on a level with his own. She wriggled uncomfortably. His grip was harder than her mother's, his chest not inviting to lean against. Mirry now squeezed in beside them.

'Look, Glory, this is a sight you will never forget – The Crystal Palace is on fire . . .' her father told her quietly.

In the distance, high on Sydenham Hill, there was a vast red glow, with a dazzling white-hot core, and shooting stars like the fireworks displays that had entertained so many visitors to the palace over the years. Brock's wonderful, colourful fireworks were visible for miles around and children grew up in the sure knowledge that they would have their weekly excitement which cost their parents not a single penny.

Crystal Palace: once great and glorious – the inspiration not of an architect, but a gardener, Joseph Paxton, who sketched his original design on blotting paper. It had been in decline, but the present general manager had worked ceaselessly to restore its reputation and the visitors had begun to flock once more to see the new attractions, like the motor-racing track. The great Handel organ still thrilled the music lovers, the sparkling fountains still entranced, the tropical plants still flourished under the acres of glass, and the prehistoric monsters, which had been recreated in the grounds, were still there to be exclaimed over and marvelled at.

The palace was illuminated by electricity for the first time in 1891, and when eventually many homes in urban areas followed suit, there came the exasperated cry of the householder to extravagant kin: 'What d'you think this is, the Crystal Palace?'

'I bet Clive's there with his notebook and camera – I wish I was too . . .' sighed Bar now.

'You're not thinking of going – oh, you mustn't, Bar!' Mirry insisted fearfully.

'I don't suppose you could get anywhere near, anyway,' Bar sounded regretful.

'Never been the same, really, since it was used as a barracks by the RNVR during the war,' Fred observed. 'It might have seemed the ideal place to have the Imperial War Museum in 1920, but it completely changed the atmosphere for me: all those displays of guns, tanks and even parachutes – shades of the great balloon races of the past.

'I think it was amazing the palace wasn't bombed and razed during the war, being such a landmark.'

'What are *you* thinking about, Glory?' Mirry whispered in her daughter's ear.

Glory yawned and closed her eyes. 'Can I go back to bed now?' she asked sleepily. Many years later, she would declaim dramatically: 'I saw the sky all lit up with a great fireball, on the 30 November 1936 the night the Crystal Palace burned to the ground . . .'

'There was an awful, eerie silence,' Clive said quietly to Bar, having rapped on the door just after seven next morning. 'Then a sort of sighing, a snapping, as the final glass and steel supports writhed, shivered, toppled down . . . Just twelve hours since the first warning of fire at seven yesterday evening . . .'

Bar, tousle-haired, and with an apron tied round her dressing gown, cracked two eggs into the sizzling fat in the frying pan. Clive looked ashen himself, she thought, unshaven and red-eyed.

'I couldn't go home after – not right away – anyway, I'll have to get my copy to the office – I had to see you, Bar,' he added. 'The national papers will already be spreading the news: ours being a weekly paper, even though local, well . . .'

They had all stayed up until the early hours, mesmerised by the funeral pyre of the great glass edifice. Upstairs, Bar's family slept on, unaware they had a visitor.

'The orchestra, who were rehearsing in the concert garden hall amazingly unaware that the fire was out of control, Bar, had to run for their lives as the roof caved in, an hour after the fire began. That wonderful organ – they say terrible sounds came from the pipes, just like death throes . . . People were praying in the streets, when I arrived – they say Winston Churchill, who was going home to Chartwell from the Commons, was one of the crowd watching from the Parade. The Duke of Kent was there, traffic was at a standstill . . . I stood by the statues on the terrace, despite the heat, feeling as cold as stone myself, and for a time I just couldn't bring myself to write a word, it just seemed impossible to describe it all, Bar. Rare and beautiful birds from the aviary were set free to take their chance, soaring and fluttering through the pall of smoke. And, horrifying all who saw it, a hideous grey mass of rats abandoned the Palace, too, moving in unison across the grass . . .' They both shuddered in revulsion.

'You have described it – made me see it, Clive,' Bar said simply. She put the comforting food before him and turned on the second bar of the little electric fire she had put in the hearth. 'Was anyone hurt?' she asked, resting her hands lightly on his shoulders, standing behind his chair, feeling how tense, how upset he was.

'By a miracle, no. It is a sight, an experience I will never, ever be able to forget . . .' He let his fork fall with a clatter and Bar realised that he was crying silently. 'Surely not even a war, a battlefield, could wreak destruction like that . . .' His head sagged back against her yielding breasts, and she held him very close, not saying anything.

They sprang apart when Fred came in, followed by Glory, trailing her teddy bear, Timothy Tapps, by one leg.

'What's this?' Fred exclaimed sharply. He looked cross, unusual for him. 'You might have put a match to the fire, Bar, instead of being extravagant with the electricity – you don't have to pay the bills, after all. And if you were going to cook, you might have done enough for us, as well. You might have woken me up too.'

'Sorry, Fred,' Bar said. She hoped he hadn't misinterpreted their closeness, when he saw her hugging Clive. 'I'll put some more bacon on, the fat's still hot . . .'

He'd calmed down when she came back with breakfast for him and Glory, who was already happily dipping bread into Clive's egg. The fire was crackling in a satisfactory way.

'I didn't mean to snap,' Fred said.

'I know, it's all right, Fred. Is Mirry still asleep?'

'I believe so.' He took a gulp of tea. 'Good cup, young lady. Thank you.'

I should go, Clive thought.

'I'll see you out,' Bar told him. 'Then I must get dressed.' They hugged briefly in the hall, by the door.

'It's the first of December, Bar . . . When you said, you know, it was all right . . .'

'Mmm?'

'That's what Crystal, daughter of Sir Henry Buckland, manager of the Crystal Palace . . .'

'Wasn't she named after the Palace?' she asked.

'Yes. She said to her father apparently: "Cheer up, Dad. Everything will be all right."' They looked at each other.

'There'll never be another Crystal Palace, though. How could there be?' Bar opened the door. 'Hurry home – go there before the office. Your mum and Iris will be worrying if you are all right . . .'

* * *

'Landmarks, great buildings like that, destroyed by fire or war or even by the ravages of time, well, after a while, they might never have been there at all, even if they are well recorded, once they are no longer in living memory,' Fred observed, wiping Glory's sticky hands. 'Before the Crystal Palace, Bar, there was the Royal Beulah Spa and Gardens. The spring had drawn many to it for its curative properties for countless years before it became the fashionable place to go, when it was designated a pleasure garden. One hundred years ago, not only did rich and poor folk alike drink the saline water for their health, but there was entertainment for everyone just like the Crystal Palace. There were brass bands playing, a maze to get lost in, beautiful gardens and lakes, an archery ground, even the odd fortune teller, too. My grandfather and his brothers used to walk there from Herne Hill as lads – he actually met my grandmother there. There were fireworks and balloon displays, just as at the Palace, but by the time the Palace rose up on Sydenham Hill nearby, well, the spa was out of favour. A few years later the buildings and grounds were auctioned and some of the area was built on. Were you aware of any of that?'

'No,' Bar said slowly. 'I know Beulah Hill, and Spa Hill of course, but I never wondered why they were named that . . . Now, it's part of local history, I suppose, not in living memory, as you said.' She combed her hair before the mirror over the mantelpiece.

'Go and jump on your mummy, Glory,' Fred told his daughter, who had been listening dreamily. 'Tell her, we're off to work . . .' He looked at Bar. 'We'll go by car, I'll give you a lift.'

'I'll catch the bus,' she said. It still rankled a bit with her, Fred jumping to conclusions like that, about her and Clive. It was almost as if he were jealous, she thought, but instantly dismissed the idea as ridiculous.

'Don't be silly,' he said lightly, 'get your coat and hat.'

'I suppose *our* lives will be part of local history, one day,' Bar said reflectively.

'Beulah, Beulah, Beulah Spa,' hummed Glory. 'I like that name, don't you Mummy?'

'What are you going on about, Glory?' Mirry yawned, surfacing from sleep at last.

CHAPTER ELEVEN

IN THE SPRING OF 1939, Glory was six years old. She had now been at school for eighteen months, having got off to a flying start, because her mother had taught her to read and to print, and to work out simple sums.

The second baby Mirry and Fred had been hoping for since Glory was around two, was still a dream it seemed, at the time of Glory's birthday last year. Because he could see that Mirry was fretting, Fred suggested she might give piano lessons. Her advertisement in the corner-shop window brought not only three pupils, but a request from Anna Boam to play for the Saturday morning dancing class she had recently started for children.

It was an agreeable exchange: in return for Mirry's services, Glory could have free lessons. Ballroom dancing no longer paid, that was obvious, but Miss Boam was as versatile as her mother had been, it seemed. Mirry nursed secret fantasies that her Glory, so bright, so bubbly, so talented, would one day be a star of stage and screen.

Glory was certainly the star turn of the end-of-term entertainment. While the chorus line obediently shuffle hopped-one-two in their red tap shoes, Glory's flying feet literally twinkled. She could sing too: perhaps more Shirley Temple in style than Deanna Durbin, whose films both she and Mirry adored, seeing them two or three times over at The Palace.

The best thing of all was, once she was busy and not worrying about it, Mirry suddenly fell pregnant at last. The new baby was due in July. Both she and Fred were like young newly-weds, over the moon.

Bar was actually now a fully fledged secretary and still being courted by Clive, as Mirry archly put it. She would soon be twenty-one – Clive was already twenty-three. They both still lived at home, with not a mention of marriage, let alone an engagement. Mirry cut out pictures of brides from her magazines, but Bar didn't take the hint. She longed to fashion yards of slippery white satin, to see Glory in a special bridesmaid's outfit, attending her young aunt ... But a wedding would have to wait now, she thought, until the new baby put in an appearance. Because Mirry wanted to look wonderful, too.

There was much talk of impending war when Fred, Clive and Jim got together. They were far too interested in politics and world events. It was a dread Mirry put firmly to the back of her mind. Whenever Laura mentioned such things she exclaimed: 'Oh, it will never happen! Mr Chamberlain promised, didn't he?' Not with King George VI on the throne, a reassuring presence like his dear kind father, after all the upset of the Abdication. She skimmed over the serious items in the newspapers, the ominous mentions of rearmament, the general feeling of foreboding.

Her life was Fred, Glory and her home. She couldn't understand Laura, once her children were at school, going back to work part-time for her old boss, though Laura's widowed mother now lived with them to be there for the children, when Laura was not. Three times a week a sleek black motor stopped outside the Sims's. Then she was whisked away to another world. Surely there was no need? Jim was head cashier at the bank now and earned a good salary. They had been to the Isle of Wight on holiday last year, and Laura had told Mirry casually, only the other day, that they were thinking of going to Europe this summer, 'before it all blows up . . .'

* * *

They were painting the empty classroom next door. The children from there had to be crammed in with Glory's class, three instead of two to a desk, under the flashing gaze of Miss Lancaster, Glory's teacher.

If you stared at Miss Lancaster when she stood by the window in a bright patch of sunlight, then screwed up your eyes, Glory discovered, in an idle moment one day: Miss L's image was still there, even with your eyes shut. The dark silhouette, with beaky nose and large ears; the tight bun of dragged-back hair, the jutting chin made her shiver, but she wasn't really frightened, because she knew she was Miss L.'s pet. She played on that naturally, but she was also aware that Miss L. could at times be over-strict with her, because she expected much more of her than the rest of the class.

Now, she raised her hand, after the register was called, before they all filed off to morning assembly in the hall.

'What is it, Gloria? Surely you don't need to be excused this early in the morning?' Miss L. demanded, brows beetling.

'I – I feel sick Miss . . . I always do, when there's wet paint. Daddy says it's the lead in it . . .'

'Rubbish! No one else is affected.' Miss L.'s gaze, sweeping over the rest of the class, dared them to complain. She also registered the fact that Gloria's face was as white as the chalk she threw with deadly accuracy at any inattentive child. 'However, perhaps you had better stay in the classroom, just in case, we don't want the morning service ruined . . . Can I trust you to behave?'

'Yes, Miss . . .'

'Class, follow me – you revise your spellings, Gloria, eh?'

When they had gone, Glory opened her dictionary. She couldn't seem to focus on the print. There was an awful pain in her head. She slumped down, put her face against the cool pages of the book . . .

She didn't remember afterwards the caretaker carrying her home, or her mother's alarm when she answered the door.

She was vaguely aware of the doctor bending over her, gently unbuttoning her pjyama jacket and placing his cold stethoscope to her burning, scarlet chest. She heard Mirry crying, then her father's voice, which wasn't right, because he didn't come in from work until six in the evening. Her head hurt so much she couldn't speak.

Strange men wrapped her in coarse red blankets and rolled her on to a stretcher. They fastened straps round her cocoon so that she would be safe while they handled the stretcher down the stairs.

'Just one night, darling,' her mother whispered, holding her hand before they lifted her into the ambulance and drove her away. 'You'll be back tomorrow, I promise . . .'

Mirry sobbed her heart out in Fred's arms. 'You shouldn't have said that, Mirry,' he reproved her quietly. 'The doctor said she could be six weeks or more in the isolation hospital . . .'

'Oh, Fred, why couldn't I have nursed her at home? I looked after her perfectly well when she had the measles so badly, last year – you know I did.'

'Scarlet fever is much more serious, Mirry. She needs very special care. So do you.' He kissed her wet face tenderly. 'Now you're expecting again, at last. And the civil service rules can't be got around. Any notifiable illnesses like this in the family mean the patient must be isolated.

It's in my contract, you know that. The house, the contents must be fumigated.'

'I don't think I can bear it, Fred!' The worry she had felt recently, when the streets in town were washed down with carbolic because of a typhoid scare over the drains, paled into insignificance against the reality that Glory had been taken away from them like this.

'You must try to be calm, Mirry – think of the baby.'

'It will be another ten weeks before it arrives – it's Glory who matters now. If anything happens to her – we haven't even told her about the baby yet . . .'

'I said we should tell her, didn't I?'

'I wanted it to be a wonderful surprise.'

'It will be, dearie, it will be.'

CHAPTER TWELVE

FOR MORE THAN TWO WEEKS Glory's small body had been racked with fever. She was unaware that on several occasions her parents had watched her from behind a sheet of glass in the observation area at the hospital. They went away even more upset than when they arrived; leaving fruit, fresh eggs, butter to supplement her diet and their daughter's favourite comics. None of these had been given her yet, in fact, the food had been shared out as was hospital policy among those who were recovering but whose parents could not afford such luxuries.

Mirry wrote to Glory every day. A sweet young nurse with a Scottish accent read these letters to Glory when she judged the child to be having a lucid moment. She took it upon herself to answer the letters. It was some days before these reached Mirry and Fred, because anything going out from the hospital had to be baked first to kill germs.

Dear Mr and Mrs Hope,

Gloria was very pleased to have your letter. As soon as she feels a little stronger, she will write to you herself.

She is doing very well. She asks me to thank you for the comics and the fruit jellies. She sends much love to you both and to her Auntie Barbara.

Yours sincerely,

Nancy Mackintosh (Nurse, children's ward)

Every night before she went off duty, Nancy Mackintosh kissed her young patients goodbye and wished them 'sweet dreams'.

Glory would never forget, when at last she was permitted by the bossy senior nurse to sit up in bed, how Nurse Nancy plumped up the pillows, and combed her hair so gently, strand by strand, so as not to exhaust her. But, she would be able only to conjure up a presence, a warmth, not to recall Nancy's face or form.

'Such pretty soft hair you have, Glory – and curls, you lucky girl, just like Shirley Temple.' Then Nancy sighed. 'You look so much better, dearie, thank the Lord – but I must say I feel like a few days in bed myself right now.' She straightened up, her face very flushed. She pressed one hand to her temple. 'What a headache.' She swayed slightly on her feet.

'You must come to tea,' Glory said, 'in my house, when I get home, Nurse Nancy . . .' She knew her family would like Nancy as much as she did.

'Oh, I promise you I will.'

It was another promise that could not be kept. Glory never saw her friend to speak to again.

She had been feverish again, sleeping heavily all evening, for her temperature fluctuated wildly, when she awoke to the sound of muffled, agitated voices.

A trolley was being wheeled down the centre of the long ward to an empty bed right at the end by the far door. A bundle was transferred to the bed, the curtain pulled immediately, concealing all, by the night nurse.

Glory lay wondering and listening. The impatient older nurse now hurried past her bed. She wasn't usually on duty at night. She walked on the sides of her feet, for she suffered from painful bunions. To the less-sick children this was amusing; they didn't realise that this was the cause of her illtemper, allied with sheer exhaustion, for there had been an epidemic of scarlet fever locally. Behind her followed a doctor, which was unusual at night.

She must have drifted off to sleep again, for she woke to hear crying, and a sharp voice saying: 'Pull yourself together, Nurse. There was nothing we could do. It takes them like that sometimes. Come with me now, while I make the necessary arrangements. There is no point in staying here.'

The nurses came alongside her bed. The older nurse glanced at Glory, shining her torch in her eyes, making her blink. 'Go to sleep, you bad girl, at once!' she hissed furiously.

As Glory closed her eyes against the light, the younger nurse wept again: 'Poor Nancy, after all she tried to do for the children – how cruel, to die of the very same thing herself . . .'

Her teeth rattled, she shook violently and tried to locate the bell-push above her head. It was no use: she was unable to stop herself from soaking the bed. Then she was sick.

She lay in a soggy, rancid-smelling mass of sheets and blankets, at first warm, then horribly chill by dawn, when there was the rattle of the washing bowls and bedpans on the trolley and the clumping of the nurses' feet.

Glory heard the exclamations of dismay, felt the bedcovers ripped off her: then the nurse who had been in charge last night was towering over her, grey faced and harshly accusing. 'Why didn't you ring the bell? How could you do this, today of all days? You're a very bad girl! Whatever would your mother say if she knew?' Glory closed her eyes again, feigning sleep in her terror.

She was pinioned by tightly tucked bedclothes in her clean bed. Her pillows had been removed; she lay flat, immobile, disgraced. Even the comfort of the comics in her locker was denied her, for the locker had been moved a few inches out of reach, beyond the firmly drawn curtains. The fever had diminished, she shivered now because she was so cold. She was aware that she had done the unforgivable, she had soiled her bed. This was her punishment. 'Don't you dare try to sit up,' the senior nurse had warned.

The hours went slowly by. A sympathetic nurse smiled, but shushed her: lifted her head to spoon in liquid nourishment and medicine. Several times the bedpan slid into place beneath her. It was difficult to manage, when she was not permitted to sit up. Her disgrace was absolute, for her own soft pyjamas had been taken away, and she wore a coarse hospital nightshirt, gaping open at the back. She cried silently, hopelessly, then at last she fell asleep.

Matron, a tall lady in a splendid uniform and frilled cap, was making her rounds. She paused by the bed with closed curtains, pulled these aside briskly and discovered the sleeping child.

'Why is this patient without pillows?' she demanded.

The nurse with the bunions, who was accompanying her, mumbled some explanation.

'How can a child who is gravely ill be punished for something which is beyond her control?' A cool hand touched Glory's brow, the tear-stained face was noted. Glory opened her eyes. 'Fetch some pillows – at once!' Matron ordered.

The bedclothes were loosened, Matron herself made the child comfortable, saw to the pillows. There were tears in her own eyes; mingled compassion for the young patient and anger that a member of the caring profession could do such a thing.

Matron had a basket of sweets and fruit with her, which she dispensed to the patients. Glory waited hopefully. She was invited to choose. A banana, her favourite! Then Matron bent and unexpectedly kissed her, just as Nancy had done, only yesterday . . . 'Is – is Nurse Nancy – all right?' she asked hesitantly, turning her head to look down the ward at the unoccupied bed, clad only in a thick, red rubber sheet.

Matron cleared her throat, swallowed hard. 'Nurse Nancy has been taken from us, Gloria.' Then she rustled on her way.

Glory walked on wobbly legs, holding tightly to the hand of the nurse, along the walkway high above the grounds, which connected one part of the hospital to the other. She was going to the convalescent ward. She would be allowed to have a bath, to have her hair shampooed: best of all, she could now wear her own clothes. If all went well, she would be home in a week or two.

This was a small ward, with open windows, a balcony for sitting out on warm days. There were toys, a dining area, and a wireless. Oh, the joy of listening to *Children's Hour* again, she thought. She was not expected to stay in bed, just to lie on top of the bedclothes if she became tired during the day. Best of all, was the bathroom; using the soap and flannel in her own sponge bag, and smelling of Pears Transparent after she had bathed, not hospital carbolic.

The nurse brushed her hair, pulling at the tangles. Glory tried not to wince. She wore the knitted skating outfit her mother had made her last Christmas. Not that she had ever skated, of course, like Sonja Henie, the film star, with her round, smiling face and powerful legs, but the skirt was short and pleated, the jumper trimmed with soft angora wool at the neck and cuffs. She had shot up in height in the weeks she had been so ill. Her legs looked long and spindly. Her hair had grown, too. Mummy wouldn't approve of that, she knew. Nurse made a fuzz of it, she hadn't time to brush each curl round her finger.

There was a letter waiting for her on top of her new locker, together with some small packages.

Darling Glory,

We can't wait to have you home! We have a wonderful surprise for you!

Bar is going to celebrate her twenty-first birthday with you, she says, isn't that nice of her to wait? The liquorice skipping ropes and the Enid Blyton book are from her and Clive. The brown eggs are from us and the pocket dictionary is from Miss Lancaster – bet you guessed that! Grandma sent a postal order. You can enjoy spending that when you get home. Auntie Laura says Junie and Don can't wait to see you. You were the only one in the Infants to be ill but the big school was closed down, it's a real mystery, isn't it?

See you soon! All our love and kisses,

Mummy and Daddy xxxx

'Your parents sent you this notepaper and envelopes: you were too poorly for us to give it to you at the time. Can you write, or would you like me to help you?' asked the nurse.

''Course I can – I'll be seven soon,' Glory said proudly.

Dear Mummy and Daddy,

Thank you for your lovely letter. I have eaten the lickerish already, please say thank you to Bar and Clive. Nurse says it will save me having a good dose of syrup of figs tonight!

I am not allowed to read for too long because it might be bad for my eyes. We have to rest on the bed in the afternoon.

I am going to have a boiled egg for my tea.

I will write to Grandma to say thank you. And Miss Lancaster. I will send the letters next time for you to post.

I can guess what the surprise is! It is just what I want!

Love from Glory xxxx

'You spell well, you don't need that dictionary,' Nurse said approvingly some time later. She paused before taking the letter to bake. 'What's the surprise, then?'

'It's a puppy – it must be! I've been wanting one for ever and ever,' Glory said. It would have to be a small dog, of course, and not too hairy, because Mummy always said pets made so much mess, and Daddy didn't like germs either.

CHAPTER THIRTEEN

'Whipdapple, Whipdapple, my nice big juicy apple,' the children sang shrilly, clattering on the floor with their steel taps. The ballroom-dancing surface was quite ruined now.

Mirry was willing the end of the session to come. She was full of suppressed excitement. She winced as the baby butted her hard and she played off key for a bar or two.

'Are you all right?' Anna Boam asked, waiting tactfully until the last of the troupe trooped out, laces untied and hair ribbons missing after their exertions. More fairy elephants than little Ginger Rogers. But Miss Boam lived in hopes, as always, of discovering that elusive star quality. She wore a practice tunic in pale green, the same one she had worn all those years ago when her mother took her in hand and taught her how to dance. Her hair hung in a long thick plait down her back. Anna Boam imagined she was seventeen again . . .

'Oh yes,' Mirry replied, 'Glory's coming home tomorrow. We're to fetch her after lunch.'

'My dear, you really shouldn't have bothered to come in today to play for the children – I could have put on a record. How happy you and Fred must be.'

'We are, but I thought it would help to take my mind off it – nearly seven weeks, Anna, it's been like a lifetime to us . . .'

'I must say I am looking forward to having my star pupil back again, too.'

'Maybe not for a while, it will depend how she goes on,' Mirry told her. 'And I'm afraid this will be my last time at the piano until after the baby. I do hope you don't mind?'

'No, of course not. As long as you do come back, both of you, eventually. Good luck, then, Mirry.'

Anna looked her age today, Mirry thought compassionately. She had never seen her without makeup, but the fine lines were harder to disguise now, the lovely hair deeper in tone – Miss Boam must be determined not to let the grey show through . . . Her eyes were bright though, but as if with unshed tears. This was puzzling. What could be the matter?

'How is your father?' she asked suddenly, gathering up the music sheets. 'I haven't seen him in ages.'

'The same as always. Sometimes, well, I think it would be better for us both if . . .' Miss Boam did not finish the sentence.

'You must come over and see Glory, when she's settled in,' Mirry said, to fill the silence.

'I will. As I said, good luck!'

'You are free to go now, Clive dear,' Miss Phillips said quietly, taking tiny sips of the brandy he had poured for her. There was always a half-bottle in the house, but until now, it had been kept exclusively for Maisie's use. She had no need of it, any more.

The undertaker had departed, taking her sister to the Chapel of Rest. The end had come suddenly, unexpectedly: she had been so ill for so many years. She would miss Maisie. They had never been apart, even during her sister's marriage. There had been times when she had almost hated her for the hold she had over her, the shared secret, but Maisie's frail health had meant that she could be *almost* a mother to Clive. She must be grateful to her for that.

'*I know*, Auntie Iris,' Clive said. He was a man now, she thought and somehow the knowledge surprised her. He was not conventionally handsome but he had a nice face, a keen, clever look, and he actually was both nice and clever. She was so proud of him and what he had achieved so far, having relinquished her own early ambitions.

'You had that offer of a job in Fleet Street, didn't you? Is it too late to accept that now?' she asked. They were in the living room. Clive had lit the fire, because despite it being the middle of June, they both felt chilled to the marrow. Shock, she supposed. She had woken this morning to find Maisie dead in bed beside her. She could not believe she had slept through it all, but the doctor kindly told her that Maisie had just slipped away in her sleep. She was endeavouring to take that in.

'The job? Oh, I can't think about *that* today ... No, I meant that I know that *you* are my real mother ...' the words seemed to hang in space between them. He looked very intense.

'Oh, Clive, how could you know that? Did she – did she tell you?' she faltered. She had known that now *she* must tell him, and soon, but this was unexpected.

'I needed my birth certificate when I started work. Mum gave it to me, without comment. *Mother – Iris Phillips, spinster – Father –* left blank. But I put two and two together. My dad – was my dad, wasn't he?'

She nodded, took a sudden gulp of the brandy, almost choked, but it warmed her, gave her courage. 'We didn't carry on Clive, under Maisie's nose, you must believe that: he was a lovely man. Your mother – my sister – was unable, through no fault of her own – she was stricken with tuberculosis you see, soon after they married, and the doctor advised ...'

'You don't have to go into details. He gave me his name, didn't he? I do understand. These things happen.'

'Ah, but they shouldn't!'

'You always seemed much more my mother than she did. I was upset, of course, when I found out, but I couldn't bear to hurt either of you by asking you about it.'

'What a kind young man you are, Clive. I'm – so proud of you.'

'Thank you.' He rose quite suddenly, went to Iris and knelt beside her, hugging her tight round her narrow waist. 'I love you. I loved her and I loved Dad, too . . .' His voice was muffled.

Hesitantly, Iris stroked his hair. 'I meant it Clive. I don't expect you to stay here – stifled – you've been dutiful enough – you must move on. Marry dear Barbara! Together you'll make a great success of your lives, I know it.'

He straightened up. 'Bar doesn't want to marry me. Well, not yet. I asked her, on her birthday. She wants a career of her own first.'

'But – I always thought – you are so right for each other, Clive. You've been together so long.'

'I thought so, too. But there's no one else, that's the important thing, and as I am the one who was always urging her on in further education, and at work, well, I have to accept it, for now, anyway. We do love each other, Auntie Iris, you know.'

'She'll change her mind – I know she will.'

'I hope so. I told her that if and when we marry she will have my backing in whatever she wants to do. There's going to be a war. Everything will change then. It always does.'

'Your hair!' Mirry exclaimed, looking at the unruly frizz on Glory's head. They sat together in the back of the car, and Mirry hugged her close as if she would never let her go.

'Now don't go washing her hair and curling it, the minute you get indoors,' Fred advised wisely, knowing his Mirry so well.

'I can't wait to see the surprise . . .' Glory said artlessly. Mummy looked different somehow; much fatter, and she kept wiping her eyes and squeezing her, which hurt a bit, because she'd got so skinny.

'You will have to wait a bit, I'm afraid,' Mirry told her hesitantly. 'It isn't here yet.' She shouldn't have said anything in that letter, she supposed. But she'd only tried to prepare Glory for the big change in their lives next month.

Then they were drawing up outside their house, and Bar had the door open and there was a banner stretched across the front window: *WELCOME HOME GLORY!*

Clive was there, too, and nothing was said, tactfully, about his bereavement, for this was Glory's day. The table was laden, and there was a big cake, iced in pink and white with decorative silver balls spelling out 'G' and 'B' and the number '21' and bowls shimmering with red and green jelly.

'My birthday tea!' Bar told Glory. 'And your coming-home-safely celebration, all rolled into one.'

Glory looked round the living room. She'd thought Mummy was teasing when she said it wasn't here yet – the surprise. She went into the kitchen and looked in there.

'No puppy . . .' She stood there, howling, and then Mirry was sniffling, too, and Fred was trying to comfort them both, when Bar asked her: 'Whatever's wrong, Glory?'

'Mummy – said – I would have a little puppy – when I came home – from hospital . . .' Glory gulped.

Fred looked at Mirry. 'Let's all sit down and have a chat, before tea, shall we?' he suggested quietly.

'I don't want a new baby! I don't want to call it Shirley if it's a girl – you always say *I'm* your Shirley Temple. I don't want curls anymore . . . I . . . hate . . .'

'We'll get you a puppy. Very soon,' Fred promised. His little girl clung to him now, leaving poor Mirry being comforted by Bar. Clive stayed quietly in the kitchen, supposedly brewing the tea. It would be well and truly stewed by now.

'You really mean it, Daddy?' Glory wiped her nose on his shirt front.

'I mean it. You can choose the puppy yourself. But now I want you to give Mummy a big kiss and say you're sorry for shouting, because expecting a baby makes her tired and all weepy and we don't want to upset her, do we? When the baby comes, it'll be the best surprise ever, you'll see, and it doesn't have to be Shirley. Suppose it's a boy, eh? And you can choose the baby's name, can't she Mirry?'

Mirry murmured, 'Yes . . .' Then Glory turned and flung herself at her mother and Mirry tried not to flinch.

'Does it *hurt* – Mummy, that big lump?' she asked fear-fully, tentatively touching the bulge.

'No, Glory, but Daddy's right, it makes you feel very tired indeed, because your back and your legs ache so . . .'

Glory's arms went tightly round her mother's neck. 'I'm going to call my puppy Pip and the baby can be . . .' The name came out of the blue, a stirring of memory, the day after the Crystal Palace burned down. 'The baby can be Beulah Spa!' she said, inspired.

'I should forget the Spa, but Beulah's nice,' Clive said, and he added with a determined grin: 'And if it's a boy, Glory, how about Clive, after me?' He'd arrived on cue with the teapot.

CHAPTER FOURTEEN

MIRRY LOOKED DOWN AT THE BABY which Nurse had put back into her arms after the weighing and wiping. It was not yet six o'clock in the morning, and she had been in labour since teatime the day before. She felt utterly exhausted, but also very happy, because, this time, Fred had been with her every inch of the way. Even Nurse had admitted that she would have found it difficult to manage without him. Now, she rustled out, her starched apron crumpled, to see how Bar was getting on with the ritual tea-making in the kitchen.

'Thank you, Mirry,' Fred said softly. He planted a chaste kiss on his wife's damp forehead. 'You've been a brick,' he added. This was his way of saying she had been wonderful. Thank goodness it was Sunday. When Nurse had gone, he would get back into his bed. Nurse would banish him if she guessed his intention, of course, but he rightly guessed that a gentle cuddle and whispers of love would do his Mirry a world of good.

'You don't mind it's another girl, Fred?'

'Of course I don't. But, that's our lot Mirry. I can't let you go through that again.'

'We'll see,' She didn't sound very convincing, it was far too soon, after all. 'Will you wake Glory, dear, and bring her in?'

Glory, in her pink cotton pyjamas, peeped solemnly at her new sister. 'She's *very* little . . .' she said finally.

'She looks quite like you, darling, when you were just born. Well, aren't you going to name her for us?'

'Beulah – I haven't changed my mind.' She put out a finger and gently stroked the baby's cheek. 'She snuffles. Just like Pip.'

'Beulah. Yes, that's nice – goes with Gloria, I think.' Fred mused.

'You'll love her, just like I love Bar – there's almost the same age difference.'

'You go on at Bar sometimes, Mummy,' Glory said frankly. 'And at Daddy afterwards if he says doesn't Bar look pretty today . . .'

'You'd better go down and let your puppy out in the garden, hadn't you?' Mirry said swiftly, not looking at Fred, but knowing he was grinning.

'Ask Bar where the tea has got to, please?' Fred called after Glory as she went out, holding on to the waist band of her trousers. 'And ask her to find you a new bit of elastic, eh?'

Pip sniffed his way round the crazy paving path, and finally performed near the rockery. He was a poodle-cross – crossed by what, was a matter for conjecture. Worth every penny of the five shillings asked, Clive reported back, having been dispatched to look at the litter of puppies. 'Curly hair, just like Glory, too!' He and Bar took Glory to choose one for herself. Pip was coloured fawn and white, and he had dainty pussycat-style paws and a tail which curled firmly along his back. He had been with them two weeks, and even Mirry was smitten with him, although she was determined that Glory should realise from the start that she was the one to train and look after her pet.

'Come on, then, I want to get back to bed,' Glory yawned. Why didn't babies choose to arrive at more reasonable times? she wondered. Beulah, my sister Beulah, she said to herself. And I'll get them to add the Spa bit, if I can, 'cause it goes together . . .

The pup bounded over the kitchen step and dived into his cardboard box. Glory spread out fresh sheets of newspaper, washed her hands at the sink as her father insisted she must, then gave Pip his reward, a puppy biscuit. 'Be good! I'll take you out for a walk round the block later.'

Bar was waiting at the top of the stairs. 'Nurse is busy with Mummy and the baby just now – come into my bed, and I'll tell you a story. I brought you up your milk, and shush! a chocolate biscuit each, and I'm dying for my cup of tea.'

Bar was lovely: she was always there to talk to when you needed her, and she was more relaxed about grubby hands and no elastic than Mummy. She would understand that it was more exciting for Glory to have a puppy of her own, than a new baby. Babies couldn't do anything, really, but *puppies* – well, they were the greatest fun!

'When will you and Clive have a baby?' she asked innocently.

Bar actually blushed. 'Never you mind . . .' she said.

* * *

The little car was bursting at the seams with all the baby paraphernalia. 'We'll have to make do with one pair of shorts and a couple of tops each, and hope to goodness it doesn't rain,' as Mirry told Fred and Glory. They were off on a summer holiday, the third week in August.

The chalet bungalow was almost teetering on the cliff edge, which caused Mirry to twitter anxiously, until Fred pointed out that there would be four of them to keep an eye on Glory, when Bar and Clive arrived later in the day. They were travelling here on the motorbike. Anyway, Glory could be a sensible child when she chose, and there were steps carved out to the sandy beach below and a handrail which was, well, adequate. As for baby Beulah, at six weeks old the only demands she would make were the middle-of-the-night 'Hurry up and feed me, Mum!' cries, and a long line of nappies blowing like white flags against a perfect blue sky, for the swooping seagulls to target and splatter.

They were on the east coast, in a windswept place with far-reaching views, and the red flag flying more often than not. But it was just the place for shrimping, with plenty of rock pools for Glory to paddle safely in, with water warmed by the sun. In the lanes around, the scarlet poppies waved among the long grass at the edge of the fields, the sails of the tall white windmill turned and the church spire gleamed gold, like the corn. Clusters of cottages with neat gardens with peasticks and sweetpeas intermingled with cabbages and cabbage roses. Wooden shacks, which were dark and cool within, with fish laid out on marble slabs, still bright-eyed and shiny. The post office sold stamps and sweets and opened and closed at the owner's whim. They were in Poppy Land, Mirry fancied. She didn't know that was what the locals already called the place.

Clive put up his green ridge tent in the small rough place they had described as a garden in the brochure. He unfolded his camp bed and set up his Primus stove and kettle. He was equipped for the week. There were only two bedrooms in the bungalow: Mirry and Fred had the baby in with them and Bar and Glory shared the other smaller room. No bathroom, just a cold tap over the kitchen sink, but a butt full of soft water by the back door to boil, for washing folk and their clothes. Clive was to eat with the family in the tiny living room, with its pile of mouldering, ancient magazines for reading in bad weather, rickety chairs, and the sand, which crept in everywhere, especially in the cracks between the floorboards, together with tiny lizards. Pip soon learned how to pounce. 'Poor little tail-less lizards!' Glory cried reproachfully to him as they wriggled away, leaving their tails behind them.

Fred, designated head cook for the week, got out the frying pan. There would be a lingering odour of bacon all week. But they looked forward to eating plenty of local fresh fish, too.

The thoughts and the imminent threat of war were always there for the adults. But they were all determined to make the most of what might well be their last family holiday for a long time. Who knew what lay ahead?

Glory was content with the clear water in the little pools, the sand oozing between her toes, her bucket and spade. Pip splashed beside her, shaking himself vigorously, tongue lolling, and panting furiously when the sun was at its height. She was in her own small, perfect world. Mummy and Daddy dozed in their striped deckchairs – Daddy with his hanky on his head, tied at the corners and his bare arms and legs all sunburnt, which made Mummy scold him; Mummy, shaded by a parasol, tied to a long stick with its end stuck in the sand, with Beulah quite swamped in a too-big sunbonnet, like a limpet, most of the time, as Daddy said, latched on to Mummy's bosom, discreetly bared. Glory did not waste time in watching this performance, it was repeated far too regularly.

She had continued with her rapid growth spurt after her illness. She was no longer a chubby little Shirley Temple look-alike. She was skinny with knobbly knees and sharp elbows, her face had fined down and she wore her hair in bunches now, with just a curl on the ends.

Bar and Clive seemed to spend most of their days going for endless walks along the beach. They didn't ask her to go with them. They went past, hand in hand, and smiled and asked her if she was attempting to build the tallest sandcastle ever. That was a silly question because anyone could see she was making a mountain to jump from into the water.

She ran towards her parents, eager to display the tiny crab hiding beneath a trailing, floating fragment of brilliant green seaweed in her red bucket, then she tripped and dropped it, cutting her knee on the sharp edge, and it was Bar who ran back, in her faded blue cotton dress, who scooped her up and carried her on her strong young back up the steep incline into the shady confines of Clive's tent where there was a first aid kit. It was Bar who sponged her wound and bandaged it, while Mummy was still puffing anxiously upwards.

'She'll live . . .' Bar said reassuringly, and Clive boiled a kettle on the Primus and made them all a cup of tea.

The stop-me-and-buy-one ice-cream man pedalled his trike and stopped by the group of chalets. It was just the right moment for him to arrive.

'My treat,' Clive insisted. On top of the hot tea, they licked blissfully and pushed up the dripping water ices in their cardboard casings.

It was a magical holiday that Glory would recall fondly whenever she noticed the silvery crescent, the small scar on her knee, in the bath.

But then, none of them could know that a very few years after the end of the war that was yet to begin, the primitive holiday bungalows would vanish into the sea, together with much of the cliff.

CHAPTER FIFTEEN

BAR STOLE QUIETLY FROM the bungalow, and met Clive as he emerged from the tent. Tomorrow would be the last day of their holiday. They were going back to London, first thing on Saturday morning. It was getting on for midnight. She had waited until the rest of the family were asleep, even young Beulah.

She followed Clive down the steps to the beach. He had checked that the tide would be on the turn about now. His shoulder blades jutted as he moved forward, she noted idly. He wore the old khaki drill shorts she remembered from their early cycling club days, as he did not possess swimming trunks. They both carried clothes for after their swim: Clive, shorts and shirt, rolled in his towel; Bar, the old blue dress which was easy to slip on, buttoning down the front, rolled into a towel, too.

Bar wore her new swimsuit. Ruched white cotton sprigged with rosebuds, with narrow straps over her shoulders – cheap and cheerful really, she thought – she was glad it wasn't daylight for she felt self-conscious. She had never revealed so much of her body before to Clive, after all. They hadn't even been swimming together, not even during this holiday. Her towelling cape swung from her shoulders, her thick hair hung loose, but she had a rubber cap to put on later. She trod with care over the shingle strip to the sand, in her bare feet.

By unspoken consent, they walked in the moonlight, some way along the beach, until they were out of sight of the row of bungalows. They laid their things on a convenient rock, then ran down to the sea and plunged in, exclaiming and laughing at the shock of the cold water swirling round their waists.

Bar was an inexperienced swimmer; she had not ventured to the swimming baths since her schooldays. She floundered a bit, flapping her arms, trying to find a comfortable stroke. She felt Clive's arm go round her bare back, supporting her. He was a strong swimmer himself, that was soon obvious. They floated forward on the swell of a wave then trod water as they felt the sucking-back of the next. It was exhilarating. Bar began to giggle, then her teeth chattered, so that Clive said, concerned: 'Had enough? D'you think we should come out now?'

He guided her on to the beach. She shook herself all over him, just as Pip did, then allowed him to chase her up to the rocks where she grabbed her robe and covered herself.

'Let me help to rub you dry . . .' he said quietly. She sat there obediently, shivering violently now as he towelled her shoulders and arms vigorously. 'Your straps have marked your shoulders,' he observed. He fingered them aside, rubbed at the red lines where the strap had been.

What happened next was inevitable, she told herself later, acknowledging that she had no notion of resisting. They had, despite all the years of familiar banter, known all along that sooner or later this would occur. It was just that the opportunity had really never arisen before. There was always someone, usually family, around: not only that, there was the strict moral code with which both had been instilled from adolescence.

It all seemed so right, the urgency of the moment, their damp, slippery embracing. The silver pencil line of moonlight on the water, the shushing of the waves, the shadowing rock, the passion, the loving.

They walked slowly back along the beach, arms clasped round each other. He stopped, kissed her lingeringly again. 'You're still trembling. D'you forgive me, darling Bar?'

'There's nothing to forgive. I wanted to, as much as you did.'

'You'll marry me now, Bar, won't you?' he pleaded. 'I'll join up, you know, directly war is declared. It could be any minute. We could get a special licence ...'

She put her hand over his lips. 'I may *have* to marry you, Clive,' she joked wryly. 'But I can't answer you tonight. We'll tell the others we've decided to go back tomorrow, eh, we'll stop off somewhere and spend the night together. We can work it all out then . . .'

'I love you so much, Bar.' He buried his face in her long, salty-wet hair, for she had disregarded the rubber helmet when they had plunged once more into the sea, before drying and dressing. 'D'you think they'll guess?'

'Fred might, but he's a dear, he won't tell. Anyway, dear prim Mirry wouldn't believe her sister could succumb to your blandishments like that. Yet it's the most natural, wonderful thing in the world, isn't it, and it's made me realise I'll love you till death us do part, so I don't care!'

'I hope you can think of a good excuse for our abrupt departure,' he teased her.

'Oh, I will, don't worry. I'm an abandoned woman now, remember.'

'You're Bar, you're beautiful, and I'm so happy it hurts,' he said. 'How can I ever leave you, after this?'

Mirry guessed after all. She had gone in to Glory after Beulah's early-morning feed, when she had heard her cry out in a bad dream. She saw at once that Bar's bed was empty.

'Bar, are you sure you're doing the right thing? What-ever would Mum say?' she asked, when she managed to corner Bar in the bedroom as she packed her few things.

Bar rolled the damp swimsuit inside the towelling robe and stuffed them in a carrier bag. 'Don't worry Mirry – I'm going to marry him – but I haven't told him yet. Not the smart wedding you dreamed of, I'm afraid, but a special licence – not because I think old Fred will demand he makes an honourable woman of me.'

'Please don't joke about it Bar,' Mirry jigged Beulah on her hip. Fred and Glory had taken the hint and gone for a run along the beach with Pip.

'Darling Mirry, I'm all grown up now – don't be upset! We just have to make up for lost time, you see . . . Clive is going to enlist the moment . . .'

'It might never happen!' Mirry exclaimed. She couldn't bring herself to call it War.

'Oh, it will. I'm sorry, but we all have to face it. I may join up myself or I will certainly find something useful to do – women will want to be just as involved as men, this time. The last war showed what they were capable of.'

It was time for another confidence. 'Fred told me some time ago that his department is to be evacuated to the West Country. I shouldn't tell you, really, it's all supposed to be secret, until . . .'

'What about you, Mirry, what will you do?'

'I haven't wanted to think about that either, but Laura intends to go to the country with the children and her mother. Her boss has offered them the use of a large house he bought some years ago, in Surrey. It hasn't been modernised, but Laura says there would be plenty of room for me, Glory and Beulah. Fred insisted I should accept the offer gratefully.'

'Of course you should! What about Laura's Jim? And have you considered Mum?'

'Jim'll be in a reserved occupation, he'll have to stay put. Anyway, he's over forty. And Mum intends to do just that, too, whatever we consider is best for her: she says the zeppelins couldn't make her leave London twenty-five years ago, and nor will Herr Hitler.'

'Well, let's forget the sandbags they are filling right now in town, the talk of gas masks and bombing, you just enjoy the rest of your stay here, you four, and don't worry about Clive and me. We couldn't be happier, I promise.'

'Bar, everything's changing so fast, it's all so bewildering but, I just want you to know – if you ever need me, I'll always be there for you . . .' Mirry's glasses were misting over.

'Mirry, I know. That means a great deal to me.' Bar paused. Then she added quietly, 'I feel like the big sister now, Mirry – I'm afraid for you, the children, the future – but I can't help feeling so happy as well, you see.'

CHAPTER SIXTEEN

BAR HELD TIGHT TO HIM AS they sped along on the motor-bike. The slipstream whipped the cheery whistling from his mouth and made her eyes water.

They stopped in a little street in an Essex village, with houses built one against the other over centuries; cottages with duck-and-grouse doorways and interior ceiling beams, uneven floors and a through draught from front to back. The coal fire in the main room meant the family crowded that small space in the winter months and regarded the rest of the house as cold as charity.

It was late afternoon: they went into the tearooms for refreshment and to ask if the proprietor knew of a place where they might have an evening meal and put up for the night. Here, they ate warm scones and spooned on home-made raspberry jam. They drank tea from delicate cups and stirred in sugar cubes with tiny silver apostle spoons. There was a strange, unexpected shyness between them.

'Mr and Mrs?' asked their prospective landlady, eyeing them from the front porch of her pink-washed cottage with wisteria climbing the wall.

'Almost . . .' Bar answered honestly. She smiled, and the wary look directed at them evaporated. 'Next week,' she added. Clive squeezed her hand.

They were shown to a long, low room under the thatched eaves, with a washstand, jug and basin, and a brass-railed double bed already made up.

'Would you like supper brought up?' the landlady asked. Her husband was not keen on strangers at the supper table. This was his wife's business.

Even as Clive hesitated, Bar said demurely: 'That would be lovely, thank you.'

'Ham and salad do? I made a fresh batch of bread today.'

'That will do very well indeed,' Bar replied.

When the door closed, she sat on the bed and bounced once or twice, pronouncing: 'Not bad, one or two wonky springs, but who cares?'

'I care,' he said quietly. 'I care about you. This might be the only honeymoon we get, Bar.'

'I know that . . .'

'Did you mean it? What you said, about next week?'

'Oh, I did, Clive, I certainly did!'

'You're not lying there awake, are you, Mirry? You should grab the chance of sleep while you can. I don't remember Glory being such a wakeful baby at nights, do you?' Fred asked, yawning twice in swift succession.

'I can't help thinking about Bar and Clive, Fred,' Mirry murmured.

'Well, don't. It's really none of our business, is it? I think they've shown remarkable restraint over the past few years.' He sounded quite sharp. While Mirry was sorting out the baby the night before, he had got out of bed to adjust the skimpy curtains over the window, for the room was flooded with moonlight. He had seen Bar and Clive arrive at the tent, embrace, seemingly hesitate, then they both went inside. He had said nothing to Mirry then, nor since, although she had confided in him tonight, her discovery of the empty bed last night.

'Fred!' Mirry was shocked at this suggestion. But after all, she and Fred had married after a much shorter court-ship, she thought. Could she have held Fred at arm's length for much longer than that?

'We'll be parted soon, Mirry. We've got to make the most of every moment together, just as they have.' He wasn't at all his usual light-hearted self. He drew her close, rested his chin on her hair. Mercifully, she had given up the steel armoury months ago, at Laura's suggestion, in favour of a simple, silky straight bob with a fringe. Without her glasses, her green eyes were wide, large and lustrous. 'It was the best thing I ever did, marrying you, Mirry . . .' he whispered.

'Fred!' she said again, but in a very different way.

* * *

'I'm delighted at your news,' Iris Phillips told them. Less formally, she added: 'It's just what I was hoping to hear.'

She had been surprised to see them back so early on the Saturday morning, not knowing they had not travelled the full distance this time. They did not tell her that they had left the bungalow the previous day.

'Bar knows, Auntie Iris, about us,' Clive told her quietly.

'Oh,' she faltered.

'It makes no difference to me, I'm glad you're Clive's mother. It will take a little time to think of you as that, but we're already friends aren't we?' Bar put in impulsively.

'I'm extremely fond of you, Barbara.'

'As I am of you! Can we drop the Miss Phillips, please? Would you mind if I called you Iris and d'you think you could manage to call me Bar, after all this time?'

'I'll try,' Iris fumbled for her handkerchief. 'Well, you'd better get the wheels rolling on that special licence, Clive.'

'You don't think I'm going to give her the chance to change her mind, do you?' Clive joked.

'Where will you live?' Iris asked next. 'And I'll tell you right away that I don't expect you to start your married life here with me.'

'We haven't the faintest idea,' Clive said frankly. 'Bar's sister intends to take the children to the country very shortly, and Fred will have to go where the civil service decrees. So they will be leaving their house indefinitely, within the next week or so, and, I haven't changed my mind about what I'm going to do.'

'I don't know yet what I shall do, Iris. What about you?' Bar asked.

'I can't move, after all this time, from here. I shall stay put,' Iris told them firmly.

'Then we'll always have somewhere, and a welcome to come home to, won't we, bless you,' Clive said for both of them.

Mirry couldn't believe that she had achieved all that packing, survived all the rushing around. It had affected her milk unfortunately but, in a way, she was relieved that Beulah had taken to the bottle so well, and that she seemed more contented. Glory had been no trouble really, apart from refusing to go to school and miss all the fun, these past two days. Mum had come over to wish them a tearful farewell and to help with the last-minute crises. Fred had taken her home last night. Now it was Bar's turn: she was to be married from Mum's next week. Mirry would miss her sister's wedding; that was more of a blow than the rest put together.

Bar was collecting her pots and toiletries from the bathroom shelf and cabinet. Mirry caught up with her there.

'Seven years,' Mirry said helplessly, 'seven years, we've lived here together, Bar. You've grown up under our roof...'

'Under your protective wing, you mean,' Bar said with a grin, opening a jar of cream to see if it was worth taking or not. 'Thanks for everything,' she added. 'It's goodbye to Number Five for me for ever, I guess. I'm homeless now, eh?'

'Oh, don't say that!'

'I'm joking, Mirry. Clive and I will get something sorted out soon. But at the moment, it's more important to just be together, we feel, before the inevitable parting.'

'That's nothing to joke about, Bar, believe me. I just don't know how I will cope without Fred, I really don't.'

'Maybe it'll actually do you good, Mirry, you'll find out just how strong you really are.'

'He's always been there for me, since we got married. He can always cheer me up, when I feel down. He and Glory are close, because they're alike. She'll miss him so much, too.'

'Of course she will.'

'Bar, I know it's awful of me, and I wouldn't confide this in anyone else, but I'm afraid, you see, that when we're far apart, well, Fred might be tempted . . .'

'To find comfort elsewhere?' Bar's eyes actually flashed. 'You should be ashamed of yourself, Mirry, even thinking such a thing! Fred has an eye for the ladies, maybe, but he'll never stray. We all know how he adores you.'

'I really don't know why.'

'Who knows why? I've loved Clive for ever, it seems, sometimes, I've never had another boyfriend, although I have had my chances. But it's only in the last few weeks I've been, well, passionate about him. If I started worrying about what might happen when we're parted, well, that would make me miserable, not deliriously happy, as I am.'

Mirry hugged her suddenly. 'You're right, I am ashamed of thinking that Fred could ever let me down.'

'Don't forget, Mirry, you're not infallible. How do you know you might not stray yourself? War, they say, turns everything upside down.'

Mirry drew away, shocked. 'Never!' she said vehemently. 'Fred will always be the only man for me.'

'Packed to the gunwales,' Fred said lightly. They drove at a fair lick towards London. Then his grip tightened on the steering wheel. 'Bar, I'll miss you, you know.'

'I'll miss you, too, all of you,' she replied, suddenly wary. 'But all good things come to an end, and now I'm going to marry Clive, aren't I?'

'He's a good chap. I suppose, if we must let you go, you couldn't do better.'

'You're right there.'

He kept his gaze steady on the road ahead. 'You must know how much I care for you, Bar?'

'What are you trying to say, Fred?'

'I love Mirry, of course I do, I know that. She's given me two wonderful little daughters. She's been the best wife a chap could have.'

'Then, what?'

'Sometimes, just sometimes, Bar, I, well, imagine, what it would be like being married to someone like you . . .'

There was a long silence. They were approaching the flats. Uncle Stan would be waiting outside to give them a hand with all Bar's luggage. Bar and Clive were staying with them on a temporary basis. They all agreed it made sense at such an uncertain time. Clive had had to work today.

Then she said: 'Please forget you said that, Fred. For Mirry's sake. You're her whole life, you see.'

'She always keeps something back from me – she's not impulsive and . . .'

'Passionate? You married little prim Mirry, Fred. There's plenty of warmth there, if you want it. Believe me . . . Here we are. Don't ever ask me to betray my sister.'

Mirry crossed the road to Lahana. She must say goodbye to Anna, she told Fred.

She knocked twice: she could hear voices, but no one came to the door immediately. Then, through the glazed panel in the door, she saw a figure approaching. The door opened, and the major stood there, swaying, with an old jacket over his combinations, dingy grey, like his complexion, she couldn't help thinking.

'Oh,' Mirry floundered. 'I just – is Anna in?'

He appeared much older, not at all the Galloping Major they had so blithely dubbed him seven years ago. His sleeve flapped – no artificial hand . . .

The major cleared his throat, but his voice still came out hoarsely. 'She's coming – I just wanted – I never said, what a lovely young lady you are – to wish you good luck, myself . . .'

'Thank you.'

'Get back to your room, Father!' Miss Boam's voice was icy. She too looked dishevelled, her hair hanging down her back, her lipstick patchy, her dress obviously unsteamed. As the major moved aside, she leaned forward and planted a kiss on Mirry's cheek. 'I shall miss you, dear little Mirry. You are going – everything is going – gone – no one wants dancing lessons now, you see . . .'

She's been drinking, like her father, Mirry realised with a shock. She backed away slowly. She managed a smile, a wave at the gate. 'See you soon, I hope. It may never happen, as they say.'

'As they say,' Miss Boam echoed derisively, then she slammed the door shut.

Mirry scurried back over the road.

'Ready?' Fred asked. 'Or do you want to take one last look around the house?'

They had sent the big theatrical trunks, which Miss Boam had lent them, ahead by train. Fred loaded the boxes, the cases, the dismantled cot into the car. The pram had to be secured to the roof rack. Baby Beulah was already asleep on the back seat. Glory had insisted on having one last go on the swing suspended from the big branch of the apple tree, while Pip snuffled around his favourite patches of the garden.

They had only been home from holiday a week. Fred had his marching orders, as he called them. Jim and Laura were already on their way to the refuge in Surrey. Fred and Mirry and the girls were about to follow them.

There were still snowy net curtains in the windows of Number Five Kitchener Avenue. All was clean and polished within. But the gas would not plop, the fire would not leap in the grate, the beds displayed bare mattresses, the crocks, the ornaments, the wedding silver were safely locked away in the cupboards. Outside the apples would drop, scabby and sour in due course, and nestle in the unmown grass.

The Phoney War was about to begin.

PART TWO

1939–42

CHAPTER SEVENTEEN

THEY MOTORED THROUGH GODSTONE, where Bar and Clive
had so often cycled, past energetic young men in dazzling
cricket whites on the green, and before long forsook the
main Brighton road for winding country lanes and farm-
land. It was less populated even than Poppy Land, Mirry
thought apprehensively. Not a shop in sight. The church
and the school, which the children would attend after the
summer holidays, must be a good mile away from their new
home, even across the fields, in the nearest village.

The house was old, but not at all as she had imagined.
A couple of hundred yards back, they had cruised hopefully past a gracious house set well back in its grounds.
Graylings, the home of Laura's boss, the film magnate. He
was of Eastern European descent, as were so many in the
world of pictures, Laura had confided. Gray was the name
he had taken on entering this country. Mirry was naturally
intrigued: but Fred had joked that he probably resembled
Peter Lorre, more short, moody and menacing, than tall,
monocled and magnificent.

It was a square, plain house with a slate roof, and small windows draped with drab curtains. Laura had omitted to tell them that it was the former farmhouse on the estate, that it was still surrounded by cowsheds, with a rough garden inadequately fenced off from the farmyard and the pasture where the cows lifted inquiring heads to blink at them as they stepped from the car. Mirry immediately felt fearful. They loomed so large. She hoped fervently that there wasn't a bull among them.

There was a ditch running alongside the front hedge, and a board walkway across to the gate. Mirry recalled the carbolic in the streets during the typhoid scare, for the stench from the ditch was really awful. She looked away quickly from the murky, shifting water; surely, it wasn't sewage? Next door was a modern bungalow and just up the lane from the farmhouse was a line of farm cottages, on a rise, where she suspected the ditch probably commenced.

The front door swung open and Laura and Jim came out to welcome and help them with the luggage and, simultaneously, Donald and Junie came running round from the back, scarcely recognisable as the smart town children they had waved off from home much earlier that morning. They were now clad in sensible, baggy dungarees, already grubby, and they displayed great, happy grins. They looked more like twins: tomboyish Junie was already as tall as her brother, with her short fair hair brushed across her forehead and shingled at the nape of the neck. 'Come on

Glory, come and see the cows! She can, can't she, Auntie Mirry?' she called out.

Glory made her own mind up, and was instantly hanging over the fence like her friends, in danger of ripping her pretty dress, holding up clumps of grass with clinging clods of earth to the cows. Pip leapt up and down, barking and blustering. The cows didn't budge. 'They're a special herd of cows, Glory,' Don told her, 'Friesians. They come from Holland. They don't milk them into a bucket here. The cowman says Mr Gray intends this to be a model farm. These cows are milked by machine!'

That impressed Glory as he had intended, but she was really none the wiser. Milk came from cows, of course she knew that, but back home it was left on the doorstep at dawn in glass bottles embossed with the name of the local dairy, and sealed with a cardboard disc, from which you licked the cream, when Mummy wasn't looking. There didn't seem much connection between that and these black and white creatures with their bony, ridged backs, odd way of chewing, swishing tails and cartoon eyelashes. She looked wide-eyed at their pendulous udders. Gosh! She murmured to herself. She thought of Mummy nursing Beulah, and decided it was just as well her baby sister took her milk from a bottle now.

Fred, humping the cases from the car, as Mirry still stood there, holding the baby, interpreted her shocked expression. 'Don't worry, Mirry – good old country smells – you'll thrive on it, I expect!'

'Not quite what I expected either,' Laura confided. 'I never ventured further than Graylings before this morning. And I only went there once, because the studios are a few miles away from here. The bungalow, by the way, is occupied by the farm manager and his wife. Their son is the cowman. Bernard had that specially built for them. They moved in two years ago. No one's lived here since . . . Mrs Dean came round earlier and brought us a huge meat pie, bread and a basket of fresh vegetables from her garden – wasn't that kind? Come and see the kitchen, it's not so bad, but the range will take a bit of getting used to, after cooking by gas, I reckon. Mrs Dean wished us luck with it. Still, once Mother gets here, she'll soon have us organised.' Mrs Hardes was coming by train later in the week. She had insisted firmly that she must await Jim's return so that she could instruct him on how to survive on his own – to cook decent meals for one.

The kitchenette of Number Five would have fitted several times within this vast room, Mirry thought. It was clean enough, but depressing, with dark brown paintwork and dingy wallpaper. There was an overpowering smell of bleach. Mrs Dean had been busy with her mop and cloths, no doubt. The stone-flagged floor was unevenly worn; the range smoked ominously. Despite the heat of the day, someone had kindly chopped a big box of kindling, and heaved in a hod of coal. There was a big table on turned legs, an assortment of chairs, plenty of cupboards full of old-fashioned crazed crocks and hefty iron pans; a cool larder, almost bare, except for jugs of milk and a bowl of brown eggs; a deep sink with pails beneath and next to this a copper adjacent to another long working surface, boxed in by wood panelling.

'Lift the top – see, it hinges! And there, Mirry, is our bath,' Laura demonstrated, laughing. 'You have to fill it from the copper, of course, and then bale it all down the sink. At least we'll be nice and warm having baths in here during the winter months, even if we do have to cultivate a warning cough. The water is pumped up from a well – fortunately that's safely covered – and at least we have a tap over the sink, eh? There's a wash-house of sorts outside, with another sink and a very ancient mangle, but we might just as well heat the water in the copper and do the laundry in here, I think.'

It was fine almost camping in the holiday bungalow, Mirry thought – fun, indeed, because you knew it was only for a week or so, but this, well, this was a return to the Dark Ages. 'Where . . . ?' she asked hesitantly.

'Outside, I'm afraid, down the cinder path at the back, but there is honeysuckle growing round the door,' Laura said, 'and Mother insisted I bring a proper toilet roll.'

They could hear the men tramping up and down the wide, curved stairs. The trunks had been left in the hall, awaiting Fred's assistance to manoeuvre them.

'We'll eat our meals in the kitchen, I suppose,' Laura said. 'There's a nice sitting room, even some fairly comfortable furniture. And a piano for you, Mirry. You'll keep the children up to their practising, won't you? The rest of the stuff came from the attics. There's quite a lot still stored up there apparently, and we're welcome to help ourselves. Oh, and that door over there leads to the cellar – we must keep that locked, to discourage the children from exploring down there – I know my two only too well.' Then she added, in a lower voice: 'That's where we're to go, you know, when the siren sounds . . .'

'I ought to change Beulah, and feed her,' Mirry murmured faintly. Could she ask Fred to take them straight home again?

'Follow me, there are four bedrooms upstairs and two more in the attic. But only these two are ready for occupation, so far. We'll have to see to another one, before Mother arrives. But plenty of beds and bedding, that's the important thing, eh?'

There was a double bed in Mirry's room, which was a relief, for Fred was staying overnight and leaving early to travel west, tomorrow morning. There was a single bed at the other end of the room for Glory and Fred had already assembled the baby's cot. A huge, forbidding wardrobe revealed plenty of hanging space and shelves and room to stow the cases and boxes. On the washstand there was a basin and jug and, in the cupboard beneath, Fred revealed a pair of chamber pots, festooned with spider's webs. Mirry shuddered.

On the dressing table, Fred had thoughtfully put out her hairbrushes and pots of cream, the flagons of Evening in Paris and eau-de-cologne; her hand mirror lay face down on the ugly yellow wood surface. There was a cracked swing mirror.

She laid the wriggling baby on a flannel piece on the big bed, and removed her damp nappy. A gloomy, fly-blown picture of an angel stared down at them from the wall above. Mrs Dean must have mislaid her duster up here, she thought wryly. She wondered if the bedding had been aired.

Fred passed the pail, and fetched warm water in a jug. He closed the door behind him, but Laura and Jim had gone downstairs to see what the children were up to, and to organise their lunch.

'Fred, it's awful, we can't stay here,' Mirry said miserably at last. ''Specially without you,' she added, 'we've never been apart since we got married.'

'Then you should think how lucky we are,' he replied quietly, 'Bar and Clive won't experience married life as we have known it, yet awhile. I'm relying on you to be brave, Mirry, to take care of the family while I'm away. I'll write as often as I can, and later on, when things are clearer, of course, I'll be able to come and see you, now and then. You're doing this for me, Mirry – for us all – please try to make the best of things. You and Laura get on so well, that's an advantage, isn't it?'

'Oh, she'll be back at work soon, she says – though the film industry will be in an uncertain state for a time – anyway, she can look forward to seeing Jim most weekends.' The mention of films reminded her that she had left The Palace behind too, which seemed the last straw.

'Laura's mother will be here soon, she'll keep you company while Laura's away,' he tried to comfort her, aware that it would not be at all the same as being with her own mother. Laura's mother was not cosy and kindly, more, efficient and organising. No wonder Laura was in a hurry to resume work.

A tap on the door: Laura with the baby's bottle, which she had kindly warmed.

She looked keenly from one to the other. 'I can guess how you're feeling, Mirry, but we'll be fine, really we will. You must send old Fred off with a happy face.'

'What's Glory up to?' Mirry asked fearfully.

'Glory is in her element – she'll need a bath tonight, like my two, I'm afraid. But, they all love it here. Make the most of a quiet moment with Fred while you feed Beulah: then lay her down for her nap. Dinner will be served at one, madam.'

'Thank you, Laura, you always cheer me up.'

'That's what friends are for, duckie.'

Mirry clung to Fred that night as if they were to be parted for ever. They whispered, because Glory was a light sleeper.

The bed was like a rock, the blankets coarse and itchy: Mirry wondered fearfully if they were harbouring fleas. She had seen a large cat lurking in the garden, and Pip was already scratching frantically behind his ears with his back paw. They had had to harden their hearts to leave him in his box in that cavernous kitchen when they went up to bed. The pup had buried his head in Fred's old jersey and whimpered plaintively. He was only a baby, like Beulah, after all.

'Don't cry, Mirry, please don't cry . . .'

'I can't help it, I want to go home!' she sniffed.

'It'll all be over before you know it,' he assured her. He felt her rubbing away the tears on his shoulder. His grip tightened protectively. 'You're making me all damp, Mirry, come on, cheer up . . .'

She suddenly pushed him away. 'Not tonight, Fred, please . . . What if I got pregnant again so soon . . . I . . .'

'I just wanted to hold you, show you how much I love you, how much I'll miss you . . .' he reproached her.

'Fred, darling, I'm so sorry,' she whispered back.

Fred lay there, wakeful, long after she had fallen asleep. Despite the fact that she was nestled against him once more, the feeling of hurt lingered.

He couldn't help it – he thought of Bar and Clive together.

Dawn came far too soon, with a cock crowing, stridently the cows reminding the cowman next door that it was time for the early milking, and Beulah seeking their attention with protesting hiccups of her own. Only Glory slept blissfully on, lulled by the good old country air gusting through the open window, oblivious to the buzzing of a giant bluebottle, caught up in the billowing window nets.

CHAPTER EIGHTEEN

ON SATURDAY, 2 SEPTEMBER, at eleven in the morning, Bar and Clive were married in the local register office. There was a long queue of other couples waiting for the same service.

The witnesses were Mum and Iris. Only two others attended, Bar's aunt and uncle. The bride wore her office costume, light grey, nearly new, over a frivolous blouse in pink organdie with a bow at the neck, and a matching small hat with a cheeky feather. She had rashly purchased silk underwear and shiny stockings and Mum had polished her black court shoes to a wonderful gloss. Her hair gleamed, too, with brilliantine, hanging in deep waves to her shoulders. She had applied pink lipstick, then almost blotted it away, because Clive didn't care for too much makeup. He wore his best suit and Iris had bought him an expensive silk tie which he would probably never wear again, and knotted it neatly round his neck.

'Don't you fiddle with it, I know what you are with ties, Clive, always skew-whiff,' she warned him with a special little smile. It was a great pity her sister wasn't here to see him married; he was, of course, as much Maisie's son as he was hers . . .

By noon they were enjoying lunch in a local restaurant, surprisingly deserted for a weekend. Even the waitresses seemed distracted, and the food was barely hot.

'I do wish it could have been in church,' Mum lamented, breaking her bread roll with her hands, scratchy and work-worn despite rubbing them with plenty of glycerine and rosewater lotion.

'Mum, dearie, there really wasn't time to arrange it. We'll have a blessing in church later on, I promise.'

'Tasty chops,' Uncle Stan remarked, at the same time as Aunt Alice grimaced: 'Bit fatty!' She sprinkled on another dose of salt.

Later on, back at the flat, Mum produced one of her 'hasty' cakes as she called them, full of fruit and spices but minus marzipan and royal icing. Aunt Alice made a strong cup of tea and eased off her tight shoes thankfully. She had already unhooked her corset around the waistline, deftly through her clothes, an art long perfected in the pursuit of comfort. She thought no one realised what she was up to, but of course, they did.

Clive squeezed Bar's narrow waist. 'No armour plating here,' he whispered in her ear.

'Hardly a soul about,' Uncle Stan observed, lighting his pipe after a sidelong glance at the ladies. 'But the exodus is about to begin . . .'

'We all know it will happen now,' Clive said. 'The Munich Agreement last year – old Chamberlain's assurances – changed nothing, did it? As Winston Churchill told the country then, we were defeated without even going to war. Last month's pact between Germany and Russia; this news about Poland – well, nothing can stop the conflict starting.'

They were all silent, thinking about the latest sharp shock, for Germany had invaded Poland yesterday. Polish airfields had been bombed by the German airforce, many planes were destroyed, even as Hitler's crack troops stormed the frontiers before dawn.

Clive lifted their cases, one in either hand. 'We'll be with you in good time tomorrow morning, keep the wireless tuned for the news, for the ultimatum,' he told the family. 'I've booked us in at the hotel for four days at least. We're both due back at work on Monday, but I'll be reporting on the London scene for the paper. And Bar will be nice and near her office. I'm glad you're staying the night here, Auntie Iris.'

'I'll run her home tomorrow afternoon, don't you worry,' Uncle Stan promised. Iris was one of the family now, as Clive had long been.

It was more of a guesthouse than a hotel. Bar could show her wedding ring with impunity this time. Again, they elected to have supper served in their room. Time was precious, parting was very near.

It was another unprepossessing room, with a hard bed, but, unexpectedly, there was a jug of red roses with ferns to greet them, prominently placed on the dressing table, with a card, covered in spidery handwriting: *WISHING YOU EVERY HAPPINESS AND GOOD LUCK. MISS WANDLE. LANDLADY. CATKIN HOUSE.* Miss Wandle's rather superior demeanour obviously concealed a romantic streak. She wouldn't divulge that she had been engaged and about to marry when the last war began. Her fiancé had been killed early on. He had proposed on a country ramble and presented her with a bunch of catkins, not roses. She didn't forget.

This nice gesture gave them hopes of a special supper even though the hotel was the cheapest they could find at short notice. Clive didn't tell Bar that he had ordered a bottle of wine with the meal. They must celebrate, despite the onset of war.

I can't believe I'm really Mrs Joy, Bar thought. Naturally, Fred had to joke about her new name in the card he sent from 'the west', adding, 'will advise address, later'. Top secret, Bar supposed? He'd trotted out his favourite 'O be joyful!' naturally.

She said to herself, I didn't intend to settle down until I'd made a real career for myself, and here I am, only twenty-one, just the same as Mirry was when she and Fred got spliced. But there won't be any babies for us, no normal married life, until we've won the war.

Clive hummed the chorus of the song they had danced to only last night, cheek-to-cheek like all the other couples, in a smoky, poky dance hall, where they had gone to bid farewell to their single state.

Who's taking you home tonight
Darling, it's plain to see
I'm pleading please let it be me
Let it be me . . .

He presented Bar with a box of Black Magic chocolates. They sat on the bed while she opened them. They were melting a bit because it had been a warm day and he had left them in the sun at the flat. 'We're well suited Bar, you like the hard centres and I like the soft.'

'Oh, Clive, I haven't got anything for you!' she exclaimed contritely. She licked her fingers. 'Mmm . . .'

He drew her close. 'Yes you have!' he said wickedly. She had removed her wedding clothes and was about to unpack a pretty dress from her case, as Clive had suggested a stroll round the streets before supper. Bar guessed rightly that he wanted to soak in the atmosphere, to observe those out and about, to listen in to what they were saying. He would be itching to write it all down on their return. Despite the general feeling of foreboding, it was an exhilarating time for a young reporter. Even one who had just got married.

His hands slipped on her silky petticoat as his arms encircled her. His lips brushed her throat, her smooth young skin. She smelled fresh and sweet. Of soap, sham-poo, brilliantine, Pond's vanishing cream and lily-of-the-valley scent dabbed extravagantly behind her ears. There had been no 'carrying on' as Mum referred to it, since their return from holiday, by mutual, unspoken agreement.

'You're making me all chocolatey,' she said dreamily, as she loosened his tie.

The British people were, as Mr Chamberlain gravely told them, through the medium of the wireless, 'once again at war with Germany'.

They gathered in small groups of family and friends, like Mirry and Bar, in Surrey and in London; or went to packed churches where the morning service was specially interrupted at quarter-past eleven. It was a relief to know that the decision had been made at last. The majority had been aware for months that this day must come.

There would be the mass evacuation of children from London to the country; mobilisation; factories already making armaments would step up production; those young men who had been training in the militia had already been called up. Winston Churchill would shortly return as First Lord of the Admiralty; the people were united in their determination to deal with, as speedily and as courageously as possible, the situation they were now meeting head on. As the prime minister told the nation: 'Our conscience is clear.'

The children took a basket, a walking stick from the hallstand, and went in high spirits up the lane to pick blackberries for pudding. 'Not too far! No further than the cottages,' Mirry warned them. 'And no paddling in that dreadful ditch.'

Glory wore a pair of Don's khaki drill shorts, belted tight round her narrow middle and rolled up at the bottoms for they hung below her knees and made her look like a comic character, as Uncle Jim told her, with a wink. Mummy had not unpacked all her things yet, and she said with uncustomary sharpness that the shorts Glory had worn on holiday were put away for next year. One thing they must buy soon was a pair of wellingtons each – Mummy's dainty galoshes wouldn't stand up to country mud, as Auntie Laura pointed out, and her own little red rubber ankle boots were not long enough in the leg for walking to school in the winter – no pavements here, you know.

Mummy was still sniffling about Daddy going away last week, but Uncle Jim had motored here for the weekend: he had brought the wireless from home, in case the set here didn't work too well. Glory wasn't sure why the grown ups wanted to sit round the table listening so intently to the news in that gloomy old kitchen, when they could be meandering up the lane as they were, pulling down the brambles and getting scratched, and mouths and hands all purple with blackberry juice, while the sun beat down overhead.

Don had Pip's lead wound round his wrist: 'I'll train your dog for you, Glory, if you like,' he offered grandly. His gran frowned on pets. But Pip was nothing compared to the cows. Gran shrieked if one just looked at her over the fence.

Glory liked Don. As long as you let him be leader and boss you in all the games, he looked after you when you were crossing the field where the young bullocks were, and he'd had a fight with the boys from the farm cottages on the second day they were here, and now they were friendly, even towards her – well, almost . . .

Junie was a bit superior. She scoffed at Glory's hair, so she'd made Mummy plait it this morning. Then Junie laughed at the big satin bows Mummy tied on the ends of the plaits. 'Little Shirley Temple!' she mocked. Glory was really fed up with Shirley. She wanted to look like Judy Garland in The Wizard of Oz, and to sing like her, too. Mummy had made her shut her eyes tight in the graveyard scene, and she'd found some of the film frightening, but once Judy burst into Technicolor, she seemed so real, you could almost touch her. Glory longed for some sparkling red shoes, with heels. This was the last film they'd been to see at The Palace before they came here.

Glory didn't care much for Auntie Laura's mother. She wasn't gran-like at all. She wore smart town clothes and clicking heels and complained about having corns, and she insisted on doing all the cooking. She'd decreed: 'You girls can do the housework between you and you children must take turns with the washing up and make your own beds.'

'Old Gran Hardes – hard old pastry, hard old carrots, she can't cook for toffee nuts!' she sang under her breath as she popped another juicy blackberry in her mouth.

Mirry stayed indoors, giving Beulah her bottle, while the rest trouped outside to see Jim off after tea. She was envious, she knew it, because Laura could see Jim every weekend, while she was parted from Fred. He had imparted very little about his digs in Somerset, apart from observing that his landlady could over-cook fatty mince in grey gravy with lumpy mash. Was it awful of her to hope that the landlady was fat and lumpy and grey as well, and considerably older than she was? And, of course, she missed Bar, too.

This wasn't home – she didn't think it would ever seem so. Tomorrow the children were going to school, and Laura back to work. She dreaded being under Mrs Hardes's thumb.

I should have insisted on staying at Number Five, she thought. Nothing's happened yet. Well, not in this backwater . . . Just one false alarm, the siren sounding, and us all going down into that horrible, dank cellar and me more frightened the baby would get a chill than the Germans were coming . . . There are mice down there, I know it, and boxes stored in dark corners and dripping candles. Laura said we must furnish it with camp beds and blankets, chairs and iron rations in a biscuit tin when we can get around to it – no hurry, eh?

Now, Laura came in grinning and said: 'Guess what? I asked Jim what he'd got lined up for his supper when he got back and he said, "liver sausage!" Nice and simple. No cooking, just butter two slices of bread and stick it between 'em. Mum looked really horrified.' Cut meats from Alberto's Deli, the cornershop, were notorious for causing gippy tummy.

Mirry smiled at last. 'I hope Alberto washed his hands before he cut the sausage.'

CHAPTER NINETEEN

Mum went with Bar when she received notice of her
medical for the ATS. Clive was already undergoing his basic
training in the Army. Her employers had tried to discourage
her from leaving, but she was determined. If Clive was going
to war, so was she.

Uncle Stan seemed to regard it all as a big joke: 'One
look at you, my girl, and they'll say: "No thanks! Next!"'

Auntie Alice was worried about her hair. 'They'll make
you have it all cropped off, I reckon.'

'Only if she's got nits,' Uncle Stan put in breezily.

'Stan!' Auntie was scandalised.

'Oh, I mustn't have my hair chopped – Clive'd have
kittens. I guess I'll have to put it up, eh, Mum? One of
those bands, you know – you tuck it all neatly in place.
Very unflattering, mind . . .'

'Maybe just as well,' Mum said, 'you being a young
married woman. You don't have to go, dearie, do you?'

'I know what you're getting at Mum. Being married's
no excuse. Sorry to disappoint you, but there'll be no

more grandchildren, from us at any rate, until we've won the war.'

'Not much chance of that anyway,' Uncle Stan said frankly, tapping out his pipe in the grate, which had Auntie Alice reaching immediately for the dustpan and brush. 'From you, or Mirry, with your men away . . .' He added, surprising his niece: 'Good luck anyway, young Bar. To tell the truth, I was only joking – I reckon they might just make a soldier out of you.'

Bar and Mum were at the medical centre all day. It was gruelling, tiring and embarrassing in parts, particularly for one so recently married and Bar wished fervently that she had heeded Mum's advice and not worn her expensive new underwear. She had instantly noticed the nurse's expressively raised eyebrows when this was revealed. She was thankful though that she had braided her hair primly round her head. 'Lucky you're dark, Bar, if you was blonde they might mistake you for a fraulein,' as Uncle Stan had said. He was off himself to be looked over that afternoon, adding: 'They say us old 'uns can play our part, in civil defence. We'll show them old nasty troops what's what, if they invade round here!'

However, Bar was passed A1, with the proviso that she should visit an optician to be fitted with reading glasses. If she couldn't afford the cost, she could be issued with a regulation pair. One look at the steely glinting glasses on the bossy officer shuffling some papers and she plumped for the former option. She was wondering by that time, what on earth had she let herself in for, but the Army struck while the iron was hot. She was sworn in by a lofty colonel: Bible in hand, she solemnly promised to serve King and Country and was promptly issued with a one-way ticket north.

'I'll be advised within three weeks, the date I'm to go. And I've already got cold feet.' She squeezed Mum's arm and echoed Uncle Stan. 'To tell the truth, Mum and I'm not joking – I'm scared stiff.'

Mum rose to the occasion. 'You won't let the side down, dearie, or Clive, or your old Mum.' She was stiff from sitting so long on that hard chair, heavy handbag on her lap, waiting around without even a nice cup of tea to refresh her. The staff had been rushed off their feet, with all those eager girls parading in their unmentionables.

'I'd better visit Mirry and the little girls, before I take off, eh? D'you know, I was really disappointed to hear that because I'm married I won't be sent overseas – not without Clive's permission anyway.' They were walking along the street now to the newsboys' shrill cries of '*Star, News'n'Stannard*! All the latest on the war!' Not that there was much to shout about at the moment, it all seemed a bit of an anti-climax here in Great Britain, even though the Navy was vigorously pursuing German U-boats. And Chamberlain was still prime minister.

'Which permission I hope very much won't be forth-coming, my girl,' Mum said firmly.

'They're in urgent need of shorthand typists it seems – they'll probably chain me to a desk,' Bar told her ruefully, 'so all those years at night school won't be wasted.'

They boarded the bus. The driver was elderly, the chatterbox of a conductress, a young girl wearing trousers. The regular team had already joined up – couldn't wait, the girl informed them. Like Clive, Bar thought. He was still writing for his paper: 'Not yet dispatches from the front, Bar, but no doubt that will come . . .' She knew his letters off by heart.

Bar read the papers avidly now; listened to the news bulletins on the wireless. The defeat of Poland was absolute for, on 17 September, Russia had joined Germany in partitioning that country. Also, Russia was now making ugly threats to Finland, which was grimly holding on to land north of Leningrad, and the other Baltic states.

She couldn't help an involuntary trembling as she realised that there was now no turning back for her, either . . .

*   *   *

The school was in the centre of the village street. It looked nicer from the outside than her old school, Glory decided, but inside, she discovered, it was much the same. High windows, opened and closed by a pole with a hook on the end, double desks and a swing blackboard and globe. But there was a fireplace, not radiators, promising a cheerful glow in the winter months to come, with a stout guard hooked in place, ideal for drying damp outer garments and, as Glory was shortly to discover, wet knickers belonging to an unfortunate child who was teased unmercifully by some of her classmates. The latter meant that there was always an unpleasant whiff in the classroom from autumn to spring. Glory felt instinctive sympathy for Jenny Stokes, remembering her own unkind treatment in hospital.

Jenny lived with her three older brothers in the farm cottages. The boys strode out ahead on the walk to school, while Glory, Junie and Don followed, immediately after they had bolted their bowlsful of Force Flakes and downed their tumblers of frothy new milk each morning, under the watchful eye of Mrs Hardes.

Jenny trailed behind, with her canvas lunch bag and coat pockets bulging with spare pants, looking utterly dejected. Glory soon got into the habit of walking alongside her, but Jenny rarely spoke, just sniffed and hung her head. 'Bit slow, our Jenny,' one of the boys informed the newcomers laconically.

Mummy had accompanied them on the first day, of course, to introduce them to the teachers, who were harassed enough already, for there were other unexpected evacuees, refugee children without their parents, who had been brought together in a requisitioned house which had been empty since the owner died some months previously.

Very few of these young foreigners, as the locals called them, could speak good English yet, but it was decreed that they should have special tuition at the school in the afternoons. After lunch, to make room for the new intake, the village children, whose group, to their surprise, included Glory and her friends, engaged in various activities, like dancing, PT or craftwork in the hall in wet weather; games in the field when fine; or what were termed 'nature walks', with the rector's unworldly daughter. Glory enjoyed these explorations along the lanes, but she soon twigged that it was an opportunity for some to sneak off on other pursuits of their own choice. Numbers rarely tallied when they returned to school to collect their things, and to say prayers. The rector's daughter always looked surprised and apologetic.

Extra teachers had been roped in, too, like one particularly ancient lady with a wispy bun of hair and glasses mended with grimy sticking plaster on the bridge, who catnapped during the scripture readings, and who could blame her? There were some singsong readers, and sulky girls only in her classes, for the boys were privileged, as Glory told her mother enviously that first evening after school. The boys helped with the work on the school farm, while the girls had to work their way through all the begats in the Old Testament – oh, that wasn't fair was it? Animals in the Bible readings were mainly sacrificial goats, but on the farm there were pigs and sheep, and calves and rabbits – her voice rose indignantly.

'At least you don't smell like Don does this evening, after all that mucking out,' her mother said thankfully. 'And girls can help in the school garden, can't they?'

'During the lunch break. And you know I don't like worms, Mummy.'

Glory could have added that she didn't like the children at school either, and that the feeling was obviously mutual. They mocked her accent, they stared resentfully at her when the teacher praised her reading, writing and spelling. She had her hair pulled from behind, which brought tears to her eyes, but she hadn't squealed.

That first day, she was cornered against the school wall by a gang of taunting girls when she was innocently bouncing her ball and wondering why no one would play with her. She did not shine at netball like athletic Junie, who was promptly put in the team, on displaying how she could shoot all the balls smartly into the net. Blots appeared mysteriously in her exercise books; the fountain pen Daddy had given her disappeared from her desk and someone sliced her rubber into bits. She really wished she wasn't clever, but it wasn't something she could change.

Then there was the walk home. Following the big Stokes lads, with their cropped heads, who Uncle Jim called 'Chucklenuts' which was a silly name, Glory thought, because they weren't ones for chuckling much. She disliked their loud voices, their great boots kicking stones on the road, and worst of all, the ordeal of the stream, which meandered across the lane at one point and deepened alarmingly in rainy periods. The Stokeses leapt its width scornfully then spun round, waited and watched, ready to jeer. Junie and Don took a run at it and landed easily beyond the water. Poor little Jenny tried and always fell short, so got her feet soaked, and no doubt wetted herself in fright at the same time. But Glory put her nose in the air and waded through. She wasn't going to let them see that she was worried, or risk ignominy like Jenny: this way, she was considered devil-may-care. Mummy soon bought her those wellington boots in dull old black rubber, at her request. The village Co-op didn't stock any other sort anyway. She dismissed the dream of Judy's red shoes: they really wouldn't do here, for their magic only worked in the Land of Oz.

She had been at the school just a couple of weeks when she found a newcomer ensconced at her desk. Until then she had sat alone. No one wanted to share with her.

'This is Horst,' Miss Stevenson said. 'He speaks quite good English, and we feel he can easily catch up on reading and writing in his new language. The teachers both here and at the hostel have discussed this, and have decided that it would be better for Horst to begin at a primary level in English and that we should select a bright, younger child . . .' Glory winced, guessing what was coming. 'Yes, you, Glory, to encourage him. I don't imagine you will have your pupil very long, he should soon be able to move up to the top class with his contemporaries.'

Horst, with his long legs awkwardly constricted under the desk, smiled gravely at Glory. 'I hope you do not mind, being my tutor, Gloria,' he asked politely. He was ten years old, but was unembarrassed at the sight of his young teacher.

His parents had sent him to safety from Germany a few months before the war began on a ship crammed full with other youngsters. 'I miss them very much. But I must work hard and do well, it is expected of me.'

He reminded Glory somewhat of Clive, with his floppy hair and angular features. His smile revealed rather crooked but good teeth. He stood out from the other boys, in their hand-knitted jerseys and flannel trousers. Horst wore a tweed jacket and matching short pants, a suit, Glory supposed, with a shirt and tie. The outfit was tight and short in the sleeves. 'We are given our clothes, people are very kind,' he said gravely, when he caught her looking at him.

'Where are your parents?' she asked him in the break. 'Did they get away from Germany, too?' Surprisingly, he had stayed at her side in the playground and did not desert her to join the bigger boys in wrestling or kicking the ball. He was tall for his age, obviously strong. The other boys did not bait him as they usually did newcomers. Glory felt safe at last beside Horst. She had found a protector. Don and Junie quickly deserted her at school. She had not told her mother that. Mirry fondly imagined they took care of Glory.

Horst did not smile this time. 'I am afraid – I do not know. My father lost his post at the university in our town. His view on politics was unaccepted, but he was merely a lecturer in Mathematics … My mother's family are American. I can only hope they are safe, and will come for me, when they can.'

Glory thought: it's awful, Daddy being away. But it's not like it is for Horst. Mummy wants to go home, she doesn't like it here. But, even though it's beastly sometimes for me here at school, I want so much to fit in, because I think living in the country is, well, good …

CHAPTER TWENTY

It was strange, opening the door of Number Five and going inside. The hall smelt musty, the rooms were just as they had left them. Bar looked around downstairs then went to collect the things from Mirry's bedroom that she had asked for.

Jim was calling for her in half an hour, to drive her to Surrey for the weekend. They'd met up in London after working this Saturday morning at their respective offices. It was Mirry's idea for her to come here first. Bar was leaving for her new life next week.

She went into her own room, opened a drawer or two. They were mostly empty. All her clothes were at Mum's now. She came across her shorthand books, hesitated, then put them in her bag. She might need to practise to increase her speed, she thought ruefully. At the publishers, her work was now interesting and varied, shorthand was only a small part of it.

There was a little diary poked to the back of the drawer. She opened it, curiously. 1933! A momentous year in Germany, which had led to all *this*, she thought.

She flicked over the pages. *Glory stood up all by herself today; Clive and I biked with the Venturas to Godstone and he kissed me! Saluted the Galloping Major in his corns – hope nobody saw me – or him!! Then: I can type at 30 wpm – hurray! Miss Boam wants to know, when are we coming back to dancing classes?* She tucked the diary in the bottom of her handbag. Childish, round handwriting, no profound thoughts, but memories, all the same. Who would have guessed then, the significance of that first kiss?

Miss Boam! She returned to Mirry and Fred's room and looked out of the window at Lahana. Although she half-fancied to see him, it still gave her a start to observe the major, at his window, staring back at her. At least he had exchanged the *corns* for a dressing gown, she thought, grinning, unless they were hidden underneath. No saluting today . . .

She closed the front door, left her bags on the step, and impulsively crossed over the road. She knocked tentatively at first, then loudly. No answer. She turned to see Jim standing in the gateway. The car was parked outside Number Five. He had guessed where she was.

'Haven't seen her in weeks,' he said quietly. 'I suppose she must go to the shops sometimes, for they have to eat, surely? Ready Bar? Got everything?'

Bar walked away from Lahana. Just as she was about to get into the car, she glanced up once more at the window where the major had been framed earlier. The curtains were now pulled across. If he still stood there, he was unseen, she thought. She bit her lip. It worried her. Something was not right there, she was convinced of it. But what could she do? She didn't live here any more. Jim started up the engine. They were off.

* * *

Mirry was tired, but so happy to hug her sister. She would keep the grumbles for bedtime confiding. It was slave labour, she thought resentfully, keeping such a big house clean and tidy. Laura was working most days now, although, thankfully, she made sure she was back before the children returned from school. She reminded herself that, because of Laura's connection with Mr Gray, they were living here rent free: they split the housekeeping money between them. Mrs Hardes accounted for all the food: she frowned on snacks of bread and cheese and buns between meals. She had also commented acidly on the dinginess of Beulah's nappies, but Mirry couldn't boil them in a bucket as she used to do at home, because she was not allowed to use the stove for that purpose. 'Suppose they boiled over?' Mrs Hardes asked. 'Not nice, Miriam, alongside cooking food.'

Thank goodness Beulah was a good baby now and Glory obviously thrived on the country life. Mirry hardly saw her elder daughter: always up a tree, or romping with Pip in the meadow with Junie and Don, when he wasn't out and about with those Stokes boys – up to all sorts of mischief, no doubt. She was glad she had daughters.

Fred's letters came by the first post most days. When she did manage to sit down for five minutes, she added to the weekly diary she was keeping for him about the family – she posted this off every Monday. She couldn't write as intimately as she longed to, but she hoped Fred knew just how much she loved and missed him.

'Oh, good, you've got a piano here, Mirry,' Bar observed, being shown round the house. 'Any pupils?'

'Our children, of course, though I'm afraid it's difficult to pin them down to practising their scales nowadays. Oh, and the school have asked me if I will take on a young refugee, called Horst. Glory's already helping him with his English. He starts next Saturday afternoon. I'm not sure how advanced he is in his music studies.'

Glory came rushing in. 'Bar! I do love you!' she proclaimed breathlessly. She too wore dungarees out of school now. Mirry was glad she had brought her precious sewing machine with her.

'I love you, too! Goodness, Glory, you've changed – braids, eh?'

'So have you! Your hair's different too.'

'Up for the ATS, duckie! All hair above the collar, so they say.'

'I wish you'd worn your uniform . . .'

'Haven't been issued with it yet. Got that pleasure to come. Well, Mirry, don't you want to check I brought everything on your list. Jim took the bags straight upstairs, didn't he?'

Then Bar sniffed. 'What's that – smell?' she exclaimed.

'Laura's mother's making something special for your supper,' Mirry told her, tongue in cheek.

'Better hold your nose when you swallow,' Glory said candidly, leading the way up the stairs. 'This is it, Bar, we're all in together, ours is the biggest room. You'll be sharing with Mummy tonight, as Daddy's not here.'

Bringing up the rear, Mirry glanced through the open door of Laura's bedroom. Junie now shared with her grandmother in the third bedroom, and Donald was on his own in the box room. It was Mirry's choice to keep her children with her at night.

Mirry was embarrassed by the glimpse of Laura and Jim embracing. It wasn't fair, she thought. It was getting on for two months since she and Fred had been close like that. She felt a sense of shock, too, for she realised that she had always thought of Jim as a typical bank cashier, steady and seeming middle-aged, not romantic and eternally boyish, like Fred.

Even as she averted her gaze, she couldn't help over-hearing Laura's almost whispered words: 'That's enough, Jim. Not now.' And his reply: 'You always push me away nowadays. What's up, Laura? Is there something you ought to tell me?'

Mirry recognised the fear in the question, the underlying jealousy. After all, didn't she worry that Fred, despite the length of his letters, the love and longing expressed, might, if their parting went on too long, have something to tell *her*, that she would rather not hear?

Then Bar's arm went round her, squeezed her shoulder, pulled her into Mirry's room. 'I know Mirry – I saw. Clive and I are apart too, remember. Just that short time together, as man and wife, but I ache terribly, just as you must do, for Fred . . .' She suddenly kissed her sister's flushed cheek. Perhaps she shouldn't have aired her feelings like that – not to dear inhibited Mirry.

She saw, yes, Mirry thought, but thankfully, she didn't hear what they said.

'Who's got toothache?' Glory asked curiously. 'Did you remember my skipping rope, Bar?'

'I did – and here it is,' Bar pulled it from the carrier bag. 'And I brought you some liquorice skipping ropes, too. Share them with the others, mind. Hello, little Beulah-baby, did I wake you up? Sorry, Mirry! May I take her out of the cot? She looks all rosy, smiley and cuddly.'

'Time she woke up, or she won't sleep soundly tonight,' Mirry said.

'High tea – fish pie – I added some diced carrots to give it a little colour; I always feel it looks rather insipid, don't you?' Mrs Hardes ladled some of the gooey mass on to Bar's plate.

'I hate fish,' Glory muttered, putting her hand over her plate.

'Rubbish!' Mrs Hardes retorted sharply.

'That's what I meant!'

'Glory, how could you be so rude? Say sorry to Mrs Hardes,' Mirry rebuked her daughter. 'Anyway, you ate fish and chips last Saturday without making a fuss.'

'That's different. It tastes nice.'

'*Glory!*'

'Oh, all right, sorry. Just a spot then, please . . .'

'You can go without – *one* slice of bread and butter, remember – this isn't Liberty Hall.' Mrs Hardes looked really cross as Glory heaved an audible sigh of relief.

Bar remembered her niece's suggestion earlier and held her breath as she swallowed the next mouthful. Glory was right – it was horrible.

Jim directed warning side glances at his giggling children. 'There'll be rationing shortly, you'll be jolly thankful for fish pie then, no doubt.'

'There might well be a shortage of fish, too,' Laura added, 'with all those U-boats about.'

Glory folded her bread and butter and demolished it in two bites. 'Can I get down now, please?' she asked, with her mouth full.

Mirry sighed. 'Here, take Beulah from me. It's difficult for me to eat with her wriggling on my lap but you're not getting away scot-free, Glory, you can help with the washing up when we're all finished.'

Bar deftly transferred a fishy lump to her serviette as she dabbed at her mouth. Then she gently shook the linen square in Pip's direction as she replaced it on her lap. It was very convenient that he lurked quietly under the table, concealed by the overhang of the tablecloth.

It was Bar who managed to smooth down Mrs Hardes's ruffled feathers. 'Let's put on an impromptu entertainment as our thank you to the cook, for all her hard work on our behalf, eh?' She suggested cheerfully.

Glory was dispatched to find her tap shoes, the rugs were rolled back in the sitting room revealing the unpolished boards: 'Look,' Bar pointed out, 'she can't hurt the floor.' Thus encouraged, Glory immediately demonstrated that her taps could strike sparks. Don and Junie looked at her with new respect, mixed with guilt, for she hadn't reproached them for leaving her to cope alone at school.

Mirry put the baby to bed while clearing the table and washing up was in progress: now, she sat down willingly at the piano, for her back was aching, and leafed through the sheet music Bar had brought from home today. Everyone knew the choruses, she thought: she'd work her way through the most popular in the *Smallwood's Tutor* which she hoped might inspire the more reluctant pupils among them. 'The easiest to teach and to learn from', was one of the homilies to be found at the bottom of each page.

So, they danced and sang loudly, and tapped, in Glory's case, to:

You're as pleasant as the morning
And refreshing as the rain,
Isn't it a pity that you're such a scatter brain?
When you smile it's so delightful,
When you talk it's so insane,
Still it's charming chatter, scatter brain . . .

Even Mrs Hardes was smiling by the time they finished that, as Glory executed an exuberant cartwheel and then slid into the splits. She really was a scatterbrain, Mirry thought fondly, but brilliant with it. The secret fears, which had haunted her since Glory was so ill a few months ago, were at last banished.

Just then the sulky fire which Jim had tried to coax into life earlier flared up with a sudden whoosh! and they pulled up the chairs, plumped up the feather cushions cased in worn orange velvet, and basked in its warmth and light. The heavy new blackout curtains shut out the night. Much later, when they were all husky from singing all the old favourites, and the children began yawning, their mothers decreed it was time for bed. 'No buts, just look at the time . . .'

Mirry closed the music, rubbed her eyes, for she had strained them to see the notes by the light of the candles Jim had stuck helpfully into the brass brackets on the piano. As if on cue, there was a wail from upstairs. Time to make Beulah's bottle. A hand ruffled her hair, as if she was Glory's age, she thought startled. Just for an instant, she had imagined it was Fred. But he was far away, still being fed grisly, gristly grub, as he put it in his letters. At least she'd be able to write a cheerful end to this week's diary for him, thanks to Bar suggesting tonight's fun. That's if she could keep her eyes open to write, in bed, and if Bar didn't want to yarn for hours.

'Thanks, little Mirry,' Jim said. He smelled of tobacco. She wondered if he had found out that Laura had taken up smoking now too. She had the feeling that like Fred, he would be disapproving. She had discovered Laura's secret by accident: looking out of her window one night she had seen a shadowy figure and the glowing tip of a cigarette. For a moment she had been alarmed, fearing an intruder, then she heard Laura's familiar little cough and the closing of the front door.

'I'll go and give the baby a cuddle and hold the fort till you arrive with the Cow and Gate,' Bar offered. 'And I'll check that Glory took her tap shoes off before she dived into bed.'

Then there was just Mirry and Laura left to push the chairs back and put the guard round the dying fire.

They had never discussed what Mirry thought of as 'the private' side of marriage, despite their long friendship.

But now Laura sighed: 'Did you hear Jim tell me to "hurry up"? He just seems to have one thing on his mind, these days.'

Mirry didn't know what to say at this unwelcome confidence.

She met up with Mrs Hardes in the kitchen, filling her stone hot water bottle. She crossed her fingers, mentally, that all the boiled water hadn't been used. No friendly, fast gas here.

Screwing in the stopper and rubbing the bottle over with a towel, Mrs Hardes looked at Mirry as she measured milk powder into the jug. 'Mirry,' she actually sounded diffident.

'Yes?' Mirry was surprised. She always addressed her as Miriam.

'I'd like to thank you for all the pleasure you gave us tonight, with your lively piano playing. I can't remember when I enjoyed an evening more. Oh, and Mirry, I do appreciate your hard work in the house, my wretched rheumatism plaguing me as it does. I'm sorry, too, that Laura doesn't pull her weight. It's my fault, really, I brought her up to be so ambitious, to want a career – there's no stopping her now, it seems. Jim has always indulged her, of course. Your mother must be proud of you, Mirry – you always put your family first . . .'

Mirry hoped that her face did not betray her surprise at these unexpected compliments. 'Thank you,' she said simply.

'Good night, my dear.'

'Good night!' Mirry echoed, feeling all aglow.

CHAPTER TWENTY-ONE

BAR WAS ONE OF TWENTY-FOUR recruits – the only females in a barracks full of men. It was really quite unnerving, she thought. The last part of their journey, the most uncomfortable, from the station, had been by lorry. They were herded like cattle, as one of their number indignantly complained. It was certainly a bone-shaking ride and the sergeant driver actually appeared to relish their discomfort.

After their first meal in the mess hall – fat bangers oozing grease, mashed potato and a great dollop of swede, followed by plums and custard, which they made short work of because they were all hungry – they kept a tight grip on their newly presented knife, fork, spoon and mug, having had it dinned into them that they would have to keep these for the remainder of their service, however long that might be.

Then the bewildered girls were marched smartly to the Quartermaster's stores to be kitted out.

'You're lucky,' they were told tersely, 'the first intake had to drill in their civvies – bloomin' ridiculous they looked, too.'

Bar wondered miserably if she would ever find her way around: all the buildings looked the same. Huts with corrugated iron roofs. It was a vast, unlovely place, and at the end of October, wind seemed to gust unkindly round every corner. There were eyes watching them everywhere, she thought ruefully.

On the journey from St Pancras, after she had waved goodbye, leaning perilously from the train window, to Mum and Iris, who were trying to smile through their tears, she had soon got chatting to some of her fellow recruits. One of them, a tiny, lively girl called Eileen Raffery, with freckles and frizzy chestnut-coloured hair, had started off the singing, as they rattled along the rails. As she followed Eileen's spirited lead, Bar thought of Clive, and how he had probably sung the same words, dozens of times already with his army pals.

Her lips quivered: he must be thinking of her at this moment, too, aware that she would be on the train, no doubt wondering just how she would cope with such a different way of life.

There's cheese, cheese, with shocking dirty knees,
In the stores, in the stores,
There's lard, lard, they sell it by the yard,
In the Quartermaster's stores . . .

Now, here she was, in the middle of a long line advancing on the counters, being chivvied by the gruff, grizzled sergeant and echoing in her head were the words of the chorus:

My eyes are dim, I cannot see,
I have not brought my specs with me,
I have not brought my specs with me!

Had she remembered to put her glasses in her bag, she wondered unhappily? She wasn't accustomed to wearing them yet. Oh, don't say she might yet be fitted with a steely pair!

She reached the first bay. Just in front of her was Eileen. They had to state their size. Neat piles of garments, three of everything, apart from tunic, skirt and greatcoat, were slapped smartly on the counter before them.

Bar's eyes widened incredulously as she stared at the amazing underclothes. White vests and underpants – so ugly, large and thick that both she and Eileen had to stifle hysterical giggles.

'You'll be glad of 'em when it gits cold, and the going gits tough,' the sergeant said reprovingly. He didn't miss a thing.

The pièce de résistance was the khaki locknit knickers with elasticated legs: baggy bloomers fit for a pantomime dame, together with the matching stockings. 'They'll come up to me armpits,' Eileen whispered.

'Just the job for scrambling over barbed wire,' Bar returned, 'the enemy won't believe their eyes. They'll wave the white flag, eh?'

Laughter was bubbling up in them again. The corporal behind the counter winked sympathetically. He looked nicer than the sergeant.

The queue was halted briefly while shoes small enough to fit Eileen's tiny feet were searched for and then produced triumphantly. 'Oright, Shorthouse? You won't suffer from corns in those. Move along then, and no more complaints.' Bar, who took an average size five, received her two pairs of shoes immediately. With their bullet hard toecaps it was obvious they would take quite a bit of wearing in, she anticipated ruefully. Blisters would be inevitable, particularly when they began drilling. 'Spit and polish, that's it, young lady,' Uncle Stan had demonstrated his expertise on his own boots before she left the flat. 'Helps if you know the wrinkles, gal.'

No brassière, the Army obviously didn't consider this garment necessary, or frowned on it as frivolous, and worse, no pjyamas were issued. Bar had already realised that these would be much appreciated in the draughty hut, for she was bedded down a fair distance from the stove. No doubt the non-commissioned staff, who would shortly occupy the room off the main dormitory area, would have more comforts, she thought. She was thankful that Mum had insisted on packing some wincyette pyjamas which went back to her schooldays. They had been told only to bring a small case with them, just the bare necessities, because everything else would be issued on the first day. What about boot polish and brasso for buttons, she wondered? They'd soon be queuing at the NAAFI, too. The one shilling and fourpence they'd been advanced wouldn't go far, that was obvious.

Clutching their new possessions they were lined up again while the sergeant checked all the items against their names on the list. 'One greatcoat; one tunic; one skirt; three shirts; one cap,' he recited monotonously, then: 'One packet of handkerchiefs,' he added nonchalantly, a neat euphemism for that essential item for every young woman there. Despite this unexpected display of tact, each new recruit blushed.

'Blimey!' Eileen the irrepressible whispered. 'We'll have to learn to talk in French when we want to say something private, eh?'

They had made their ablutions, as they learned to call them, in the primitive block with its lack of privacy, insufficient hot water and puddly floor, and then were glad to tumble wearily into bed. It had been a long, long day.

They were still awaiting a woman officer-in-charge. The sergeant, who had daughters of his own at home, just a few years younger than these girls, actually felt a sympathy he dare not show. A tall girl called Coral, somewhat older than the rest who were mostly around Bar's age – Eileen was only nineteen – with a cut-glass accent and the unself-conscious air of one who had been head girl of her school, was instructed to see to the putting out of lights and to the strict rationing of the coke supply for the stove.

Eileen had bagged the bed next to Bar's, by unspoken agreement. The first friend you made was going to be very important. They both knew that.

'You asleep, Bar?'

'No . . .'

'Like a bit of choc'late?'

'Cleaned my teeth, remember!'

'Oh, go on!'

'All right then – thanks.'

'Coo, the bed ain't half hard.'

'Not as hard as the one I slept on, on my honeymoon . . .'

'Don't suppose you cared then, eh?'

'Can't say I did . . .'

'You miss him, I reckon . . .'

'Yes . . .'

'Been married long?'

'Nearly two months. Clive joined up just after the wedding. He didn't wait to be called up.'

'I got engaged on my birthday – two days after war was declared. My boy's been in the Navy since 1938. Haven't seen him since that last leave. We had such a party, I tell you. I don't know where he is right now, except he's on board ship, of course, and he'll have no idea I'm here. Just made my mind up one day, and that was it.'

'Putting the lights out – now!' Coral called. She wore a brocade dressing-gown over satin pyjamas and a turban concealing her curlers.

'Bossy boots: thinks she's Jessie Matthews I reckon. With them pencilled eyebrows and that fringe. Bet she can't do a high kick like Jessie though: did you see her in *The Good Companions*? It was about a troupe of travelling artistes. 'Course, it's quite an old film, the only sort we get at our local fleapit.' Eileen turned over and thumped her flat pillow. 'They're right to call these biscuits "hard tack" I reckon. Why can't we have a decent mattress, not bags of bleedin' straw . . . Bossy B. should've had a tight perm like me. I'm hoping it'll last the war out . . .'

'I bet my sister's seen that film, she's a real fan,' Bar yawned so widely, she made her jaw click. 'Ouch! that really hurt . . .'

'Makes a change – not sharing a bed for once . . .' came the last mutter from Eileen. Bar smiled ruefully to herself, thinking of her brief married life so far.

It wasn't quite dark, because there were chinks of moonlight filtering through the cracks here and there in the walls. But Bar was glad that Eileen and her neighbour on the other side, an adenoidal girl called Renee, couldn't see that she was crying her eyes out. She wasn't sure who she was missing most – Clive, of course, but they'd spent so little time actually living together she thought, wiping her eyes on the thin sheet, maybe Mum, or Mirry . . . Then she became sharply aware that she was not alone in her desolation. Every single girl in that stark hut, with blankets pulled up round her ears, was weeping too, as rain splattered then drummed relentlessly on the iron roof.

They were a motley crew, in uniforms which fitted where they touched – in Eileen's case nowhere at all on her skinny six-stone frame. 'How they ever passed you Al, I'll never know,' the sergeant exclaimed. They were quick-marched to the M.O. for their jabs, as he called them. They were not too sure what these were for but were tersely informed: 'You'll all get TT and TAB whether you like it or not.'

'TT – sounds like the Isle of Man motorcycle race,' Eileen sauced the sergeant. 'You'll feel as if you've been bowled over by a motorbike shortly my girl,' he returned, as if he relished the thought.

As Bar wrote to Clive later:

I'm positive I'll always remember that 'orrible sergeant growling: 'In you go, sleeve rolled up – out you come, form up in threes and the first one what dares to faint, I'll really have it in for.' Naturally I did – and he did. Ooh, it was such a strange sensation, Clive – I just sort of floated away. Don't worry, I'm all right now.

*(And no, I'm not 'in the club', as the girls call it. I
wouldn't keep that from you – and I wouldn't be here.)*

*Eileen, a girl I've palled up with, a real Cockney
sparrer, but her parents are Irish, fanned me with her
cap, so he's got it in for her, too. She said it might be
preferable to suffer from lockjaw and malaria than
have his evil eye on us, but I don't intend to let him
have me beat . . .*

*Actually, I think he considers female soldiers a bit
of a joke. We've got a lot to prove. But, we'll do it. Oh,
Clive, my feet don't half hurt! How are you doing?
Whose idea was it to serve King and Country? I must
be mad, if it was mine . . .*

Sore feet paled into insignificance that night as the injec-
tions took effect and arms swelled like pumpkins and
throbbed, fiery red. Bar achieved a momentary relief by
gingerly moving the tender part against the cold, hard
iron of the bedstead. She was just drifting at last into an
exhausted sleep when the bugle call warned it was time to
rise and shine. Shine? More like groan, she thought, winc-
ing. How on earth, she wondered, were they expected to
swing their injured arms today?

Meal times proved daunting for the girls. All those fellows,
making the floor echo with the pounding of their great
boots, lining up eagerly with their eating irons and stained

enamel mugs. Bar suddenly pictured Glory clattering in her tap shoes and the sparks flying on wooden floorboards not so very long ago.

She'd send a few sparks flying herself she thought grimly, if she could summon up the nerve. The soldiers dipping their none too clean mugs into the tea urn really turned the girls' stomachs. Bar wondered what Fred would have said – him and his standards of cleanliness. Mind you, it sounded like a prison camp where old Fred was, from the couple of letters he'd written her. No going in or out without passes, just like here. And she'd rather be in the army than the civil service any day. She hadn't replied to the letters yet, because she wasn't sure if Mirry was aware that he, too, was keeping in touch with her sister. She was still fond of Fred, nothing would change that, for he'd been so kind and supportive of her over the years, but his admission of his real feelings for her, on the day he took her to London, was hard to forget.

Her chance came sooner than expected, when the orderly officer, observing them from the end of the long table, asked the routine question: 'Any complaints?'

Eileen gave Bar a nudge. 'Why me?' she muttered.

''Cause you've made such a song and dance about it, that's why!'

Bar rose. 'Yes, sir,' she cleared her throat.

'Speak up, I can't hear you.'

All eyes were on her as she said loud and clear: 'We don't fancy drinking the tea after all those dirty mugs have been dipped in it.'

'Ah . . . Food meet with your approval, I hope?'

'Yes, sir, we're so hungry we'd eat anything.' She sat down, scarlet cheeked. This was very true, for all the unaccustomed exercise meant that they fell upon everything that was dished up.

To her surprise, someone gave a whistle of approval and there was laughter from the soldiers on the nearby tables. 'That's right, you tell 'em, girl!' one called out.

The following day a mug was tied to the urn and there was a notice informing that this was for ladling out the tea. And Bar was paid another unexpected compliment, by one who had hardly spoken to her until now.

'You've got what it takes. I admire your spirit. We might just survive with you around to champion us, Bar,' Coral told her, as they filled their mugs with unsullied tea.

She's nice, Bar thought, surprised. I do believe I've made another friend.

CHAPTER TWENTY-TWO

MIRRY HAD BEEN DREADING the thought of their first Christmas away from home but, now it was almost here, she told herself she must make the most of it. Beulah was too young to realise what was coming, but Glory, naturally, was excited and busy with secret painting and glueing both at school and in the farmhouse.

'Mummy, you're peeking!' she accused, every five minutes.

'What about you? Who was hunting about in the wardrobe yesterday, eh?' Mirry countered, smiling.

Laura arrived home one afternoon with some exciting news. 'Bernard's back in business. He's been asked to make some short films – public information and advice, with a good storyline . . .'

'Propaganda, you mean?' Mrs Hardes was doggedly scraping huge carrots, brought round this morning by kind Mrs Dean. 'Waste not, want not', was certainly her motto, even though those orange torpedoes had been neatly holed by some pest.

'Well, I suppose you might call them that but more facts than fantasy, Bernard insists. He wants to feature evacuees in the first feature. I was bold enough to suggest: "How about us?" He was rather doubtful, I suppose because we're not typical.'

'You mean, we didn't have labels tied round our neck and weren't torn away from the bosom of our family and sent to the ends of the earth,' Glory interrupted dramatically.

'Don't be silly, Gloria,' Mrs Hardes reproved, chopping the carrots into big chunks and guarding them jealously from the eager outstretched hands of the children, just in from school and hungry as usual. 'These are for the casserole. Laura, don't forget that many evacuees have already returned to London and other cities which were said to be certain targets for bombing; so far, this appears to be a war at sea, not in the air.'

Laura rolled her eyes meaningfully at Mirry, who was jigging a fretful Beulah on her hip. The baby was cutting her first teeth and, as a consequence, Mirry had dark shadows under her eyes. She couldn't stop yawning either. She thought ruefully that when Glory was this age, Fred had willingly done his bit, getting up in the night and rocking the cradle.

'Would we get paid if we were in the film?' Junie wanted to know. Don muttered cheekily that they could pay him not to take part, acting was for sissies, or sisters anyway.

'Bad enough being in the Nativity Play at school. I told them I was too big but they said they wanted someone tall, and old.'

'Goodness no, we wouldn't even have our names in the credits, but we'd be doing our bit for the war effort, wouldn't we?' their mother reproved them.

'Gloria is the only one of you who has any talent for acting,' Mrs Hardes said unexpectedly, opening the oven door and letting a welcome blast of hot air into the cheerless kitchen. It was really wintry outside now. The children had come in with flakes of snow clinging to their hair and eyebrows. 'After all, hasn't she been chosen to be Mary to Donald's Joseph?'

Don didn't need to say anything this time, his expression told exactly how he felt about that.

But Mirry felt a little rush of excitement and pride.

Laura said: 'I told Bernard about Glory, and he said he'd really like to meet her and judge for himself – so I promptly invited him to supper on Saturday evening.'

'You should have asked me first, Laura,' her mother said crossly. 'Two days – to get this place looking spick and span, so he doesn't wonder why on earth he let us loose here; a cake to bake – and, what about Jim?' It was becoming obvious to the other adults that, now they were apart so much, Jim was rather huffy about the time his wife devoted to another man, even if it was in the course of working together.

'He's on firewatch at the bank this weekend. Mother, please don't fuss.'

'I'll make a sponge cake, we've got plenty of fresh eggs, and there's that bramble jelly we made from all the blackberries the children picked in the autumn; just right for filling a Victoria sandwich,' Mirry offered diffidently. Was it unkind of her to be secretly glad that Jim wasn't coming this Saturday? She liked him, of course she did, but it seemed so unfair, when she and Fred were still apart. She might really have something to write to him about after Mr Gray's visit – like their daughter embarking on a film career, eh?

'Mummy's cakes are the best, so Daddy says,' Glory added artlessly. 'D'you think Mr Gray will want to see me tap dance or sing?'

I must wash her hair, Mirry thought, and maybe she'll agree to ringlets – just this once.

'Ouch!' Glory protested indignantly, as Junie gave her a sly pinch. Jealousy was not confined to the older generation.

Horst came round as usual that Saturday afternoon for his piano lesson. As he sat down on the stool, Mirry noted with motherly concern that his legs were painfully chapped where the wind had caught at the bare skin between flannel shorts and long woollen socks. She fetched the round cardboard ointment box containing the soothing zinc and castor oil cream which she used at nappy changes for Beulah to prevent any soreness, and she whispered tactfully in his ear: 'Rub some on your knees. Haven't you got any long trousers for winter?'

'Thank you, Mrs Hope, you are very kind. It is not allowed. We wear the short ones until age fourteen.'

'That's ridiculous!' she said loudly now, for the family, apart from Glory, were busy with their own pursuits elsewhere. 'You're tall for your age. Your mackintosh is not long enough to cover the gap. Tell the ones in charge *I* said so.'

'It will make no difference,' he said equably. 'We follow our own school rules, even in this country. Shall I play now, Mrs Hope?'

As he bent his head over the keys, she saw the chilblains on his ears, and bit her lip. And she complained about the draughts in this house . . .

Glory, dressed and curled, and warned to stay put on the sofa, to be ready for the more important visitor due in a while, as usual did not miss a trick. 'We've got chilblains too, on our toes, haven't we Mummy? Coo, they don't half itch! Mrs Dean next door told Mummy to cook a turnip and mash it, then stir in some powdered mustard and grated horseradish – with a spoonful of olive oil, only we hadn't got any of that, so we used liquid paraffin – then, Mummy grated her knuckles when she found a root of horseradish, all withered and gruesome, at the back of the shelf in the larder. Then she had to make a poultice – but can you imagine keeping *that* on your toes, when you're lying in bed?'

'I expect he can imagine it all too well,' Mirry said wryly. There really wasn't much she could teach Horst on the piano – just provide the music sheets, listen, encourage and comment. It was a pity she could not give him her undivided attention today: she couldn't help wondering if Beulah, strapped in her high chair in the kitchen, supposedly entertained by watching Mrs Hardes bake scones, was dribbling down the front of her clean outfit.

She glanced covertly at her watch. 'I'm sorry Horst, but I'm afraid I must cut your lesson a little short today – you see, we are expecting someone shortly. Would you like to finish with a piece of your own choice?'

He looked up, smiled. 'Of course, Mrs Hope. *Volti subito*, eh?' he added, riffling the pages.

'Turn over quickly,' translated the know-all on the sofa, somersaulting on the cushions. 'Play the *Blue Danube*, Horst, I like that.'

Mirry faced the inevitable. Glory was far too lively today, it was no use reminding her why she was supposed to be sitting all starched up, as Mrs Hardes had remarked earlier with a quirk of the lips.

She held out her hands impulsively, inviting her daughter to waltz to Horst's accompaniment. She was almost as uninhibited as Bar had been, dancing with Fred as Mirry herself played this, back at Number Five – was it really only a year or two ago?

'Bravo!' observed the man who had paused in the doorway to watch them, in amusement.

Mirry whirled round, flustered. Laura, her hair much blonder now that Jim wasn't here to frown on the strength of the Hiltone bleach, came up behind the visitor. As she ushered him in, Mirry noted with surprise that Laura, who usually favoured slacks, was wearing the pretty crêpe dress in shades of blue, bought by Jim for her last birthday and hung in the wardrobe with the comment: 'Very nice but I don't suppose I'll have much opportunity to wear it here out in the sticks.'

'Bernard,' Laura said, 'meet my friend, Mirry Hope, and her daughter, Glory. Oh, and this is Horst, the boy I was telling you about. All of you, this is my employer, Bernard Gray and our benefactor of course, regarding the house.' She sounded a little out of breath, and Mirry saw that she had buttoned her bodice awry. She must have changed at the last minute, Mirry thought.

Shaking hands with Bernard Gray, Mirry had to admit that Fred had been right – he wasn't tall and distinguished, but short and thickset. But there was something a bit disturbing about him, the way he looked at her. Such a deep, attractive voice, heavily accented, too . . . He likes women, I can tell, she thought, in confusion. I believe he'd even try to charm a little mouse like me. She would have been amazed if she had known how attractive she appeared to him, all flushed from dancing round the room. Mirry was definitely blossoming now she was approaching thirty.

'I am a little early? I came by car. You are taking a piano lesson?' he asked.

'It is finished. I am going home now. Thank you, Mrs Hope,' Horst put in politely.

'Why don't you stay Horst, so I can talk to you, also? I am very interested in your present situation, which mirrors my own, you see, some years ago,' Bernard Gray suggested.

'You are very welcome to have tea with us,' Laura said quickly.

'Thank you, but I promise to return to the house where I stay, before dark, Mrs Sims.'

'Then, tell them there,' Bernard Gray said, 'that I shall call, with regard to a film I am to make. It concerns evacuees, far from home.'

'I am a refugee, sir.'

'So. Yet you also have to integrate in a new community ... We will discuss. Goodbye for now.'

'Goodbye, Horst,' they echoed, as he retrieved his cap from the hall table.

Mirry went with him to the door. She found Bernard Gray's gaze somewhat unnerving. She asked Horst to wait for a moment. She went into the kitchen to find a bag in which to put the soothing ointment. She had a new box upstairs. Mrs Hardes was arranging scones on a plate. Junie and Don were washing their hands at the sink. She had obviously called them in from the garden.

'Caught us on the hop, Mirry,' she said ruefully. 'And I'm afraid the baby dropped off to sleep in her chair while I was busy – sorry. I did put a cushion behind her head. She won't go to bed after tea now . . .' Beulah's cheeks were like red apples, her mouth hung slightly open. Her bib glistened with dribble.

'Never mind . . . Please, can you spare a scone or two for Horst to eat on his way home? He didn't get his usual cup of tea and biscuit.'

Mrs Hardes actually split the scones and buttered them, wrapped them swiftly in greaseproof paper. She didn't even add that it was bad manners to eat in the street. Not that one could call a muddy lane a street, Mirry supposed. 'I'll be straight back to make the tea,' she offered, 'and help lay the table.'

'Laura can play hostess very nicely by herself, no doubt,' Mrs Hardes said shrewdly. 'Go on you two, make yourselves known to Mr Gray – for Gloria's already beaten you to it.'

'This is very kind of you,' Horst said. He slung his gas mask over one shoulder, took the two paper bags.

'Hurry on your way,' Mirry told him. 'See you soon.'

Mr Gray lavished praises on the scones and on Mirry's delicious sponge. He did not patronise the children, but included them in the conversation. He made them laugh, with humorous asides. Nothing more was said, however, about the proposed film, to their disappointment, and eventually it was time for Beulah to be put to bed along with the older children. Mirry and Mrs Hardes went to oversee all this and returned later to tackle the sinkful of washing up in the kitchen, and to prise Pip away from the stove and out into the freezing garden, all hangdog. 'We've got to make a last trip out there, too, you know,' Mirry told him.

They could hear animated voices emanating from the sitting room. He was an amusing man. Flirtatious. Even her mother's raised eyebrows had failed to alert Laura to the mishap with her buttons. Mirry had noted Mr Gray's quizzical, frankly appreciative glance.

'This is so typical of Laura,' Mrs Hardes said sourly, wringing out the dish cloth. 'Well, I've finished entertaining for tonight. I'm off to bed. You can join them if you like. No one would think they saw each other only yesterday. His wife left him recently, you know – that doesn't seem to have upset him much, eh?'

'Has he any family?' Mirry asked.

'Not with this wife. A grown-up son by one of the others, I believe. Turkish cigarettes,' Mrs Hardes sniffed suspiciously. 'Can't you smell them, Mirry?'

Mirry shook her head, feeling guilty. Her first loyalty must be to Laura. Still, she thought uneasily, you really didn't know someone properly until you lived with them: all those years of easy, uncomplicated friendship, based on their similar circumstances, and now she was discovering things about Laura she'd really rather not know.

'I think I might go up, too,' she said, 'I'll just say goodnight.' Surely he'll take the hint, she hoped, it's past ten o'clock.

* * *

Mirry came downstairs some time after midnight to fetch the gripe water. Beulah would choose tonight to be restless. All was quiet, apart from the baby's spasmodic wailing.

There was a glimmer of light showing under the sitting room door. She paused. Had Laura left the light on, or the fire unguarded? She had better check.

She pushed the door, it was not quite closed, feeling for the switch on the wall just inside. It was off: but the fire was still burning well in the grate and by its glow, she saw the couple stretched out on the long sofa. In one of Mirry's romantic films this would have been instantly recognisable as the seduction scene – that thought came immediately to mind, together with the shocked realisation that Laura was not struggling but obviously enjoying the experience.

Stunned, she stood there for a long, long moment, then she gently pulled the door to and fled, thankful that she was wearing soft slippers, praying that they had not noticed her. She remained in the kitchen, shaking, in the dark. A wavering beam of torchlight suddenly appeared.

A hand touched her shoulder. Laura's mother whispered in her ear: 'Come back upstairs, Mirry. I can guess what you saw in there. I followed you down to say that I put the bottle of gripe water in the larder, earlier, in case you wondered where it was.'

'You – you don't seem surprised?' Mirry managed.

Mrs Hardes sighed. 'I had my suspicions, I'm afraid. It was like this before she married Jim – he was married to someone else then. I was so thankful to think she had settled down, and I hoped that would be the last we heard of Mr Gray. But, she would go back to work for him again, as you know, and I don't think Jim suspected a thing – then. She seems to like playing with fire.' She propelled Mirry towards the larder. 'By the bread bin, dear. Got a spoon? Mind, Beulah seems to have given up and gone back to sleep now. Try to forget this, Mirry. It's for the best.'

CHAPTER TWENTY-THREE

DRILLING: SWINGING ARMS EVER higher, marching, marching, *marching* – wheeling left when the sergeant bawled 'Right turn!' The suffocating smell of the rubber masks donned for gas drill. Physical jerks, merciless exercise in the quest for the peak of fitness, again with the feeling that all eyes were on them in this male-dominated camp. Mental agility, too: poring earnestly over pictures designed to detect colour blindness; aptitude tests. Fear, ever present, but immediate, absolute obedience to commands, as Bar and her friends crawled resolutely through rooms set on fire and full of choking smoke.

They had been assigned a woman sergeant towards the end of the training period, a veteran of the last war, before the ATS evolved from the Women's Auxiliary Army Corps. She had a moustache almost as bristling as their old sergeant's, who remained in overall charge of their training. She intimidated the men as much as the girls. 'Who are you smiling at? Why are you standing there doing nothing? Don't you know there's a war on? Are you volunteering for fatigues? Any of you men lay a finger on one of my gels and I'll make you suffer for it, that's a promise . . .' Even the sergeant grinned wryly at her shrieks.

'Blimey!' Eileen muttered, after Medusa, as they'd named her at Coral's suggestion, on account of her wild, wiry, cropped hair, frog-marched a nice young soldier away on the grounds that he had been loitering outside their quarters. Fortunately, she was unaware that he had half a pound of streaky bacon donated by the cook house in his pocket, which he had been delegated to slip to Eileen for a fry up on their stove, knowing that the girls were always hungry. 'Hope poor old Peter can withstand her interrogation, or I'm for it, eh?' Eileen said disconsolately.

Eileen's friend had obviously led a sheltered life before joining up. He had not long left his grammar school, proudly clutching his Higher School Certificate, and been but a few months with the sober Gas Light and Coke Company.

Bar managed to have a brief few words with him the following morning when he beckoned to her urgently round the side of the mess hut. 'She warned my lot that most of you girls were innocents straight from civvy street and she told us in the most coarse language exactly how we were expected to conduct ourselves. I'm not saying that I haven't heard all this foul-mouthed stuff before, from some of the regulars among us, but this is the first time I ever heard a woman swear like that and it left most of us feeling shell-shocked. She didn't comprehend that quite a few of us young chaps were innocents too – most of us still are – chance'd be a fair thing! A couple of months ago . . .' He produced a crumpled newspaper package. 'Here, take it quickly. At least she didn't search me.'

Medusa did not emerge from her room that night as Bar and Eileen took charred potatoes gingerly from the stove and fried the bacon to a crisp in an old tin can. Just a mouthful or two each, for everyone must have a share, but hot and satisfying, because it was illicit. 'Learned how to do this in the old Girl Guides,' Eileen grinned, 'before they drummed me out for smoking in the latrines.' Bar thought nostalgically of Fred's fry ups.

'I can hear her snoring.' Coral, watching the inner door, informed them, giving them the thumbs up. She was accepted as one of the girls now, being Bar and Eileen's mate.

'Well, at least we know she's got no sense of smell,' Bar said licking her fingers clean of fat, so she wouldn't make splodges on Clive's latest letter which she was going to reread by torchlight. No one asked then: 'What's he got to say?' It was a precious time, almost as if they were actually together . . .

It was time for the Passing Out Parade. The sergeant made his own eagle-eyed inspection on the parade ground, with Medusa at his heels, before the colonel arrived. He tweaked a cap here, glared there. Bar quaked in her shining shoes as he paused between her and Eileen. Had she buffed her buttons to the requisite gleam? Her hands still reeked of metal polish despite all the scrubbing.

'I should've brought a bloody clothes brush with me, Shorthouse!' he growled. He pounced on a single red hair clinging to Eileen's shoulder, flicked it disdainfully into the wind. There was a concerted expelling of held-in breath.

Yet he betrayed his obvious satisfaction as the colonel walked approvingly along the line. Even Medusa bared her teeth in a smile. 'Well done, gels!'

They had all 'passed out'! With the colonel safely out of earshot, Bar dared to call for 'three cheers!' Did the sergeant have a bit of grit in his eye, she couldn't help wondering, or was he actually rubbing fiercely at tears of pride?

'Well,' he said, after blowing his nose like a trumpet. 'I did my bloody best to make soldiers out of you.'

The girls were now being split up. They would go to various parts of the country, they would do different jobs. They would become cooks, orderlies, drivers or join the Pay Corps. Some of them would go out to France to swell the ranks of the British Expeditionary Force: some would become gunners, *almost* equal with the men, although, at this point, they were not actually permitted to fire the guns. All were sad to part with those who had become such good friends during the training period. There were many promises of: 'We'll keep in touch!' But they all knew that their paths were diverging and that soon they would make new friends in new places.

But to Bar's relief, she, Eileen and Coral were still together. After their leave, they were going to Command HQ – Bar's prediction had come true: she was actually to be a junior secretary to a major-general, no less! Coral's appointment was even more illustrious. She was assigned as personal assistant to a member of the top brass. Eileen grinned: 'Reckon I'll have more fun – and more chance to slack in the copy-typing pool!'

Even Medusa turned a blind eye to the celebration party on their last night as a group. They ate fish and chips straight out of the paper, shared a few smuggled bottles of cider and shandy, stoked the stoves and nearly set the hut on fire, borrowed a gramophone from the mess hut and half a dozen scratched records and skidded about to Victor Silvester and his dance band on the newly polished floor. ('Leave the place as you found it' – well, they could do better than that, with torn-up blanket polishers attached to their feet . . .)

They sang too, encouraged by Eileen. It was Bar who suggested the final chorus, which nearly raised the roof, and prompted Medusa to emerge from her room at last and actually join in. They made such a racket, that they were heard by the soldiers, and the song was taken up and echoed all over the camp.

Ginger, you're barmy!
You ought to join the Army!
They'd knock you out
With a bottle of stout –
Ginger, you're barmy!

Clive's embarkation leave coincided with the last three days of Bar's. She spent the beginning of her leave with Mum, at her aunt and uncle's flat. Now, Uncle Stan drove her back to Number Five in the late afternoon, with a box of provisions and a bag of kindling in the sidecar. There was enough coal left in the bunker outside to light the fire and air the place. He lit that first, then the Valor stove, the one Clive had taken on holiday. 'Get the kettle boiling, young Bar, eh? I turned the water on. Don't forget to ask Clive to turn it off when you go. Oh, and be careful with the candles, Bar – and remember the blackout: pity we couldn't get the gas and electric back on at short notice, but I don't suppose you two'll mind being in the dark.'

'Uncle Stan!' she mildly reproved him.

The whole area seemed deserted. They were not the only folk to have left home at the outbreak of war. Of course, they could have stayed with Iris, but it was she who had tactfully suggested they come here instead. Iris would be along tomorrow afternoon, early closing, to see them, she'd said in her letter, and she hoped Bar wouldn't mind her suggesting that she put a hot water bottle in the bed.

'Time to go to the station, to meet your lad,' Uncle Stan said. 'I'll drop him off at the gate, so I'll say cheer-ho, my girl, to you now. I'll collect the bits and pieces over the weekend, I've got the spare key, just leave 'em in the kitchen.' He gave her one of his bear hugs. 'Will you be with us for Christmas, duckie, I wonder?'

'I'm not sure yet, Uncle. Thanks for everything!'

'You keep on writing, as you do. It means a lot to your Mum, you know.'

'I know.'

'Means a lot to your auntie and me, too – us not having a family of our own.'

'Dear Uncle Stan – you've been like a father to me, bless you – look after Mum and Auntie for me!'

"Course I will,' he said stoutly.

Over the road, the dusty curtains shifted. Anna and the Galloping Major were still in residence.

* * *

They huddled over the sulky fire. The house already reeked of paraffin. The December chill had not yet dispersed. They sipped their tea, feeling like strangers, ridiculously shy, for they were both in uniform. Clive's hair was starkly clippered short; Bar's own flowing locks were wound tightly round the hairband. She saw him looking: knew he didn't like her hair like that.

'Hungry?' she asked after a while.

He shook his head. 'I ate on the train. Shan't want much for supper, Bar. How about you?'

She patted her middle ruefully. 'A big dinner at one. You know Mum. I'm not too sure we can produce anything edible on the stove. Anyway, we must ration the oil.' She added: 'I hope the bed's aired. I did as Iris suggested – put a bottle in between the sheets . . .'

He placed his cup in the hearth, reached out and took her empty cup from her hands and placed it beside his. 'Might be warmer in bed,' he told her.

'Yes,' she agreed, 'but . . .'

'It's only just past seven o'clock? Have we got to sit here for three more hours making polite conversation, Bar?'

'No!'

'All brass buttoned; soldiers, both of us,' he said softly. 'D'you suppose we're the same young people underneath?'

Bar's smile lit up her face, as she thought of her service-able underwear – not that she hadn't been thankful for it those last draughty, chilly weeks on the camp – then she pulled off the restricting hairband and shook her hair free. 'There, is that better, Clive?' She jumped up. 'You see to the fire, and I'll take up a tray of biscuits and milk!'

* * *

I wish we could stay here forever, like this, ignore the fact that the country's at war, Bar thought. She studied her husband's face as he lay asleep. She nestled against him. No clashing of brass buttons now, as embarrassingly there had been when they clasped each other and kissed, in the hall, after his arrival. The bed was still clammy, toe-curlingly cold on either side of them. But thinking of the loving warmth of their reunion made her oblivious to that. Plenty of time to make the tea, cook up breakfast, pull the blackout to see grey skies: lying here in Mirry and Fred's big bed, together, was all they needed right now. Clive was going to France – she would soon be pounding a typewriter again, not much change there . . .

He opened his eyes. He pulled her even closer, the covers up round their ears. 'I don't suppose the fire kept going all night, Bar, d'you? Cold water to shave in, I suppose,' he murmured. 'Well, I'm used to that. There was a dearth of hot water in my barracks. D'you mind my bristly chin?'

'I love it,' she said.

CHAPTER TWENTY-FOUR

GLORY SHOT OUT OF BED, pulled up her bedsocks which she was in danger of tripping over, and dived for the bulging pillowcase dangling invitingly from the bed knob.

'You didn't wake me up!' she called reproachfully to the hump in the other bed.

It was just light, and the nightlight still burned. Beulah's cot was empty as usual, and she could hear muffled squeals and laughter from Don's little room next door, where, no doubt, his sister had joined him for the ceremonial unwrapping of presents.

'How about saying "Happy Christmas"?' her mother asked.

'Oh, Happy Christmas! Can I come in with you?'

'Of course you can.'

Glory humped the pillowcase across the floor, as her mother sat up, warning finger to lips.

'Don't make too much noise, Glory.'

She was too late. Glory's shriek would have woken the deepest slumberer. There was Mummy, on her usual side of the bed, and Beulah's little round head on the pillow beside her, and –' Daddy!' she cried in joy.

He seemed to have difficulty in opening his eyes. Then he smiled at her, still lying there, hair all rumpled, then he yawned widely. 'Hello, sweetheart,' he said at last. 'Pleased to see me?'

The knobbly sack landed on his legs, and Glory wriggled in beside him and gave him a big hug. 'Now I know it's going to be a *really* happy Christmas!' she said.

'Daddy wanted it to be a surprise for you but he hoped to arrive much earlier, before you went to bed.'

'It took much longer than I anticipated, driving with muffled lights and all the signposts gone,' her father said wryly. He'd told Mirry about the horrors of the journey, of course, at a snail's pace when it became really dark last evening, but now he just wanted to put it out of his mind and make the most of this Christmas with his family.

Beulah stirred, struggled up, and looked wide-eyed and uncertainly at her father.

'Hello, baby,' he said softly, 'remember me?' He gently touched the fluff on her head. 'You've grown some hair, since I last saw you . . .'

Beulah clutched at Mirry, let out an alarmed cry. Fred tickled the nape of her soft, pink neck.

'Don't frighten her, Fred,' Mirry said in mock reproval. She smiled at him over the baby's head, now burrowing against her breast. 'I'll get her changed before she soaks our bed, eh, and you help Glory unpack her presents . . .'

'*I* recognised you, Daddy, *instantly*,' Glory said brightly, as she pulled the first package from the pillowcase. 'Oh, look – felt slippers from Grandma – she made them herself, I suppose – and look, jolly Father Christmases sewn on the toes – he's got a longer beard on this one.'

'They'll keep the chilblains at bay,' Fred told her. 'What's in here, I wonder?'

There was soon tissue and wrapping paper strewn all over the bed, books and toys piling up, and chocolate all round Glory's mouth from the gold- and silver-wrapped coins.

'Don't do that – can't you wait to use a brush?' Mirry said helplessly, as Glory wetted a finger and rubbed it over the blank pages of the magic painting book.

Beulah just sucked hard on the teat of her bottle and watched from her mother's arms.

'Your present from Mummy and me is downstairs – I couldn't manage that with my bags to bring up,' Fred said mysteriously. Instantly, Glory wanted to jump out of bed to go to find it.

'Wait until breakfast,' her mother said.

There was a tap on the door, and Mrs Hardes appeared with a tray of biscuits. 'Merry Christmas one and all!' she said brightly. 'I hope you're going to tidy all that mess up, Gloria, before you go and see what Don and Junie are up to. I've told them the same, of course . . . It was a good idea,

Mirry, putting the turkey in the oven overnight, I must say – it already smells most promising. And thank you for a nice surprise – you did a really good job with peeling all those potatoes and sprouts.'

'I had to keep myself occupied,' Mirry said ruefully, 'while wondering where on earth Fred had got to: Merry Christmas to you, too!'

'Hilda,' Mrs Hardes said unexpectedly. 'We needn't be so formal over Christmas, I think. I'm glad you got here, in the end, Fred.'

'So am I.'

Glory stuffed presents, paper and ribbon haphazardly into her pillowcase. 'See you later – and don't be too long, will you, coming down for breakfast.'

'Oh, go and look in the hall, then,' Mirry told her, 'and let that dog out, while you're about it . . .'

'A doll's pram!' Junie said in awe, as the three of them stood shivering in their pyjamas while Glory ripped off the brown paper and string.

'Just like Beulah's – only brand new – she inherited *her* pram from me,' Glory said with satisfaction. She bounced the pram on its springs, both hands on the handle, then hooked the elastic fastening on the rain-cover on the sides of the hood. 'Maroon; I'd rather have had a blue pram, but never mind. Look, it's even got a little mattress, a pillow and a blanket.'

'Which dolls are you going to wheel out in it?' Junie asked. 'Oh, you know I don't play with dolls much – Timothy Tapps, I suppose, my teddy . . .'

'I've got a better idea,' Don suggested, feeling rather bored with the object of the girls' admiration, and in Junie's case, envy, for a satchel, even a leather one, from your parents didn't compare with the coach-built pram. 'Put Pip in it.'

'Put on some clothes, you lot,' Jim told them, opening the sitting room door. 'While I get the fire lit, and then you can spread yourselves in here.'

There was an unexpected visitor after breakfast – little Jenny from the farm cottage. 'Can I speak to Glory, please?' she asked in a tremulous whisper.

Glory invited her into the kitchen. Jenny looked round, at the women folk chatting and washing up at the sink, at the paper chains looped stickily round and pinned here and there to the walls, at the trays of mince pies and sausage rolls, glazed with egg, waiting their turn in the oven.

'D'you want to come and see all our things?' Glory asked, tactless as always.

Jenny shook her head. Then she felt in her pocket. 'For you,' she managed.

Glory took the packet of fruit gums, which had obviously been opened. 'Thank you, Jenny! I have got something for you,' she wondered wildly what she might give Jenny in return. She gave a beseeching look at her mother, instantly interpreted. Mirry departed discreetly.

'I only ate one,' Jenny said.

'Have another,' Glory offered. 'And I'll have one, too. I like the green ones best.'

In the sitting room, Mirry had quickly emptied the red crepe stocking she had made for Beulah, and refilled it with Junie and Don's generous donations, following the prompting of their father. 'Here, what about this?' Fred suggested, pulling a book from his bag. 'I didn't get time to wrap or sign it, as I bought it at the very last minute.' Mirry wrapped the *Film Fun Annual* in smoothed-out holly patterned paper.

'I'm afraid Glory will be disappointed,' she said, 'it was on the list she sent up the chimney . . .'

'Glory has so much; she will learn something today, I think.'

The two girls sat at the kitchen table, while Jenny carefully took out her presents, one by one. She said nothing, but she smiled as she touched the crayons and pencils, the cardboard cut-out dolly with paper clothes, the pipe-cleaner people to hang on the Christmas tree, the lollipops, the orange and walnuts.

'You must write a message in the book, Glory. Here, use this pencil,' Mirry told her.

TO JENNY, HAPPY CHRISTMAS, 1939, WITH LOVE FROM GLORY HOPE, Glory wrote carefully on the flyleaf.

The look on Jenny's pinched little face was indeed reward for the sacrifice, Glory thought, but she could hardly tell Mummy that Jenny couldn't read or write yet, and that she suspected the Chucklenuts would pinch it from their sister, the minute she got home.

It was a good day, plenty to eat, with the thought of rationing looming up in the New Year – a day for lounging round the fire, reading, not playing games, or singing round the piano. Fred was too tired after the dreadful journey, to want to stay up long after the children at last had gone to bed. He undressed quickly: 'Coo, it's freezing up here, Mirry – bet you miss the gas fire in our bedroom at Number Five, eh?'

'Do I . . .' Mirry said, with feeling. She was glad to get to bed, too. They hadn't had time to talk on their own yet. She was secretly pleased when Glory had wheedled: 'Can I sleep in with Junie tonight, oh, please?' She was getting a big girl to share her parents' room at nights, after all. It was all right when Mirry was on her own. Beulah didn't count, in that respect, of course; she was sleeping soundly, at the far end of the room.

Fred clambered in, reached for her, hugged her tight. 'Different from our usual Christmases, Mirry – I missed Bar, didn't you? Shame she couldn't get leave.'

'Oh, she volunteered to stay on duty, Fred – what with Clive being overseas – Mum invited his Auntie Iris to stay with them, you know.'

'That was nice of her . . .' he murmured. 'Anything up, Mirry – with Jim and Laura? Things seemed, well, a bit tense between them, I thought.'

Mirry decided that it wouldn't be disloyal to tell Fred. She outlined simply what had been going on. Not that there was a lot to tell. It was easier to tell tales, as she couldn't help thinking, in the dark.

'Darn shame . . .' Fred sounded regretful.

'It'd never happen to *us*, Fred would it?' she asked anxiously.

'Of course not,' he assured her. He kissed her in a most satisfactory fashion. 'Happy now?' he teased her, later.

Her passionate response surprised him. 'We *must* make the most of every moment!' Yes, it was a time for giving, for loving, for being together. And for throwing caution to the winds.

The children had divided into two camps now. Junie and Don went around with the Chucklenuts out of school, and Glory and Pip looked out for, and protected, little Jenny.

One Saturday afternoon in March, when Horst came round for his piano lesson, Mirry was looking pale and distracted. She had taken an aspirin for a bad headache. Glory was grumpy, too, because the other children had gone out without even a perfunctory: 'Want to come, Glory?'

'Why don't you call for Jenny? It's not a bad day – cold, but if you wrap up warmly . . .' Mirry suggested. How could she concentrate on teaching Horst if Glory kept rolling about on the rug, and moaning, 'There's nothing for *me* to do' like that?

'Can I go fishing?'

This was a new pastime. The Chucklenuts were skilled with bent pin and string, cane rod, jam jars full of greenish water and wriggling tiny fish. Glory had tagged along a few times, at a distance, and a couple of weekends ago, she and Jenny had gone to the big pond on the farm by themselves. As they had heeded Mirry's warnings about the danger of water, Mirry saw no reason why they should not go today. She had no idea that the pond was a large one, more like a lake.

'Ask Mrs Hardes for some dough bait then, and don't be more than an hour, be back well before dark.'

'Oh, thanks, Mummy!' Glory had brightened up considerably.

'It is kinder to put the fish back,' Horst suggested. 'They only die, if you bring them home.'

Jenny's brothers, naturally, used chopped worms. The thought of that made Glory shudder. She let Jenny peep in the bag at the little balls of dough, and the crusts of bread. There was a brief skirmish between Pip and the Chucklenuts' lurcher, then the girls went off to the pond.

'Hope the boys ain't there,' Jenny said fearfully, wiping her runny nose on her holey glove. She chewed the fingers of the gloves so that her whitened fingertips poked through.

To their relief the meadow was deserted. A watery sun shone on the murky waters. They put their bag down under a dipping willow. Then Glory spotted something, drifting on the edge of the water, tied by string to an overhanging branch of the tree.

'It's – a *raft*, Jenny! Look, old oil drums, and rotten planks. We could go out on the water, and fish where it's deeper . . .'

Jenny looked alarmed. 'Boys . . .'

'Your brothers made it, d'you mean? They won't mind if we borrow it, will they?' She knew the answer to that, of course. 'Anyway, they aren't here, so we can do what we like.'

The look on Jenny's face meant that her bladder had let her down yet again.

'You can't get any wetter,' Glory thought she was being tactful. 'Come on, Jen, let's have a *real* adventure . . . this long stick'll do as a pole. It's not far to the other side, we can paddle with our hands . . .'

The raft was surprisingly stable, and they soon found themselves bobbing gently in the middle of the pond. 'Here,' Glory offered, 'you have the first cast, Jenny. See all those ripples? This is where all the fish are hiding.'

The bait was continually taken, but not a single fish was foolish enough to be caught. It was disappointing, but they persevered.

Jenny was shivering. 'It's cold. Can we go home now?' She must have been hungry, too, Glory thought, for she'd eaten most of the crusts. Pip's whining intimated that he was fed up, too.

Which bank should they make for, Glory wondered? The shouting took them unawares, the stones plopped in the water around the raft. The Chucklenuts, together with Junie and Don, were jeering and pelting them. Pip barked bravely, scrabbling his feet on the splintery planks.

'Paddle like mad, Jen – let's go to the other side – they can't reach us there,' Glory yelled. She was wrong, for the bigger children pounded round the pond to meet them. The stone throwing resumed.

Then Jenny was swaying on her feet, causing the raft to rock alarmingly and the dog to leap overboard, yelping and splashing towards the bank.

The stone struck Jenny behind the ear and to Glory's horror, she saw blood spurting and staining Jenny's fair hair bright red. There was a thin, ear-splitting scream from the injured child, then she lost her balance and fell backwards into the water.

'Jenny, oh, *Jenny*!' Glory went on hands and knees to the edge of the raft stretching out her hand in a vain attempt to catch hold of her. She could hear angry, raised voices from the bank, then, even as Jenny emerged from the water, gasping and spewing out foul pond water, clinging desperately to the jutting plank on top of the drums, someone swam towards them, caught hold of her, and hauled her aboard.

Jenny's eyes were closed now, her face deathly pale. Horst, minus his jacket and boots, swam to the bank, pushing the raft ahead of him, until it grounded in the reeds with a shudder. Don and Junie – for the little girl's brothers had scarpered when Horst came running up – yanked on the trailing string, tied it to a stump, and then helped Glory to scramble on to safe ground. Horst lifted Jenny carefully, hoisted her weight over one shoulder, then strode off, without saying a word.

They followed at a distance. He was taking Jenny to the farmhouse. As they approached the gate, Horst said curtly to Don: 'Go and warn your mother and Mrs Hope, we are coming. They heat water already for your baths, I think. *Jenny* will need the hot soaking, now.'

Junie was sobbing: 'Oh, Horst, you've got blood all over your shirt.'

'And *you*, who threw stones, you have blood on your *hands*, I think . . .' he said bitterly.

Jim gave his children a furious ticking off for their disgraceful part in the affair. Laura, grim-faced, followed them upstairs: they were to go straight to bed, she said, and they needn't think they'd heard the last of it from her . . .

The bath was filled with hot water, and Jim, after ascertaining that Jenny was not, thankfully, badly injured, although still mute with fright, took Horst, the hero of the hour, now uncomfortably attired in dry spare clothes, courtesy of a scowling Don, home by car. He would collect and do the same for Jenny, he told them, on his return. 'I shall have something to say to her parents about her brothers' behaviour, as well as apologising for my own children.'

Glory, trembling, was waiting for Mirry to reprimand her for persuading Jenny to go out on the pond in the raft. She was ignored, while Jenny was coaxed to undress and step into the bath. The bleeding had been stemmed by Mrs Hardes's quick thinking: she had applied pressure to the wound, which was not deep.

At last Mirry turned to her daughter: 'Go upstairs, get undressed and off to bed. I can't believe you could be so foolish, Glory, but at least you had no part in throwing stones. You are *never* to go near that pond again – d'you hear me?'

'Yes! I'm sorry, Mummy ... Will Jenny be all right?' Glory sobbed. She thought that Junie and Don would hate her now, for telling what happened. Jenny – and Horst – were her only friends now. Oh, and Pip, of course. He had raised the alarm, rushing home, arriving just as Horst was leaving after his lesson, which made Mirry ask him to run to the pond to see what was up.

Then Mirry sat down abruptly, her face as drained of colour as Jenny's had been.

Mrs Hardes looked at her keenly. 'Are *you* all right, Mirry? Off you go, Glory, and don't wake Beulah, she's asleep in her cot.'

'I haven't . . .' Mirry said faintly, 'even told Fred, yet. I'm expecting another baby – and I've got such – an awful pain . . .'

CHAPTER TWENTY-FIVE

'Why didn't anyone let me know?' Fred asked reproach-fully.

It was Glory, naturally who, in her innocence, greeted him breathlessly as he stepped from the car the following weekend, joyful at his unexpected appearance, with: 'Mummy's been ill, Daddy, she's been in bed all week, and it's all *my* fault 'cause Jenny fell in the pond – but *I* didn't throw stones. really . . .'

Laura's mother escorted him immediately upstairs, closed the door firmly and shooed Glory back down into the kitchen. 'You can amuse your little sister – get into the playpen with her, she likes that.' She looked at Laura, rinsing potatoes in the sink, pale-faced because she had been rowing with Jim most of the night: 'We'll leave the two of them alone, eh, until lunchtime . . .' Jim had wisely taken his children for a long walk. They weren't talking to Glory much, still smarting from what they considered the injustice of receiving most of the blame for what had happened to Jenny.

Mirry lay flat on her back in the bed, neatly tucked in like an invalid, with the obvious signs of nursing care on the bedside table: medicine bottles, spoons, a jug of water capped with a tumbler. She looked pale, weary but not really ill.

'Fred, it's *lovely* to see you – how on earth?'

'Can't say too much . . . Well, we were suddenly told to take leave sooner rather than later, so here I am. I was worried stiff because I hadn't had the usual letter from you last week, too. What on earth's up, Mirry?' He knelt by the bed, rumpling the rug, and scrutinised her closely.

'I had a threatened miscarriage,' she told him simply.

He looked at her in disbelief. 'You didn't say anything – why not?' he calculated mentally swiftly. 'Christmas? Last time I was home . . . Oh, Mirry, I'm *so* sorry!'

'Don't be, Fred! *I* was the one, who . . . Of course, I was upset at first – what with Beulah being a baby, in nappies still, and perhaps not even walking by September. But then I thought, Fred might even get his little son, this time – and he'll let me go home now, because I don't want to have a baby here. I want our nice nurse, to be nearer my dear mum. I *can* go back to Number Five, can't I Fred?'

'Not this moment, you can't, old girl, that's obvious.' He squeezed her hands in his. 'I'm proud of you, taking it like that. But just suppose the war hots up, eh?' He broke off. He mustn't say too much about that.

'I told you. I just long to go home: I know Jim would take us, if we asked, and keep an eye on us, too. The atmosphere is horrid here every weekend: Laura and Jim are still at odds. The children can hear them quarrelling at night. That's not good for them is it? And the other two have turned against Glory, because of something that happened last Saturday, so *she's* unhappy – if it wasn't for Hilda, Laura's mother, I'd be really depressed . . . She's looked after me this week, and the girls.'

'You're *really* going to be all right?' he asked anxiously.

'Yes: honestly! A warning, to slow up: I'm not to do any lifting, I'm to go easy on the housework, the doctor says. But Glory's getting big enough to help a bit, isn't she? And I'll be *so* happy when we're back in our normal routine . . .'

'We'll see,' he said, 'I'll talk to Jim about it . . .' Then he bent and kissed her. 'An unexpected blessing, Mirry – I'll never forget how we were, together, you know, last Christmas,' his voice was husky with emotion.

'Nor will I,' she said, her face flushing hotly. She clutched him close to her. 'Oh Fred, if only you didn't have to go back to Somerset . . .'

Rationing was not too stringent here in the country. There were always fresh eggs and plenty of milk, even the odd pat of butter. Sugar never seemed sufficient though, and the adults soon decided to drink their tea without.

'Thank goodness they haven't rationed tea, yet,' Mirry said, one Monday morning: 'I couldn't do without my cup every hour.' She rinsed out the dregs from the breakfast potful.

'You should drink more milk,' Mrs Hardes said sternly.

Mirry patted her slight bulge ruefully. 'The boy prefers tea, it seems . . .'

'Don't be *too* set on a son, Mirry. Wouldn't you like another dear little girl just like Beulah? Sisters, close in age, they'd probably be inseparable you know. Of course, Junie and Don are a similar distance apart, but they don't get on so well, now they're growing up, being boy and girl.'

'They don't hit it off with Glory either nowadays,' Mirry sighed.

It was now almost the end of March, and she had been back on her feet for a week or two. She had been secretly sorting and packing up in her bedroom, and she hoped that Jim would be prepared to take her and the children back with him this Sunday.

Fred had agreed to their return home after Jim wrote, at Mirry's prompting, that Mirry and the children would be welcome to make use of the Anderson shelter in his back garden if there was an alert, whether he was there or not. 'When I'm at the waddling stage, there's always under the stairs . . .' Mirry wrote to Fred herself. Everyone knew that was the safest place in the house if you hadn't got a cellar. The Hopes, being away, had missed out on the free issue of what the cartoonists made to look like a mud igloo, even though it was fashioned from sturdy steel. Jim also promised to check that they were all right, each evening he was at home. Backing Mirry up, he assured them that public shelters, those alien structures which had first appeared in 1938, had been reinforced, should they be caught out and about in a raid.

Mirry decided to spring her proposed departure on Laura at the last minute, for Laura had obviously felt slighted when Mirry hinted at what she might do: 'It hasn't really worked out, Mirry, has it? Oh, I know you've got very chummy with Mum, goodness knows why, for I thought you agreed with me that she's an old tartar at times – but I imagined you appreciated *my* moral support ... Have you thought, how you'd cope, with the school still closed and rationing – what about all the extras you come in here for? Most of the neighbours have gone away, too – just the dubious ones left, like the Boams. And you know how het up you get when you practise putting Beulah in her gas mask! I'm hurt, I admit it, that you confided in my mother about the new baby, before me ...'

'I had no choice, Laura.'

'That may be, but we were such good friends once.'

Mirry wanted to say that they still were, but she knew it was untrue. Laura had been unfaithful to Jim, she thought, she might be self-righteous, but she couldn't condone that; she wouldn't discuss it with Laura, either. Laura still slept with Jim, so despite the flareups, their marriage was continuing uneasily. But for how long, Mirry wondered? She didn't want to witness any further breakdown.

Now, she put the tea towels in to soak, and wondered, in excitement, how Glory was enjoying her morning, for today the filming would at last be under way. Glory was assured of a part, for the camera would record her ostensibly helping Horst, although he had moved up from her class some time ago.

Glory was a star after all. She had combed out those wretched ringlets in the cloakroom before she went into class, but there was nothing she could do about her nails. Since they had come she had started biting them and it was a habit she didn't seem able to break. Mirry had painted her nails with something called bitter aloes: it made you grimace when you first got the horrible taste in your mouth, but if you used your imagination, Glory promptly decided, well, there was a faint recall of cracking plum stones with your teeth and sucking hard on the juices, so the stuff in the little bottle was unlikely to stop you chewing.

Mr Gray recognised her at once. He looked down at her sensible school shoes, then back at her, and winked. So she knew he remembered her tap dancing, which was nice.

Horst grinned, in an 'oh, well . . .' sort of way. They sat together in a different desk, because of the camera angle, although Mr Gray said they were to ignore it, because he wanted them to carry on with their school work as usual, and not to act any differently because they were being filmed.

Of course, it was different, for they didn't usually read aloud their compositions on a Monday morning. That was a treat reserved for the winding-down of Friday afternoon. Glory acted out her poem for all she was worth. Poetic licence, and a touch of Edward Lear:

Jenny and Me
by Gloria Anna Hope, age 7

Jenny and Me,
We went to sea –
In a most peculiar craft –
A plank and oil drum raft . . .

Jenny, behind her, sucked her collar in an agony of embarrassment; a dark, damp patch grew around her feet in their scuffed, oversized shoes, inherited from her youngest brother. Junie and Don looked wary, wondering what was coming next. Thank goodness, the Chucklenuts were in the top class, they thought, but someone was sure to tell them, of course.

Then Horst read his essay which was entitled: 'My Life in a New Country'. He did not use dramatic effects like Glory, but spoke confidently and quietly. The children were hushed. It was quite a revelation. The snide attacks on him in the playground, and outside school, for being different, he mentioned these, but without resentment, or names. The children did not look at one another. He was grateful, he said, for the chance he had been given, to continue his education, to be free. The people here had been so kind. There was an awkward pause, then a burst of enthusiastic clapping. Mr Gray beamed.

The filming went on all day. Glory didn't have to endure lunchtime play: 'You come with us, eh, Glory?' Mr Gray suggested, 'as interpreter,' when everyone knew that was a joke. So she sat in the staff room and had lunch with the Head, Horst and the supervisor from the hostel, while the camera rolled. She chattered away, quite unselfconsciously hogging the limelight. Her burbling amused and entertained: Mr Gray winked at Horst this time.

When Horst was joined by his compatriots for their afternoon shift in the classroom, Glory was asked again to stay, to participate in the lessons. Through the window she could see the village boys playing football, and the girls shooting balls into the net. A mad March wind stirred scraps of lunch paper, lifted skirts and blew hair into tangles. She thought how proud Mummy would be when she told her she had played such a prominent part; however, the camera would depart the school after today, to record life at the refugee house. After all, the film was about Horst and his friends. But she couldn't help dreading the thought of the walk home after school. She knew that the others would resent her even more for what they regarded as blatant showing off. Even Jenny had looked frightened and not responded when they met up briefly after lunch, looking over her shoulder as if expecting a Chucklenut to say: ''Ere, take no notice of 'er – she's a telltale tit.'

'Your daughter is a natural, a born actress.' Mr Gray would confirm Mirry's aspirations, on Saturday, when they came to film Horst at his music lesson.

Glory did not know then, that the very next day, they would load up Uncle Jim's car and go back to Number Five just in time for alarming, devastating developments both in the war and on the home front – Dunkirk, the Battle of Britain and the Blitz . . . These would all be a reality before the end of this year.

CHAPTER TWENTY-SIX

'THIS *WONDERFUL* VIEW!' BAR EXCLAIMED, holding on to her cap in another mad March wind. She had been walking the city walls of Chester with her friends. They looked out to the Welsh hills, filled their lungs with fresh, intoxicating air. Despite the tall, beautiful timbered buildings, ornately decorated in black and white, the pinnacles and gilded spires, the crowded streets below, here was peace, a feeling that this place would be the same for ever. Sometimes, Bar felt it was not right that she had struck so lucky with her posting – living and working in a very different environment from the one she had imagined, when she joined the ATS to do her bit in winning the war. The arduous training, the draughty barracks seemed like a dream nowadays.

Bar, Eileen and Coral were billeted, with two other girls, in a fine old town house, from which the many servants had long since departed. The owners of the house were twins, ladies in their late eighties, the only remaining members of the family living there. The girls were invited to call them Miss Drusy and Miss Lucy and they were determined to do their utmost to see that the girls were comfortable and happy. No more illicit feasts cooked in old cans – the kitchen, the stove, the tins of food squirrelled away over several years, some minus labels, some rusted slightly, some suspect, but most perfectly edible, meant that their guests could be fed well and their rations supplemented. The twins had been living in genteel – gentle – poverty; now, the allowance they received enabled them to entertain, to be generous.

The beds were soft, with meticulously darned linen, satin-edged blankets; the bathrooms were large and luxurious, in particular, the one assigned to Bar and Co.

'A sunken bath!' she exclaimed in awe, when she first saw it.

Eileen brushed away a cobweb or two, shuddered at the spiders poised motionless on the grubby ledge behind the ornate taps. 'It'll need a good clean before milady Coral will deign to step in, I daresay.'

'D'you mind!' Coral said with a grin. She had soon got used to Eileen's teasing.

'Bet you wish Clive was here, to share it with you,' Eileen continued with a sly twinkle at Bar.

'I certainly do,' Bar said airily. She wasn't going to tell Eileen that she felt hot all over at the very thought. She suspected that she was far less experienced in matters of the flesh, as Mum coyly referred to it, than their housemates, even though she was the only one married. Sometimes she had to look at the gold band on her finger to remind her-self that this was so. She wondered if Clive felt the same. Letters were a comfort, but not enough. One of the other girls had remarked tactlessly the other day that: 'Our boys, they say, are having the time of their lives in France – more whoring than warring, I heard the colonel say.' She trusted Clive implicitly, of course she did, but it worried her all the same.

They were going back to the billet now, anticipating sinking, in turn, in lovely hot water. They'd draw, of course, to see who would have the privilege of being first, and the 'oh well' of being last, because they had to be economical with fuel for the boiler. They had a real cause for celebra-tion and, after the bath they would be staying in, not going dancing, as they usually did, on a Saturday night.

'What do you think, Bar?' Miss Drusy asked, holding out a kilner jar full of unidentifiable black objects floating in either syrup or brine. 'I couldn't get the top off, your young wrists are stronger than mine – it might be plums, though I don't recall cook bottling any for a good few years. Perhaps tomatoes, eh?'

Bar didn't try too hard to unscrew the cap on the jar. She heeded Coral's hiss: 'Botulism, Bar!' while being thank-ful that Miss Drusy was rather deaf. She was murmuring about finding a cache of these jars right at the back of a cupboard she had decided to clean out: 'About time, my sis-ter said – it's all right for her, when we split the household duties between us, I seemed to take on anything requiring a scrubbing brush and soda. Any luck, dear? If it is tomatoes, they'll go very nicely with the macaroni cheese.'

The other girls, Margie and Marie, friends from way back, who drove the officers' staff cars, both had boyfriends and were rarely in to supper. Sometimes they stayed out all night: as Margie, a big, bouncing-bosomed corporal, who had answered the call to join the ATS in 1938 and consequently considered she knew it all, which did not endear her to Eileen, in particular, said: 'Make hay while the sun shines, before the balloon goes up, before we all get posted again.' But she heeded Miss Lucy's advice to take her whistle with her in case she was grabbed at in the blackout.

So, they were five sitting down to supper in the dining room, with the long table covered with a treasured tablecloth and fine china, even if some of it was chipped now Miss Drusy mostly washed up. The silver was tarnished, but there were napkins in ivory rings and brandy goblets filled with water. There was nothing much cheesy about the macaroni, but they scraped the dish clean and ate with good appetite, thankful that the kilner jar had apparently remained firmly closed.

When Miss Drusy triumphantly brought in dessert, Bar saw that they were mistaken.

'Margie popped back to change and, as she's a big, tough girl, I enlisted her help. I boiled them up well, then we tasted one, didn't we Lucy?'

'Victoria plums,' Lucy said complacently. 'A bit sharp, but the custard's nice and sweet. Not sure there's enough for five, though . . .'

'*You* have them!' the girls chorused quickly.

'We're full up,' Bar added. 'I'll make the tea, shall I?'

Later, when they were running the bath, she said: 'I hope they'll be all right. Was it cowardly of us not to have some?'

'Don't worry about it,' Eileen said blithely, stripping and throwing her clothes in a heap in the corner as she was to bath first: 'They've been eating up all the preserves dear old cook made, ever since she went to make pies in the sky, and I gather that was some years ago. They must have cast-iron gullets. I'd rather die a heroine, in action, than have my mum and dad informed: "She passed away from poisoned plums." '

Bar was used to Eileen's banter, but she couldn't prevent an involuntary, horrid cold shiver. 'Don't make jokes like that, Eileen.'

'Because,' Coral finished drily, 'You never know, do you?'

They sat there and chatted to Eileen while she lay back and soaked herself, not worrying in the least about an audience. 'We're all the same, aren't we?' as she said, the first time they had bathed in this house.

Not only water shared, but a huge, thick bath towel, almost adequate for a whole army of bathers, Bar thought, grinning. This was living life on the grand scale, she decided. If only Mum, Mirry – and Clive – could see her now!

Damp hair pinned up, rosy-faced from the steam, they let out a whoop! as they appraised each other. They wore brand-new blue and white striped pyjamas, issued only yesterday, two pairs per girl, cut in extravagant army fashion, so that they were swamped in them. Eileen, with rolled-up sleeves and pyjama trousers, looked just like: 'Little Orphan Annie,' as Bar said.

'About time, I don't know what they think we've been wearing to bed until now, those dreadful bloomers, I suppose,' Coral inspected herself in the long mirror in their shared bedroom. 'Reckon they're men's pyjamas, girls?'

'No bras yet,' Eileen moaned. 'Margie says she might be able to get hold of a parachute, seeing as her boyfriend's a fitter in the RAF, and then we can cut it up quick and make some things like that before we get found out.'

'You don't need any support anyway,' Bar sauced her tiny friend.

At eight-thirty, with half an hour to go before Miss Drusy called them, 'Ooh-hoo, ladies!' for cocoa, they wound up the gramophone, rolled up the rugs, and pushed the beds together against the wall.

'I'll teach you to tango,' Bar offered, pouncing on an old record, courtesy of their landladies. 'I'll lead!'

Memories of dancing nights at Lahana; of Chas's hot hand clamped on her back, Miss Boam's voice calling: 'Bar, will you give the gramophone a quick wind, please, dear?' And of Clive, at sixteen, stumbling over her feet, determined to be her protector. She'd give anything to have her toes trodden on again like that.

They laughed until they cried: until Eileen's trousers unwound and tripped her up. Then they danced wildly by themselves until they all fell in a heap on the floor, with the worn needle stuck in the groove and the music repeating over and over. Then they scrambled to their feet, and adjusted their pyjamas, now covered in fluff, and conga'd perilously one behind the other down the many stairs, in order to sup cocoa made with boiling water and a mere dash of milk.

Tonight they were like schoolgirls: in just a few days' time they would have to take a deep breath and grow up.

CHAPTER TWENTY-SEVEN

LESSONS WITH MISS LANCASTER again: Glory's teacher, being only a few months off retirement, had not gone with the school to the country. Already, some of the children had returned, and Glory joined them in the improvised school-room in Miss Lancaster's house, where the ceiling reverberated, not to sounds of war but to the insistent rapping of her aged mother's walking stick.

While Miss Lancaster was attending to her mother, the children got up to all sorts of mischief: whirling the great, faded globe of the world on its base, clashing swords, well, rulers and aiming blotting paper soaked in ink at each other. One day they surpassed themselves. It was only meant as a bit of excitement, but it ended in tragedy.

The canary was released from its cage, and the moth-eaten old tabby, who watched the children with baleful eyes and swishing tail from the top of the bookcase, actually attempted to pounce, but the little bird expired with fright anyway. The stricken look on the teacher's face, when she cradled the still-warm bundle of feathers in her bent, arthritic hands, quelled her pupils immediately.

'I thought better of you Gloria . . .' she said at last.

Glory wanted to tell her that she had tried to stop Binnie, the girl who had opened the cage, but the fear of having her classmates turn against her, as they had in the village school, kept her silent. She knew, too, that she was just as guilty as the others of taking advantage of Miss Lancaster's absence – the ink pellets were her idea.

Years later, Glory would recall these antics with shame and remorse; she also wondered how Mrs Lancaster had coped, unattended, when her daughter was away all day at the school. There would have been no point in knocking for attention then.

Now, she didn't notice the tired, puffy eyes, only the cross voice, the strictures, the strictness. No approval for poems by Glory, as there had been just a few months ago, but jabs of red ink indicating spelling errors, and the comment: 'You can do better.' Glory was no longer teacher's pet.

She missed the countryside, the walks, the explorations, even the school. Life was full of restrictions back at home: no going out to play, much more awareness that there was a war on. There was also the puzzling news that Mummy was expecting another baby. Mirry wasn't springing it on her this time, but hoping she would gradually become used to the idea. But, Glory thought, why did Mummy need a new baby when they'd got Beulah? It wasn't the same here without Daddy and Bar, either.

Uncle Jim popped in when he wasn't on fire-watching duty in London; then Mummy said why didn't she cook him his supper? Silly for him to be on his own and a single ration book didn't go very far. Uncle Jim looked sad, and all he wanted to talk about was his own children and how he didn't feel welcome any more at the farmhouse. He even cried one evening – he hadn't meant Glory to see, but he was talking to Mummy in the kitchen while she dished up his dinner, and Glory had come down to ask for a drink of water because her calls hadn't been answered. 'She wants a divorce,' he said, and Mummy put the plate down and said: 'Oh, Jim, I'm *so* sorry!' and she put her arms round his waist and hugged him close to comfort him. That made Glory feel really funny. It didn't seem right . . .

Glory turned and tiptoed back upstairs then. However, when Uncle Jim went to Surrey next for the weekend, on his return, he brought Glory an unexpected letter from Horst.

The film will be showing soon, Glory – they did not cut your part at all! They are nice to me now, at the school – I am famous for five minutes, as they say! I have good

*news of my family. They are safe in America. I shall
join them one day when this is possible.*

We must keep in touch.

Your friend, Horst

The only letter Bar received this week, was from Fred, agonising over whether he had done the right thing in allowing
Mirry to take the children back to Number Five. She could
hardly believe that they had been so foolish, when she read
the surprising news about the new baby, and Fred's fears
whether all would go well, because of the fright Mirry had
earlier on. He asked if it was possible for Bar to get leave, just
to reassure him everything was all right. 'She misses you, I
know, Bar, as I do – the three of us have always been so close.'

It was all rather worrying, plus the fact that she hadn't
heard from Clive for a couple of weeks now. Some of the
other girls she worked with had also been without letters
from their loved ones in the forces overseas. She could get
a forty-eight-hour pass, even though she would have to pay
her own fare, she thought ruefully. Fred hadn't timed his
request well. Last month she had used her travel pass home
to see Mum and Iris; the usual seven days' leave granted
every three months, except in emergencies, of course,
which hadn't occurred so far.

'I'd come with you,' Eileen offered. 'Except I've only
got a couple of bob left – not enough for the train fare to

London, eh – but we could hitchhike – with two of us, we'd be safe enough, I reckon.'

'Well, I must admit I'm hard up, too,' Bar agreed.

'Don't do it,' Coral advised wisely. 'Think of Margie, and that lorry driver . . .'

'She knocked him out!' Eileen said admiringly. 'And, he lost a front tooth.'

'Maybe. But she lost all the buttons on her tunic.'

'Well, that was all she lost – but she's not good at summing up a bloke, like yours truly.'

'He seems to expect a lot of you, I think, your brother-in-law,' Coral said astutely. 'After all, your sister is near your mother again, isn't she?'

'Yes, but – well, Fred's always been very good to me – both he and Mirry have – it can't have been easy, as newly weds, sharing their home with a lively fourteen year old, can it?'

'Going by the number of letters he sends to *you*, I get the feeling that . . .' Eileen dodged the pillow which Bar threw, with some force. They always had these more private chats in their bedroom.

The arrival of Margie and Marie saved Bar from making excuses for Fred.

As usual, Margie had what she regarded as the perfect solution. 'Marie's Captain Snowball is driving himself up to London late Friday night, I reckon he'd take you, if Marie was to be, you know, obliging, when she asked him.'

'I can guess what you're thinking,' the more stolid Marie said, her sallow face impassive. 'But you're wrong.'

'To put it bluntly,' Margie said brightly, 'it wouldn't take much to change his name, just one letter . . .'

'All right,' Bar said quickly, 'in other words, he's harmless!' Eileen was often saucy, she'd got used to that, but Margie was far coarser, she thought.

'Ask him then. We could always have a kip while he's driving, or take it in turns to chat to keep the Cap awake,' Eileen decided for them both.

'Ooh-hoo!' came the call as a duet from their landladies.

'Supper! Wonder what grisly feast they've cooked up for us tonight,' Margie sighed. She heaved herself up from Bar's bed where she had plumped down on her arrival.

As Margie led the way downstairs, Marie beckoned to Bar and Eileen. 'All I have to do, honest, for he's a perfect gentleman otherwise, is, well, give him a glimpse of my passion-killers – no more than that – he doesn't say anything, and nor do I – but they have to be regulation issue . . .'

'Knickers, to you!' Eileen murmured to Bar.

Captain Snowball lived up to his name. He had prematurely white hair, watery blue eyes behind rimless glasses, a sharp pink-tipped nose and he was indeed, it seemed, a perfect gentleman as Marie said. In civvy street, he was a Professor of Languages at Cambridge, which is why he found himself, with a commission, translating documents in German, French and Russian for the Army. He also had a habit of clearing his throat nervously before he spoke. It was very irritating.

He called for the girls after supper on Friday evening, and Eileen offered (generously, Bar thought) to sit in the front alongside him for the first lap of the long journey.

It all went smoothly, despite the slow driving because of the blackout. Buses, they said, would soon have to run on coal gas: the captain carried cans of petrol aboard.

He insisted on delivering Eileen to her door in Lambeth, and carrying her kitbag for her. As Eileen's mother opened the door in surprise, by the flashing light of her torch, Bar, looking out from the car window, saw Eileen, when taking her bag, deliberately catch at her skirt, so that it lifted well above her knees, as the captain turned to salute her.

Captain Snowball still had the bemused look on his face, when he slid back into his seat. 'Now to get you home, my dear,' he said.

Well, Bar thought, he's had his reward, I couldn't do that to save my life. She had a real job to suppress her giggles.

It was not much past two-thirty in the morning when they finally drew up outside Number Five. It was still pitch black. Bar said goodbye firmly to the captain at the gate, shaking his hand. He said he would pick her up on Sunday evening at eight. He was driving back to London to see his brother, who was a doctor at Barts.

As she fumbled with the latch on the gate, Bar felt something brush her back. She whipped round, immediately wary, tensing herself. A hand grabbed at her shoulder: she struck out instinctively, using her raised knee as they had been taught in self-defence. She had hit the spot: her assailant staggered back, was gone.

Shaken, Bar made for the door, and despite the hour, hammered on it desperately. Inside, Pip answered with frantic barking.

Mirry, in her nightie, torch in trembling hand, clutching a crying baby on her hip, thoroughly alarmed, opened the door and ushered her in. 'Oh, Bar darling, it's *you*!'

'It wasn't the major thank goodness, much shorter and thicker-set than him,' Bar said, sipping tea.

'He doesn't go out at all nowadays, Anna says . . . I suppose it could have been the warden on patrol – I imagine he'd have been too . . .'

'Surprised?' Bar bit her lip. Maybe she had struck out at someone with a legitimate excuse for being out and about in the early morning darkness.

'Winded. To say anything,' Mirry said, trying to jig the baby back to sleep.

'I'll pop over and see Anna in the morning, and have a chat,' Bar decided. 'You need someone to keep an eye on *you*, Mirry, when Jim's not around . . .'

A wide-awake voice said, from outside the dining room door: 'Can I come in? Is it really you, Bar?'

Mirry made a little face. Say no more about it, she intimated. 'Oh, come on Glory, and I hope you're wearing your slippers?' she called.

CHAPTER TWENTY-EIGHT

THE WAR STILL SEEMED UNREAL to many people. Life went on much as before, for those who, like Mirry and her little girls, had returned to their homes. Rather to her family's surprise, Mirry was coping very well without their support. She did miss her once regular visits to the Pictures; but even though she knew that Anna would sit the children, she did not ask. *She* had sole responsibility for them now, she thought.

Rationing was accepted cheerfully: children continued learning, conventionally or otherwise; the most positive thing to come out of all this was that there was now very little unemployment. The unfamiliar became acceptable, normal: like shelters in suburban gardens, and squares of lawn dug up and planted with vegetables; pet rabbits and chickens in makeshift hutches and runs, with an eye to possible food shortages in the future, but not if the children could help it . . . Mirry pointed that out to Glory when she wheedled to have a rabbit: 'Neither of us would be able to eat it, when the time came, Glory – and it's hard enough finding scraps for Pip, you know that.'

'Pip's a guard dog,' Glory said, in a huff. 'We'll never eat him – even if we have to withstand a siege!'

Sandbags, security measures and inspiring slogans were all part of the war effort. The women at home were immensely proud of family members in HM Forces but Mirry shared their unshakeable belief that it would all be over, before they knew it . . .

'There's the Channel between Britain and France, isn't there?' Mum said confidently to Mirry, visiting one day. 'That always makes me feel safer somehow, the water between us.'

Mirry was much more aware nowadays – she listened to the news on the wireless, read the papers avidly – she had learned to make her own mind up about things, now Fred was away. She said: 'The Germans would have invaded Britain months ago, Mum, if they were going to.'

As always, the British navy seemed supreme, despite the increasing threat of German U-boats. The national shock, horror and disbelief at the sinking of the *Royal Oak*, moored in Scapa Flow, so early in the war was vindicated when the German battleship, *Admiral Graf Spee*, scuttled herself in shame after the disastrous Battle of the River Plate the previous December.

The unexpected invasion of Norway and Denmark on 9 April marked an ominous new stage. It was a vicious stab in the back and the Danes were forced to capitulate. Norway fought fiercely on to guard her coastline. The massed might of the German airforce tipped the balance: British troops were landed to reinforce the defence, but had to be evacuated within a couple of weeks; the Royal Navy manoeuvred courageously at Narvik in the north but, inexorably, Norway, too, was taken.

At home, this signalled the final demise of Chamberlain's government. Winston Churchill became the new prime minister of a government, formed from all the parties, who were unanimous in their support of his leadership. He roused the country to renewed fervour, with his prophetic words, that there was nothing to offer but 'blood, toil, tears and sweat'. Mirry let the tears flow when she heard that stirring message on the wireless. It was a rallying call, she thought, and like everyone else listening, she took courage . . .

On the day Churchill took office, 10 May 1940, more invasions swiftly took place. Holland was forced to capitulate after four devastating days of bombing, but British and French troops fought doggedly in Belgium, unaware of German strategy, until the French defences were breached and the Germans stormed through into France. The British, cut off from the main French forces, had no alternative but to withdraw from Belgium – on 27 May, the Belgian army surrendered. There was a big picture of King Leopold on the front page of Mirry's paper: such a handsome man, she'd always thought, with film-star looks . . .

The BEF, with the remaining French units, retreated, fighting a bloody, defiant battle all the way to Dunkirk, while the German Stukas dive-bombed indiscriminately – refugees, soldiers, ambulances were hit – buildings and bridges were blown up, and there was a great pall of billowing black smoke from burning oil tanks to stumble through, retching and choking, deafened by the terrible screeching of the planes and the explosions, to the evacuation points on the beaches. Everywhere there was the stench of death. Those who somehow survived, like Acting-Sergeant Clive Joy, staggering to a dug-out with the support of two pals, would have to live with the sights and sounds of this for the rest of their lives. Later, he would not need to transcribe the compulsive, pencilled shorthand symbols in his torn notebook, for the memory of the pain of recording it all was more intense than the awful wound in his stomach.

Agonising over Clive, for she was acutely aware, through her work, that his unit would be in the thick of the fighting, Bar bent her head over her typewriter, working for Captain Snowball at his request, her fingers moving speedily, automatically over the keys; she was determined to keep the signals flying. Like the rest of the women during the Emergency, she stayed in the offices, on duty like the men, snatching brief periods of sleep on a narrow camp bed, and did not go back to her digs. It was secret, shocking stuff; she was thrilled to know that she was involved in vital communications, but secretly she longed to be out there – with Clive – part of the blood and tears – part of what would become known as the Miracle of Dunkirk, of the little ships . . .

What seemed like an impossibility was accomplished. An unlikely armada sailed; rust-buckets, pleasure craft, tugs, barges, some hardly seaworthy, spluttering defiantly, spurred on by anger and determination, there was even the splash of oars. Great Britain was going to bring our men, and our women, back home. It took nine days, and amazingly, ironically, Hitler had a hand in its success for he inexplicably ordered the German army to halt and to leave the fate of Dunkirk to his Luftwaffe. Blazing battles in the air were fought by British and German pilots as those troopers who could wade out, or who could shoulder a wounded comrade, were hauled aboard the smaller craft and ferried out to the waiting destroyers.

To those who anxiously awaited their return, the threat of invasion was now very real; the relief was euphoric when the first trainloads of soldiers steamed from Dover.

Flags flew on the washing lines, propped high, in gardens backing on to the tracks, women and children waved and cheered as untidy heads poked from carriage windows, and broadly grinning soldiers gave the thumbs-up.

Captain Snowball delivered the message to Bar personally. She didn't care what the other girls in the office thought, she flung her arms around that nervous academic, startling him with her cry: '*Clive*! He's *safe*! He's in hospital, but he's *alive*, thank God!'

Clearing his throat, the captain said huskily: 'I'm glad it was good news, Barbara.' He added: 'Dunkirk must *never* be classed as a defeat, with such a victorious outcome . . .'

It was a few days before Bar could take compassionate leave, to travel to Kent to visit her husband. She was comforted by the knowledge that Iris had been able to go to him sooner, and had a room booked in a house which they could share.

He was very pale, but smiling, bandaged below his armpits, the sheet tactfully covering up the extent of the swathing. Bar wanted to hug him close, feel him respond, but all she could do was to sit beside him, and squeeze his hand.

'I'll come along a little later, you need some time on your own . . .' Iris was tactful as always.

Bar smiled ruefully. They were in a long ward, crowded with beds. No chance of being on their own, she thought. Even with screens pulled round, you were aware of all the other patients.

'I've lost one or two bits,' Clive tried to make light of it. 'Spleen, for one . . . Nothing vital, don't worry . . .' He winced.

'Are you in much pain, darling?'

'Well, a kiss might help, as long as you don't lean on me.'

She knelt down, and their lips met briefly. She hoped he wouldn't know she was struggling to hold back the tears.

'I'll survive,' he told her, holding her hand again. 'I'll be here a few weeks, I'm afraid, but then I can convalesce with Auntie Iris – maybe even get up to Chester to see you – I do hope so.'

'Will you – will you – be invalided out, Clive?'

'Not if I can help it! France will fall shortly, that's certain. We'll be standing alone, then, Bar. Like old Kitchener said last time, "Your country needs you." '

'If you are going to fight again, well, so am I. I shall put in for a transfer to active service,' Bar declared.

When the German forces crossed the Seine, Italy joined the conflict, on their side. Paris fell, and Germany and France signed an armistice on 21 June.

But the British people, as in the rousing speech by their charismatic new leader, were set to 'defend our island, whatever the cost may be' and were unanimous that 'we shall never surrender'.

There really was 'a white glow', as Churchill would write in retrospect. Both Bar and Clive experienced it then.

CHAPTER TWENTY-NINE

'WHY DID MR CHURCHILL TELL old Hitler we don't want peace?' Glory asked, puzzled, after poring over her half of the paper. Mirry had taken to dividing the *Mirror* in the mornings, so she could read in peace at the breakfast table. Fred would have been surprised at such relaxation, she mused ruefully, but sometimes Glory's incessant chattering first thing made her feel even more weary after a night of Beulah and her teething. It was hard being both mum and dad, she decided – Fred was always so patient with Glory, and with the baby. Would she be able to cope with three? It was the middle of July now, and only eight or nine weeks to go before the new baby put in an appearance.

She thought about her answer for a minute. Glory would repeat it, no doubt, to Miss Lancaster, who would soon correct any inaccuracies. 'We'd be giving up, Glory: we have to go on fighting for what we believe in. Daddy might be home this weekend, that's good, isn't it? Why don't you read the comic strips? You don't want to worry about the news – Mr Churchill knows what he's doing.'

'Mummy, look – Jane's got hardly any clothes on!' Glory said, wide-eyed, losing interest in matters of war.

Jane, the *Mirror*'s delightful curvaceous blonde, with her German sausage-dog Fritz, was certainly doing her bit to boost morale, while the enraged Hitler now marshalled his crack troops to board the invasion barges in the harbours of northern France and Belgium.

But, first, the Luftwaffe was ordered to pave the way to submission by bombing Fighter Command – the British planes, sitting ducks on the airfields because of the need to conserve precious fuel, were to be destroyed on the ground. They were to target, too, those suspicious, puzzling, great masts erected all along the south and east coastline of Britain.

The two months after Dunkirk, during which Hitler failed to strike, proved a valuable breathing space. There was the formation of what would become the Home Guard, a voluntary army of determined veterans; munitions factories worked night and day to produce more planes and weapons: Britain was prepared for the worst. Alone.

Captain Snowball, whom Bar had grown to admire and respect, disregarding his occasional odd behaviour because his foible obviously did not apply to her, kindly drove Bar himself to visit Clive. The hospital was allowing him to spend a precious night with his wife in Dover, before Clive was taken to a convalescent home in the country. He was among those patients able to be moved now from the danger zone, but the rest were also being prepared for sudden evacuation. Yet Dover seemed much as it always had, a cheerful, bustling port. It was a beautiful summer, the sun like a great golden ball in a cloudless sky: the famous cliffs like the soap advertisement, shining, Persil white.

His recovery had not been as straightforward as they had both optimistically imagined it would be. Clive had suffered relapses and infections. It now seemed extremely doubtful that he would be able to rejoin his remustered unit, but he would plead to stay in the army, in whatever capacity he could be of use, he told Bar firmly.

It was a room very much like the one in which they had spent their wedding night. Plainly furnished, but clean. No sea view, and certainly no flowers, but a comfortable bed, on which Clive, looking pale and disorientated, immediately stretched out. Bar saw how his hand rested lightly on his abdomen. He did not complain but she knew he was in constant pain. He suffered recurring abscesses on the site of his many stitches.

She lay down beside him, kicking off her shoes under the bed. Very carefully, she moved so that she could feel the warmth of his breath, from parted lips, fanning her face. He turned his head and they kissed, lingeringly, longingly. Her arms gently encircled his chest. He smelled unfamiliar, of hospital, of antiseptic. She stroked his hair;

unoiled, longer, obviously fresh-washed with strong soap. 'Oh, Clive, I love you *so* much,' she whispered.

'Bar,' he said slowly, 'I'm so sorry, darling, but I'm afraid, I can't . . .' She saw the anguish in his eyes.

'It doesn't matter, I understand . . .' She cradled his head to her breasts as she had that morning he came to her in distress, after the night of the Crystal Palace fire. That was when she realised just how much she cared for him.

'This damn war,' he said helplessly.

*   *   *

There were myriad spiders' webs trembling on the bushes, even in suburban London. They glistened, silky, strong, looped at the corners – they asked to be touched . . . Plain privet was transformed. To Glory it looked like Fairyland.

'Leave them alone, Glory,' Mirry warned. There were rumours that the webs had floated down from German planes, that the merest touch could burn, for they were said to be impregnated with acid. These were the new superstitions, half-believed by the credulous. You couldn't be too careful.

An amazing, wonderful, even foolhardy battle was being fought in the skies above south-eastern England this August. It began on the morning of the twelfth: the radar stations and airfields were bombarded by German planes. The devastation they effected was dreadful: everywhere was tinder-dry that blazing summer. As at Dunkirk, the black smoke rose above the roaring red of the fires. The airstrips were pitted with craters. Day after day, the attacks continued, peaking on the fifteenth, with courageous, determined WAAF personnel plotting the position of the enemy planes while the youthful RAF pilots scrambled to become airborne.

Glory, of course, knew nothing of this. She looked up, dancing with excitement, at the white streaks, ribbons in the sky, at the Spitfires and Hurricanes, vastly outnumbered, taking part in a magical ballet of their own, ducking, diving, weaving; whooping like the other children as a plane, which they always assumed to be a German fighter, spiralled with a kite-tail of smoke and flames, then plummeted to the ground, who knew where, but not here, or in London itself. She certainly didn't connect the enthralling death throes of the aeroplane to the terrible, tragic ending of the lives of those who piloted it, whatever their nationality.

Once a week, they caught the bus to Grandma's and Mummy, Grandma and Auntie Alice talked babies, which was boring, but while they were exclaiming over Beulah's latest achievement, like feeding herself messily with a teaspoon – she only obliged because she liked chinking it against her front teeth, not to please Mummy, Glory knew – Uncle Stan winked at her and said, 'Shall you and me go to the Pictures, Glory?'

Then, right in the middle of what they called the Battle of Britain, a German pilot, off course, jettisoned his load in London. On a church, too, which was terrible, poor St Giles in Cripplegate ... When our bombers retaliated, hardly successfully, on Berlin, the fate of London was sealed: the Blitz was about to begin.

CHAPTER THIRTY

I am not going anywhere! I am having a baby in less than a month's time – remember? Jim shouldn't have written to you like that, I don't want to go back to the farm. Anyway, Hilda wrote that a German plane crashlanded in one of the farm fields. The crew weren't killed, but they ran off and it was some time before they were captured. Hilda tried not to let the children out of her sight until then, but she says Don seems to do what he likes these days, since all the trouble with Laura and Jim. He biked over with his pals and got some bits from the plane. I don't want Glory to run wild. Look at that trouble with Jenny.

You mustn't worry! Mum will be staying with us indefinitely from tomorrow, you know that.

Dear Fred, I don't mean to sound cross. But I am so very hot and huge and if only you were here everything would be all right . . .

Sighing heavily, mirry folded the letter, written in the heat of the moment, and sealed the envelope with a thump of her fist. 'There! It's nice of you to offer to go to the post, Anna – could you get me a bit of shopping, too?'

'Of course,' Anna said, draining her cup of tea and taking it out into the kitchen to rinse. She called back: 'Are you feeling all right, Mirry? You look rather – flustered . . .'

'Don't you start!' Mirry said in a quite un-Mirry like way. Here she was, in a voluminous blue smock, which creased like billy-o, with swollen ankles and a desire to spend a penny every ten minutes or so. And Anna, all done up to the nines, with her hair short and curly and wearing a brand new dress – perhaps in honour of the attentive warden?

'Glory can come with me to the shops, then back to mine to practise her steps. We'll take Beulah with us, in the pram, shall we? Handy for the shopping. Then you can have a bit of a rest.' She looked up expressively. 'All quiet on the Western Front, as they say, this afternoon, Mirry.'

Still, Mirry thought guiltily when she had gone, for it was too late to retract what she had written to poor old Fred, and he was only showing how concerned he was for their safety, wasn't he? Still, I'm glad Jim asked Ted the warden to help him shift our double mattress and all the bedding under the stairs . . . We'd never get to his shelter in time, with me like this, in the middle of the night especially.

I guess I will take up most of the space, and Mum will have to squeeze in beside the children. But I must admit I'll be glad when she's here . . .

The Few – so few – were almost at the end of their tether when the Luftwaffe were ordered to attack London. On 7 September 1940, in a massive daytime strike by bombers, accompanied by fighter planes, the docklands were set on fire. Those on radar watch, in the plotting rooms, responded magnificently, but that night there was a second wave of bombers, guided by the still blazing Thames-side warehouses, intent on destroying the country's vital supplies of food and other commodities. The conflagration could be clearly seen by those desperately manning our defences on the coastline opposite France. Invasion was surely imminent.

When it did not come, there was renewed resolve, sheer bloody-mindedness; Spitfires and Hurricanes again made daredevil swoops, anti-aircraft guns now blazed with deadly accuracy, but still the bombers came.

The night raids were the worst. The unearthly, urgent wailing of the siren; the sinister, heartstopping droning of the enemy planes intensifying in brilliant moonlight – then the reassuring *crump*! of the defending guns.

Mirry and Mum lay awake, cramped and sweating, in their refuge under the stairs, clutching the sleeping children to them. Above their heads on the shelf were the torches, the gas masks, a tin box containing chocolate, Horlicks tablets and boiled sweets, a flask of tea. They had taken off their shoes, but hadn't undressed, because, as Mum said: 'I'm not being carried out of here in my nightie by some strange man.' The dog curled up on their feet. Fleas and all, who cared? Mirry thought wryly. There was a covered pail for emergencies, in the meter cupboard.

In the early morning, after the all-clear sounded, out in the streets, the full horror of the night was starkly revealed. Bomb Alley, the locals called it; on the way to London – where bomb loads were jettisoned at random – and incendiary devices caused havoc. In the capital itself, fires still roared, the firefighters battled on; a choking pall of dust rose from the rubble and there was the sound of shattered glass being briskly swept by bent-backed old shopkeepers. Postmen arrived with the mail, milkmen delivered the milk, and the public, too, went to work, if their workplace still existed.

Mirry had drifted into an uneasy sleep, now she awoke with a start. 'Mum, my waters have broken . . .' she hissed.

Mum sat up cautiously, shifting Beulah nearer Glory. The bombers sounded ominously overhead. 'We'll have to do the best we can, dearie – can't run for the nurse in this. Jim not home, either. If the warden comes, we'll see what he suggests. Any pains, yet?'

'Not yet,' Mirry lied. She buried her face against Mum's broad shoulder, gripped her hand, smothering a gasp. Fred, *Fred*! Where are you when I need you? she cried silently. Then she struggled to the end of the mattress, staggered to her feet. She urgently needed that wretched bucket. Then the world seemed to cave in around her as the whole house shook and the heavy front door crashed inwards and struck her a terrible blow, knocking her flat. There was an almighty whistling in her ears, but strangely, no pain. Then a man came scrambling through the gaping hole where the oak door had been, shouting encouragement.

The screaming came from her mother, and the children.

The hospital ward was dimly lit. It was night again and Mirry came to, to hear the familiar drone overhead. Fred sat by her bed, which was strange, because he shouldn't be here, surely, she thought, bewildered.

She was wearing a coarse white gown. Instinctively, she felt her stomach, winced. It was flat, heavily bandaged. 'The baby?' she whispered.

'We thought we'd lost you both . . .' Fred said, his voice thick with emotion. 'You had to have an emergency operation, Mirry . . .'

'But I was already in labour!' She tried to make sense of it all. 'The children?' she asked sharply.

'It's three days, darling, since ... Anna looked after them until Jim could take them back to the farm – I know you didn't want that, but ...'

'Mum?'

'She's – all right. She'll be joining them very shortly. Don't worry, she says ...' How could he tell Mirry that the same night they were bombed, there had been a direct hit on the block of flats where Aunt Alice and Uncle Stan lived. There were no survivors. If Mum had been there: but it didn't bear thinking about.

'The baby – what was it?'

So she knew the baby was dead. 'He – he was stillborn, Mirry – he didn't stand a chance. I thought I was going to lose you, too,' he repeated.

'Don't say there'll be other babies, Fred. I was right, you see, it was a boy.'

'We've still got a baby,' he reminded her sadly, 'Beulah. You must get well for her, and for Glory, now – and me. You'll go back to Number Five one day, Mirry, I promise you. The bomb went through the party wall between our house and next door. The house is still standing ...'

'Who got us out? I didn't know him, he was a stranger – quite thick-set, but he was so strong and kind ...' Suddenly, Bar's voice seemed to echo in her head: 'It wasn't the Major ... much shorter and thicker-set ...'

'It's a mystery, no one seems to know,' Fred said. 'But he was there at the right time, Mirry.'

The lights went out. Staff came running. Fred helped carry his wife on the stretcher down echoing stairs. Those patients who could be moved were being taken to another hospital. He sat beside her, in the ambulance, holding her hand, trying to comfort her. *She knew.* There would be no more babies for Mirry. She herself would recover physically, they had assured him of that. But how long would it take for the mental scars to heal?

There was a brief report in *The Norwood News*:

The badly burned body of a man found among rubble in a gutted house has still not been identified. It is believed the stranger carried an elderly lady to safety, before going back into the inferno for her son.

There had been reports to the Police recently of a stranger lurking in the vicinity of Kitchener Avenue, in particular the Victorian Villas. A woman walking home in the blackout complained that she had been grabbed outside the dancing academy. Fortunately she broke free and ran to her home further along the road.

There is conjecture that 'the strangers' are one and the same. Earlier, there was another miraculous rescue, when 'a stranger' carried an injured, heavily pregnant woman from her bomb-damaged home, Number Five, Kitchener Avenue. 'If he is the same man,' the local warden said, 'I have to think he is both Saint and Sinner.' But he added that he would continue to keep an eye on vulnerable women in that area, especially the proprietor of the dancing academy, who cared for her invalid father.

CHAPTER THIRTY-ONE

LIKE BAR, AFTER DUNKIRK, EILEEN had asked for a transfer to more active duties. She had volunteered, when the call came, to join an anti-aircraft battery. 'Just fancy, Bar, men and women all mixed up together, training side by side – we'll show 'em, eh?' she exclaimed, determinedly bright. Her fiancé had written, breaking off their engagement, saying he could not tie her down, when at any moment he might go down with his ship. Broken-hearted, all she'd said then was the trite: 'Plenty more fish in the sea,' but Bar knew how she really felt. They had been through a lot together, they were mates.

'I'll miss you, Eileen . . .' Bar told her.

'You've still got Coral. She's not budging, it seems, from here. What did old Snowball say when you asked him why you hadn't heard?'

'He said, I should wait, in case Clive is invalided out, and I'm needed at home. In other words, the army will decide where my duty lies.'

They were cleaning their shoes in the kitchen.

'Well, he must come first, Bar, they're right there.'

'I know that, of course I do, but Clive doesn't agree. If he can't fight again, there's no reason, he says, why I shouldn't carry on . . .'

'Gosh!' Eileen said admiringly, 'your Clive really believes in equality of the sexes, doesn't he?' She spat on her toecap and buffed it vigorously. 'How's your poor sister?' she asked.

'Not too well . . . Fred had to tell her about our aunt and uncle being killed – the same night as they were bombed. She's left the hospital now, and gone back to where she was evacuated before. Mum's with her, so she's got plenty of people looking after her.'

'I worry about *my* mum and dad,' Eileen said, lacing her shoes and straightening her stockings. 'No let-up in the bombing. I can't wait to get my finger on the trigger, Bar.'

'Give 'em a blast from me,' Bar said strongly.

With much clearing of his throat, Captain Snowball polished his glasses on his handkerchief. Bar waited patiently the other side of his desk.

'Your release,' he said finally, tapping the sheets of paper he had been studying. 'I'll be very sorry to see you go – invaluable contribution . . .'

'I'm sorry to leave,' she said quietly, 'at such a time.'

There was no let-up in the bombing, and the range was ever-widening; the great cathedral cities, the industrial towns, had all been blasted.

More hrrumphing. Then Captain Snowball asked: 'Where will you go, Barbara?'

'I'm not sure,' she answered honestly. They could go to Iris of course but, after Mirry's experience . . . 'The only home I had was at my sister's and that's been bombed.'

'This might provide a solution, if you agree,' the captain said diffidently. He opened a drawer, took out a bunch of keys, attached to a luggage label, and a sealed letter. 'I took the liberty . . . I own this little cottage on Dartmoor, Barbara – left to me by my grandmother, y'know . . . I stayed there, from time to time, before the war – very peaceful – if rather remote; a good few miles from Plymouth and the docks, which is just as well, with all the bombing, eh? You'd be doing me a favour – keeping an eye, hmm, hmm, caretaking, if you like – I'd be glad to waive rent if you would be willing to, hmm, hmm, to give a lick of paint here and there, where necessary . . . it's where I shall retire eventually. What d'you hmm, hmm, say, Barbara?'

Bar read the label: 'Ivy Cottage, Church Hill . . . Can you hear the bells?' she asked, then felt rather foolish.

Captain Snowball smiled. 'You can hear the bells, yes. In peacetime, that is. You'd like to go to Devon then?'

Bar nodded, quite overcome.

'The letter will introduce you. The rector has the other set of keys, he and his wife will help you settle in, I'm sure. You may stay as long as you like. I'll arrange transport, naturally, for you, and your husband.'

'You are really kind, thank you, Captain Snowball.'

'Cecil,' he told her. 'You see, I – have become, ah, very fond of you, Barbara – oh, nothing – hmm, hmm – I assure you . . .' His pink-tipped nose twitched in embarrassment.

After you, Claude, no, after you, Cecil. A catchphrase, which she had often heard on the wireless, but she didn't smile now. Captain Snowball really was a gentleman, she thought gratefully.

Dartmoor was bleakly beautiful in November. The picture-book cottages, the little hump-backed bridges, the stone walls, the winding lanes, the great moors cropped by shaggy ponies, cows and sheep, the towering tors. 'But where are the trees?' Bar exclaimed. She had never been so far west before.

'Trees, my lover?' Their driver was a local chap who had jumped at the chance of a brief visit home. 'In the valleys, by the streams, bending like, all covered in lichen . . . Like crystal, the water: rushing over the stones. But you'll need to wrap up warm – the rain might get you down – once it starts it forgets to stop. And you can expect to be snowed in after Christmas.'

Bar was sitting next to Clive in the back of the staff car. Not the most comfortable of vehicles, she thought wryly, hoping that the bumpy ride had not exhausted Clive too much. The driver had spread a rug gallantly over their laps. She felt for his hand, squeezed it. 'Nothing will get us down, will it? Not rain, or snow,' she whispered, as the driver noisily changed gear. 'It's our honeymoon, Clive, better late than never, darling.'

'I wish it had been – before . . .' he answered slowly.

The Reverend Stoop was actually upright, middle-aged, bushy eyebrowed and bald; his cassock rather grubby and held together, here and there, with large safety pins. He had a rumbling laugh which inevitably left him gasping and wiping his eyes. He did not stand on ceremony: 'My wife calls me Ginger.' Bar's face must have shown her disbelief, for they were treated to his laugh for the first time; he finished hoarsely: 'So I retaliate by calling her Delilah,' he tapped his head ruefully, 'draw your own conclusions, eh – but most folk round here call me Rector, to my face anyway, and . . .'

'Call me Delia,' Mrs Stoop obliged. She was much younger than the rector, with coal-black hair hanging halfway down her back and narrowed sloe eyes. She had a voluptuous figure, obviously unrestrained, a rich local accent and she laughed a lot too. 'You approve of your new home, I hope,' she asked. 'Apart from being near the top of the hill, like the rectory and the church?'

They had hardly put their bags down before the Stoops arrived, letting themselves in with their key.

Bar looked round the living room, at the uneven walls, sagging ceiling, old pitted beams, the well-worn furniture dating back to Captain Snowball's late grandmother, no doubt – still covered with her crocheted, multi-coloured blankets; at the rag rugs, which Mirry, she thought, would have rushed outside to shake vigorously; at the unrubbed horse brasses decorating the mantel. Then she stared at the fire burning well in the grate, sending out warmth and cheer, just asking for the chairs to be pulled up close, and feet to be rested on the fender.

'Do sit down, you must be tired after all that journeying. I'll soon get the kettle boiling and make us all a cup of tea,' Delia said, as Ginger moved the chairs into place.

Not only tea, but still-warm scones, and rich butter were served. Later, Delia promised, she would call with a chicken casserole: 'We had a bit o' luck, my lovers – old Bob Bowden, good as gold he is, you'll see him very soon, I don't doubt, for if he can help, he will – he brought round a hen, first thing . . . He does our garden for us, grows all the veggies, Ginger being taken up with the spiritual, like. His little wife obliges in the house – I do my own cooking, though: Ginger feeds the spirit, and I feed the body, I say.'

Escorting Bar up the steep stairs: 'I hope your husband can manage these, my lover,' to show her the two tiny bedrooms, with both beds made up. 'You take your choice, eh?' Delia confided: 'I'll be glad to have some younger company. I'm Ginger's second wife, you see. I did nurse his first, for five years. I qualified in Plymouth, but I had enough of hospitals – too much skivvying for my liking. His son and his daughter are both in the forces. I can lend you a bike, if you like, but, just a little hint, my dear – don't be going too far afield – there's things going on, since the war, you don't need to be too curious about . . .'

'Do you – mind, Bar,' Clive asked, having made that exhausting climb to bed. 'If I sleep in the other room? I get so restless, you see – it's not fair to you – just for a night or two, I expect.'

She helped him into bed, tucked him up tenderly. 'Goodnight darling,' she bestowed a light kiss on his forehead. She recognised the relief in his eyes at her acceptance and she managed a smile. She placed a bottle unobtrusively by his bed. There was no bathroom, of course. Oil lamps, which could be turned down low, though, which was a blessing. 'Sleep in as long as you like,' she added, as she turned to go. 'I'll be sure to hear you, if you call . . .'

'I won't call,' he said, but he sounded uncertain, like a child.

Despite her fatigue, she lay awake until the early hours. Clive was right. It wasn't the time for a belated honeymoon. This place, so quiet after the communal life, with her friends, over the past year: would she be able, could she, adapt to her new life? Like Mirry, she was a townie, she thought. She cried silently, because she would hate Clive to know that he had upset her by deciding they should sleep separately. I don't expect to pick up married life, loving, where we left off. I'm prepared to wait, be patient – but, I can't bear it – if he rejects me . . .

CHAPTER THIRTY-TWO

IN SLACKS, THICK JERSEY, WOOLLY HAT, mitts and scarf, Bar set off on her borrowed bike; free-wheeling perilously down the hill, just preventing herself from whooping, as if she were Glory's age.

There was a riming of frost on the verges, on the hedges, and frost in the air, too, pinching her cheeks scarlet, making her eyes water, but the sky above was cloudlessly blue. I'm happy when I'm biking . . . she thought, and surprisingly, after a sleepless night, she realised that she was light of spirit.

Pump, privy and grumpy stove, it's the primitive life for me! she improvised.

Dogs leapt up at the gates set in the craggy stone walls, barking as she whizzed past. Spotless washing billowed between clothes posts, and black-haired buxom lasses like Delia, wearing old-fashioned wrap-around aprons, felt in their pockets for pegs, or wiped the runny noses of their infants, and some of them waved a greeting to the stranger.

She made herself known at the shop, in the central dip of the village, built of the same grey stone as the surrounding cottages, facing a little stream, glistening with ice, and beyond that, a rise of meadow. She filled her basket with necessities. It was a puzzle, juggling with their ration books, she soon discovered, but there was plenty of eager advice to be had. 'Look here, my lover!'

She had left Clive still in bed, having put the jug of hot water for him to wash and shave on the washstand. She mustn't be too long, she thought. What vague cooking skills she had once possessed had long been forgotten, apart from frizzling bacon in old tins. It was going to take time to become a proper housekeeper, like Mirry or Mum and Aunt Alice. At the thought of the latter, her lips trembled. What had dear old Uncle Stan said? They just might make a soldier out of you, Bar . . . Well, they had, and she'd never forget the experience but she and Clive had to find a new purpose to their lives now. There was always voluntary war work.

She unwound her scarf, took off the bicycle clips which she had discovered in a kitchen drawer, and stacked the groceries on the table. She was still deciding where everything should go, when she felt his arms tentatively encircling her waist. He nudged her cap off with his chin, kissed the back of her neck. 'I missed you, Bar,' he said in a muffled voice. 'I thought you'd run away – after last night . . .'

She waited, standing there with a blue bag of sugar in her hands, her heart beating fast.

'Put that down,' he said. 'We need to talk ...' He hadn't yet dressed and shaved, but wore the moth-holed dressing gown which had been left, gathering dust, on the hook on the bedroom door. 'Let's go in the living room, by the fire. It's not smoking like this old range.' He coughed. 'Must be blocked somewhere, might be better to use the oil stove for a bit, and ask Old Bob to look at it.'

She had lit the fires soon after dawn – at least she was capable of that, due to all her training. Old Bob, Delia had mentioned, had chopped the splendid pile of wood in the shed, and poked his brushes up the chimney: 'He won't ask for payment, but five bob is usual, my dear.'

They sat in their chosen chairs, facing each other side on. 'Do you forgive me?' Clive asked.

She looked at his pale, drawn face, the shadowed eyes. She observed the way he sat down, with care, and she knew he was still in discomfort, that it had been a real effort for him to descend the stairs on his own. 'There's nothing to forgive, Clive. I love you.'

He put his head in his hands, and his shoulders heaved slightly. 'I'm afraid, Bar ...'

'I'm here,' she said quietly. 'Perhaps you should have had a day in bed, to get over the journey. I'm sorry I didn't realise that ...'

He looked up then, and she got a glimpse of the old Clive as he smiled at her. 'Only if *you* come back to bed with me!'

She had a present for him: five fat exercise books, the shop's entire stock, and a bundle of pencils. 'You're going to write a book, Clive,' she told him firmly. 'You always said you would, one day.'

'Bossy as ever,' he returned, but he took them from her, and spread them on the table. 'What's the alternative?'

'Reward, d'you mean? We'll see! One of my special cakes?'

'What special cakes? You've never made a cake, as far as I know . . .'

'That's what will make the first one special!'

'It's good to joke again, isn't it?' he said. 'You're a real—'

'Dose of salts?' she teased. She could just see Uncle Stan's approving grin. A good laugh never hurt anyone, gal. Never let life get you down.

'No – tonic: which room shall we sleep in tonight?'

'We'll take it in turns,' she said demurely. She thought, I'm going to be happy here, after all. Good old Captain Snowball for thinking of it. I must write and tell him so, but I can't tell him all . . .

* * *

Glory, much to her surprise, found going back to the village school no problem at all. She was the centre of attention:

285

all the children wanted to hear what it was like to live in Bomb Alley and to be bombed out. She was quite a heroine, it seemed. The business of the pond was forgotten. Besides, wasn't she a film star? And wasn't it a pity Mr Gray had gone away from here to make films for the forces, but at least he'd let them stay on in the farmhouse.

She was disappointed to discover, however, that Horst was no longer at the hostel, or the school. After he had written, he had heard that he was to go with other children to America, to be reunited with his parents. She hoped he would write again, it was lucky they were back at the farm, as the postman wouldn't be calling at Number Five for some time to come, she thought. Anyway, he didn't know her address there.

Jenny gripped her hand tightly and smiled happily, the first time they walked to school again together, and the Chucklenuts said: 'Wotcher!' off handedly and then walked ahead, as always, with Don and Junie.

They were nice to her again, too. And Auntie Laura had greeted Mummy with a big hug, and said how much she had missed them, and how lovely it was to have them back. Mummy was quite calm, like she'd been ever since she came out of hospital, and no one mentioned the poor little baby who would never be at all. Then Auntie Laura looked at Uncle Jim, and she was crying, and Uncle Jim looked funny, too. He put his arms round her, and said in a chokey voice, 'It's all right, Laura, it's all right . . .' Granny Hardes fussed over Mummy a lot, and she eyed their grandma a bit as if she wasn't too sure who was boss, now, and Grandma, who was used to Auntie Alice's ways, smiled, and asked what she could do to help: before you knew it, they were firm friends.

Glory couldn't believe she'd never see Auntie Alice or Uncle Stan again, or hear him say, 'Shall you and me go to the Pictures, Glory?' but she knew they must have gone straight up to heaven, no question of that.

Daddy was home again for Christmas; he had to sleep downstairs in the sitting room on the sofa, because Grandma shared Mummy's big bed now, of course. Still she and Beulah, whom Daddy had started calling Boo, for short, went downstairs at the crack of dawn and woke him up with hugs and kisses and demands that he watch them empty their stockings. 'O be joyful, Daddy!' Glory cried encouragingly. And Daddy grinned wryly, yawned and said, 'Chip off the old block you are, Gloria Anna . . .'

It was nice now Boo was on her feet and could climb and jump around, even if she did land on her bottom, with a thump, quite often. She looked so surprised then, that Glory got fits of giggles. She was beginning to chatter, too, but Glory was the only one who knew what she was trying to say – but then, as Mr Gray had said, she was an interpreter, eh? Grandma said she looked just like Bar at that age, with those gypsy black curls and mischief written all over her.

Uncle Jim was lucky, Auntie Laura had plenty of room for him, in *her* bed.

It would have been nice if Bar and Clive could have been there, too.

Laura and Mirry managed a brief five minutes on their own when they were seeing to the Christmas pudding and stirring the custard in the kitchen, while the rest of the gathering sat expectantly at the table in the dining room, the older members looking sheepish in homemade crêpe-paper hats, courtesy of the children.

'I didn't think we'd all be here together like this, did you, Mirry, this year?' Laura asked, whisking at the lumps in the custard.

'No.' Mirry stuck the sprig of holly on the upturned pudding and poured on a generous measure of brandy. It was ready to set alight; carry to the table in triumph.

'Everything – all right between you and Fred?' Laura didn't look at her.

'Of course. Fred's been wonderful, as always, about – you know . . . I know how lucky I am. And you?'

'I've got a confession to make – I must, Mirry, it's been bothering me, you see. When Jim didn't come to see us; when I learned, from your letters to Mum – that you were cooking for him, and that he was spending time with you and the children – well, I felt jealous. I thought maybe you were both trying to pay me out . . . When Bernard told me that he was moving on, but that we were welcome to stay on here – when he didn't ask me to go with him – I knew it was over. If I'd lost Jim, too, I don't know what I would have done . . .'

'You never had any cause to think there was anything between us,' Mirry told her simply. 'He's a good man, Laura, don't let him down again . . .' I told her things were all right between me and Fred, she thought – but, they're not. How could they be?

* * *

Bar and Clive walked up the slippery slope to the church on Christmas morning, arm in arm like an old married couple. Last Christmas, she thought, she'd been larking about with Coral and some of the other girls who hadn't been able to go home. They'd had a real Christmas dinner in the NAAFI, and sung carols and danced to the gramophone in the evening. She'd missed Eileen, back in London, but she'd tried not to think too much about Clive, in France, because then she wouldn't be able to stop moping.

This Christmas, it was just perfect, the two of them together. Naturally, they'd asked Iris to join them, because they worried about her, alone in Bomb Alley, but she decided to go to an old friend and former colleague, long retired in Buckinghamshire. 'I might stay on there, I could get a transfer, I expect. Muriel suffers badly from bronchitis, and needs me right now and I admit I miss having someone to keep an eye on! We've always got on very well. You enjoy this first Christmas, just you two, my dears. I'll come and see you in the spring: meanwhile, keep those letters posted.'

They had been invited for Christmas dinner at the rectory that evening, which was quite a relief, for they had eaten quite a few burnt offerings from the sulky stove. Clive had cooked the breakfast on the oil stove, but paraffin was in short supply nowadays. The cottage smelt like Number Five, Bar thought, wrinkling her nose, the day they were reunited, the day their brass buttons clashed. Oil was all pervading, it seemed. Thank goodness the wireless Mirry and Fred had kindly sent them for Christmas worked by batteries.

The church was only half-full: they already knew that the village was a stronghold of the chapel. But the gleaming brasses, the candles, the greenery, the joyous carols, made the service very special.

'Did you enjoy it?' Delia asked, smiling, as they waited to shake the rector's hand at the end.

She hadn't mentioned it to Clive, in fact, the idea had only just come to her. Bar said: 'Oh yes – and Delia, what do you think? We got married, you see, in a rush as war broke out: we said we'd have a marriage blessing later in church – d'you think?'

'Of course, my lover! I know Ginger will agree – you must have your blessing here!'

Bar held tight to Clive's arm. 'We'll wait until Iris can come and possibly Mum, too.'

'It's a wonderful idea,' he said.

CHAPTER THIRTY-THREE

THREE LETTERS THIS MORNING, delivered by Old Bob; Bar and Clive had soon discovered that his regular employment was as village postman. 'Get plenty of spare time, you see, for my other interests,' he beamed, the first time they met, when he pocketed five bob, cheerfully dismissing the fact that he had so much of his day free courtesy of his before-light start.

As he cycled off, Bar waved from the door – there was no letter box, so Old Bob knocked, then they exchanged pleasantries about the weather even if it was snowing hard and the postman's one remaining long lock of hair, carefully spread over his scalp, lifted in the spring breeze in a farewell salute.

She carried the post up to Clive on his breakfast tray. It took him a long time to get up in the mornings; they had slipped into a comfortable routine – Bar cooked breakfast, and Clive saw to the other meals. He was still the better cook, she thought, glancing with a grimace at her stodgy porridge, but at least she wasn't likely to spill it on the bed, for she liked to eat with Clive.

'One from Iris – still postmarked Bucks, I see – you have that first; one from Fred, I'll save that for after my cup of tea – poor chap's still worrying about Mirry I expect; and, O be joyful! this one's from Eileen:'

Guess who I've met up with again? Peter from our training camp! Ack, ack! True love at second sight! He asks to be remembered to you; says he's never forgotten the day you stood up and spoke up about the dipping-in of mugs in the tea urn . . .

We're still kept very busy here, but that's all I can say about that. It must be wonderful to be in such a peaceful place, with such a lovely feller! Do hope Clive is recovering well, and that I'll get to meet him one day.

Still miss you, dear old Bar! We did have fun, didn't we? I hear from Coral now and again. Did she tell you Marie got her discharge, because she was in the family way? Bet Drusy and Lucy are clicking the old knitting needles, eh?

Which reminds me, when are you and Clive going to make me a godmother?

Much love, from your old pal, Eileen

'You didn't read the last bit out,' Clive said, scraping his blackened toast, then scraping on marge.

She passed the letter over, without comment. He scanned it, put it down and crunched his toast before he spoke. Then he asked lightly: 'Well?'

'Clive, you know we agreed – not until after the war.'

'I don't think we actually said that, Bar. Let's face it, I'm not going back to the fighting, you've got involved in village affairs with Delia, the welfare clinic, the WVS. The war could go on for years.'

'I'm not sure I'm the maternal type,' she floundered. She rose from her perch on the side of the bed, piled the plates on the tray. 'Better get washed up, I suppose. I'll bring your water up.'

He caught hold of her skirt, as she turned to go. 'You wouldn't have to give anything up, Bar. I know you'll still want a career, when the time's right but I'll be at home for the foreseeable future . . . I could look after the children . . .'

'More than one now, is it?' she teased. 'Eileen's really stirred things up, hasn't she? Let's not rush into anything Clive: remember, we'll have to leave this place one day, it doesn't belong to us, after all. You'll go back to journalism, I'm sure of that – and, now, get on with that book!'

They held the weekly clinic in the Memorial Hall, dedicated to those who had lost their lives in the last conflict. Local names were inscribed on the polished wooden plaque,

Trelawney, Trembath – names repeated now in the new generation of babies.

Wearing a starched white overall, with her hair tied neatly back, Bar took wriggling armfuls of plump babies with peachy skin and long-lashed dark eyes and weighed them in the scales. She held them while the doctor vaccinated them, and comforted them when they wailed with indignation at being jabbed; she issued baby milk, advice, and cod-liver oil, and she listened when their mothers confided their worries. There were the expectant mothers, too, keeping ante-natal appointments. She learned to test the samples and to whisper tactfully: 'D'you think you could manage to wipe the Daddy's Sauce off the rim of the bottle next time, please?'

Delia, as a qualified nurse, was in charge. Bar saw how the mothers loved and trusted her as one of them. They were still a little wary of her though. There weren't that many strangers living hereabouts, she discovered: those, like the rector, married to a local woman, were welcomed, but not quite integrated.

As Delia told her privately, before her first session at the clinic: 'Never probe into relationships, my lover, you might hear some surprising things. But, a baby's a baby, and nearly always accepted. You might see a likeness here and there, that shouldn't really be, but I respect their privacy, as they do mine.'

Mum couldn't leave Mirry and the children, she said, writing:

> *Don't say anything when you reply, Bar, but I think she's having a bit of a nervous breakdown. Fred does worry so, poor man. Hilda and I keep an eye on her, and try to cheer her up. We'll think of you in the church, and I'm glad Iris will be with you.*

Iris had the most surprising news to impart. She was engaged! Her friend's brother had come to stay, after being bombed out. They'd taken to each other right away. Harold was in his early sixties, ten years older than Iris, a bachelor – 'But not at all crusty. There doesn't seem any point in waiting – we're going to fix the date, when I go back: I just wanted your approval, first.'

Bar hugged her tight. 'Oh, Iris. I'm thrilled, aren't you, Clive?'

'Pass her to me!' he said, 'of course I am.'

Bar helped her unpack. Iris had endured a long journey by train, sitting on her case in the corridor because the carriages were full of service personnel, predominantly naval. The rector had taken Bar to meet her at Plymouth, where security was tight. The docks at Devonport had been hard hit by the bombers. They were a prime target. It was Bar's first visit to the city where Drake had played bowls before battling with the Spanish Armada, and she was shocked by the damage inflicted there. They heard the enemy planes going over, of course, heard the distant guns, saw strange lights in the sky, but they were in such a quiet backwater here.

'This is for you, Bar, I hope it's not too crushed,' Iris said, handing her something wrapped in layers of tissue paper. 'I had it by me, in a drawer, thank goodness,' she added.

Bar carefully unwrapped a wedding dress, ivory now, once white, she knew. Old fashioned, but beautiful, with tiny pearl buttons on the bodice and on the cuffs.

'My sister's . . .' Iris told her simply. 'I know she wanted Clive's bride to wear it, to keep it. Would you – wear it for *me*, tomorrow?'

Bar hugged her again. 'Darling Iris, of course I will, if I can squeeze into it, that is! We were going to tell you this evening – we're going to have a baby in about seven months' time!'

Iris looked at her, eyes bright with tears. 'Oh, Bar, I'm so happy for you both.'

'Quite a twenty-third birthday present, Iris, eh? The doctor confirmed it then, last week . . . The only thing is – it's due around Christmas Day!'

They sat round the fire, which they still lit in the evenings, for the house was always cold; the three of them, drinking celebration cups of cocoa and munching Delia's scones.

'You won't be Auntie Iris any longer,' Clive said reflectively. 'You'll be Grandma, or whatever you choose to be called, like Bar's mum . . .'

Bar's new friends, her young mothers, helped to fill the church. No bells, but the jerky wheezing of the harmonium, and the two of them sitting on chairs before the altar to be blessed, because Ginger had guessed it would be difficult for Clive to kneel. Bar was right, the dress was strained round her middle and hips, and she thought ruefully that it would probably set tongues wagging.

She felt Clive sway slightly as they stood outside the church in the May sunshine and Iris took precious photographs with her box camera with the last roll of prewar film. This day has its own magic, she thought: then she smiled to herself because only the two of them were aware that she wore once more that special silk underwear. Recalling that other simple wedding ceremony, and what followed, was still very evocative.

The wedding breakfast was at the Rectory, well, a tasty liver and bacon hotpot. The bride sprang her surprise, to the delight of their friends, and then it was back home and early to bed, because the bridegroom looked pale and tired.

Bar suppressed a twinge of fear when she kissed him goodnight. 'Was it worth going through all that again?' she asked, as lightly as she could.

'I'd marry you over and over again, if I could,' he told her fancifully,' if you looked just as you did today . . .'

Young Eileen Raffery, so delighted to hear the good news that her friend was expecting a baby, knitted a pair of pale blue bootees and reminded them that she intended to be the baby's godmother.

A few days after the parcel arrived, and they smiled over the fact that one bootee was larger than the other, another letter arrived, from Captain Snowball. He regretted having to impart bad news, he said, for he knew how close the two girls had been, but Corporal Raffery had been killed on duty with her battery. She had showed exceptional courage: they were all very proud of her.

'Darling, you'll make yourself ill, you must think of the baby,' Clive said helplessly, as Bar curled herself up in a ball under the eiderdown on their bed, and wept and wept.

When, at last, she had cried herself out, she lay there still, holding Clive's hand, and she remembered all the happy times – Ginger, you're barmy! – Eileen waggling the sleeves of her oversized tunic – tripping up in the blue and white pyjamas, and dancing downstairs. She saw the pain on Eileen's face when she read the letter from her fiancé, and she was glad that her friend had found new happiness with Peter. But to die at twenty-one years old . . .

Little Eileen, so full of life, had laughingly suggested her own epitaph:

I'd rather die a heroine, in action, than have my mum and dad informed: 'she passed away from poisoned plums'.

Another Ginger, the rector, and Delia came to offer comfort, at Clive's request. The prayers, the kind concern, did help, just a little.

CHAPTER THIRTY-FOUR

SOMETHING MUST BE DONE about Mirry, the extended family at the farm decided. It was Laura, bored with being at home all day, who offered to find a solution.

Walking along the lane, early one afternoon, pushing Boo in her chair, with Pip's lead fastened to the handle, they paused to look at the cows, out to pasture.

It was October, the children were back at school after all the fun of helping with the harvest. The three of them had become brown as berries, and Glory had asked to have her hair cut short like Junie's, because: 'I get all in a muck sweat, Mummy, even with my hair in bunches.'

Mirry, shocked, had reminded her: 'Horses sweat, Glory, little girls perspire.'

'Well, I'm out with the horses, aren't I, and I sweat, just like them,' came the retort.

Mirry was relieved to see that Glory once again resembled the younger Shirley Temple – although even *she* was in her teens now – with those springy short curls all over her head. But, wisely, she kept quiet about that.

Boo bounced about in the pushchair, pointing in excitement when a young heifer ambled over to the hedge to see what they might have to offer. Pip had learned respect for cows. He sniffed about the verge, pretending he couldn't see the large creature staring curiously over the gate.

Laura seized her opportunity. 'I've been thinking, Mirry, we ought to get a job. We're superfluous to requirements as they say, with two mums in charge, aren't we?'

Mirry looked at her, puzzled. 'I know you miss going out to work, Laura, but . . .'

'I know, you haven't worked since you got married. Don't you want to do something for the war effort, Mirry?'

'Well . . . I've still got Boo to consider, she's too young to leave.'

'Oh, you know jolly well she'd be perfectly happy looked after by those doting grandmothers!'

'Have you got something in mind? I don't think Fred would be too pleased.'

'Fred wants to see you happy again, we all do. You need to try something new – make a fresh start – rather like me and Jim . . . Look, if I don't get something useful to do, with the children getting older – Junie's nearly ten, remember – I'll be drafted into war work anyway. Yes, I have made inquiries: the chap who delivers the milk for the farm has been called up. They're desperate to find a replacement. When they said it wasn't really a job for a woman, I said, "How about *two* women?" They'd have the churns ready on the cart, and the old horse, they say, knows when to stop and start – I don't mind being the one to hold the reins. You have to start early in the morning, of course, but the mums can see the children off to school, and we'd be home by midday. What could be easier – you dip your measure in the churn and fill the jugs people leave out for you! Well, Mirry?'

Mirry looked animated for the first time in months. 'You've already decided, haven't you? It sounds easy, and as it's only a part-time job . . .' She pulled up a clump of grass for the waiting heifer.

Laura crossed her fingers behind her back. She wouldn't mention that it was barely light at six o'clock in the mornings, or that Mrs Dean had said their fingers would get frozen in the winter, and that there were some nippy dogs on the round. Mirry wouldn't have time to mope, and read those endless library books, as she did all day now, and that was important.

'We'll call and tell Mrs Dean the good news on our way back,' she decided. And she lit another cigarette. She deserved a little treat for making Mirry smile, she thought.

Mum knitted Mirry a cap, scarf and fingerless mitts like she had for Bar. She nudged her daughter out of her warm bed at half past five, and mentioned that she wouldn't half like a nice hot cup of tea, if the girls were making one.

Mirry was glad of the stout boots and the trousers she had adapted from an old pair of Fred's. She was so thin now, since she lost the baby, they needed to be bunched round the waist with string. She felt like a real country bumpkin.

They giggled their way to the dairy, fighting over the torch, and treading in goodness knows what, only it was soft, squishy and smelly, Mirry thought, moving the scarf up to cover her nose. She skirted the horse warily, and climbed aboard the cart. Laura took the reins as if she was an old hand, and the horse ambled off through the farm gate and turned right towards the village.

By the time they had filled all the receptacles obligingly left outside gates on wormy, wobbly old tables for the scattering of cottages as isolated as their own, the sun was coming up, and the horse was stopping at all the familiar places, and they were tired from hopping on and off and bending over the churns. They were greeted now by folk setting off for work themselves: 'Milk ladies, is it now?'

'Same horse, same milk!' Laura called back cheekily.

They sat at the kitchen table, with their sore feet soaking in bowls of hot water and a dash of mustard, elbows on the table because they were too fatigued to sit up properly, and Boo, in her high chair, chinked her teeth with her spoon and stared wide-eyed at her mother in such funny clothes, while Mirry ate the best meal she'd had in ages. Mum had tactfully improved on Mrs Hardes's offerings since her arrival.

'Not ready to give up then, Mirry?' Mum asked casually.

'No fear!' Mirry said, moving her sore feet cautiously so as not to splash the contents of the bowl on the floor. 'But I don't know what Fred will say when I write to tell him his wife is a milk lady!'

* * *

Bar, despite her increasing girth, was still out and about on her bike. 'Delia says it won't hurt me, as long as I don't try to race uphill,' she told Clive when he demurred.

Sometimes she felt a pang when she thought how well she was keeping and how haggard he looked. She didn't want to remember what the specialist had said, that they must be realistic and not expect much improvement in his condition. Clive's early self-assessment of his injuries was what he wanted to believe. That he would be back to near-normal one day . . .

'Make the most of your long honeymoon here, together, my lover,' Delia said perceptively one bright autumn day, as they cycled over the moors to deliver a bundle of clothes to an elderly couple who had gamely taken on several evacuees. 'You know, Ginger and I feel t'would be best if you both came to us for the birth and lying-in – we've plenty of room, running water and a bathroom. You need to keep newborn babies warm, too, and your old cottage is so draughty. You ask Clive what he thinks. I can keep an unobtrusive eye on him, at the same time, eh?'

They were made welcome at the far-out farmhouse: plied with pasties and dough buns, split and filled with real clotted cream. The evacuees, a young mother and three children under five, from the east end of London, obviously revelled in their new life. 'Putting on weight, reg'lar puddin's we are,' the girl said proudly.

Delia weighed the baby, born since their arrival, after being bombed out, with her spring balance, and expressed her approval. 'Well done my lover! Still feeding well?'

'Longest I've ever managed feeding a baby, myself,' the girl said. 'Must be all the milk missus pours down me! Good grub, here, in't it?'

'Certainly is,' Bar smiled. 'I reckon Delia will have to give me a leg up on my bike.'

The afternoon was already drawing in when they started for home. Bar wasn't really worried, as Delia of course, knew the way, but she hoped Clive wouldn't get in a stew, as he sometimes did, if she was away longer than he expected.

The moors loomed, and suddenly they were aware of voices. Even as Bar thought, surely not Americans – here? Delia dismounted and motioned to Bar to do the same. She whispered: 'We'll walk this stretch, in case we get spotted . . . They can see I'm a harmless village nurse then. Canadians, must be, Bar.'

They didn't speak again, even when they were startled by the sound of rapid gunfire. It was eerie, they couldn't see a soul.

Later, as they climbed wearily up church hill, pushing the bikes once more, Delia said: 'As I once told you, my dear: there are things going on in these parts we don't talk about – not even to our husbands.'

Bar felt a little shiver down her spine. Somehow, she thought, the war had begun to seem to her rather unreal, remote from here. Could you really be safe anywhere?

They moved in to the Rectory three days before Christmas. Welcome parcels had arrived from Mum and Iris – the new baby would be cosy in the flannel nighties and crocheted shawl – and from Mirry, a box full of little clothes worn by Boo, and lovingly put by for the baby she had lost last year. That made Bar sniff and wipe her eyes, and she read the enclosed letter several times:

Dear Bar,

I am thinking of you, and wishing I could be around for your great day, as you were, when Glory and Boo were born. Now the bombing is easing off, Fred hopes to have a longer Christmas break.

Mum suggests I go back with him for a week or so, on my own, and then it wouldn't be so far for us to travel to see you, Clive and the baby. Love to you both, and a very happy Christmas 1941. Don't forget to send that telegram, tell Clive!

Much love again from us all, Mirry

PS Will you buy a present from us, with the enclosed postal order, please? It's nice to have some pin money, I must say, now I'm a working girl again.

'I can't picture Mirry delivering milk – on a horse and cart especially,' she said to Clive. 'And I can't picture us with a baby! Stuff your fingers in your ears, if I yell too hard, won't you?'

The bedroom seemed vast, after the one at the cottage. There was what Bar immediately dubbed a bridal bed big enough for a double wedding, and another smaller bed, 'ready for action'. There was a coal fire, and stone hot water bottles in the beds.

'D'you always have to bounce on beds, Bar?' Clive said in some alarm, as she subsided, laughing, like a beached whale on top of the rumpled covers.

'I believe the baby likes it!' she retorted.

She must have been right, for the baby seemed in no hurry to put in an appearance. Christmas Day came and went, she even waddled to church. The four of them enjoyed a goose dinner courtesy of a grateful parishioner.

Three nights later, she woke sharply and nudged her sleeping husband. 'Clive!' she hissed. 'Fetch Delia – *hurry*!'

She did yell, when the pain was at its height, and Ginger persuaded Clive to come downstairs, to continue the game of chess they had set out in his study, and he poured him a stiff measure of whisky. 'I promised Bar I'd stay with her,' he said helplessly.

'Didn't you hear what she said, old man, "Clive, get out of here!" My late wife was the same – I haven't told anyone this before, but she threatened to hit me, directly the baby was born. Delia knows what she's doing. They call her the wise woman, hereabouts. She'll be fine, she's young and fit. It's you we worry about, you know . . .' He looked with concern at Clive's grey face.

'Maybe we shouldn't have had this baby – a crock for a father . . .'

Ginger cleared his throat: 'Your move, I think, Clive.'

Bar was exhausted. She was past caring now, if she screamed or not. She had been in labour for hours, it must be morning by now, she thought.

'One more push, my lover,' Delia encouraged. 'Don't give up – the baby's coming . . .'

The baby slithered out into her waiting hands, already crying, and Bar gave a big sigh and lay back on the pillows. She felt suddenly dizzy, but elated, even though it wasn't quite all over yet, and the pain was still gripping her fast.

'A little boy, Bar dear – beautiful! Hold on, while I cut the cord and tidy him up – then we'll see to the rest of it, quick as we can, and you can give him a cuddle while I call that husband of yours to see just how clever his wife is . . .'

* * *

Clive fingered the shawl from his son's red face. 'Bar, you were so brave, darling.'

She couldn't disillusion him, she thought wryly. When he bent to kiss her, she told him: 'You've been drinking, Clive!'

'Wetting the baby's head – Ginger insisted,' he smiled sheepishly. The whisky had given him a better colour, dulled that constant pain. 'I do love you both . . . Well, have you finally decided on his name?'

'Robin – Robin Raffery – for Eileen, is that all right?' she asked anxiously.

'Robin Raffery Joy – it has a certain rakish feel to it – a good name for a journalist, Bar.'

'Oh, you've got his future mapped out I see! I bet old Fred will immediately call him Raff.'

'It's snowing outside, you're in the best place,' Delia observed later, deftly removing Robin Raffery's nappy and looking pleased: 'Everything's functioning well – the first dirty nappy of many.' Then, handing the beshawled bundle back to Bar, and tucking them up warmly, she added: 'Treasure him, my lover – I can't have babies of my own but bringing them into the world is the next best thing . . .'

CHAPTER THIRTY-FIVE

'HE LOOKS JUST LIKE YOU, Clive,' Mirry said, more than a week later. Her lips trembled as she lifted Robin from the cradle.

They were still at the rectory, but Bar had soon insisted on coming downstairs: 'I'm lonely up there in the bridal-cum-maternity suite.'

'I'm glad of that!' Clive joked, but the sisters exchanged anxious glances. He looked so frail, not the vigorous twenty-five year old he would have been if he hadn't gone to war.

'Quite a journey we had,' Mirry said quickly. 'But the snow must have been worse here. More still to come, I suspect. Time for me to go home. Still, we were determined to see you at the start of 1942. D'you realise we've been apart for more than a year now, Bar? We didn't see you at all in '41.'

'You'll stay overnight, of course,' Delia said, bringing in a tray of tea things.

'Are you sure?' Fred asked. 'We could put up at the pub – we need to make an early start for Surrey.'

'We insist,' Ginger said, handing round the biscuits.

'Don't I get a turn with young Raff?' Fred asked, and then wondered why everyone laughed.

Mirry thought, watching as he held the tiny baby against his shoulder: our little boy would be just about toddling by now, that's if he was as forward as his sisters. But I'm glad Bar and Clive have a son – even though I can't help wishing he was ours . . . Mum was right, this time on our own, just Fred and me, has been good; making love again wasn't easy; I was so afraid, but Fred was patient, so understanding, and given time . . . He's right, we've got two wonderful daughters, we're more blessed than some.

She said aloud: 'Number Five is all patched up, Bar. I'm trying to persuade Fred to let us go back there in the spring. Things are getting back to normal, the raids are few and far between; the Jerries are too busy in Russia they say; the schools are re-opening and people are returning home. Laura thinks it's a good idea too. Don's coming up to scholarship age, you see. I might get a bit of opposition from Glory, I suppose: she really loves country life now.'

'What about Mum?' Bar asked.

'Oh, Mum and Hilda have agreed that if we do go back to Kitchener Avenue, they'll get a flat together – near enough to call on in an emergency, they say. They've got used to sharing a kitchen, it seems. Like Laura and me, they miss the bright lights.'

'No bright lights yet, old girl,' Fred put in.

'No, but there's the Pictures – I miss them! And Anna wrote that she has re-opened the dancing school because quite a few of the girls from that factory off the High Street were knocking eagerly on her door. They don't mind dancing together. People are going out and about in the evenings again, she says. And the warden, Ted, who had been helpful with the major, she said, had somehow acquired quite a few modern records for her, so things are looking up.'

'Please excuse me,' Clive said suddenly, 'if I go off for a bit of a rest, I'll come back later, of course.'

'I'll help you up the stairs,' Delia offered.

When he had gone, Fred said, concerned: 'Has he seen the doctor lately, Bar? He looks really groggy.'

Bar didn't answer. She got gingerly to her feet, for despite her insistence otherwise, she was still wobbly on her legs, and followed her husband and her friend out of the room.

The baby hiccuped, brought up some milk on Fred's jacket.

'Here, give him to me,' Mirry ordered. 'And pass me that muslin piece to mop him up.' I'm glad he looks like Clive, she thought, not like one of my babies – it makes it easier for me to love him for himself. She wiped the milk away and gave him a tender little kiss.

Clive was already stretched out on the bed, when Bar came slowly into the room. Delia looked up and gave her a little warning wave to stay where she was. She was unbuttoning his shirt, the wasitband of his trousers. There was a moment's silence, then she said: 'Fetch some towels from the airing cupboard, Bar – he's passing blood . . . why did the poor chap keep quiet about it? He must have been worried sick. And call Ginger, he'll have to go immediately for the doctor.'

* * *

'I wish we didn't have to go, leave you at such a time,' Mirry lamented next morning.

'The family will be expecting you and, Mirry, please don't tell them Clive's not too well, will you?' Not too well, she thought, still feeling dazed by the enormity of it all: renal failure the doctor said. They might still rush him off to hospital . . . or . . . 'She pressed her shaking hands to her breast.'

Mirry clutched her close, misinterpreting this gesture. 'Bar darling, you must take care of yourself. I know how my milk went, when everything went haywire right at the start of the war.'

'Robin's feeding well, Mirry, honestly. Delia will look after us. We'll stay on here until Clive's better.'

'Can I just look in to say cheerio?'

'Better not, I'll give him your love and best wishes. He's asleep.' She fervently hoped this was right, that he was not unconscious. His face now had a bluish tinge, and when she'd touched his hand it had been icy cold. I wish they'd go, she thought, it'll be a relief – I can't concentrate on anything except Clive . . .

Fred had poured boiling water in the radiator. The car was ticking over. He came in, followed by Ginger, who had helped with the cranking. 'Well, old girl, ready to go?' he asked Mirry. Then it was his turn to hug Bar. 'Take care of yourselves . . . Where's our Raff?'

'Wide to the world . . .' she said.

She cuddled the baby to her in the big bed. When Bar insisted she wouldn't leave his side, Delia told her to rest. Clive lay in the bed where Bar had given birth, moved nearer the bridal bed at her request. Delia sat beside them, watching quietly.

The doctor called twice, then talked to Delia outside the door. When she returned, Bar wanted to say, but couldn't: 'Tell me! I've a right to know. Is Clive going to die?'

In the early hours of the next day, she, Delia and Ginger kept vigil. The rector prayed continuously, Bar knelt beside him, and he put a comforting arm around her sagging shoulders.

'You should try to get some sleep,' Delia said, looking weary and pale herself.

Bar shook her head. 'No, I can't.' Despite herself, she felt her eyes close, and she laid her head on the bed, still stubbornly kneeling.

'He's gone, Bar, my lover.' Delia's voice seemed to come from far away. She helped her friend to her feet, guided her back to the other bed, gently persuaded her to lie down, and put the baby in her unresisting arms.

The baby stirred, seeking his own comfort. Bar put him to the breast, and lay there, dry-eyed, not saying anything at all.

* * *

'Come back with us, Bar,' Iris said after the funeral. She had been very brave, and her husband was very supportive. Bar was glad Iris had someone like Harold to care for her. She deserved it, after all those years of selflessness.

'I can't go anywhere, yet, Iris. It – hasn't really sunk in, you see – that he's not here . . . I will go back to the cottage, when I feel I can – Delia and the rector have been wonderful to us, but . . .' It wouldn't seem like home to her without Clive, she knew that. Nothing there really belonged to her, apart from a few personal belongings – even the cradle was borrowed. She could just walk away from her honeymoon home with a couple of cases and her baby. Clive had left her that one precious thing. No money, apart from his savings in the post office – just five fat notebooks, only three of them written in – a fragment of a book.

One day in April, she opened these notebooks at last. It wasn't what she expected, a story of a young man going to war, but a love story – their story.

Bar wheeled the old-fashioned pram, which had been used by the rector's children more than twenty years ago, down the hill to the shop. She went straight to the post office counter. 'I'd like to send a telegram please – to Mrs Miriam Hope.'

She was going home, with Robin Raffery, as Mirry and Fred had urged, to Number Five.

Delia and Ginger drove her to Plymouth to catch the train.

'I don't know how to thank you for all you've done for us,' she said. 'And I'm grateful that you will care for Clive's grave.'

'You'll come back to see us, won't you?' Delia appealed.

Even as she said yes, she felt she wouldn't return. There would just be the memories of that wonderful year together. *But that part of her life was over.*

PART THREE

1943–47

CHAPTER THIRTY-SIX

MIRRY REJOICED WHEN THE United States entered the war on their side. She didn't want to dwell on the outrage of Pearl Harbor, or the Japanese conquests in South-East Asia. The thrilling Battle of El Alamein over ten days – late October into November with the general they called Monty commanding the Eighth Army, our Desert Rats, against the German General Rommel – captured the public imagination. The Suez Canal was safe. On 8 November, the British and American forces routed the German army in Algeria and Morocco, and that same month the Russians began their counter attack to drive the enemy from their soil. Now, in 1943, the Allies were back in Europe at last, after the landings in Sicily. Italy surrendered unconditionally, but almost immediately was invaded by Germany. The war was by no means over yet . . .

This September was a turning point, too, for the family at Number Five. Glory went off to the grammar school, new leather satchel bumping on her back, wearing her uniform proudly, courtesy of the generous donation of clothing coupons by her parents, her grandmother and her aunt. Fred was at last coming home – not to Whitehall, but to a safer location which would mean taking a bus after the train, a more lengthy journey than the prewar one. The little car had finally conked out, as he put it. And Bar decided it was time to look for a job.

'The three of us,' Fred said, putting his knife and fork together after his welcome-home meal. Meat pie, with suspiciously red meat, which Mirry had queued patiently for in Croydon at what used to be called The Cats' Meat Shop. 'You, Bar and me, Mirry – and the kids, of course – just like it used to be . . .'

Mirry flashed him a warning glance. Bar was always so determinedly cheerful, you tended to forget why she was here.

'You'll need to get early nights, Fred,' she reminded him, 'with having to rise at six.'

'Back in the old routine, eh, with a nice cup of tea in bed every morning for you ladies?'

'And for *me*!' Glory was diligently doing her homework at the table after clearing it, which was considered to be her job. Inspired by the story of Archimedes in class today, she decided to illustrate her essay on the subject. Ingenuously, she had drawn a bony figure in a hip bath, hair standing on end like a mad scientist, with water splashing overboard, and a cartoon bubble declaiming: 'Eureka! I haf found it!'

Unfortunately, she did not show her mother, who would have advised her to erase it: double quick.

Then Bar sprang her bombshell. 'If Mirry agrees, of course, because it would mean her looking after Robin, I think it's high time *I* contributed more for our keep: I'm going for an interview for a job tomorrow . . .'

'Bar, you *know* I wouldn't mind having Robin – he and Boo are a real pair anyway, aren't they, but . . .'

'You think I should stay at home and look after him myself. What about the time you were a milk lady, Mirry?' Bar appealed.

Fred couldn't say what he really thought: women wanted to work nowadays. They'd got a taste for it he supposed. Not the sort of work their mothers' generation had been forced to undertake, when times were hard, but jobs that went some way towards proving the equality of the sexes.

'What do you have in mind, Bar?' he asked.

'Ah, that'd be telling . . . I don't want to tempt fate. I'll tell you all about it, if I get offered the job.' She rose. 'I'd better go and make sure my little lad's not playing around in his cot and keeping Boo awake. Then I'll have my bath.' She'd stay upstairs, to give Mirry and Fred time together. They didn't use the front room at all, unless there was an alert, because the large indoor shelter took up most of the space. Fred had insisted on that before Mirry set up home there again.

'Finished your homework, Glory? Then off you go. You can read for half an hour, no more,' Mirry told her elder daughter.

'Come and sit on my knee, we'll listen to the wireless, it's ITMA tonight,' Fred suggested, when Glory had departed. He hadn't forgotten how to wink.

'Oh, Fred!' Mirry said fondly, thinking: ITMA – It's That Man Again – and here *he* is, about to whisper sweet nothings in my ear . . .

Lady Makepeace's School for Girls had been built in the late '20s. It was a spacious, light and well-equipped school, with an attached flat for girls to learn how to keep house, a library, splendid cloakrooms, a gymnasium and a great assembly hall with an impressive stage. Outside, the playing fields were being encroached upon for Dig For Victory and a substantial shelter had been built on the net ball court.

The only drawback from the girls' point of view was that the school was situated in a not-too-salubrious area of Norwood. They had to run the gamut of nasty little boys running and jumping and trying to dislodge their pudding-basin velour hats. Any girl caught without her hat by the teachers was instantly reprimanded severely. Glory did literally sprint the last hundred yards to the safety of the school gates – but, if you were caught doing that you were in line for – well, lines, as she soon discovered.

Miss Tiptree was all aquiver with indignation this morning. 'Disgraceful, Gloria Hope!' she fumed, waving her homework book at the class.

Glory looked up in surprise. She had been studying Miss Tiptree's stout legs, encased in thick lisle stockings, set wide apart under the table, for the girl in the desk behind had prodded her in the back and whispered: 'Hey, look, you can see her bloomers.'

'Yes, you, Miss Hope! How dare you deface your book with – such rudery – don't you know there's a shortage of paper? You will stay in at break-time and rub this . . . this . . . out, then you will write fifty times, "I must not draw in my books." Is that clear?'

'Yes, Miss Tiptree,' Glory bit her lip. She was learning the rules fast. But she wanted to add: 'Why was it rude? I thought it was funny. And isn't writing lines a waste of paper, too?'

She couldn't know that, earlier, in the smoky haze of the staff room, the teachers, including Miss Tiptree, had found her drawing very funny indeed. 'This is a girl with imagination,' Miss Tiptree declared, taking a last drag of her cigarette, to give her strength, before going off to take her class.

Bar wore a neat pinafore dress with a white blouse, her last pair of unladdered stockings and the shoes she had worn to her wedding. She sat in another fuggy room, taking shorthand verbatim and then typing it up on a machine which neatly holed the letter and gummed up the works with what looked like confetti. She was aware that she was being closely watched by the two men who had interviewed her – grizzled types, with shirt sleeves pushed up with elastic armbands, lounging back in their chairs with socked feet on their desks. How had Clive stood the mingled odours in this dark, cramped office, she wondered, of sweaty feet and strong tobacco?

'Yes, I can ride a bike,' she said demurely, when she was suddenly asked this question. Of course, Clive had been out and about most of the time, in his quest for news.

The younger of the two men swung his feet to the floor, stretched out a hand. 'Welcome to *The Norwood News*, Barbara. You'll soon learn the ropes and we're desperate for a junior reporter.'

'Thanks. Tom, I won't let you down.'

'I know you won't. And, we're not taking you on just because we thought so much of young Clive. You've got the will to succeed, just as he had.'

'He'd be proud of you,' the chief reporter said, and he began rattling away on his typewriter, as he had been when she arrived. He was a man of few words. He'd started with the paper at fourteen and stayed with it for fifty years.

'When can you start?' the editor asked, packing the bowl of his pipe.

'Soon as you like. But not today. I've got to break the news to my sister, first.'

'Make it officially the day after tomorrow, eh – but bring that little boy of yours along to see us before that – like Clive, is he?'

'He's Clive all over again.' Bar said proudly.

'It won't be too much for you, will it?' Fred asked, after lights out that night. 'It'll all be down to you, Mirry, the cooking, the housework, the shopping, the children – young Raff still in nappies . . .'

'He's an easy child, Fred. Adventurous, I have to keep my eye on him, but no more than Boo was at that age.'

'It won't be long before she's at school. Think about it, you'll still be tied with a little one, Mirry, not much time for yourself.'

'If our little boy had lived, well, it would have been the same.' It still hurt Mirry to talk about her loss. 'I love little Robin, Fred, he's like my own. It's Bar I worry about. She'll be losing out, not being with him all the time. I don't think she's fully realised that.'

'You do what you think is best,' he told her, cuddling her close. It was so good to be home again.

* * *

Bar could hear the murmur of their voices through the wall. She knew she should put Robin back in his cot once he fell asleep but she loved having him close: the warmth he radiated, with his head on the pillow where Clive's should have been.

He was her responsibility, but as Clive had understood, she needed her freedom too. Mirry was so good with Robin, he was obviously contented and integrated in the family – the girls were like older sisters. He needed that, as an only child, but she thought: it's different now Fred is back. It would be all too easy to revert to the role of young Bar, we three, as Fred had said . . .

CHAPTER THIRTY-SEVEN

LAHANA DANCE CLUB. OPEN EVERY NIGHT. ALL WELCOME so proclaimed the new sign.

'Any evening any day . . . You'll find 'em all, doin' the Lambeth walk – Oi!' the dancers within sang shrilly, faces flushed, feet stamping, bouncy curls newly released from the Saturday torture – steel curlers concealed by natty turbans. Then, as if by magic, they switched to the current favourite song: 'You'll never know just how I much I love you – you'll never know just how much I care . . .'

It didn't matter that the only man around was Ted the warden, and he had to listen out for the siren call to duty. The sedate waltzes, the smoochy foxtrots were still popular – the quickstep even more so, but Anna was moving with the times: a nubile young girl called Joyce, who had been out with a Yank or two, was only too pleased to demonstrate the jitterbug and the jive and her nylons were the envy of all the girls.

The symbolic cutting of her hair, the fashionable clothes, the greatly enhanced income due to the craze for dancing: the new Anna was enjoying life, particularly now her friends over the road had returned. Glory was tapping away as merrily as ever: long legged now with the suspicion of a bust, at the Saturday morning sessions. And the two little ones, Boo and Robin, always a couple of steps behind, had great fun trying to copy her flying feet as Mirry played the latest sheet music with equally nimble fingers.

Bar wore a tin hat as she cycled along, with her gas mask hanging in its brown cardboard box over her shoulder. Her notebook and pencil were in one pocket of her mac, a comb, powder compact and lipstick in the other. So equipped, she was ready for any assignment the editor might throw at her. The London dailies had all the war news from overseas: their small paper still concentrated on the lives and fortunes of the local community. It was all scaled-down, Bar thought, but there were still inspiring stories of courage. There was plenty of humour, sadness; a touch of exposure (occasionally indecent), outrage – a reflection of how life was carrying on at home, coping with minor crises.

On Tuesday, the chief stated laconically: 'That's it. I've had enough. I'm fed up with being Uncle Charlie for the kids. I took that on when I was still a spotty youth myself when Uncle Desmond retired. I can't relate to the little sods any more. You take the Children's Corner over, Bar. And good luck to you!' He rolled another sheet of paper in his typewriter, didn't bother to adjust it, and hammered out: *UNCLE CHARLIE SAYS GOODBYE AFTER FORTY-FIVE YEARS* and *GOOD LUCK TO AUNTIE JOY*. 'There you are, Bar, I've even chosen a pseudonym for you.'

'Talk about being thrown in at the deep end,' Bar murmured, grinning.

'You can do it – Clive declined,' Tom, the editor, said in passing.

'I bet he did,' Bar returned smartly. It was good that Clive was often mentioned casually in this way. It might sound trite, she thought, but he really did seem to be with her, in spirit.

'But before you get down to composing the topical rhyme of the week – that's obligatory, by the way – get on your bike, and follow this up. Darts champion, Mrs Peggy Wiles, with unerring aim, stops sneak thief in his tracks . . .' Tom called out from his cubbyhole of an office. The door was always open.

'Sounds painful,' Bar said, taking her bicycle clips out of the biscuit tin, which only contained crumbs, 'like *my* bottom after a day in the saddle.'

There was a nice tea waiting for her when she got home around five. 'Surprising what you can do with one egg, and some powdered milk whipped up to a froth,' Mirry said, passing over a plate with a golden pancake nestling on it. No lemon, of course, but a dash of the baby's concentrated orange juice, courtesy of the USA. She made lovely light cakes too, with glycerine in them – you could no longer get liquid paraffin from the chemist for the same purpose – this was now strictly under the counter for those who needed it for legitimate reasons.

Glory wolfed her pancake down. 'Any more?' she asked hopefully.

'Sorry,' Mirry told her. 'Fish paste sandwich?'

'I suppose so – thanks. Eating this the wrong way round, Mum, but – who cares? School dinners are awful – you ought to write about them in the paper, Bar.'

'No she shouldn't! You should be grateful for them, Glory – I'm relieved to know you get a good, hot dinner every day, it certainly helps with rations.'

'It's not worth threepence . . . Ugh! Miss Tiptree was on dinner duty today and she caught Jean and me putting our gristle on the ledge under the table. We didn't get a chance to bury it out in the allotments as usual. Jean went and told her that's what we do, and she said, "Right, report to me at break, and I'll show you where to dig, if you're so keen on gardening."'

Bar mused to herself, I will write it up one day, Clive would have enjoyed that. I did the right thing, leaving Mirry in charge here. Mirry enjoys the challenge of making something from almost nothing – I'd just find it frustrating.

Her sister was tactful in other ways. Boo and Robin had to share a bath of course, because you had to be careful with water, but this enjoyable task was left to Bar. This evening, she soaped them both, rinsed them well to squeals of laughter, allowed them to 'swim' with her hand supporting their supple little backs. She lifted Boo out first, while Robin seized the chance to splash and suck the flannel, and gave Boo's curls a brisk rub with the towel, before enveloping her in it. Then she called 'ooh-hoo!' just as her land-ladies had done oh, moons ago, she thought, to Glory to collect her little sister, to be dried and pyjama'd by the fire.

Bar sat her little wriggling son on her lap, and cocooned him in his towel, while she let the water out of the bath, and she tweaked his hair, straight and floppy like Clive's had been, into a coxcomb, and hugged him close and wiped away the tears on her rolled sleeve . . .

'Is Bar crying?' a muffled voice asked curiously.

That set her off again: Robin was calling her Bar now, copying Boo – how long would it be, before he called Mirry, Mummy?

Fred ate his supper by himself, officially that is. The little ones hovered hopefully by his chair, waiting for titbits, while Pip concealed himself under the table to catch what they dropped. Glory sat at the other end of the table, sighing over her maths homework. 'You'll have to help me, Dad, hurry up . . .'

Dad, Bar thought, having a cup of tea before taking Robin up to bed. Glory's growing up. I suppose the other girls at school call their parents Mum and Dad, not

Mummy and Daddy. She must conform, I know I did. But like me, Robin's not even going to begin by calling his father Daddy. I can't remember my father, and it will be the same for him . . .

'Penny for them,' Mirry said softly. She really looked like a mum these days, rounder and contented, she even twisted a turban round her head when she went out to join the endless queues at the shops.

'Oh, nothing really. Was there any post today – I'm expecting a letter from Iris.'

'Yes, sorry! From Chester, though – Captain Snowball, I wonder?'

'More likely Coral . . .' Bar reached the letter down from the mantelpiece, behind the clock.

But the first letter *was* from the captain, inquiring after their health and welfare, and there was an enclosure. This letter took Bar completely by surprise. She opened it and read it in silence. It was from Peter, Eileen's boyfriend.

Dear Bar,

I imagine you will think, Peter Who? I must apologise for taking so long to respond to the very kind letter you wrote after Eileen's death. I did appreciate this. We were about to get engaged when it happened. It has taken me a long time to come to terms with her loss. She was a wonderful girl, and, I know a great friend to you.

I have only just heard about your own bereavement from Coral, but she did not give me your address. (She said she might be moving shortly, so I will send this c/o your captain.)

You have my deepest sympathy. Coral tells me you have a little son – I know how much this must mean to you.

Remember the episode of the bacon? And she-who-was-in-charge? Eileen and you were such sports. I fell for her then, but, of course, I couldn't say, as she had another sweetheart.

I have a spot of leave coming up shortly. Would you mind if I came to see you for old time's sake? If yes, please advise your address. Letters mean so much when you are away from home, as you know.

But I shall understand if you would rather not keep in contact.

God bless,

Peter Howe

Bar folded the letter, looked at Mirry's inquiring face. 'Yes, it was from Captain Snowball . . .' she confirmed. She couldn't for the life of her think why she was being secretive.

CHAPTER THIRTY-EIGHT

MIRRY AND LAURA WERE AT The Palace, elbows in because the cinema was packed, there was even a queue standing in the aisle, waiting for seats to be vacated. No sitting round to the end of the main film again as used to be general practice prewar, as the eagle eye of the elderly usherette was on you, Mirry thought.

Laura had a few hours off to relax between shifts: she was doing her bit for Britain these days, as a quality control inspector in the local factory. Don and Junie attended different schools from Glory, but Laura had been magnanimous about Glory being the only one of the three to pass the scholarship. The children's friendship had waned now they saw little of each other, but Mirry and Laura were almost back on the old footing and, of course, the easy relationship between Fred and Jim had never faltered.

The black and white film had been starkly realistic: the crew in the lifeboat clinging desperately to life and hope on the angry swell of the Atlantic, the blazing guns, the flaming oil, the lurking U-boat menace, had gripped their imagination, tightened their insides with apprehension. You couldn't say it was enjoyable, more an extension of the Pathe News, Mirry mused; she had preferred the B film, a gentle story of a girl trying to decide between her sailor boyfriend and a GI on embarkation leave, with lots of nostalgic tunes. When the credits rolled for the main film, there was spontaneous clapping for survival against the odds. Produced by Bernard Gray, Mirry read, still in a dream. Then she jerked, knocked Laura's arm. 'Oh, *sorry*! But we ought to go, the usherette is waving her torch in our direction . . .' She wasn't sure whether Laura had noticed Mr Gray's name or not. It had been three years since they parted, after all. Unbelievably, she thought, it was now another new year, 1944.

'Let me just finish this cigarette,' Laura said. 'At two and four for twenty I can't afford to stub 'em out half way.' She sounded perfectly normal, to Mirry's relief.

Outside, in the January chill, they turned their coat collars up and linked arms, shivering. 'Let's have a cuppa at the teashop,' Laura suggested. 'A few more minutes on our own before we collect the little ones from our mums, eh?'

'The children will be back from school in an hour . . .' Mirry worried.

'Glory's got a key, hasn't she? My two have, of course, because they usually have to come in and get their own tea.

She's getting on for twelve, after all, Mirry – oh *come on*!'
They crossed the road to the shop which, like the cinema,
was crowded. Folk seemed to prefer to be part of a group
nowadays.

'Just ten minutes then,' Mirry said firmly. 'I'm always
home for Glory, you see . . .'

The buns were stale, currantless, unsweet: not a patch
on Mirry's homemade cake. The tea was weak, but at least
it was hot. It was elbows in again, as they wedged themselves at the back of a little table.

'I know why you tried to hurry me out of The Palace.'
Laura fished a tea leaf out with her thumb and deposited it
on her saucer. 'Proof that there was actually some tea in the
pot, I suppose. It gave me a strange feeling, Mirry, to see his
name at the end of the film. I didn't tell you, because I knew
what you'd say, but he wrote to me a few months back. Of
course, I kept it from Jim. You'd have thought there never
had been anything serious between us, it really was just a
friendly letter. He said he'd never found a secretary half
as good as me since I left his employ. He even mentioned
Glory – said he expected to see her name in lights one
day – that he would be delighted to write a warm recom-
mendation if, later, she decided to go to drama school – just
contact him, he said.'

Mirry was thrilled and flattered at this, but she knew
instantly what her advice must be. 'You didn't write back,

did you, Laura?' Laura shook her head. 'Then you mustn't! You'll only regret it, if you do . . .'

But as they walked home, she kept thinking, one day, my daughter will be a star – I just *know* it!

Mirry was flustered when she saw Glory waiting at the gate, well, hanging on it and swinging, which would do it no good at all. Still, they were lucky to have a gate; being wooden it had escaped the fate of iron gates and railings, given up to boost munitions, or so it was said.

'Where've you been, Mum? I've been waiting *ages* – can't I have a key?' Glory asked, but she didn't sound resentful, only full of barely suppressed excitement. She ushered the little ones inside and divested them of coats and hats, exchanged their shoes for slippers. 'There! Grandma used to make *me* toe-beaters like yours, but guess she thinks my feet are too big, now, eh? Any biscuits, Mum? I'm starving!'

'You always are,' Mirry returned. 'No biscuits until tomorrow I'm afraid – but I made some honeycomb with golden syrup – just hope I haven't overdone the bicarb, it doesn't taste nearly as nice then.' She indicated the plate on the kitchen table.

Glory and the little ones soon had their mouths full. 'Delicious!' Glory managed, eyes rolling upwards blissfully. 'Sticky, but full of holes, like real honeycomb . . .'

'Just a toffee mixture, until you stir in that magic spoon-ful of old bicarb . . .' Mirry smiled to see them enjoying her sweet-making efforts. 'Save some for Bar and Dad,' she added.

Glory was so good with Boo and Robin, Mirry thought. She removed her coat, but kept on her hat. She'd have to go outside to the shed to get more coal to ginger up the fire. Then she must start on the tea. 'Get changed into your siren suit,' she reminded Glory, 'and sponge that honey-comb dribble off your school cardigan – two more days to wear that, remember.' Mirry was very proud of the siren suits *au* Winston Churchill, which she'd made the chil-dren from a nice length of maroon fleece, dressing gown material, she guessed, that Anna had donated. Long, baggy trousers were so much more practical for both boys and girls, she thought. You could sleep in them, if you had to. Mind you, Fred had said he hoped she wasn't going to make a suit for herself – he saw little enough of shapely legs nowadays – look at Bar, biking all round town, cycle clips and all.

Glory couldn't contain herself any longer. 'I'll *bust* if I don't tell you – I was going to wait until Bar and Dad were here, but I can't! Miss Fitzbarn, you know, the new history teacher, the one we call Miss Fizzbang, is starting up a drama club after lunch on Tuesdays and Thursdays. It's supposed to be for girls in the third form upwards, but anyone very keen, in the first and second years, can audition – so I am! Tomorrow!'

'Lucky you sponged your woolly then,' Mirry said, knowing it was a funny thing to say, but she just couldn't express her excitement as she would like. This was something to tell Laura, eh? Maybe she would be writing to Bernard Gray in a few years' time on Glory's behalf . . .

There was another letter for Bar, and it was Fred who asked curiously, as he cut hopefully into his corned beef pasty: 'From one of your old army friends, Bar?'

She folded the letter, slotted it back into the envelope. 'Sort of . . . Remember Eileen? Peter Howe – he got his commission, he's a lieutenant now, about my age, I think – they were going to get married, when . . . Well, he'd like to come and see me, this Saturday evening, take me out for a meal or a drink, he says, but . . .' She looked over at Robin, playing on the hearth-rug with a row of paper dollies cut out by Glory to amuse him.

'We'll look after Robin, it'll do you good to go out,' Mirry offered at once.

'It hardly seems fair, Mirry, you care for him every day except Sunday, as it is.'

'Or your friend can, of course, spend the evening here with us. He'd be most welcome,' Fred said.

Bar bit her lip: 'Well . . .' she began awkwardly.

Glory butted in, as usual. 'I expect he wants to see Bar on her own, Dad, not to have these two jumping all over him, and asking for the potty while he's eating. It's a date, isn't it Bar? How exciting! What does he look like?' she demanded.

'He looked very young, wet behind the ears, as they say, when I last saw him – just as I did, because we met at the training camp. The only date about it, Glory, will be the one on the calendar . . . We'll be reminiscing, I expect, that's all,' Bar told them all firmly. She wasn't even sure she wanted to revive memories of that time, but she did know that she would rather talk to Peter on her own, than have the family listening in.

'This is Robin,' Bar said, feeling absurdly shy when, not long after finishing work on Saturday afternoon, she answered the knock on the door, still wearing her slacks and jersey with her hair tied back, and her young son in her arms.

His face was familiar, but this confident young officer was very different from the Peter Howe who had been shocked at the strong language used by Medusa, and who had so diffidently offered her that greasy packet of bacon. 'I hope I'm not too early – but I also hope you're going to ask me in. Hello, Robin, I'm Peter,' he said. He took off his cap, and Bar saw that he still had that thick thatch of blond hair, the darker eyebrows over amused blue eyes.

Robin, who often stuck his thumb in his mouth when confronted by strangers, indicated that he wanted to be put down, and offered his hand to Peter. 'Come and see!' he exhorted. 'Come and see! Train set going!'

Glory had obligingly arranged the rails of the clock-work train set which Bar had bought Robin second-hand for Christmas, because toys were in short supply, of course, just where the unsuspecting visitor might trip over it, in the dining room. Peter skirted this hazard without blinking, and Bar hurriedly introduced him to her family before excusing herself to get changed for the evening out.

She ran the obligatory five inches of water in the bath, level with the mark Fred had painted, hurriedly stripped and plunged in, soaped and rinsed herself, then out: no bath salts, but soda crystals to soften the water, so she recklessly added a dash of eau de cologne.

She pulled the drawer out in her haste, had to jiggle it back on the runners of the chest, removed the tissue-wrapped bundle which had been at the back. The famous silk underwear, she thought ruefully, worn less than half a dozen times since her wedding day . . . Dear Mirry! She had laid her best stockings out on the bed for her to wear. What made them both feel this was a special occasion? What a pity she had only one decent outfit these days: the dusky pink woollen pinafore dress slipped over the one, two, three, slip one, of the mock Fair Isle jumper Mum had made for her for Christmas from odd lengths of pastel baby wool. The ribbed cuffs and collar were, by happy chance, almost the same pink as the pinafore. She combed her hair briskly, looking solemnly at her reflection in the mirror. It was way past her shoulders just as Clive had loved it, but usually, of course, she tied it back severely or put it up – flowing locks were frowned upon nowadays, she thought ruefully. She powdered her nose, dipped a finger in the baby's Vaseline, and anointed her eyebrows and eyelashes. The last touch was Tangee lipstick, a mere stub, but that went with anything . . . She'd been over half an hour despite her haste.

He was on his knees, winding up the engine for Robin and Boo, when she opened the door. He looked up, smiling at her, and she could tell that he approved of the change in her appearance. It was absurd, she felt a little breathless, almost, she realised, as if she was going out with a young man for the first time . . .

'Pretty Bar!' Robin approved, too. She gathered him up in her arms again and hugged him tight.

'You've made a big splodge of lipstick on his face,' Glory told her cheerfully.

'Kiss me!' Boo shouted in glee. 'I want lipstick!' So Bar obliged.

'You won't be too late, will you?' Fred said, as they went out; he ignored the irate pinch from Mirry. 'The roads might be icy later tonight.'

Peter had come by car. They drove to the West End. The shows were all booked: London was busier than ever despite the still-present threat of bombs. Not everyone slept down the tube shelters now, though – confidence was growing.

'I'm staying at a hotel – we could have dinner there, maybe dance a while,' he suggested.

'That would be nice,' she said, 'but I'm not really dressed for dancing, Peter.'

'It's all very informal nowadays,' he assured her, 'and don't get *too* excited about what we might be served for dinner, will you?'

'Don't you go to your parents' house?' she asked, remembering that he had come from north London.

'My father is in the army, too. My mother is in Wales with my sister and her family. I usually go there, but I wanted to see you, Bar.'

'Oh . . .' She felt the pressure, the warmth of his hand on her back as he ushered her into the hotel foyer.

It was not one of the plusher hotels, Bar was relieved to see. They sat at a table for two and suddenly it was easier to talk, especially of those they had lost.

The soup was delicious. And there were savoury ducks to follow, sort of rissoles. The unaccustomed wine went straight to Bar's head.

'Eileen wrote to me, you know – she said, "Ack ack! Love at second sight." She made Robin some bootees, but she wasn't the world's best knitter, bless her.'

'I loved her very much. She was such a cheerful little soul,' he said softly. 'But, I've been thinking, you see, that life has got to go on, you've got to stop grieving some time, Eileen would be the first to tell me that . . .'

'I'm sad for you, that you didn't have as long together as Clive and I did – we knew each other since we were children, really: I wish I hadn't kept him waiting before we married, but even then, we were *so* young, Peter – I was twenty-one and he was twenty-three. It was good we had that last year together in Devon, despite him being so ill.'

'Are you over it now?'

'Do you *ever* get over losing someone you love so much?'

'I know I'll always miss Eileen, as you do, your Clive.' He looked at her for some time. Then he said lightly: 'You've smudged your lipstick, Bar . . .'

'It's a tango,' she said uncertainly, when he asked her to dance.

'Oh, Eileen taught me – I might surprise you with my expertise!' he joked.

'And *I* taught Eileen!' she said, rising from her seat. Seductive music she thought, and the first time a man had held her so close for more than two years . . .

It was almost midnight when they drew up outside the blacked-out houses of Kitchener Avenue. Bar felt in no hurry to get out of the car.

'Would you mind,' he asked, and there was something of the diffident young man he had been when they last met, 'if I gave you a chaste kiss goodnight?'

Ack ack! she seemed to hear Eileen chuckle. Impulsively, she felt for his face in the dark, slipped her arms round his neck. 'Just a brotherly peck,' she agreed. 'Because I had such a lovely evening, Peter . . .'

It was an unexpectedly long and satisfying kiss. She felt warm and good about it. They were mates, she thought, as Eileen always said the two of *them* were.

'I'm glad we've met up again,' she said at last, as they moved apart.

'I can see you tomorrow, can't I?' he asked. 'I only have three days, Bar.'

'Yes, come round tomorrow,' she told him. 'Come for the day as it's Sunday.'

'Where have you been?' Fred asked wrathfully. 'And what were you doing outside all that time in the car?' He had confronted her in the hall.

'You're not my keeper, Fred,' Bar said furiously, for he had dispelled the magic, the warmth of it all. 'I'm going up to bed – *good night*!'

CHAPTER THIRTY-NINE

MIRRY EASED HERSELF CAUTIOUSLY out of bed, shifted the eiderdown to cover Fred's back; groped for the torch on the bedside table. Whatever time was it, she wondered? The stealthy footsteps going downstairs had alerted her. She pulled the bedroom door to, began her own cautious descent.

Bar was in the kitchen, waiting for the kettle to boil. When she turned in surprise, shining her own torch at Mirry, it was obvious from her reddened eyes that she had been crying.

Mirry put her torch down on the draining board, then, her arms round her sister. 'Bar darling – that wretched husband of mine – how *could* he be so sharp! Robin was no trouble, he never is: I was happy to think you were having a nice night out ... Trouble with Fred is, he doesn't remember you're all grown up.'

'Kettle's singing,' Bar sniffed, but she hugged Mirry back, before she went to rinse the teapot.

Mirry watched her, perching on the wooden stool, as she made the tea. 'Did you have a good time?' she asked. They were keeping their voices low. Neither of them wanted Fred to come downstairs to see what was what.

'Yes, I did. And don't tell Fred, Mirry, but – we actually kissed goodnight! Nothing more than that . . . He's coming over here today, I said he was welcome, but, now I'm not sure he is.'

'I'll talk to Fred,' Mirry said firmly. 'I would have jawed him last night, but I didn't want to wake the children. It – it hasn't been all plain sailing, you know, Bar, since Fred came home . . . I'd got used to looking after the children on my own, making up my own mind about things you see – I don't . . .'

'Defer to him, like you used to?'

'I suppose that's it. But I have to remember it's been difficult for him to adjust too.'

'I'm afraid I've complicated things, haven't I, coming here with Robin?'

'Oh, Bar – *no*! It's the opposite, really; Fred believes that we are all back where we were. You, the little sister he's always been so fond of – he seems to have put it out of his mind that you were married, just like us. Peter, suddenly appearing, has made him think you could leave us again, just when he thinks we're all getting back to normal – pour one out for Fred, too, there's a dear – I'll take it up to him, we really shouldn't be lingering down here – I'm shivering in my slippers.'

'Nice cup of tea, Fred,' Mirry said, getting back into bed, and putting her cold feet on his, which had him groaning and sitting up immediately.

'Whatever time is it?' he grumbled.

'Devil's dancing hours – oh, dear, I shouldn't say that on a Sunday. Half-past five – drink up, before you discover it's iced tea, I should.'

He gulped the tea down, then went back down under the covers, pulled her close. 'I suppose I'll have to warm you up. Why are you up so early?'

'I heard Bar downstairs: you really upset her last night, you know, Fred.'

'I'm sorry about that – I *mean* it – it's just that . . .'

'You think she's still a giddy fourteen year old, don't you? She's a mother, like me, and she works hard for her living, and she's been really brave and good about losing the love of her life – and, she's asked Peter over today – and, *he's* just a friend, really and . . .' His gently caressing hands tickled, distracted her. He was intent on disarming her as usual, she thought wryly.

'You want me to apologise, and make him welcome – well, I will. Now shut up little peacemaker, and let's make the most of an undisturbed hour, I hope, all to ourselves, before first light . . .'

'Coming with us for a walk, Glory?' Bar asked casually, after lunch. She had deliberately not dressed up today, but she had left her hair loose. She was glad that Peter had changed into civvies, too.

'Got to finish my homework, or Miss Tiptree will tear her hair out,' Glory said regretfully.

'We could take Boo,' Bar offered next.

Mirry said quickly: 'She's tired, she'll only grizzle. She should go down for a nap – I'd put Robin in the pram, if I were you, he needs a sleep, too ... off you go; Fred and I can have a snooze then, like all old married couples do.'

'Wear your gloves,' Fred said with a wink. He had apologised to Bar after breakfast, when the two of them took their turn with the washing up. 'Or you'll end up like the butcher – remember? The mincing machine ...'

'Yes, sir,' she returned demurely.

Peter pushed the pram as if he was experienced at so doing, although, when they reached the kerb, he said: 'You'd better take charge, Bar, I don't want to tip Robin out.'

Robin gave a squeal of protest, when his mother gripped the pram handle. 'You be quiet, Robin Raffery,' she said, with a grin. 'Peter can have you back, and welcome, in a minute.'

'Robin Raffery – I'm glad you called him that; Eileen would have been so pleased.'

'I'm glad you agree, Peter.' The wind whipped a long strand of hair across her face, obscuring her vision. Peter brushed it back, tucking it behind her ear, pulling down her woollen cap. He had taken off his glove and now he lightly felt her cheek.

'Mmm. Cold face, but warm breath,' he observed. 'Let me steer again, then; not many others braving the elements today.' Actually, they had only seen one other couple, hurrying home from the pub for a late lunch, perhaps.

'We're going on a long walk: there's a special place I want to show you,' and she held on to his arm as the wind buffeted them along the deserted streets. It was just as she had imagined she and Clive would walk together, with Robin in his pram. She was thankful she was wearing the coat Mirry had made her from a fine blue blanket, with darker blue velvet edging the collar and revers, and fastened military style with round silver buttons which Mum had discovered in her bottomless box, as she called it.

They walked along the Parade. 'Just imagine, Peter,' she said, comfortable with the awareness that now he was pushing the pram with one hand and had slipped the other round her waist. 'On Sundays long ago, the nobs rode their horses along here, and grand ladies paraded in gorgeous crinolines. I wish I'd been alive during the heyday of the Crystal Palace. To look up at those great balloons shimmering in a blue sky – not the barrage balloons that have taken their place in this January greyness.

'When the Palace blazed, in 1936, Clive made his way through the crowds massed here in the Parade. He was just twenty, a very junior member of the paper I now work for.' They stopped. Looked over at the ruins. No crowds today, no blazing furnace, but evidence along the way, of

Hitler's grim follow-up destruction, with the gaps, the craters where fine old buildings had been.

Peter looked at Robin. 'He's asleep at last,' he said softly. He put the brake on the pram, then moved close to her again. 'Go on . . .' he prompted.

'He was so upset,' she continued. 'He came back to our house in the early morning – I cooked him breakfast – the fried egg was hard, I remember, I never was very skilful with the frying pan. I was eighteen, Peter, I thought myself quite grown-up, but of course, I wasn't. I'd led a pretty sheltered life you see, as you once told me you had, until you joined the army . . . Anyway, I found myself trying to comfort him, and it was the first time I realised – that I loved him.'

His arm tightened round her. 'I can understand why this place means a lot to you, Bar. D'you think we ought to turn back? It'll be dusk before we get to your home. Shall I hook the rain-cover up to the pram hood? We mustn't let Robin Raffery catch cold . . .'

She turned, stretched up impulsively, and kissed him on the cheek. 'Oh, I *do* like you, Peter Howe – *I really do!*'

'You haven't got your mind on your work today, young Bar,' Tom observed shrewdly, as she unlocked the mishit typewriter keys yet again, and wiped her hands on her handkerchief. 'Not much news, nothing to send you pedalling out for, take the afternoon off . . .'

When she snatched another kiss, this time on a weathered, stubbled cheek, he exclaimed: 'Hey what's that for? I shall expect some overtime, when it comes up, in return, you know . . .'

'I know!' she returned, and she was gone out of the door in five seconds flat.

She dialled the hotel number from the first working telephone box she came to. 'Peter? It's Bar, I've got the afternoon off. I'm glad I caught you in your room, I thought you might be out and about.'

'I was just hanging around, waiting until it was time to come to see you,' he said frankly. 'I'll be with you in about an hour.'

'Have you had your lunch?' she suddenly realised.

'Hang lunch: seeing you, having more time with you, is more important . . .'

She replaced the receiver with a suddenly shaking hand. What have I done? she thought. I've let him know I'm keen, that's what. Maybe it's just as well he's leaving tomorrow. I can't believe it – I don't want to believe it! But I must be falling in love. I never imagined I'd ever feel like this again, after Clive.

Mirry guessed, when she saw her face. 'Bar, you're all *aglow*!'

'Am I? Tom said I could come home, and I rang him – Peter – and he's driving here right away, and oh, Mirry – I must get changed, and would you mind?'

'If you go out? Of course I wouldn't. Make the most of the time you've got left, Bar. I don't know what Fred will say though. I expect he'll think you're rushing into things headlong.'

'I *am*, Mirry! I feel as if I'm, well, coming alive again.'

'Peter?' Robin said inquiringly from his high chair, all covered in goo from his mashed-up dinner.

'Yes, Peter's coming, darling, and I'm feeling really happy,' Bar smiled, dodging a spoonful of mashed potato.

They sat in the cinema, holding hands, and neither of them could recall afterwards much of the films they had seen. They weren't in The Palace, but in really plush seats, because they had driven back up to London. They were going to dine again at the hotel, and Bar had solemnly promised Mirry that she would be home by eleven.

They didn't talk much over the meal, either. The fish wasn't all that fresh, and Bar was amused to see it served up with mashed potato. 'I won't throw it at you,' she whispered.

'Pardon?' Peter was puzzled.

'I'll tell you later – the waiter is in earshot . . .' she giggled.

'Would you like to dance?' he asked later. The band, well, the trio of three rather ancient musicians, was just tuning up.

'Not really,' she told him honestly. 'Couldn't we go up to your room?' She interpreted his expression. 'Oh, Peter – don't think the worst of me – but I think we need to talk, in private, that's all.'

He settled her in one of the elegant bedroom chairs, busied himself pouring the coffee.

They raised their cups to each other in a mutually shy salute. 'Cheers – good luck!'

'Now?' he inquired, when they had drained the bitter brew.

'I learned, with Clive, to say what I thought,' she said simply. 'It took me a long time, as I told you, because I was so young when we met, to realise how I felt about him. I don't want to embarrass you, heaven forbid, but I already know how I feel about you, Peter. If you haven't been struck by lightning, too, forgive me. But I had to tell you, before you went away . . .'

'I may not see you again for some time, Bar. I can't say anything about that – I'm sorry. You spoke of lightning – all I will say is, that this could well be the uneasy calm, the lull before another storm . . .'

'You don't feel the same, then,' she stood up, looked around uncertainly, as if she thought she should go.

He rose swiftly, came over to her. 'You're so wrong about that, Bar,' he almost squeezed the breath out of her, as he kissed her. Then he added: 'And you're so right, about this . . .'

Nothing improper happened, she thought drowsily later, when she lay in bed that night, thinking, and wondering about it all. I couldn't commit myself like that, and he didn't say, but I know he wasn't ready for it, either. We have to really get to know each other first . . . But we both have someone to care for again, we'll write, and when the time's right, we'll be together.

CHAPTER FORTY

GLORY WAS TIRING OF TAP DANCING; it wasn't leading any-where, apart from those little displays Miss Boam put on from time to time. She was getting too big – too busty – she thought, very aware of her new shape, to be leading little girls with leaden feet and pigtails. She wanted to be an actress. That meant projecting your voice, good breathing, believing you were someone else, not wearing silly cos-tumes, high kicking and pretending you were a prancing horse ... She knew it would be difficult to convince her mother, though, that her Shirley Temple days were finally at an end.

The drama group was practising hard for the Empire Day play on 24 May. Some of the rehearsals took place in the air raid shelters at school because there was what they called the Little Blitz – the last sting, they hoped, in the German Bombing Tail, as Miss Fizzbang put it. That hope was to be dashed, and in a most sinister way.

Glory had started as an understudy but, as her talent became obvious, she had graduated to a main part. It helped that she was now tall for her age and appeared to be so confident, but she was still childish enough to eat the iron rations in the Oxo tin, the first time they marched to the shelter. The Horlicks tablets were supposed to be made into a drink, but she soon chewed them up.

'I need a bra,' she confided in Bar, because she guessed that her Mum would say she was too young. And Bar said she thought she'd got one, from when she was around her age, tucked away somewhere, and, she had. When Glory next changed for gym, she was aware that the other girls were looking enviously at her, and she was glad she had been able to discard the despised liberty bodice at last.

Miss Fizzbang was her heroine. She looked young, but Mum reckoned she was around her age, mid thirties. She wore fishnet stockings, dyed purple, dirndl skirts and frilly blouses – she was about as different from the stolid Miss Tiptree as it was possible to be. Her sleek dark hair hung in a perfect rolled-under page-boy bob, she plucked her eyebrows, her eyes were outlined in black, and she was the only teacher to wear lipstick.

When Miss Fizzbang swept into the class, folder under her arm, calling out: 'Question number one . . .' The desk lids banged, fountain pens squirted, and it was usually question number four or five before the really desperate pupil made a mark on her paper. Glory was never ready for Miss Tiptree, but she rose to the Fizzbang challenge, and usually she managed to get going by question number two.

She was a charismatic teacher: Glory's imagination was so stirred that she sometimes got carried away, and one day Miss Fizzbang held up her homework book and said in her clear voice: 'Gloria Hope, whatever is this?'

'My essay on the life and career of Disraeli, Miss Fitz-barn . . .'

'Well, you've made him even more interesting than he ever was in real life, Gloria. *I* didn't know he had seven sons, all of them destined to follow in his footsteps.'

'Please, Miss, the books I looked in didn't mention him having a family, and I thought it was a shame, him being so brilliant and . . .'

'He was married to a lady much older than himself, Gloria,' Miss Fizzbang said drily. 'He was devoted to his wife and I don't think he looked further afield, although he did write romantic novels. However, you have his political achievements in the correct sequence, so I will ignore the progeny and award you fifteen marks out of twenty. Just remember, in future, if you're not sure of your facts, it's better not to write them down, eh?'

'Yes, Miss. Thank you, Miss.'

Miss Fizzbang renewed her scarlet lipstick in the staff room after eating her sandwiches at lunchtime. The kohl – not coal dust, a rumour which amused her – with which she emphasised her eyes, had survived the morning's chal-lenges. 'Now for the drama group,' she said. 'I hope Gloria

Hope has not embellished her lines – her part seems to get longer and longer ... I'm afraid she needs taking down a peg or two, she's been told so often, at her previous school and obviously by her doting family, that she's bright. She'll have to accept that she's a very little fish in a large pool of academic bigger fish at this school ... Did you know, Dora,' she addressed Miss Tiptree, 'that Disraeli had seven sons?'

'Did he?' Miss Tiptree blew out a cloud of smoke. 'I never heard that before.'

'Nor I. It's the gospel according to Gloria.'

'Ah, well, that explains it. Did she draw a picture of them?'

'Well, no.'

'I suppose she didn't have to: you could imagine them, too, couldn't you?'

Naturally, in her family's eyes, Glory stole the show. Mirry looked round in awe at the vastness of the assembly hall. On the far wall was a roll of honour, of scholastic successes, including those gained later at university. One day, Mirry thought, Glory's name will be added to the list. She would have been disbelieving if anyone had dared to voice a doubt.

Miss Fizzbang did not allow Glory to take a separate curtain call: when the entire cast of *She Stoops to Conquer* lined up on stage, Glory took her bow with the others, but the beaming smile on her face said it all.

Bar, reporting for the paper, said that she must be impartial, of course – and she was, but the photographer had no such qualms. There was a picture of the cast, and another with the comment: 'Gloria Hope is a talented young actress who is surely destined to tread the boards.'

But her moment of fame was brief, for there was general rejoicing because at last it was D-Day, 6 June 1944, and the Allies were landing on the Normandy beaches.

These were names to stir the imagination: the Mulberries – the floating harbours, and Pluto – the vital pipeline of petrol under the Channel. Ike – General Eisenhower – the supreme commander and our own Monty, holding the Germans at bay around Caen, while the Americans fought their way south via the Cherbourg Peninsula. Then the enemy was forced to retreat from the north and there was a second successful Allied landing in the south.

But exactly one week after D-Day, early in the morning of 13 June, the sirens wailed again and ack-ack batteries targeted a single mysterious plane which remained inexorably on course, but crashed, mercifully on open ground, at Barking. But just half an hour later a second plane followed and this time there were casualties. These were the first V-1s, soon to be nicknamed doodlebugs.

The highly secret sites had been detected and audaciously bombed by the Allies, delaying any concentrated launch over the past year, but many of these pilotless planes had survived, and within the next forty-eight hours over 200 would crash, with devastating effect, on London and Bomb Alley. This really was the sting in the tail.

Glory and her family were crammed like sardines in a tin in the Morrison shelter every night now. To the children, it was fun, but to the adults, a tiresome business, and anyway as Bar said with feeling: 'Fred and I would end up in a sorry state, if we got a direct hit, because our feet stick out in the open.' Having increased in numbers, they had to lie along the width of the mattress, not the length. And, naturally, Glory insisted that Pip must be in there, too. She'd wanted to adopt a stray cat that she'd christened Timoshenko, after the Russian general – most new pets were called Monty, but she liked to be different.

'You can feed the poor thing, though I don't know what on,' Mirry told her firmly, 'but I'm not having a general in bed with me every night.'

The sound of a V-I was blood-curdling, heart-stopping. The sputtering was unmistakable. Then came the ominous *cut*! in the engine, an eerie pause, followed by the explosion as it dived into the ground.

One night, Robin's little voice piped up unexpectedly. 'Did you hear that doodlebugger, Bar?' and even as Mirry cried, scandalised, 'Whoever taught him that?' the rest of the shelter crew shook with uncontrollable laughter. It certainly helped to ease the tension, the terror.

'D'you think it would get past the censor if I wrote and told Peter that?' Bar asked. She wanted to talk about him, but it seemed that no one else did . . .

Mirry had told Glory privately that she shouldn't ask too much about Peter at the moment: he had been involved in the D-Day landings, Bar knew that much, but – it must bring it all back to her, Clive having been at Dunkirk – and all the grief that came afterwards . . . It would be awful if – but she hadn't finished the sentence.

Glory ran to school each day: you never knew when the doodlebugs would whine overhead. When the sound abruptly ceased, she kept on running, as if trying to escape it, although she knew it was more sensible to dive into a doorway, or fling herself flat on the pavement. During the Blitz, she thought, she had been too young to feel real fear. Now she was aware of what war meant, of the brave airmen intercepting the doodlebugs, tipping their wings to turn them, and of the gunners destroying many of them as they came across the coast.

One afternoon in early July, she left school during a lull, having been in and out of the shelters all day. She came along Kitchener Avenue, and then stood, rooted to the spot, staring in disbelief across the road from Number Five to the Victorian villas opposite. Lahana was no more; a smoking pile of rubble, still being hosed down fiercely by the firefighters. There was a splintered piece of debris by her feet. She saw two painted letters: HA. An absurd thought struck her – where was the other HA? As in ha-ha.

Her mother came to the gate, chalky faced, and told her to come away, come inside, not to look. 'Are you all right? I was so worried about you. I couldn't come to get you . . .'

'I've got a note,' Glory said. 'In my satchel. The school's closing till after the summer holidays . . .'

Bar was standing in the hallway, the little ones clinging to her, her reporter's notebook clenched in one hand. She looked dazed. 'I can't do it, Mirry, it's too close to home,' she said. 'I thought I was going to be sick . . .'

Glory said urgently: 'Mum! answer me – when did it happen? Is Miss Boam all right?'

'Just after lunch – they got Anna out – they took her to hospital, I don't know . . .' Mirry looked at the children. 'I can't say, Glory – will you make some tea? The power's off, but I've got the kettle going on the little stove.'

Bar followed her out into the kitchen: 'I must get a glass of water, Glory.' The water trickled, a funny colour, she let it run before it suddenly spurted and filled her glass. 'They've evacuated the houses on either side of Lahana, but they say we are safe over here; how can we be safe, with those – things – coming at us . . .'

Glory pulled out the stool from its corner. 'Sit down, Bar. Everything will be fine.' She echoed the calm words of

Miss Tiptree earlier: 'Sit down on the benches girls. Every-thing will be fine.'

It was not until her father came home, much later than usual, because the trains were so delayed, and Boo and Robin were tucked up in the Morrison, that he told them, looking weary and dusty: 'They're still digging, but now it's dark . . . They haven't found the major yet.'

Glory thought she wouldn't be able to get to sleep, but eventually her eyes closed. In a half-dream-like state, she thought, I won't have to tell Mum now, about wanting to give up the tap dancing lessons . . .

CHAPTER FORTY-ONE

'MIRRY, MIRRY, ARE YOU AWAKE?' Fred whispered urgently. As the only male, apart from Robin and he was too young to count, he had chosen voluntary segregation in the steel fortress, pressed against the unyielding side barrier. When one turned, they all turned – it was like the old chant, he often thought ruefully. 'There were ten in the bed, and the little one said – roll over!' Except there was no danger of falling out and making more room for the others . . .

He turned, with great difficulty, and groped for her shoulder. She was shaking so much, her teeth were rattling.

The reverberation was felt by Bar, at the other end of the line, with the three children in between. It was a long minute before she managed to ease herself out of the shelter and to feel her way towards Mirry and Fred.

'What's wrong, Fred? Is Mirry ill?' she inquired anxiously.

'Is Mum ill?' Glory's voice echoed in alarm.

'Glory, I'm just finding out. Cuddle the little ones up and try to keep them asleep.'

Between them, they helped Mirry out, then Fred lifted her and carried her, guided by Bar's torch, into the dining room, where he deposited her in the armchair. Bar wrapped her round with a spare blanket. 'Where's the brandy, Fred?'

Fred managed to spoon a little between Mirry's chattering teeth, spilling some down her front. 'You smell like a brewery,' he tried to joke, 'swallow it down, that's the ticket.'

The shuddering was easing, Mirry appeared bewildered but suddenly, she seemed to come to. 'Whatever happened?' she asked.

'Shock, after yesterday, that must be it, Mirry. Don't worry, darling, you're all right now.'

'There's some tea in the flask, let's share it, eh?' Bar suggested. The electricity was still off, but Fred now lit the candle on the mantelpiece. Batteries were precious, they mustn't waste the one in the torch. 'Shan't be a tick, Mirry, I must just check on the children – we're lucky there's no alert at the moment – nothing doodling overhead.'

'You always look on the bright side, Fred,' Mirry said, accepting the beaker of tea gratefully. There was the merest tremour in her hands now, but she was still white-faced and starey-eyed, as if she'd seen a ghost.

At three in the morning, Fred tucked her up in the Morrison once more. Bar stayed in the other room. 'I don't feel like going back to bed,' was all she said. 'I ought to get on with my report for the paper.'

'You'll strain your eyes,' Fred told her.

He was right. Bar gave up the attempt, and settled back in the chair, adjusting the blanket. She might as well finish off the night here, she thought, unless there was another warning.

*　*　*

The room was suddenly flooded with light. Fred was removing the shutters. It was morning. She wrinkled her nose at the fumes from the old stove. As always, she was instantly reminded of Clive, and the fun and fry ups they had had in the past. But it promised a really hot cup of tea to come. Without milk, unless the milkman had come today.

'All quiet on the home front,' Fred observed. 'Stay where you are. No need to rush. I'll give work a miss today, I think. They'll expect it, when they know our area was badly hit. Mirry looks peaceful enough.'

'Delayed shock, Fred, it must be.' Bar didn't need to elaborate. From the last time. When the bomb hit here. When Mirry lost the baby.

Fred set her teacup down in the hearth. Then he bent and unexpectedly kissed her. 'What would we do without you, dear Bar? Don't ever leave us again, will you?'

She couldn't promise that, she couldn't confide her own fears for the safety of her new love, but this was not a problem to be faced right now. She clung to the comforting truth that Fred truly loved her sister, and that his kiss had been an appreciation for the part she played in holding the family together in these times.

Over the road, the men with the shovels resumed their sombre task.

'You're not going to say we must go away from here again, are you Fred?' Mirry was quite composed, she hadn't even mentioned what had happened the previous night. It helped that Glory was at home, too, to amuse the children: Bar had gone off to work as usual, after a brief word with the workers opposite.

Fred had just returned from walking the dog and buying a paper. It was a sparkling summer's day. He, too, paused to talk to the men.

He saw that she had the lid of the neglected piano up, and there was a smell of polish. He wasn't sure whether this was a good sign or not. Since the piano was relegated to the hall, to make room for the shelter, Mirry had not played it, as far as he was aware.

'I shouldn't really say this but, well, I have reason to think the, er, present worrying situation will soon be under control . . . Where would you go, anyway? I feel happier about you here this time, with Bar around, I must say. Ah, good-oh, the wireless has just come on, they must have restored the power. Better listen to the news, eh?'

Mirry wanted to know what was going on among the ruins of what had been Lahana. She wanted to ask, 'Have you heard anything about Anna?' But she admitted to herself that she didn't know if she could cope if it was bad news . . .

Ted spoke to the Sister at the hospital desk. 'She knows about her father, Sister. She took it well, I think.'

'You *think*,' Sister observed. Her face matched his for weariness. Her ward was full of casualties, some of them in far worse straits than Miss Anna Boam. 'You are seeing to his funeral, I take it? Miss Boam named you as her next-of-kin, as her fiancé. I'm afraid she will not be able to attend, she will not be mobile for many months.'

Could one make arrangements, when remains were unidentifiable, poor Ted wondered. There was something else troubling him deeply. The shocking rumour voiced by the search party, that there might have been another body buried beneath the house . . . There would be an inquest. What would it reveal? He couldn't help recalling the rumours around the time of Anna's mother's disappearance. Another unsolved mystery – like the still unidentified stranger who had saved lives and lost his own. Ted had not asked Anna, after all, if this could have been her long-lost lover, seeking sanctuary at Lahana for reasons Ted could only conjecture . . .

*   *   *

In August, Paris was liberated. The papers were full of wonderful pictures of jubilant girls perched on tanks, being hugged by the Free French soldiers. Other women were shamed for their supposed collaboration with the enemy, by the symbolic hacking off of their hair.

The V-1 launching sites were captured, but it was not quite the end of this menace. The flying bombs were now launched by Heinkel aircraft: some exploded prematurely, along with their host plane, but some made it over the Channel.

In September, when Glory was about to celebrate her twelfth birthday and hoping that school would resume, the Galloping Major was laid to rest. The coroner had decided that, in the circumstances, it was impossible to say whether the remains were those of one, or two, persons. What was certain was that the major's demise had been caused by enemy action.

Bar wrote a short obituary for the paper, mentioning his valour in the Great War. The major's daughter, Anna, a popular figure who had run the Lahana Dance Club, was still too unwell to attend his funeral, she added. She was now being cared for at home by her fiancé, Mr Edward Goldsmith.

Anna was kept company by Bar that afternoon. She sat in her wheelchair, quite composed, not looking like the

elegant Anna of the past at all. All her belongings had
been lost in the bombing. She wore the sensible wincyette nightgown that had belonged to the late Mrs Violet
Goldsmith, who had been some twenty years her senior, and three stone heavier in weight. Her head was
still heavily bandaged, but her face had something of its
former beauty.

She doesn't look right, here, in this stuffy little parlour,
Bar thought. Anna needs space round her, space to dance,
but that's silly, because she doesn't need room to do that,
she never will again . . .

'Thank you for coming, Bar,' Anna said suddenly. 'It
means a lot to me, to have good friends, like you and Mirry.
It's about time, isn't it?'

'Yes, I think so.'

'I'm glad it's over. For him – and for myself. Even
though I'll be, like this, for the rest of my life. My head will
be scarred, as his was, that's ironic isn't it? But they say my
hair will grow back.'

'Will you marry Ted?' Bar interjected swiftly.

'I imagine so. It's what he wants. He's a nice man, Bar.
I need him. But I can't be to him what he fondly imagines.
Don't worry, my dear – I shall never tell him that – and
nor I'm sure, will you.' She reached out for Bar's hand.
'You've guessed, haven't you? The secret of Lahana – my
mother . . . But you can't know – can't ever be sure . . .
You were such a talented dancer, Bar, I had such hopes

373

for you; you've had a far worse tragedy in your life than I have in mine.'

'I've found someone else to love, Anna. Will you be happy for me?' Bar smiled at her. 'But I want to keep it secret, special, until he comes back, you see – just my family know and now, you . . .'

'I'm glad,' Anna said.

And in September, too, there was a new threat: The V-2, a supersonic missile, more terrifying than its forerunner because it was impossible to detect and intercept, dive-bombed on British soil.

CHAPTER FORTY-TWO

'WE'VE COME THROUGH!' Mirry cried jubilantly. They all knew she didn't just mean that the war in Europe was over after six long years. She was also referring to the triumph of staying put, here at Number Five, through the fearful winter of the V-2, and emerging unscathed. Now, yet another V, one to be ranked with the V for Victory salute of the great Winston Churchill – it was 8 May 1945, VE Day. Victory in Europe. What would go down in family memory as The Great Pickled Onion Race Day.

'O be joyful!' as Fred said, when their large and happy party straggled up the heights of Spa Hill to what Mirry preferred to call the tavern, early that evening.

Glory, Don and Junie led the way, trying to keep one step ahead of the exuberant Boo and Robin, followed by Fred and Jim, then Mirry and Laura, giggling away, because they'd already been at the sherry bottle, while Bar brought up the rear, linking arms with the oldest celebrants, Mum and Hilda Hardes.

It wasn't quite all over, of course; Japan had not yet surrendered, but that would come shortly, everyone was convinced of that.

Glory felt a little shy of Don, she didn't know why. She was almost a teenager, but he seemed a young man, with his voice newly gruff and his hair all slicked back. At fifteen, he was taller than his father and he'd obviously nicked himself with Jim's razor, for his face and neck looked sore, and he'd dabbed calamine on a spot on his chin. Despairing over a blemish or two herself, she knew how he must feel about that.

She hadn't seen much of them, despite being near neighbours, since they all returned from Surrey, she thought. Don went to the tech now – he wasn't going to follow his father into the bank – Don wanted to be a motor mechanic. He intended to leave school next year and try for an apprenticeship. Junie still kept aloof, she had a circle of friends, some already fourteen and working, having smartly departed school before the leaving age went up to fifteen; she didn't need to hang around with Glory, who might look mature for her age, but was a baby as far as going out with boys was concerned. Junie was at a contrary stage: she resented parental authority and she had no intention, she told them, of going on to secretarial college and working in a stuffy old office like her mum.

'I suppose you're going on to university?' she asked Glory in what was obviously a pitying tone.

Glory hadn't lost her spark, she'd just learned to dampen it a bit under Miss Tiptree's guidance. At school, anyway. She flashed back: 'I'm going to drama school, actually. I'm going to be an actress. But I've promised Mum and Dad I'll do my exams first.'

'I bet!' Junie said scornfully. She stomped off ahead, but Glory guessed she was mouthing, 'Show off!'

Don had young Robin riding on his shoulders now, while Boo clung to her father's back. Glory and Don walked along together. She was well aware of his sidelong glances. She was pleased she was wearing the new blue skirt Mirry had finished off this morning: a skirt like Miss Fizzbang's, a style her mum agreed was nice and economical with material. It went well with the Hungarian blouse Grandma had brought home in triumph from a jumble sale – fine muslin, brightly embroidered yoke, drawstring neck and short, puffed sleeves. A bit see-through, her mum said doubtfully, so she must hitch up the straps of her petticoat to conceal her cleavage. She was proudest of her Clark's sandals: with crisscross straps in brown leather, leaving her toes bare. Another sixpenny jumble prize. She still wore her hair short – the bubble cut was becoming popular now, so she was ahead of fashion.

The pub gardens were crowded with people: children played hide and seek round the rose bushes and the men queued patiently for drinks. Junie eyed the local boys, dripping with Brylcreem, seemingly unaware of her proximity.

Mirry and Laura were still talking animatedly, only Bar sat quietly with the older ladies. Glory and Don ostensibly kept watch on Boo and Robin, while sitting on the grass, making daisy necklaces to amuse their charges.

'You've got a cherryade moustache,' Don told her.

'Better than pickled onion breath,' she retorted.

'They went down well, with that spam roll,' he said, 'disguised the taste of marge – I hate marge! When I get married, I shall order only butter in my house.'

'*If* we ever get rid of rationing, Don.'

He looked at her in surprise. 'The war's over, isn't it? Surely rationing will end soon?'

'How can it? The countries we used to import from are struggling to survive – people are starving – it will take years for the world to recover from this war.'

'You're very knowledgeable, Glory! I didn't think girls were interested in politics. Oh, I know my mum says you're too clever by half . . .'

'Oh, does she! That drop of cider has loosened your tongue I see, Donald Sims. What cheek!' But she smiled at him, because it was nice to be thought clever, even by half.

Maybe it was the illicit glass of cider, which he hadn't expected to get, although he'd grandly requested it, mainly to impress Glory, when his dad asked for their orders, but Don suddenly saw her in a fresh light. She was a pretty girl, the sort boys would fight over, and he was in with a good chance, for he'd known her all her life . . .

'Like to come to the Pictures this weekend?' he asked casually. 'There's an Edward G. Robinson film.'

Glory didn't like gangster films; she took after Mirry for musicals and love stories, with spunky heroines, of course. But – she'd actually been asked out on a date! Her very first. 'Don't see why not,' she agreed casually, then – 'Where have those two terrors got to, Don? We'd better go and look.' As she jumped to her feet, he noticed that she had painted her toenails with pink varnish and that her long legs were shapely, and golden from the sun.

Down the hill they rolled the pickled onions, gathering dust, with the smaller children shrieking their delight as Mirry and Laura continued to let their hair down. The older children, in an agony of embarrassment, kept well to the rear this time, stony-faced. The rest of the party displayed tolerance. Actually, Fred could hardly believe his eyes: there was Mirry, retrieving her battered onion from the gutter and Laura singing out: 'I've won! Loser gets to eat the champion onion!'

Boo and Robin were doing a jig of excitement.

'No fear!' Mirry replied. 'Anyway, we haven't quite reached the bottom of the hill . . .' and she bowled her onion past Laura's, where it hit the lamp post and smashed to pieces.

'Draw!' Jim said hastily. 'Now sober up, you two, those three at the back think you've gone quite mad . . .'

Bar took the two grandmothers home. 'You were quiet, Bar,' Mum observed. 'Ooh, my corns are all athrob – I haven't walked so far in ages.'

'I'll put the kettle on,' Hilda said ruefully, 'not for tea, Bar – but to soak our feet.'

When she had gone out into the kitchen, Mum said: 'You were thinking about your Clive, of course, like I was, your dad, and Alice and Stan. When you should be over the moon, dearie, you're always sharply reminded of the ones you've lost . . .'

Bar's lower lip trembled. 'You're right, Mum, you always are. It just wasn't fair – Clive dying like that, when he'd come back from Dunkirk . . . Robin needs a dad . . .'

'And you need a husband. You're lucky in that respect, I never found one to match up to your father, Bar. Heard from Peter?'

'Two days ago: he's in Germany. Sometimes I wonder if I'm reading more into this than I should. We only just began to get to know each other, those three days – and not seeing him since . . .'

'You haven't committed yourselves, then?'

Bar shook her head. 'How could we? With him away at war. I don't know when he'll be back – it can't be till the war's really over, with Japan, anyway. Mum, sometimes I feel jealous of Mirry – she's still got Fred – and now and again, I have to face the fact that she's got more to do with bringing up little Robin than I have . . .'

'There's a danger there, dearie, that our Mirry feels he's replaced that little baby she lost,' Mum said thoughtfully. 'Don't suppose it ever struck you, that I felt I'd given you up to Mirry and Fred all those years ago? I know just how you feel . . .'

Bar hugged her. 'Thanks, Mum. I do love you, you know. Well, duty calls: I'm going to join the crowds celebrating in the High Street, with my notebook in hand. They're going to switch the lights on at midnight, rumour has it.'

'Can I go with Bar?' Glory begged.

Mirry was feeling rather queasy. She said she'd put Boo and Robin to bed. Glory could go, if her dad went too, because Bar would be busy with her reporting.

'But,' Glory began, 'Don asked me to go with *him* . . .'

'Don? What about Junie?'

'Yes, Junie's going – so's Uncle Jim. Auntie Laura's been sick.'

'I'm not surprised,' Mirry said primly, just as if she hadn't been involved in The Great Pickled Onion Race, and won it, what's more, whatever Jim said. She looked at Glory's flushed face. 'What else did Don say? I thought you weren't all that friendly with them any more?'

'Oh, *he's* all right – it's that stuck-up Junie. He asked me to go to the Pictures with him too, on Saturday.'

'I don't know about that . . .'

'Oh, Mum, it's only Don!'

'Maybe, Glory, but you don't want to grow up too fast . . .'

'I don't know what you mean?' It was obvious that she didn't.

Mirry said: 'I'll think about it. Ask your dad. Now, just you run upstairs and change that blouse, it's a bit thin for you to be out in the night air.'

'It's really warm, still,' Glory told her. Really, Mum was such an old fuss pot!

The trams had come to a standstill in the High Street. As the clock in the tower chimed midnight, a great cheer arose from the crowd of excited people spilling over the pavements and dancing in the road. The lights went on in Woolworths, in the other shops – the crumpled bunting thus illuminated, dated from the Coronation, eight years ago. The local band was playing – people were singing, not necessarily the same tune: Bar could decipher a mixture of 'Roll Me Over' and 'When the Lights Go on Again'. The first aiders were busy reviving the fainting-from-excitement, the tipsy-tripping-up, and mislaid children wailed for mum. Bar could see to write now, and her pencil flew, as she soaked it all in.

As the last *dong*! faded away, and a loud voice called for those who were grateful for deliverance to 'Follow me to the church to say your prayers' Bar turned to find Fred beside her. All around them folk were kissing, crying in relief, and Fred smiled at her and said, 'Let's join 'em!' before he kissed her. It wasn't a brotherly kiss, at all. She sensed the danger in it. Just a few drinks – and he betrayed himself, like this. He would regret it, in the morning, she knew. He wouldn't be the only one, she thought wryly. The way some were carrying on, in full view of everyone else, a new generation was guaranteed . . .

She pushed him gently away. 'I mustn't stop, Fred, I've got to get this all down – the wonderful atmosphere, the lights, the flags, what people are saying, while it's actually happening . . . Then, I shall go on to the church. We all need to calm down, take a step back, think what this means and say thank you for it. You ought to go and see where Glory is, take her home, I think. I'll make my own way back, later, don't worry. So many out and about, I won't be in any danger.'

I hope Peter comes back soon, she thought. It's time for a new start, for me and for Robin.

Glory was being kissed, too. By Don, who was as inexperienced as she was, fortunately. His lips briefly touched the side of her mouth, where the dimples appeared, when she was laughing.

'Happy VE Day,' he said bashfully.

Glory didn't know whether to say thank you, or not, but suddenly she wanted to go home. She didn't want Don to look at her, all serious, she hadn't really got time for boys, she thought – she'd got homework to do, and drama club – and Pip to take out. 'Sorry, but I won't be able to come to the Pictures on Saturday,' she said. 'I've got to babysit.'

'Oh, there you are,' her dad said. 'Better get back to your mum, eh?'

CHAPTER FORTY-THREE

THE FOLLOWING SPRING, with Peter still not demobbed and stationed in Germany, Bar decided to take Robin on an early holiday, to visit Iris in her new home.

Things seemed to be more stable now, some months after the atom bomb effectively ended the war with Japan and then there was the General Election that followed. It seemed shocking to those at Number Five that Churchill had been deposed but, as Glory told them, courtesy of Miss Fizzbang, naturally, this was the way of it, when a party, the Conservatives, apart from brief interludes, had been in power for so long – 'twenty-odd years – longer than I've been alive,' Glory said. 'She reckons Aneurin Bevan's a bit like Lloyd George.'

'Lloyd George knew my father,' Fred quoted.

'Did he? How exciting!'

'You're so gullible,' Fred said affectionately. 'I've always been a Tory, and I suppose I always will be, but I can understand why those coming back from war are ready for a change ... Might be a blast of fresh air, I suppose, at Westminster. And if the National Health Act ever gets through, well, that'll be a good thing for us all, won't it? But I have my doubts about Nationalisation . . .'

There was still stringent rationing of food and clothes, the utility stamp on the latter and on the plain furniture with which newly weds now set up house. To Bar, who had never had a home of her own, it would have been wonderful to go window-shopping even for that.

Iris lived in a bustling village, with a good bus route to town. She welcomed them with hugs and a few tears. 'It's been so long, Bar, oh it really has! Robin darling, how like your daddy you are! You look big enough for school.'

'He's going in September. He'll be ready for it, even though he won't be five until the December. Mirry says she's worn out with all his chattering, all the questions, but then she says she's only joking because, isn't it wonderful, he's such a bright spark?'

'You look so well, Iris – so youthful! But I keep forgetting you're a few years younger than my mum. Robin, you haven't gone all shy on us, have you? Say hello to your Grandma Iris. She hasn't seen you since you were a tiny, new baby, you know . . .'

'Are you my daddy's mum, Gram'Iris?' Robin asked her, deciding to shorten her title and rightly guessing it would make them both smile. She poured him a glass of lemonade, and cut a large slice of cake.

Iris looked at Bar. What have you told him? was the silent appeal.

'Yes, she is and she's a second mum to me, Robin, aren't I lucky?' Bar said.

'I lost my son, but I'm fortunate to have such a dear daughter,' Iris said huskily, and then she hugged them all over again.

Harold, her husband, had tactfully disappeared upstairs with their luggage, after insisting on paying off the taxi which had met them at the station. Now, he came into the kitchen, where they had gravitated, and asked: 'Aren't you going to show them the rest of the house, Iris? I expect they'd like to wash and brush up before lunch. I do all the cooking, Bar. Iris says she has to do all the clearing up after me.'

'Can I stay with you, Grandad?' Robin asked. He had taken instantly to this large, bluff man with glasses slipping down his nose and expressive eyebrows which needed a trim.

'I don't see why not,' Harold said jovially. 'You can help, once you've rinsed your hands at the sink . . . No fancy soap down here. I told your grandma I don't fancy her favourite Knight's Castile mingling with the onions. There's the Lifebuoy – a man's soap, I always say.'

'He's so nice, your Harold,' Bar observed, as she followed Iris upstairs. 'Good with children, too.'

'Oh, he's thrilled to be a grandfather. To have a readymade family. I do wish he could have known Clive, that's my only regret. This is your room, this is ours – and this little room is for the boy – d'you think he'll like it by himself?'

'He's got to get used to it, sometime, Iris,' she murmured ruefully. If I get married again, she thought.

'Just a little house – suited the three of us very well. I was touched, Bar, when I knew that Muriel had left the house to both of us – she was so happy when we decided to marry. She had her own room downstairs – we call it the garden room, because the french doors open out there: Muriel loved looking out on the flowers, the trees and shrubs, those last months, when she lay there in bed. It's the guest room now, we keep the bed made up but, of course, you're family, so you're up here with us.'

Iris sat down on the side of Bar's bed. 'Slept well, I take it? Must be the change of air, Robin's still fast asleep – I peeped in on him ... It's pouring with rain, I'm afraid, outside, so why not stay where you are for a bit? One bachelor way Harold hasn't lost, is hogging the bathroom in the mornings. He'll be another half-hour or so. But, then, he'll cook us all a lovely breakfast, that's something to look forward to. I brought my cup of tea with me, it's a chance for us to gossip, isn't it?'

Bar sat up, reached for her own cup. 'I actually like the sound of rain blowing against the windows, when I'm all cosy in bed. It reminds me,' she took a sip of tea, 'of being with Clive in Devon, all cosy under the covers, listening to the water running off the roof into the butt. We were so happy there, Iris, despite his poor health.'

'I know you were,' Iris said softly, 'that's a great comfort to me, too.'

'It doesn't – hurt you, does it, that I've found someone else? Not to take his place, please understand that, but Peter is someone I just know Clive would have liked very much. Robin and I, of course, are treated as part of Mirry and Fred's family but, it's not the same, is it?'

'No one knows that better than me . . .'

'I'm sorry, Iris, how tactless I am . . .'

'No, it's true. You have my blessing, you can be sure of that.'

'Gram'Iris!' came the call from Robin's bedroom. 'Where are you?'

'It makes me so happy to hear that,' Iris said, rising obediently to go to her grandson. 'I know Clive wanted to call me Mum, but it was difficult, after so long, me always being Auntie Iris. Things are becoming more open, aren't they? I think it will be easy to tell Robin, when the time comes.'

They had spent the day indoors, playing games around the fire: Harold was a dab hand with the cards.

'I think it's a bit too early to teach the boy Bridge,' Iris told him, tongue in cheek, 'after all, you know I haven't mastered it yet. Clock Patience, that's more like it.' She fanned the cards in a circle on the table.

Robin was making so much noise with shouts of: 'Nearly out! Hope the last King doesn't come up, Gram'Iris – you turn the card up, Grandad – oh, please don't let it be the King of Hearts!' that they didn't hear the first ring of the door bell.

'I'll go,' Bar offered, being not so involved in the game, 'to find out who it is. I won't invite them in without your sayso.'

'Hello, Bar,' Peter said, just as if they'd seen each other two days ago, not two years since. 'Sorry I'm dripping wet – it was a long walk from the station – aren't you going to ask me in? I called at Mirry's first thing this morning, I couldn't wait to see you, I only arrived back in London last night. It was a real blow to be told you'd gone away for a week with Robin. Well, Mirry gave me something to eat, she gave me your address, and she said: "*Go!*" So here I am – getting wetter by the minute . . .'

She found her voice at last, opened the door wide. 'Oh, *Peter* – come in!'

He looked so different out of uniform. Younger again, she thought, with his blond hair darkened by the rain, and his coat collar turned up. He was too wet to hug. Perhaps it was just as well, for he made no attempt to get close to her. He put his hand in his pocket. 'Hope it isn't all damp and ruined, but I wanted to produce it like this – a present for you, Bar.'

She didn't have to unwrap the neat parcel to know that it contained half a pound of bacon.

Iris, coming out to see why Bar was so long, and who was there, immediately guessed who the stranger was. 'You're Peter, Bar's friend – you must be! Hang your wet coat on the banister, for now – and come inside and warm up. Harold!' she called. 'Put the kettle on!'

'I don't suppose you remember me, Robin,' Peter said.

'Yes I do!' Robin retorted. 'Bar's got your picture, by her bed. She says goodnight to it, and Keep Safe . . .'

'*Robin!*' Bar said, highly embarrassed.

'I've got *your* picture in my wallet,' he said, smiling at Bar's confusion, 'and one of your mummy, too.'

'Do you say goodnight to us?'

'Of course I do.'

'We must have been expecting you, Peter,' Iris told him, indicating the door to the garden room. 'The bed's made up.'

'No, really, I don't expect . . .' he said.

'You might not, but we do,' Harold told him. 'D'you take sugar, Peter? Are you hungry? Shall I fry up some of that bacon for you?'

'No – and no – and no, thank you! Why don't we all enjoy the bacon for supper?'

'Got an old tin, Iris?' Bar asked, with a happy grin.

They hadn't even kissed goodnight, Bar thought ruefully, coming out of the bathroom, ready for bed. She met Iris outside on the landing. Her expression must have betrayed her. Iris put a hand on her shoulder.

'Goodnight, dear. Robin went out like a light.'

'He didn't even hear the end of Grandad's story,' Bar agreed.

'Sorry you didn't get a chance to be on your own, Bar.'

'There's always tomorrow,' Bar said.

'Don't be shocked, dear – but there's still tonight . . .' Iris whispered, as she kissed her. 'I'll listen out for Robin, don't worry – and Harold sleeps like a log. Snores too, as you no doubt discovered last night.'

'I'm not sure,' Bar whispered back, 'that Peter wouldn't be shocked, you see – maybe it's all been wishful thinking as far as I'm concerned – maybe he's come to say just that.'

'Go down and find out,' Iris told her firmly, adding, 'and don't worry – I'm always the first one down in the mornings . . .'

'You're making me blush – but I love you for it!' Bar gave her another hug.

She felt her way cautiously through the living room, by the dying light of the fire. She tapped twice on the garden room door. Perhaps he was already asleep – he'd looked tired, she thought. She turned to go. She shouldn't have come.

The door opened slowly. He stood there, blanket obviously draped hastily round his bare shoulders. He wore pyjama trousers, nothing on his feet. She caught a glimpse of bedclothes thrown back, the shaded lamp by the bed. 'Is anything wrong?' he asked.

She shook her head. 'No, I just wanted to say goodnight, Peter.'

'I thought you did.' He looked rather bewildered.

'You didn't kiss me,' she said childishly, and she couldn't help it – she started to cry.

'*Ah*,' he said, and he pulled her inside. 'Hush! You'll wake the whole house.'

They stood there, he held her close, making soothing noises. 'Better now?' he asked after a while.

She clutched him tighter, 'Peter, did you come to tell me you're going away again, that you don't want to be tied down so soon after getting out of the army?'

He guided her to the bed, and they sat side by side. He tilted her chin with one hand. 'First, I'm going to give you that goodnight kiss. Then I'll tell you exactly how I feel – you've got it all wrong, Bar darling,' he said.

Being nearest the lamp, she switched it off. 'I'm shivering, let's get under the covers,' she answered.

At first light she woke in his arms, and saw him regarding her with a bemused smile. She'd hardly looked glamorous, she thought, knocking on his door in her serviceable pink pyjamas. One of Eileen's favourite songs: 'She'll be Coming Round the Mountain', with the refrain, 'She'll be wearing pink pyjamas when she comes!' But it wasn't the time to think of Eileen, or Clive, now . . . Anyway, the pyjamas were in a heap on the floor.

'What can I say?' she whispered.

'You don't need to say anything, Bar . . . But I will. Remember Medusa, and her pep-talk, when she caught me with the first lot of bacon?'

'Mmm. 'Course I do.'

'She warned me in no uncertain terms what my lot would be if I seduced one of her gels but she didn't say what I should do if one of those gels had designs on me.'

'Wave the white flag, Peter, surrender!' she said demurely.

And he did. Again.

Bar was back in her own bed when Iris came in with two cups of tea on the tray. 'Everything all right?' she asked.

'Everything is wonderful!' Bar said, dreamily.

'Is marriage on the cards?'

'Yes, but not yet – Peter doesn't want to go back to his old job. He has applied to do teacher training – there's a special course, a year he believes, for those who passed all the army exams. I'll stay on at home, work and save hard, and we'll be together when we can.'

'Couldn't you get married, go with him, wherever he is at college, and get a job there?'

'No, I don't think that's fair. With Robin around and all, he wouldn't be able to concentrate on his studies . . .'

'Think a bit more about it, I should,' Iris advised wisely.

Before she left, she asked casually: 'Did you – stay down there long?'

'Nearly all night, Iris . . . D'you mind?'

'I know I should say I do – but, dear Bar, I'm glad you did. Follow your own heart, they say – I wish I had.'

After the rain, a sunny, blowy day. Peter had brought a kite for Robin. They climbed a nearby hill and after a few failed attempts, the wind caught the kite and sent it streaming into the sky.

As Robin turned somersaults with excitement, reminding Bar vividly of Glory at that age, she said to Peter: 'Iris knows – about last night. She doesn't mind, but we must be discreet. How long can you stay?'

'You look like Medusa yourself – with your hair flying all over the place like that,' he said, unwinding more string. 'Three days, Bar – why does it have to be three days, again? I have to be in London, about my course, on Friday – you could come back with me, on the train.'

'We'll make the most of today, and tomorrow,' she decided. 'Iris and Harold have been looking forward to us coming for so long, it wouldn't be fair to leave early. We'll be home next Sunday, anyway.' She paused, then, as he went to run along with the kite at Robin's urging, she added: 'There's just one thing, Peter, you haven't said—'

'I thought you knew. I love you, Bar – *I love you!*' he shouted to the wind.

CHAPTER FORTY-FOUR

MIRRY CORNERED BAR in the kitchen, when she returned from work. The children were eating their tea in the living room and absorbed in *Children's Hour* on the wireless.

'Are you all right, Bar?'

'Why shouldn't I be?' Bar countered warily.

'I *can* add up, you know – you last saw Peter in April, before he went off to college, and it's July now, and—'

'I'm obviously three months' pregnant – is that what you're trying to say?'

Mirry pushed the stool at her. 'Now, don't upset yourself, that won't do you any good – I know, from experience, when I found myself in the same situation, after Fred and I got carried away that Christmas. I'm on your side, Bar, don't push me away, please; but you obviously haven't told Peter.'

'How d'you know?'

'Because he would have rushed back here from Bristol and made an honest woman of you, that's why.'

Bar's face suddenly crumpled, and she searched in her pocket for a handkerchief.

397

'Here, have mine – I haven't blown in it,' Mirry said. She reached for the teapot. 'Let's drain the pot, eh?'

'Have you told Fred?'

'Not yet. But he's bound to notice soon, and I've seen Glory giving you sly glances – she's a big girl now, remember . . . I've been worrying about you riding that bike, too. You'll have to give your job up soon . . .'

'I won't have to do anything of the sort! If Tom and the chief have put two and two together, and I don't know if they have, they'll be happy for me to soldier on as long as I can. Don't forget, I'm Auntie Joy, too. I'll ask if I can carry on with that, at home. As for the bike – I rode on an old boneshaker until I was eight months gone with Robin; Delia didn't say I must stop.'

'Promise me you'll write to Peter and tell him, Bar.'

'It's almost the end of term; I'm going with Robin to Bristol for a week then. It can wait.' Bar said firmly. 'And I shall make it clear that he must go back and finish his studies – I'm *Mrs* Joy, after all, so there shouldn't be too much talk, if that's what you're worried about.' Then she saw the tears in Mirry's eyes. 'Oh, Mirry, I'm sorry! What a beast I am! I should know you're only jawing me, because you care about me.'

'Bar, dear, I really don't know what Fred will say,' Mirry sniffed, even though she remembered that Fred had turned a blind eye to what had happened between Bar and Clive, that last holiday before the war. She thought, somewhat astonished at herself: I'm more broad-minded than I was, but I'm sure that Bar wouldn't have succumbed if she wasn't deeply in love; it'll be Fred who will be upset and feel let down by this news . . .

She was actually surprised by his reaction. They discussed their problems at night, when they went to bed, when there were no flapping little ears.

'As usual, Mirry, you'll bear the brunt of this, until she actually gets married and moves out,' he said. 'Just when you were looking forward to a bit more freedom, with young Raff going to school in the autumn, you'll have to see Bar through the birth and then help with a new baby, and all that entails.'

'You're not to worry about that,' she told him. 'I'll cope. And Mum will help out, of course. Bar's promised to tell her tomorrow – it takes a lot to shock Mum.' She added ruefully, 'We're a full house now – we might have to open up the attic.'

'Glory would enjoy swinging up there on a rope, to bed, at nights.' He patted Mirry's shoulder. 'You'll miss that little lad, Mirry, when they do go, and so will I.'

Then they were both silent, thinking how their lives would be changed, too.

The site where Lahana had stood was being cleared, levelled, at last. Ted popped over to see Mirry one day. 'The council is taking it on – they're going to grass it over, put on swings and playthings for the youngsters in the area – benches for the mums. They say there'll be a lot more children born in this post-war period and it'll be a safe place for them to play. No busy roads to cross, as there are, to the Grove.'

'Is Anna pleased about this idea?' Mirry asked.

'I believe she is. She doesn't say much about anything these days – depressed the doctor says, because she's still on crutches.'

'No wonder . . . I must come and see her, Ted, but, well, things have been a bit upside down here.'

'I've noticed young Bar wobbling on her bike,' Ted cleared his throat.

'That's a tactful way to put it,' Mirry said, but at least it made her smile.

The day before Bar and Robin were due to leave for Bristol, a telegram was delivered to Number Five. It was from Peter's parents, now settled in Wales:

Please postpone visit. Peter here. Very Poorly. Chickenpox. Writing. Howe.

The letter arrived by first post the next day. Bar read it, then passed it to Mirry without comment.

Dear Barbara,

I can guess how disappointed you must be not to be travelling to Bristol this morning – Peter was so looking forward to seeing you and your little son, and says he feels really fed up about it all. I said, if Barbara has had the dreaded c/p why doesn't she come here, to cheer you up?

But he pointed out that he would be afraid of passing on the infection to Robin through you.

What a way to catch it – on teaching practice, at a local school! But maybe it's better now, than later – even if he has to spend most of the holiday recovering, eh? These things are always more severe when you are older, it seems.

We had been looking forward to coming to Bristol to meet you, too. He has told us so much about you! We understand that an engagement is in the offing?

Peter sends his love to you both, and will write as soon as he can. Meanwhile, rest assured that he is being well looked after.

With every good wish,
Marian Howe

'An engagement in the offing!' Mirry exclaimed crossly. 'She's in for a surprise! You ought to go there, Bar – Robin could stay here with me – I don't think you could pass it on as Peter imagines, you have to have direct contact . . .'

'Don't you see, Mirry – I may have had chickenpox – I can still remember that dreadful itching and Mum making me wear gloves at night, in case I got at the spots in my sleep – but what about – this new little one? I can't take that risk.'

'You must write and tell him now, Bar – oh, you must!'

Bar took the letter back and stuffed it in her bag. 'I hope you haven't any thoughts of writing yourself, Mirry. I shall be really cross if you do . . . It's my business, I told you that – and, now, I'm off to work. Robin! Come and give Mummy a kiss,' she called.

Glory had been supervising him in the bathroom. Now, she came downstairs behind him, with Boo trailing behind.

'Bar,' she said, 'are you having a baby? No one tells me anything.'

'Yes,' Bar answered honestly, 'but I'm afraid I'll have to leave your mum to explain – I'm late for work already.'

'Thank you very much!' Mirry said, with feeling.

While Glory took Boo and Robin over to the new play park opposite, Mirry walked down the road to call on Anna. It had been surprisingly easy to talk to Glory because, at rising fourteen, her daughter was well aware of all the plain facts of life. Mirry wouldn't willingly have broached the subject when Glory was only eleven, but a letter from the Lady Makepeace School, which was sent to the mothers of each new intake of girls, had made it quite clear that this talk was obligatory. Now, she was very glad she had.

The only embarrassing moment for Mirry today was when Glory asked: 'Is the baby's father Peter?' She had merely nodded then, and Glory said cheerfully: 'I expect they'll get married soon then, won't they?' When Mirry nodded again, Glory seemed satisfied.

Anna came slowly to the door on her crutches. Slacks – something the old elegant Anna would never have worn – concealed the scars on her legs, and there was more grey than auburn in her hair now. But she wore a pretty blouse and she had put on lipstick, so Mirry thought she must be feeling better in herself.

'Shall we go out into the garden? Ted told me you were coming – he put out some chairs – he'll leave us to chat, he says, but he'll make some tea a little later. It's so good to see you, Mirry – but where are the children? School holidays: I expected you to bring them.'

Mirry could hardly say that Boo and Robin, being art-less seven and four year olds, were all too likely to make tactless remarks when they saw Miss Boam swinging pain-fully along with her sticks, or when they noticed the little embroidered Juliet cap she wore to hide the aftermath of the injury to her head, where the hair had unfortunately not grown back.

'Glory's helping them get rid of their excess energy – they have gone over to the Lahana play park, Anna. Wasn't that a lovely idea—'

'A sort of memorial?' Anna said drily, sinking down with relief in her chair on the flagged terrace which took up most of the back garden. 'To my late, lamented father, whom most children seemed to regard as a bogey-man, and to my mother?'

'But . . .'

'You imagined my mother, dear Beatrice, might still be around somewhere, is that it? No, she left us a long, long time ago. There was no point in rebuilding the house, Mirry. All the old memories are dead and buried there; I don't even have a photograph of them, you know. Ted and I are perfectly comfortable here: he just resumed where he left off – from nursing the first Mrs Goldsmith to caring for me.'

'He's a very kind man,' Mirry observed.

'Yes, he is. Ted was my first boyfriend, you know, when I was still innocent, before I met Vernon, older and well versed in the ways of the world. He wasn't faithful but to betray me with my own mother . . .' She broke off, then continued, 'Of course, when Ted and I first got together – before all this happened – he must have imagined his life was about to change for the better. Still, he never complains.' She looked at Mirry. 'Cheer up! I didn't mean to sound so gloomy, sorry. You tell that sister of yours she hasn't visited me in ages – I know she works hard, but I'd love to chat with her about the old times, when she learned to tango so exquisitely and broke all those hearts.'

'Bar's expecting another baby, Anna.' Mirry surprised herself; it just came out.

'Ah, I wondered when you'd say. Ted heard rumours on the grapevine, and put two and two together, and told me, of course. She's still full of youthful passion . . .' her voice trailed off, and she looked regretful.

'Peter, Bar's young man, is a super chap, we would be only too pleased to see them married, Anna.' Mirry knew she sounded prim.

'What's the problem, then? Robin?'

'Oh, no! Peter's out of the army now and training to be a teacher. The problem, and we can't understand it at all, is that Bar hasn't told him yet that she's four months pregnant. She was about to, when she heard from his mother that he's ill – nothing serious, but she won't be able to visit him this week as she hoped.'

They heard the hammering on the door and the agitated voices, from where they sat in the garden, then Ted appeared, with Boo in his arms, clinging round his neck and sobbing, and Glory, white-faced, carrying Robin.

'Whatever's happened?' Mirry cried, jumping up in alarm. 'Which one of them is hurt? Glory, you promised to watch them . . .'

'Oh, Mum! It's Robin, he got off his swing while I was pushing Boo on hers, and he tried to get up the slide from the bottom, and he slipped, and—'

'I banged my arm,' Robin said, holding his left wrist with his right hand, but not crying, although he looked very solemn.

'Don't scold Glory, Mirry,' Anna said quickly, 'you know how quickly these things happen.'

'Give him to me,' Mirry said, and she sat down again with Robin on her lap, and fearfully felt his limp little wrist. He winced at her touch, tried to pull his arm away.

'Even if it's broken, and I'm afraid it does look as if it might be,' Ted said, having trained in first aid, of course, during the war, 'it'll only be a greenstick fracture, at his age. Best if you and I take him straight to the hospital casualty department, Mirry; I'll get the motorbike and sidecar out of the garage.'

'Glory and Boo can stay with me,' Anna offered.

'It's so kind of you both – oh dear, whatever will Bar say? You'd better take my key, Glory, and just you be back at ours before she arrives home from work. Goodness knows how long we'll be at the hospital – it's getting on for four already.'

Robin suddenly burst into tears. 'It hurts!' he wailed. 'I want my mummy!'

It was Bar who was white with shock now. Glory whispered to Boo to go and play with her dolls and to be quiet for a bit. She made Bar sit down in Fred's armchair, and she gave her a glass of water, because Bar said faintly that was what she wanted, not tea, not yet, until Glory had told her exactly what happened . . .

It was another hour before the front door opened and Robin rushed in, proudly displaying the white plaster to his elbow. 'I gotta have a sling, Mummy, but I can wiggle my fingers – look! – and the doctor said I was a real soldier, and to tell my daddy how brave I'd been – is Peter my daddy now?'

And then Bar was weeping as if she would never stop.

CHAPTER FORTY-FIVE

IN NOVEMBER, ROBIN, his wrist now minus plaster, had been at school for two months. Bar, heavier than she had been in her first pregnancy, bowed to the inevitable, and gave in her notice at *The Norwood News*. They said they would miss her, and she was welcome back any time. Carry on with the children's page, anyway: she could do that at home – the chief said he'd no intention of being dear old Uncle Charlie again . . .

She still hadn't told Peter about the baby. She would have gone to Bristol at half-term and spilled the beans then, she tried to convince herself, if Robin hadn't had his hospital check-up booked during that week.

Peter was writing regularly again: long, but more light-hearted than loving letters. She couldn't help worrying that he might have put to the back of his mind what had happened while they were at Iris's. I don't think he would have made the first move then, she agonised to herself. I can't blame him for responding, I made it quite clear how I felt, after all. Still, he did broadcast to the wind that he loved me.

You don't know how much I am looking forward [he wrote] *to seeing you both this Christmas! Please thank Mirry and Fred for asking me. Of course I don't mind bunking down on the settee! It's great news that you are taking some time off work to be with me . . . Perhaps we could go to see my parents in the New Year?*

Little does he know, she thought, that we, Robin and I that is, won't be going anywhere, until I've had the baby. Will he be angry – hurt – at the way I've deceived him? His mother mentioned an engagement in that letter: I believed that we would get married at the end of his course. I don't know what to think now . . . Six days in all, is that long enough to be sure of someone? It took seven years for me to decide to marry Clive.

'Can I – stay – Mirry,' she asked, one Monday afternoon, as Mirry pressed the small garments she had washed earlier. 'If things don't work out, as planned?'

Mirry set the iron down, eyed her sister with concern. 'Bar darling, you know you can. You make your mind up, in your own good time.'

'It won't be me that has to make my mind up. You were right, Mirry – I was pig-headed. I should have told him. He might find it hard to forgive me, you see.'

'He'll be surprised – maybe shocked – but I don't think he'll let you down Bar.'

'He might feel I've trapped him into marriage – oh, Mirry, I'm so tired this time, carrying all this weight – just look at my mumsy ankles!'

'You ought to go to the doctor,' Mirry told her, worried.

'Can't afford it! Besides, he'll just tell me to rest – and that's exactly what I'm doing now, thanks to my lovely sister.'

'There's a surgery this evening, we'll go then. Your health is more important than the doctor's fee. Fred and I aren't exactly hard up nowadays; we'll fork out – it'll be worth it for our peace of mind, as well as yours . . .' Mirry decided. 'Glory'll see to the children, and serve up Fred's dinner . . .'

Dr Brown frowned when he checked her blood pressure, but did not comment. When he prodded and probed her swollen belly, Bar tried to joke: 'Sometimes feels as if there's a whole army pounding away in there.'

'Not an army, Mrs Joy – more likely, two babies,' he said at last. 'It's very unlikely you'll go full term and, if your blood pressure soars any higher – well, I'm afraid it's hospital for you, until the birth. You should have bed-rest from now, at home, and I will call to see you next week.'

They walked homewards in stunned silence. Mirry held Bar's arm, trying to comfort with her support. Rain had puddled the streets in the last hour, the street lamps illuminated their wet shoes, their pale, shocked faces, the leaves floating in the gutters.

Bar spoke at last. 'D'you mind Mirry – taking me round to Mum's? I'll tell her the news, while you do the same at home . . . Please, don't let Fred make a fuss. But he can fetch me home later, if he doesn't mind.'

'He won't mind, of course he won't. If he fusses, well, it's only because he thinks the world of you, as we all do.'

'I've got to hang on for three weeks – to eight months, if I can, Mirry. The babies, will have more chance then, won't they? Then Peter will be here.'

Mirry sighed. 'And you still haven't told him, have you, Bar?'

Mum made Bar put her feet up while Hilda, guessing that Bar wanted to confide in her mother, went to make a comforting pot of tea.

'What's up, dearie? Mirry going off quickly like that, and you – come on, tell your old mum all about it.'

'I'm going to have twins,' Bar said weakly. Then she started to laugh and cry at the same time.

'Hilda! Bring a drop of brandy, will you?' Mum called out. Then she sat down, too. 'Bring the bottle – we'll both need it, too.'

'I never told you, either of you this before, and now I realise I should have,' Mum said, adding her drop of brandy to her tea. 'But Mirry was one of twins – the other

– oh, dear – why I am telling you that, now?' She spilt some tea on the arm of the chair, in her distress.

'I'll fetch a cloth – don't worry about it, Elsie,' Hilda bustled out again.

'You'll be all right, Bar dear, of course you will, and so will they . . . I only meant, well, twins might run in our family, you see. You have complete rest, as the doctor says.'

Fred was wonderful, he gave her a hug when he called for her, and whispered: 'O be joyful! Two for the price of one, eh?' Then he walked her slowly home, with a firm arm round her shoulders.

* * *

On 8 December, the day Peter was due to arrive, Mirry hurried back to Number Five after taking the children to school. There was a lot to do, she thought ruefully, if she was to have the place all spick and span, the bed on the sofa in the front room made up and Bar helped in and out of the bath and her hair washed. Bar was determined to look her best, 'from the neck up', as she wryly put it. She also intended to be dressed, and downstairs to greet him. 'I won't need to say anything now, Mirry – he'll see for himself, eh?'

As she put her key in the lock, the door unexpectedly opened. Bar stood there, huge in the inadequate dressing gown, bare-footed because she could not bend to put on her slippers.

'Bar!' Mirry exclaimed crossly. 'You know you shouldn't come down without me behind you—'

'Mirry dear, please, can you run for the doctor? I – I won't be able to hang on, till Peter comes, I'm afraid . . .'

With memories flooding back of the day Glory was born, Mirry guided her sister into the front room, restored to prewar order, and helped her to stretch out on the settee. She grabbed one of the blankets from the neat pile intended for Peter, and tucked it round her sister.

'I'll be as quick as I can. Don't you dare move until I get back!'

'Anything wrong?' they heard Mum's anxious voice. 'I found the door open.'

'Oh Mum, thank heavens! In here – look after Bar while I go for Dr Brown.'

*   *   *

When the ambulance had gone, with Mum accompanying Bar, Mirry suddenly seemed to come to, to realise just what was happening, the task ahead of her. *She* was going to have to break the news to Peter – she hadn't made the beds, she hadn't washed up, she hadn't peeled the potatoes for lunch, she would have to collect the little ones from school shortly, and she was shaking like a leaf . . .

Bar moved her head restlessly on the pillow. It was evening now, and the painful events of the past hours were clouding, mercifully receding, as sheer exhaustion took over. She was in a cubicle by herself, not back in the big ward where she had been taken on her arrival at the hospital. The light was dimmed, the bustle outside muffled.

'Robin . . .' she murmured.

'Robin is fine – king of the castle back at home, as I imagine he always is.' A calm voice, a warm hand covering hers.

'Peter! Oh, Peter – what a welcome for you!' she cried, trying to struggle up in bed.

'No, Bar – you must rest – you've got lots of stitches, but not as many, thank goodness, as you would have had, if they'd had to perform that emergency Caesarean . . . You did it by yourself, Bar, I'm so proud of you.'

It was all coming back to her now. 'The babies?' she whispered urgently. They'd given her a brief glimpse, before they were whisked away to special care. Fair skinned they were, with reddish blonde hair like Peter. Just a fuzz, in their case . . .

'The little girls – our little girls – are holding their own.' He cleared his throat. 'The next few days will be crucial, of course, but the first one weighed nearly four pounds, and the second baby almost as much – they still look so tiny, to me, Bar, yet they are perfect.'

'Peter, are you *very* shocked? Do you forgive me?'

'Well, I am, but I do. It's – a lot to take in, you know.'

'I know!' Tears began to trickle down her face.

He wiped them away gently with a clean handkerchief. Then he kissed her, briefly, but tenderly. 'To quote your nice brother-in-law – love will find a way, Bar. And I do love you, you must believe that. Who is going to tell my mother – you or me?' he joked. 'And guess what? I don't have to sleep on the sofa after all – I've got your bed!'

'Wish I was in it.'

'No, you don't! But, I do.'

'Would your husband like a quick cup of tea?' a young probationer nurse put her head round the door. 'Then you must go, I'm afraid,' she reminded Peter. 'Visiting ends at eight ... Have you thought up names for your unexpected arrivals, I wonder? At the moment they are just Baby Joy, one and two – they're not identical, that's something.'

'Howe,' Peter said firmly, 'their surname is Howe.'

'Oh,' the nurse said uncertainly. She smoothed down her crackling, starched apron, to cover her confusion.

'You name one, and I'll name the other!' She sounded quite like the old, bouncy Bar, again. 'You first, Peter.'

'Crystal,' he suggested. 'How about that, darling?'

'After the Palace, I presume?'

'Of course.'

'Crystal, that's nice,' the nurse repeated, 'and?' she prompted Bar.

'Anna,' Bar decided out of the blue. 'It takes two to tango, you see . . .' she told the nurse.

Nurse, whose name was Tallulah, only she wasn't revealing that, thought they must have given Mrs Joy – or Mrs Howe? – too much gas, for she was laughing, but then, so was – whatever his name was, even though he hadn't gone through what his wife had, in producing those twins. They wouldn't be tangoing for a while, she'd bet on that. She made her escape. 'I'll fetch that tea,' she said.

Christmas Eve in the hospital, and the youngest nurses turned their cloaks so that the scarlet lining gleamed as they made their torchlight procession round the wards, singing carols. Shining unadorned faces they had; smooth, short hair, tucked behind their ears. Outside it was bitterly cold with a hint of worse to come.

They stopped outside Bar's room, knocked, opened the door, and began the hauntingly beautiful 'Silent Night'.

Bar had the baby girls with her in bed, propped up on a pillow, one cuddled in the crook of each arm. She looked like a girl herself, despite her twenty-eight years, with her long curly hair threaded by a ribbon which matched the nurses' capes. Peter sat in the corner, unable to take his eyes off this maternal scene, but at a prudent distance from the bed, with Robin on his lap. The nurses pretended they didn't see him, for children were not allowed on the maternity ward.

'That was really lovely ... thank you,' Bar said softly, when the singing stopped. She looked down at the tiny bundles; the babies were doing really well, after the initial agonising by their mother as to whether it would be easier to bottle-feed, the decision had been taken out of her hands when she developed a breast abscess and a high temperature. This had delayed her own recovery but the babies were fast making up their birth weight. However, they couldn't go home yet, and nor could she. She fretted over this, when she lay awake, alone, at night, for she thought that she and Peter needed so much to be together just now, to plan their future.

When the nurses had gone, she said to Peter: 'I wish I could be there tomorrow to see Robin and Boo open their stockings ...'

'Father Christmas is coming, don't you worry about that,' he assured her. 'I keep getting tangled up in all those sticky paper loops Glory has put everywhere. Mirry informs me I'm far too tall. I do like your family, you know, they've taken all this in their stride and made me feel at home.'

Robin had had enough of sitting still, and looking at Mummy in bed with those babies. 'Shall we go now, Dad?' he asked Peter.

Peter asked: 'D'you mind, Bar? I suppose he's put two and two together and . . .' She could detect the hint of anxiety in his voice.

'I don't mind – and I know Clive wouldn't, either,' Bar said. But tears pricked at her eyes, thinking of him. Robin had been only ten days old when Clive died. The twins were already two and a half weeks old. It was better, though, she thought, for Robin to copy Glory and call Peter Dad, rather than Daddy . . .

'We'll get married, Bar, when you do come home, I've already got the licence,' he told her. 'I'll do my best to get a transfer to a college in your area – it's what I should have plumped for in the first place – but I'm afraid you'll have to go back to your dear Mirry for a bit, until things are sorted out.'

'I don't want to get married in slippers, Peter,' she tried to joke. She'd have to tell him, but not today, that she didn't want a rushed wedding, only to have to part again almost immediately, as she had with Clive. She'd say he shouldn't jeopardise his chances of passing his exams by changing colleges at such a late stage. Number Five was splitting at the seams anyway, it wouldn't make much difference, she thought. 'Give me a kiss, you two, then you can go, because I can tell Robin's longing to get back to hang his stocking up – but don't breathe on the babies,' she said. 'I might have to eat my Christmas dinner in here, but I'm the luckiest girl in the world.'

'You're not a girl, you're a Bar,' Robin said solemnly.

CHAPTER FORTY-SIX

THE YEAR 1947 WAS A YEAR to remember, not only because of a royal wedding, which lifted the spirits of the nation, but because of the vagaries of the weather and its effect on the country. That year had it all: bitter cold, thick fogs, shortages of almost everything and, in contrast, there was a brilliant, scorching summer when many holidayed by the sea for the first time since the war. There was Christian Dior's promise of a New Look for women, who had been so long starved of glamour, even if it still seemed beyond reach for most of them.

In April, Bar and Peter were to be married. Bar had been back at her job for a few weeks helping out on the paper, ostensibly to earn some pin money towards her wedding outfit, but really because she felt somewhat redundant at home, with Mirry and Mum vying to look after the twins. Clive had known Bar so well. She adored her children, no one could dispute that, but she didn't really want to be at home with them all day like Mirry.

Glory knew that she would be the same, when the time came. She was hopeless at sewing – Mirry had had to finish the hem of her cookery apron – she only enjoyed fancy cooking which her mother said took far too many ingredients and, although she was very fond of her sister and her cousins, she'd rather read them stories and stir their imagination than become involved with the messy chores small children engendered.

'Gloria Hope, what are you doing?' Miss Tiptree exclaimed in exasperation one day, when she was in the library off the school flat and heard excessive laughter emanating from there.

Glory, skirt tucked in her knickers, domestic science cap awry, stood barefooted in a puddle of water in the bath. She was playing to an audience of two other girls. She turned, cloth in hand, and beamed at the teacher. 'Cleaning the bath, Miss Tiptree,' she said cheerfully. 'It's much easier if you get in and get down to it, if you know what I mean.' Her classmates, who had egged her on, now tried to slip out of the door, back into the big kitchen.

'I know exactly what you mean,' Miss Tiptree sighed. 'You can write fifty lines: I must not play the fool during Domestic Science lessons.'

Playing the fool, any sort of acting, was exactly what Glory wanted to do.

On Saturday mornings, now she was rising fifteen, she was allowed to go shopping in Croydon, unaccompanied by her mother, but with her little sister tagging along, in the hope this would make her feel very responsible.

Boo wasn't so bad, Glory thought; in fact, they got on very well. They soon followed a familiar routine: Surrey Street Market, with all the noise and bustle, to buy fruit and veg, which might not be available in their local shops, was the first port of call. Then Kennards, that marvellous store with its many departments and, best of all, the arcade, where shaggy Shetland ponies walked patiently up and down, with excited children on their backs, and the pets' corner, where there was an overpowering smell of small animals in cages and beady-eyed birds rushing to peck the unwary finger poked through the mesh. Poor old Pip had died suddenly after Christmas. Glory had been in floods of tears for days whenever she thought of him, but now she was intent on looking at the Kennards puppies, all adorable, even if the ones she could afford, on her half a crown a week pocket money, were of dubious parentage with large feet. Anyway, Mum had said a firm no to replacing Pip. There was enough to do, with babies all over the house, she said, without mopping up after pups. She was aware that Glory had done her bit with Pip in the past, but now she must concentrate on passing her exams next year, because most actresses were very glad indeed to have Something to Fall Back On . . .

There was a rumour that Kennards would soon be selling ice-creams again in the arcade. Dad said it was most unhygienic to have food of any sort in that part of the store, but Glory and Boo couldn't wait. 'I shall buy two,' Boo decided, 'one to hold in each hand, and lick them in turn.'

This Saturday, after the pony-ride, they left the wriggling, pot-bellied puppies with reluctance, and emerged outside, heading for Glory's touch of sophistication, Wilson's Coffee Shop. The aroma was wonderful, but Glory always warned Boo to be on her best behaviour as they entered this posh place. Good old Bar, slipping her the odd shilling or two, now she was earning again, she thought. She wasn't really sure she liked the coffee, which was very strong and bitter, but the fancy cakes were mouth-watering morsels. She kept a stern eye out for Boo's crumbs.

'Glory?' a voice inquired. She turned in surprise. A young man, wearing a sports jacket and flannels, regarded her with a smile. She blushed. She'd come here to drink coffee, wearing her new green skirt with what she fancifully dubbed cabbage-leaf straps, wide and ruched, over a yellow blouse, inherited from Bar. She was being all ladylike with crooked little finger as she raised her cup; eating cake with a fork, not intending to get into conversation with strange boys, she thought.

'You haven't changed – I'd recognise that curly head anywhere. Well, you are quite grown up, of course,' he said. 'But I see you don't recognise me: Horst – we met at school in Surrey at the beginning of the war, when you were – this must be your sister? Around this age—'

'Horst – whatever are you doing here – I thought you went to America?'

'I did. But my father came here quite a while ago to lecture, in London, you know, and we all wished to stay. I called at last to surprise you this morning. I wrote to Mrs Dean at the farm and she gave me your address and, as I couldn't wait to see you after so long, your mother directed me here: "Go to the Coffee Shop," she said, "about eleven . . ." May I join you?'

'Sit next to me,' Boo offered, making them both smile.

'Let me see,' he said, as he drank his coffee: 'You must be fifteen years old?'

'Not far off,' she answered quickly. The young Horst had been angular, all legs, big feet and hands, with untidy hair; this young man was tall, with broad shoulders and fair hair brushed back with a quiff. She hadn't remembered the rather beaky nose, but the nice smile was just the same. He had grown into his hands and feet, she thought, absurdly; thinking of his knees wedged under the desk they had shared more than seven years ago.

'And I am eighteen. I am studying music at the Royal Academy. I shall have National Service deferred until my studies are over.'

Glory suddenly realised the time. 'We have to catch the tram! Mum gets het up if we're late for lunch.'

'Mrs Hope has kindly invited me to eat with you, I do hope you don't mind?'

'Of course I don't! We've got a lot of news to catch up on, Horst.'

'I shall pay the bill,' he insisted, 'I have a good allowance from my parents.'

This made Glory feel really grown up, a young man treating her to coffee.

He said in her ear, as they boarded the tram: 'You are just as pretty as I imagined you would be . . .'

'I don't turn somersaults on the settee any more,' she whispered back. What would he think of her if he knew of her pranks at school?

'Glory's going to drama school next year, if she passes all her exams first,' Boo said proudly. 'And I'm going to be a bridesmaid at Bar's wedding next Saturday. Glory said she was far too old. You can come, if you like, I'll ask Mummy.'

'That would be very nice.' He was quite straightforward about it. 'I would like to see more of you, during the Easter vacation.' And he looked at Glory as he said that.

Bar walked down the aisle in her powder-blue costume, with the little feathered hat, holding tight to Fred's arm. She kept her eyes on Peter's straight back, as he stood beside his best man, a friend from the army. She was determined not to look at Crystal, lying wide awake in Mirry's arms or at Anna, dozing in Mum's. Five-year-old Robin sat, looking solemn, next to Glory, and Boo followed on – well, she hoped she did – behind. There were just the two families, in the church, she thought, apart from the Sims and their mother, and Glory's friend.

No Anna and Ted; Anna was not too well at present. Bar had promised to call to see her soon.

She mustn't think, at this moment, of the last time she had married – well, been blessed – in church. Very soon she would be Barbara Howe, wife of Peter, and there was still so much they had to learn about each other . . .

Then she was at Peter's side, and he had her hand in his warm, reassuring clasp, and Fred moved away slightly, as if he was relinquishing her at last.

They kept the reception, in the front room of Number Five, short and sweet, because Peter's parents were driving home that evening. They had entertained Bar and Peter to dinner the previous night in the hotel where they were staying before the wedding. Bar liked them, but she sensed a certain reserve on their part. She hoped very much that they didn't feel she had rushed their only son into matrimony because of the twins, but she had no doubts that the babies and Robin had won them over. They were already doting grandparents. They waved them farewell, and repeated their promises to visit soon. Then it was time for the newly-weds to depart for their short break from family commitments – I never manage a real honeymoon, Bar thought wryly.

'You are not to worry about a thing,' Mirry insisted. 'Glory will help with bathing the children tonight, and amusing them until you come back.'

'I'm sorry we are putting you out still further,' Bar said. They were in her bedroom, with its single bed, which Peter would have to share for the time being, until they found somewhere to live. At least he had a temporary post lined up in a school in Norwood, she thought, so they would be able to pay their way, and she could continue at the paper for the time being – Mirry wouldn't want her under her feet all day.

Robin, a bouncer on beds like his mum, was doing just that, energetically, on his little bed under the window. It wasn't going to be ideal, sharing a room with him. The babies had slept, from the beginning, in Mirry and Fred's room, because it was large enough to accommodate their cots. That wasn't the best arrangement either, Bar was very aware of that. In the beginning, she had been grateful, because it had taken her a month or two to regain her strength, but now . . .

Bar, having checked the contents of her case, clicked it shut.

'Got everything?' Mirry asked unnecessarily. Then she took off her glasses and pretended to polish them with her handkerchief. 'A bit like *Brief Encounter*, isn't it, Bar dear? You and Peter, snatching time together when you can – Peter's got a look of Trevor Howard, I always think.'

'You can hardly say I'm like the character Celia Johnson played,' Bar returned drily, 'but I do know what you mean. We'll have to make the most of tonight I suppose.'

'*Bar*! But, yes, you will. Fred and I feel the lack of privacy, too, you know, at the moment,' Mirry admitted.

'You should make the most of us not being around, too, eh? I'm sure Fred will agree: you look so pretty today, Mirry, in that pink crêpe; that soft perm really suits you. No one would believe you've got a daughter almost grown up.'

'One who seems to have acquired a boyfriend very suddenly. She made sure she caught your bouquet, you know,' Mirry mused. 'I'm glad it's only Horst, though.'

'Only Horst? She's bowled him over, Mirry!'

'Oh, she's far too young . . .' Mirry looked worried.

'As you and Fred thought I was, I suppose, when I first met Clive . . . Don't worry, Mirry, she isn't *that* grown up yet, and he'll respect that, I'm sure.'

Fred looked round the door. 'Ready? The taxi's here.'

'Ready for anything!' Bar sang out, with a confidence she didn't feel . . .

Here I am again, she thought, sitting on a hotel bed, only I restrained myself from jumping on it, for once – in a pretty white slip, not silk this time, I'm afraid, waiting for Peter to come out of the bathroom before I take my turn, and get changed into my nightie at the same time . . . We're not at ease with each other yet, that's obvious.

He said cheerfully: 'All yours . . .' as he towelled his head. He looked so young like that; with rumpled hair, no jacket, like last time, which made Bar blush, remembering that night, with the twins to show for it. 'I thought I ought to wash out the Brylcreem my mother insisted I use, to try to flatten my unruly hair – those pillowcases look all starched and prim don't they? Well, where's the pink pyjamas?' he grinned. He didn't look nervous at all.

She felt better about everything immediately. 'You're about to get a nice surprise, I think.'

'You only think? Come here, d'you realise I haven't had the chance to kiss you properly these last two days, and here we are, almost at the end of our wedding day,' he touched her bare shoulder lightly, suddenly serious.

'But at the beginning of our wedding night,' she whispered, 'and somehow, I don't think this will be a brief encounter . . .'

CHAPTER FORTY-SEVEN

Austerity was still the key word in Great Britain – the prime minister spoke solemnly of further cuts in rations – with the war already over for two years. Fred's dream of buying a new family saloon car was fast fading, with the clampdown on the use of petrol. Laura and Jim wished they had seized the opportunity to holiday abroad earlier in the year – no foreign pleasure trips would be permitted from September. And rented accommodation, Bar and Peter found, was like gold dust . . .

But in August, Mirry and Fred went back to the little bungalow perched on the cliff in Norfolk: they took Robin as company for Boo, and Clive's old tent for Horst, so that Glory would have a friend more her own age. And Mum came too, to babysit, and chaperone the young people, when Mirry and Fred felt like a night out on the town, i.e., the village pub. The weather was wonderful, and Mirry said, before she went: 'Pity you can't come, too, Bar, though I suppose you'd be worrying about the babies crawling on the sand and eating it. Are you sure you can manage on your own?'

Bar bit back a sharp retort. It was true, after all, that she had hardly ever looked after her children without her sister being there, too. This would be a testing time, she thought, with regard to future plans she hadn't yet felt able to discuss with Mirry for fear of upsetting her. 'I'll be fine – remember that Peter will be here all day, as well. I'll write my Auntie Joy bits for the paper when the girls deign to take a nap – and I just might enjoy being a real housewife for a change.' Unsaid was: And won't it be wonderful for Peter and me to have the place to ourselves in the evenings – and the luxury of your double bed!

'There!' she challenged Peter, one afternoon, displaying a dish. 'Does this look like shepherd's pie?' She had criss-crossed the potato crust with the tines of a fork. The lumpy mince and onion was quite concealed. Were you supposed to cook these first, she wondered? But Peter didn't have Clive's interest in cooking. He wasn't any more domesti-cated than she was, she thought ruefully.

'Looks aren't everything,' he teased her, crawling along the floor with his daughters clinging to his back. They were so like him, as Robin was Clive. Bar missed her little boy, but Mirry and Fred adored him, so she hoped it would be a comfort to them later, to have had him to themselves for a couple of weeks, when she and Peter broke the news . . .

'Well, you can just twitch your nose now and then to smell if it's burning in the oven, eh, while I take the opportunity to go round to see Anna Boam-as-was. I met Ted round at the butcher's today, and he said she'd been asking for me . . . Can I trust you to look after the terrible twins for an hour?'

'Easier than keeping tabs on their terrible mum,' he teased. He was a natural with children, she thought. Yes, teaching was obviously the vocation for Peter.

Bar suddenly went down on her knees, kissed two rosy, dribbly faces, and the top of his head. 'I love you, Peter, have I ever told you that?' she asked him. After losing Clive, and being so fortunate to find Peter, she had promised herself that she would repeat this often, for you never knew how long you might have together.

'You have, but don't ever stop will you? And we love you, too, don't we girls?'

'I know you do. 'Bye!'

'I'll make the tea,' Ted said, as he always did, about to disappear discreetly. 'I'll bring it in, in about half an hour, eh?'

Anna sat in an over-stuffed armchair by the window in the front room. Bar experienced quite a shock when she saw how she looked, realising that it must be some months since she had visited. In fact, it had been Mirry who had proudly wheeled the twins round in their big pram to show them off.

'You haven't brought Crystal – or little Anna?' she asked.

'I'm sorry – no. I thought – well, it's difficult to chat, when you're mopping dribble, or one of them suddenly needs changing urgently,' Bar apologised.

Anna's hair had grown again, the dye had faded and she had braided it in two silvery ropes around her head. Although now lined through constant pain, her face was still beautiful, Bar thought. She seemed much smaller, sitting here, than the tall, regal Anna who had worn those fraying stage clothes with such aplomb, and danced so gracefully round the ballroom floor at Lahana.

'Neither of us dances nowadays ...' Anna said suddenly, as if she knew what Bar was thinking.

'No.'

'You could have taken it up professionally.'

'I loved dancing, Anna, thanks to you but, well, I suppose you can say the war steered me in another direction. But another of your pupils will be a performer, we think. Glory is determined to be an actress, and who knows? The old tap dancing might come in handy, if she appears in a musical show one day. Mirry, of course, dreams of her becoming a film star.'

'You are a talented family, Bar. Mirry with her music – does she play much, now?'

'My fault if she doesn't,' Bar said, 'as she looks after my children while I work ...'

'Ah, but she will miss you all when you go away,' Anna observed.

Bar showed her surprise. 'How did you know we are going away?'

'I didn't! But I'm sure you will. I never thought you were destined to spend your life here in the suburbs. It's better if you leave soon, because it will become harder to make the break as time goes on or, as it was with me after Vernon went off, when my mother left me with my father, eventually impossible.'

'We are seriously considering emigrating to South Africa,' Bar said. 'Peter's been finding out about the pros and cons. His uncle is out there. He has already lined up a school for Peter, and there would probably be something for me, too, if I wanted it. It would be a new start, a new country, a different life – perhaps then, we would start to feel like a real family . . .'

'Oh, you must go, Bar – seize the opportunity.'

Then Ted came in, beaming, with the tray of tea.

Glory and Horst walked hand in hand along the shore, enjoying the foamy water washing over their gritty bare feet, as the tide went out. Glory was nicely tanned after almost a week of sunshine: she had tied a cotton scarf, gypsy fashion, over her head, at her mother's insistence, because she was much too old for her prewar summer hat with Mickey Mouse printed on it. She wore the Hungarian blouse, but didn't tuck it into her box-pleated faded blue shorts: something else she had inherited from Bar, she thought. Wouldn't it be wonderful when you could buy what you liked in the shops? She wanted, so much, to appear attractive to Horst.

He wasn't worried about impressing her, though, in his army-surplus khaki baggy shorts and what they called a teeshirt, brought with him from America.

'It's a wonder Grandma didn't say she was coming with us,' Glory observed, as at last they reached the beach beyond the bungalows, where the family groups were lounging, and found themselves quite alone. 'Let's sit with our backs to that rock, shall we?' Of course, she was quite unaware that this was the spot Bar and Clive had made for, on a moonlit night long ago.

Horst had a bottle of lemonade in his knapsack. They drank from it in turn. It was tepid, but they were glad of it. It was a scorching afternoon. At least they were shaded by the overhang of the rock. Glory lay back, put her head on the bag, and closed her eyes. She imagined she looked alluring, but in fact, she was soon asleep. The sun and fresh air had such a soporific effect.

Some time later, he woke her with a gentle tap on her arm. 'We ought to go back, Glory. We have been here an hour.'

'Aren't you going to kiss me?' she asked. Why else had they walked so far out of sight of the family? She'd been hoping for this all week. She would have to waste time by nodding off!

'You're shameless, Glory Hope, besides, I don't think your mother would approve, she would say you are too young.'

'I only said a kiss, you know!' she protested.

'I see that I must have the sense of propriety for the two of us,' he told her. 'You have guessed right – I want to kiss you, very much . . . In a few years' time, it will be different, I think.' His laughing face came close to hers. She shut her eyes again. He knew how to kiss all right, he got down to it straight away. It didn't take Glory long to get the hang of it.

When she got her breath back, she accused him: 'You've kissed someone before!' Surely, he must have guessed that she had not, she thought.

'Of course,' he agreed. 'I am, after all, older than you. But,' he looked at her very seriously now, 'my dear young Glory, one day, when we are both successful in our careers, I shall marry you . . .'

'That will be years and years ahead,' she cried, scrambling to her feet. 'Anyway, how d'you know I'll wait all that time?'

'Oh, I am confident, you will,' he said softly, gazing up at her flushed face, her sparkling eyes. It was just as well she couldn't read his thoughts . . .

Mirry listened quietly, while Bar and Peter told them of their hopes and plans. They waited until Glory had gone to bed, the night they returned from holiday. She said merely: 'I'll miss you, Bar dearie, we've always been together, you see, apart from—' She glanced at Peter.

'It's all right,' he said. 'I know what you mean. Being with Clive was an important part of Bar's life. I'd never want her to forget that. Any more than I can, the brief time with Eileen.'

'It's quite a shock you know,' Fred put in, 'to be told you've been going into all this, and never said a word to us – as if our advice counted for nothing.' He sounded dazed.

'It was only because we didn't want to hurt you, upset you unnecessarily, if it wasn't all going to come off,' Bar said.

'You've been extraordinarily good to us, both of you. We appreciate your kindness, your help, more than either of us can say. But you must have realised that things couldn't go on, as they are. You need, too, to adjust to being a normal family again, and we have to leave you, if we are to be the same.'

'You didn't have to go so far away, Bar,' Mirry's lips were working now. Fred, sitting beside her on the settee, put his arm around her.

'We'll come back, of course we will,' Bar tried to reassure her.

'You could have waited a day or two to tell us,' Fred said reproachfully. 'Mirry's worn out, after all that travelling, and I'm tired after humping those cases, and it's a bit of a strain looking after two young 'uns, you know, getting on and off trains. We miss the car, we could just lump most of it inside, and stick the rest on the roof rack.'

'Not Robin and Boo, you couldn't,' Bar tried to joke. 'Look, I'm sorry we broached the subject tonight, but there it is. All we want is to go, with your blessing . . .'

'It'll take some getting used to,' Fred told them frankly. 'Well, goodnight.'

'You're not still crying, are you, Mirry?' he whispered, after they were settled in bed. 'You'll wake the little girls – shush . . .'

'Fred, you know what will be the worst thing?' she whispered.

'Losing young Raff . . . But, Bar was right, you know. We've hardly ever been, just us, since we got married, have we? It would become impossible, very soon, if we tried to continue as we are, I admit that.'

'Glory's growing up so fast – Boo, too – I wish we could have another baby, Fred.'

He stroked the tears from her face with his finger. 'You don't – not really, Mirry . . . It'll be a chance for us to be ourselves again, darling; whenever I—'

There was a wail from one of the cots, followed immediately by a cry from the one alongside.

'See what I mean?' he said ruefully, 'here we go again!'

Mirry, Glory and Boo went with Fred to Whitehall very early on the morning of the Royal Wedding Day. They watched the procession from the third-floor windows of

Fred's office, fortified by sandwiches and coffee. Glory borrowed a pencil and sheets of paper and endeavoured to capture the excitement of it all with scribbled notes and many exclamation marks. The route was lined with eager viewers, some of whom had camped out overnight in the rain. There hadn't been so many flags waved, or such crowds, since VE Day.

Defying the dismal weather, a great cheer rang out to rival the bells of Westminster Abbey, when the golden state coach appeared. The wedding was to be filmed, which was exciting in itself, but the faithful wireless transmitted the whole event as it happened.

At home, Bar and Peter listened avidly, despite the interruptions of their young family. Their belongings were piled up in the hall. Next week they would be leaving for their new life.

EPILOGUE

1957

EPILOGUE

'I CAN'T BELIEVE YOU'RE really here at last!' Mirry threw her arms round Bar and hugged her tight. Behind them, the slight young girls with pony-tailed golden hair, exchanged grins.

It might be a few minutes before we actually step inside this little, old-fashioned house was the message silently received. Crystal and Anna were not identical twins, but there was certainly empathy between them.

Fred and Peter came through the gate, carrying the cases from the car. At long last, Fred had his Morris Traveller. Robin, now a long, lanky fifteen year old, 'a man of few words', as his father observed, followed shyly with the hand luggage.

It was June 1957, getting on for ten years since Bar and Peter had left for South Africa with their family, and seven years since they last came home.

'You're so slim, Bar,' Mirry told her sister, just a little enviously, as she at last ushered them all indoors, and into the front room, adding, 'We use this room every day now – we like to sit in comfort to watch the television.'

'The heat, I suppose,' Bar said, 'keeps me thin, and look, Mirry, I've gone all grey just as I knew I would, like Mum.'

'Suits you,' Mirry told her sincerely. 'But you'll see, when Mum arrives, which should be any minute, that she still deals with any grey hairs the minute they dare to appear.'

Bar wore her long hair in a fashionable chignon, showing off gold hoop earrings. She didn't nearly look her age. Goodness, had she really just celebrated her thirty-ninth birthday? Mirry realised, but pleased, because she always thought of Bar, as she was, when she went away. It was nice that she'd retained her English accent. She wore a smart linen two-piece in a peachy shade, which complemented her tanned skin.

Mirry had endeavoured to lose a few pounds in weight before her sister saw her but, as Fred said, she was too good a cook and couldn't get used to providing meals for only two, now the girls had left home, and rationing was no more, at last. His own waistline had spread, too, he indicated ruefully. Mirry surreptitiously removed her pinny, revealing her new cap-sleeved dress with the cross-over bodice in pale blue with navy polka dots. She had been shaking icing sugar on the still warm split sponge when they arrived. She wouldn't mind betting that Bar hadn't made a single cake in the last ten years, she smiled to herself.

'You're not fat, Auntie, just cuddly – and you're not grey at all, and Mum says we take after you, being short and playing the piano. Want to hear us perform a duet? Just a short piece?' said Crystal, who always spoke first.

'Fortunately!' finished Anna, with a twinkle.

'Mirry hasn't lifted that piano lid in months, since we got that television; I resisted it at first. "What's wrong with the old wireless?" I said, but after we watched the Coronation on the Sims's TV, she kept on at me, until I weakened,' Fred told them. 'Yes, you go ahead.'

'They are obviously chips off the old block,' Mirry told Bar. 'Irrepressible – just as you were!'

'Don't forget your Glory. How's the famous actress?'

'Well, she hasn't made it to Hollywood yet, but she is in the West End – a supporting role, but she's as determined as ever, so it can't be long before her name is up in lights. She and Horst—'

'Not married yet? Glory must be almost twenty-five.'

'No! We keep hoping but Horst is away so much on his tours, it's difficult for them to find the time, they say. Anyway, she's sent us tickets for the show, and is longing to see you.'

'As we are, to see her . . . And Boo?'

'You missed her by a few days, I'm afraid. She's got a summer job in a hotel on the Isle of Wight, before she goes to university,' Mirry said proudly. 'She'll be ringing up to speak to you on the phone, this evening. Fred told her to reverse the charges ... She turned out to be the academic one. Glory made up her mind what she wanted to do in life and stuck to it, though, didn't she? Boo's a real historian, thanks to the wonderful Miss Fizzbang at the Lady Makepeace.'

'When you girls let us get a word in edgeways,' Fred said, 'shall we take the luggage upstairs?'

'And I've been trying to ask what that For Sale sign is doing in your front garden,' Peter put in, just as his daughters finished their piece and swivelled round on the long piano stool to see if the company approved, fortunately not aware that their mother and aunt had been talking too much to listen.

'They're waiting for you to clap,' Robin said in his newly gruff voice. 'I wouldn't encourage them if I were you.' It was obvious he found his little sisters rather embarrassing. He made a face at them. Knock it off, girls, they interpreted.

There was a knock on the door. 'Oh, there's Mum, and I haven't even put the kettle on,' Mirry fussed.

'I can't believe,' Bar said, just as Mirry had exclaimed to her earlier, 'that you and Fred are really thinking of moving from Number Five after all these years.'

'Twenty-five, like Glory, to be exact,' Mirry smiled. There were just crumbs on the plate which had held the fat sponge, oozing jam. Young Robin had enjoyed two large slices. 'Well, we've almost paid off the mortgage at long last, and the house needs modernising, and we don't feel inclined to tackle it, *and* we've missed Laura and Jim since they retired and went to Sevenoaks, so—'

'We decided to join 'em,' Fred said. 'Not that I'll be retired for a few years yet, but there's a fast train service to London from that part of Kent; we only need two bedrooms now, of course, and we rather fancy a bungalow, with central heating, now won't that be a boon? On a new estate. We're trying to twist Mum's arm to come with us, because she's on her own since Hilda went with Laura and Jim a couple of years ago.'

'This is far enough out of London for me,' Mum insisted.

'What happened to Junie and Don?' Bar asked curiously.

'Junie got married young – that was her aim in life you could say – Laura and Jim are grandparents twice over already. Don, well, he was rather sweet on Glory, I believe, but it was obviously Horst for her, since they met up again. Don joined the Merchant Navy, didn't he, Fred?'

'And Anna?' Bar asked. 'You haven't mentioned her in your letters for a long time.'

Mirry looked at Fred. 'Anna, Anna is a little strange these days, Bar – she couldn't get any better, her legs were so badly injured, weren't they? But . . .'

'Still, I reckon she'll be pleased to see you; poor old girl, she's rather gone the same way as the Galloping Major did, towards the end,' Fred added. He didn't actually tap his head, but Bar guessed what he meant.

'I really do want to see her,' Bar said.

They sat in the second row of the stalls, soaking in the atmosphere; the elegant clothes, mingled perfumes, the dazzling footlights. They were a large and happy party, for Iris and Harold had joined them and were staying overnight in London. Tomorrow they would take Robin back with them for a few days. They had enjoyed a celebratory meal in a smart restaurant earlier, and Bar had seen Iris gazing at her grandson all misty eyed, and instantly understood. Robin was the young, gauche Clive all over again . . . It was right, she thought, that Iris should have him to herself to get to know him properly, to re-establish the bond weakened when they took Robin to South Africa. Dear Mum had suggested it: he was her grandson too, of course, but as she whispered to Bar, she'd always had Glory and Boo more or less around, hadn't she, and now, there were the twins . . .

Glory even got to sing and dance with the leading man – in one scene she wore a flame-coloured dress with a circular skirt which billowed out as she whirled round, giving tantalising glimpses of her long, lovely legs in flesh-coloured sheer nylon stockings. She didn't blush, but her mother did. Her short curly hair, under the bright lights, appeared as golden as it was when she was a child. In a sad scene towards the end of the show, when she accepted rejection with a brave smile, Glory's family watched proudly. They could sense the audience's sympathetic reaction to their daughter, as she picked up her sable stole and said casually to the handsome cad who had cast her off, 'Well, you might see me around some time, but don't count on it . . .'

It was a very pleasant surprise when Horst joined them later, hailing a taxi immediately following his own performance at the new Festival Hall.

They toasted their star in the dressing room she shared with two other girls. The first-night cards and telegrams were still pinned on the wall, including one from Bernard Gray who, it appeared, was following Glory's career with some interest.

Glory and Horst are very well suited, Bar thought happily. He's much quieter than Glory, a good, steadying influence, but they have so much in common, too . . . Why am I reminded so poignantly of Clive and me, in the old days? Peter and I have a really good relationship, but – I can't quite give him all of me . . . I know he understands that, because he said as much, when we married.

'Bar darling,' Glory said, as she hugged her, and imprinted lipstick on her cheek, 'I don't have to ask if you are happy, do I? I've missed you, you know, because we were always so close, we two . . .'

Bar saw the flash of jealousy in Mirry's eyes. So, it still hurt. She was glad she had kept that little distance between herself and Fred, though she hoped that Mirry's suspicions in that direction had long ago been forgotten.

Now, she said: 'We'll be here until the end of July, you know – isn't that time enough for you to arrange a wedding, Miss Gloria Anna Hope?'

* * *

'What I do to please you, eh?' Glory remarked cheerfully, as her mother carefully pulled the wedding dress over her head. It was the dress of Mirry's dreams, ivory silk, decorated here and there with tiny seed pearls, and she didn't mind a bit that Glory hadn't asked her to make it.

'Keep still you two,' Bar told the bridesmaids, Crystal and Anna. They might look like angels with their long fair hair and big blue eyes, but they had already creased their pink taffeta dresses, which Mirry had run up on her faithful machine, when they bounced on the springy hotel bed.

Glory was getting married in London, because all her friends were there she said, and it would make less of a rush for the evening performance. The understudy was more than delighted to take over tomorrow, Saturday, and so there would be two days to honeymoon, but it'd be back to normal, if you could call appearing on stage that, on Monday . . .

When Horst tapped on the door, there were shrieks of: 'Go away! It's unlucky to see the bride before the ceremony!' from the bride's mother.

'I only wanted to say,' he called out, 'see you in church!'

'I'm glad your sister took my advice and decided to get married, because it means I got to see you after all,' Bar said to Boo, who was chief bridesmaid.

Now she was adult, Boo didn't look much like Glory at all. She was quieter, more intense, like her mother. Too clever by half: that had always been said of Glory by her proud parents, yet it was Boo who would eventually have her name inscribed in gold on the Lady Makepeace Board of Honours. Right now, Glory seemed a hard act for Boo to follow.

Boo and Robin had slipped back easily into their almost brother/sister role, and Robin was obviously pleased to have someone more his own age to talk to. He was already thinking of returning to England if he could get a place at university, later.

'Well, I'm ready,' Glory said cheerfully. 'Haven't over-done the makeup, have I? I've got used to slapping on the greasepaint.'

'You look beautiful, Glory – your dad will be so proud of you, when you walk down the aisle on his arm,' Mirry said huskily. She was pleased they were getting married in that little old London church.

'D'you think Mum knows we've been living together for the last three years, whenever we got the chance?' Glory asked Horst, much later, after it was all over. It had been a wonderful day, she thought, and she knew how happy her parents were to see her married at last.

They were stretched out on the bed, in the bridal suite, paid for by Horst's benevolent parents, having kicked off their shoes, but they were too tired at that moment to undress and pull back the covers.

'Does it matter?' he asked, picking confetti out of her hair. 'Some things are best left unsaid, Glory. I always knew I'd marry you one day – it was you who wouldn't say when. Still, we were committed to each other, weren't we?'

'Remember the first time you kissed me, on the beach?' she asked dreamily.

'Would you like an encore?' he teased. 'You'll have to get busy with the cold cream and cotton wool first on those ruby red lips.'

'I'm anticipating a curtain call . . .' she said demurely.

* * *

'She might not know you, I'm afraid,' Ted said, 'but go on up, Bar – it's the first door you come to.'

The curtains were pulled across and, in the half-light it took Bar a moment or two before she saw Anna, propped up in the bed. 'It's me, Bar,' she said.

Anna regarded her with a frown. The devoted Ted had trimmed her hair, brushed it neatly; powdered her already pale face. She plucked at the folded edge of the sheet, a compulsive movement of shaking hands.

Bar thought, 'She looks very frail and old. Vague, too – as I remember her father was, the last time I saw him.'

'Da-da-da-da, de-da-de-da-da . . .' A wheezing travesty of the tango, to which Anna had introduced her twenty-five years ago. Then Anna said: 'She's too young and innocent for you Chas, my little friend Bar . . .'

'You do know it's me!' Bar felt a rush of relief.

'Come here, so I can see you properly – what happened to your black hair, Bar?'

'It went grey on me, I'm afraid, Anna,' she said ruefully. Like yours. But she couldn't say that, of course.

'D'you still dance?'

'Now and again,' Bar was glad she could be truthful. 'With my husband.'

'Ah. Clive . . . Such a nice boy, mad about you, Bar, but not much of a dancer.'

'Not—' Bar bit back the contradiction. What was the point? Anna was obviously living in the past.

'Can you tell me? He—'

'Ted?'

'Ted says I'm imagining it, but – did I do something – terrible once, did I?' Anna's face revealed her distress.

'No, Anna, I'm sure you didn't.' Bar stilled the restless hands with her own warm clasp. 'Believe me,' she insisted urgently. 'Whatever happened, I know it was nothing to do with you.' She hoped fervently this was true, that Anna had not been responsible . . . after she found her mother with Vernon. Had he come back to blackmail Anna during the war? Was he both 'Saint and Sinner' as Ted had said then?

'Thank you . . .' Anna's voice was faint. She closed her eyes.

From the doorway, Ted said: 'She remembered you, Bar, I'm so glad. You said what she wanted to hear. Best come away, now. I'm so grateful to you for sparing the time for us.'

'Did you guess, too, Ted?' Bar asked slowly.

'When you love someone, you just know, don't you?' he answered obliquely. 'You've never told what *you* guessed, have you, when they found *two* bodies, and nor will I, till the day I die.'

*   *   *

They walked along the Crystal Palace Parade for old times' sake, the day before Bar, Peter and their family were due to embark for South Africa.

Bar walked arm in arm with her sister, hugging close to her, because they were so soon to part again. The two men, with Robin, followed leisurely behind, and the two little girls raced ahead.

'I don't remember this,' Bar exclaimed, 'it all seems so different to the last time I was here.' They gazed over a wall at a stretch of waste ground below.

'Well, it's been like this, since they closed the rail link from Crystal Palace to City and the West End of London some years ago,' Mirry told her. 'And demolished the High Link Station.'

'It's a magic bit of countryside, look at all the wild flowers still,' Crystal called. The grass was dappled with bright sunshine, which twenty-odd years ago would have gilded the great glass dome of the Crystal Palace.

'Can't we get down to it?' Anna asked eagerly.

'Look,' Fred said, 'it's alive with butterflies and bees. Quite an oasis, eh, in the middle of all the hustle and bustle. Nature soon takes over. Yes, girls, you can get to it by a side road – there's nothing to say keep out, but I'm not too sure if we'd be trespassing or not.'

'Can't see anyone official lurking about,' Peter observed. 'All right, you girls, follow Uncle Fred.'

Across the expanse of tangled grass they trouped, and the children soon discovered a wall, all grown over with twining ivy and scarlet and green creepers.

Just like in *Alice in Wonderland*, they came upon a door, and opened it.

Here was all that remained of the beautiful old railway station, forlorn and seemingly forgotten, just the walls and platform decorated in still dazzling, colourful mosaics. It made them all catch their breath. The lines had vanished, it seemed, with that final puff of smoke from the last train to leave.

'Here's another door,' Robin had been investigating further along.

'I don't reckon we should, but in for a penny in for a pound,' Fred decided for them all.

They emerged into an unfamiliar part of the Crystal Palace Park where there were workshops and sheds. Through a dusty window, they saw piles of headless and limbless statues and a flight of wide marble steps.

'Better go,' Mirry worried, 'we might get caught . . .'

'We haven't touched anything,' Bar said. 'Those poor statues, the steps – must have been salvaged from the fire . . . Come on, then, you lot, time to go home for tea, I suppose – and remember we're going to have crumpets toasted by the fire, which Uncle Fred has promised to light specially for us.'

'Why are you crying?' Peter asked softly. They were back in the old single bed, having turned down the offer of Fred and Mirry's room, so they couldn't get much closer. His arms were already wrapped around her, so that she wouldn't fall out. 'It's because we went to Crystal Palace, isn't it?'

At least they didn't have to share a room with Robin this time; he would have been horrified at the very suggestion, and didn't mind stretching out on the settee downstairs, especially as he got to watch more television, until it closed down for the night. The girls, of course, had Glory and Boo's old bedroom to themselves.

Bar nearly squeezed the breath out of him, then she kissed him, in a thoroughly abandoned fashion.

'Hey!' he said, laughing, 'what's that for? Have you forgotten how thin these walls are?'

'I wanted to show you how much I still love you, Peter – even though we've been married all these years,' she said fiercely.

'You feel guilty, don't you, because you were weeping for Clive – because of all the old memories which have surfaced today – well, you mustn't worry, Bar, because I know it doesn't alter how you feel for me – how I feel for you.'

'I think I let him go, you know, at last – in that place . . .' she whispered.

'Get to sleep now,' he said wisely, 'it's a long, long way home . . .'

* * *

Mirry and Fred didn't look back as they drove away from Number Five that afternoon in late September. Soon there would be another young couple, expecting their first child shortly, exclaiming with delight as they explored the possibilities of their very first home. The red brick Victorian villas stared over the road in their lofty fashion. Two little boys swung recklessly on the swings in the Lahana Play Park. Would the Galloping Major have disapproved? There was a plaque on the back of a new oak seat: *PRESENTED IN MEMORY OF ANNA BOAM*, 1893–1957.

In the garden of Number Five the last shrivelled, sour apple fell with a plop! in the grass.

'O be joyful!' Fred said, as they gathered speed. 'Just you and me, Mirry, the way it'll be from now on . . .'

'Just you and me,' Mirry echoed. Wasn't that always what she'd wanted? And she regarded him with love.

ACKNOWLEDGEMENTS

My grateful wishes to Win Luck, who told me 'how it was' when, like Bar in the book, she left home at a tender age, to be a soldier . . . I hope my story reflects her happy – and sometimes sad – memories of those times.

And to my cousin David Whiley, 'an innocent, straight from the sober Gas Light & Coke Company' who also joined the army at the outbreak of war – but happily managed to play plenty of cricket whilst fighting for his country . . .

I must also thank family and friends who shared their pre-war, war-time and post-war memories with me, in particular my husband and my mother.

The wonderful Crystal Palace may blaze in Part One, but its memory, its shadow is always with my characters. My thanks to Joan Garratt, who lived near the Palace for many years, and others who shared their memories, including Mr R J Hamshere for a newspaper report of the fire. Also to Gladys Pattemore for her vivid stories of the deserted station.

Thanks, too, to Janet Chambers, the intrepid reporter of *The Diss Express* for a touch of inspiration! And to my history teacher a long time ago, still my friend and mentor, Freda Feasey. (I hope she thinks the character of Miss Frizbarn, although fictional, of course, has *just a touch* of her own inimitable 'fizz' ...)

Welcome to the world of
Sheila Newberry!

Keep reading for more from Sheila Newberry, to discover a recipe that features in this novel and to find out more about what Sheila is doing next . . .

We'd also like to introduce you to MEMORY LANE, our special community for the very best of saga writing from authors you know and love and new ones we simply can't wait for you to meet. Read on and join our club!

www.MemoryLane.club

Meet Sheila Newberry

I've been writing since I was three years old, and even told myself stories in my cot. So it came as a shock when I was whacked round the head by my volatile kindergarten teacher for daydreaming about stories when I was supposed to be chanting the phonetic alphabet. My mother received a letter from my teacher saying, 'Sheila will not speak. Why?' Mum told her that it was because I was scared stiff in class. I was immediately moved up two classes. Here I was given the task of encouraging the slow readers. This was something I was good at but still felt that I didn't fit in. Later, I learned that another teacher had saved all my compositions saying they inspired many children in later years.

I had scarlet fever in the spring of 1939, and when I returned to our home near Croydon, I saw changes which puzzled me – sandbags, shelters in back gardens, camouflaged by moss and daisies, and windows reinforced with criss-crossed tape. Children had iron rations in Oxo tins – we ate the contents during rehearsals for air-raids – and gas masks were given out. I especially recall the stifling rubber. We spent the summer holiday, as usual, in Suffolk and I remember being puzzled when my father left us there, as the Admiralty staff was moving to Bath. 'War' was not mentioned but we were now officially evacuees, living with relatives in a small cottage in a sleepy village.

On and off, we returned to London at the wrong times. We were bombed out in 1940 and dodging doodlebugs in 1943. I thought of Suffolk as my home. I was still writing – on flyleaves of books cut out by friends – and every Friday I told stories about Black-eyed Bill the Pirate to the whole school in the village hut. I wrote my first pantomime at nine years old, and was awarded the part of Puss in Boots. I wore a costume made from blackout curtains. We were back in our patched-up London home to celebrate VE night and dancing in the street. Lights blazed – it was very exciting.

I had a moment of glory when I won an essay competition that 3000 schoolchildren had entered. The subject was waste paper, which we all collected avidly! At my new school, I was encouraged by my teachers to concentrate on English Literature and Language, History and Art, and I did well in my final exams. I wanted to be a writer, but was told there was a shortage of paper! True. I wrote stories all the time and read many books. I was useless at games like netball as I was so short-sighted – I didn't see the ball until it hit me. I still loved acting, and my favourite Shakespearian parts were Shylock and Lady Macbeth.

·MEMORY LANE·

When I left school, I worked in London at an academic publisher. I had wanted to be a reporter, but I couldn't ride a bike! Two years after school, I met my husband John. We had nine children and lived on a smallholding in Kent with many pets (and pests). I wrote the whole time. The children did, too, but they were also artistic like John. We were all very happy. I acquired a typewriter and wrote short stories for children, articles on family life and romance for magazines. I received wonderful feedback. I soon graduated to writing novels and joined the Romantic Novelists' Association. I have had many books published over the years and am over the moon to see my books out in the world once again.

Dear reader,

I hope you have enjoyed reading this book as much as I enjoyed writing it. When my mother read the first draft she exclaimed, 'Sheila, it's us!' Although not actually based on myself and my family, the book is set where we lived at that time and some of the things that happen to the characters did happen to us during the war. I believe they would have been our friends if we had met them . . .

It is not a conscious thing when I am writing, but I do, of course, draw on my own experiences of the times I have lived through. Mum must have recognised herself in 'The Great Pickled Onion Race' when we celebrated the end of the war. The Lady Makepeace School is also based on my own school. I confess, as well, that there are similarities between the young Glory and myself. But she achieves stardom on the West End stage while I appeared in amateur dramatics. I still recall the pantomimes I wrote and acted in, in a village in the Weald of Kent. I could sing and tap dance to my heart's content.

My characters 'tell me' what they want to say. I suspect other authors experience the same excitement when a story writes itself. As my Dad always said: 'You let your pen run away with you, Sheila!'. I am often asked how one can learn to write. That's a hard one for me to answer. I was reading and writing stories from the age of three, so for me it's just something I have to do. I have learned, though, the importance of knowing the period you are writing about, which often requires a lot of research. However, in the books that I write, it is important not to over-burden the story with too much historical fact that is not directly relevant to the characters. I think you have to write from the heart and make the characters feel like real people, which I do by drawing on my own experiences.

As a mother, grandmother and now great grandmother of a large family, there are children and much-loved pets in my books. When I am asked how I coped with having such a large family – six children before I was thirty and then three more to follow later! – my answer is always that I just blew the dust off the mantlepiece and joined in the fun. We lived then in a large, shabby house with a lovely orchard, where the children climbed the trees and picked the fruit. After supper, when my husband, John, was home, he took the older children outside and they played cricket, football and tennis, with twanging racquet strings and an old net he mended. This was when I relaxed with a book – after putting the babies to bed, that is.

All of these memories form the characters I create and the stories I tell, and I hope there will be many more to come.

Best wishes,
Sheila

A Recipe for a Celebration Fruit Cake

This cake is still a favourite with those family members who recall my mother's boiled, eggless fruit cake – fondly referred to as 'Bella's Cake'. She always made one when visitors were expected, long after the end of wartime austerity. The Hope family must have made their version of this cake too.

Ingredients

– One breakfast cup of mixed dried fruit – or a block of dates. You can add glace cherries, dried apricot pieces or chopped walnuts if available.
– One breakfast cup of demerara or soft brown sugar.
– One teaspoon of mixed spices, or ginger if preferred.
– Half a teaspoon of bicarbonate of soda.
– Two breakfast cups of self-raising flour.
– Three ounces of margarine.

Method

– Put all of the ingredients apart from the flour in a saucepan and bring slowly to the boil.
– Simmer for ten minutes.
– Allow to cool and then mix in the flour.
– When thoroughly mixed, spoon into a prepared cake tin. Bake at 160°C for one and a half hours. Check regularly until a skewer comes out clean.

· MEMORY LANE ·

Don't miss Sheila Newberry's next book,
coming May 2020 . . .

THE MEADOW GIRLS

August 1914. Twelve-year-old Mattie and her little
sister Evie lead an idyllic life in the Suffolk countryside,
playing in the meadows and picking watercress in the
streams. Living with their family in Plough Cottage,
little do they know that this perfect childhood will soon
come to an end as the first World War hits England.

As the years pass the girls go on to live very different
lives. Mattie travels from Suffolk to Plymouth and
then to Canada and America, whilst Evie remains
in England and pursues her career. But through
marriages, deaths, births, war, heartbreak and
distance, their bond remains strong.

More than fifty years later, will the two sisters
finally be re-united to have their time
in the meadows again?

**Sign up to Memory Lane to find out more and do
follow us on Facebook and join in the conversation
 MemoryLaneClub.**

Want to read
NEW BOOKS
before anyone else?

Like getting
FREE BOOKS?

Enjoy sharing your
OPINIONS?

Discover

**READERS
FIRST**

Read. Love. Share.

Sign up today to win your first free book:
readersfirst.co.uk